THE CHRONOCIDE MISSION

THE CHRONOCIDE MISSION

Lloyd Biggle, Jr.

WILDSIDE PRESS

In memory of
JOHN FLORY,
who asked for it.

THE CHRONOCIDE MISSION

An original publication of
Wildside Press
P.O. Box 301
Holicong, PA 18928-0301
www.wildsidepress.com

Songs Quoted in the Text:
"We'll All Remember Janie," words and music
copyright © 1976, by Lloyd Biggle, Jr.
"Counting All the Stars," words and music
copyright © 1976, by Lloyd Biggle, Jr.

First Edition: April 2002

NOTE FOR THE READER

Much of this book's action takes place in the future, and the characters taking part in that action are, of course, future characters. In the more than three hundred years postulated between the present and the novel's setting, with a massive catastrophe in between, a great deal would have happened to our language. It may well have become unrecognizable to the reader of today.

As a reminder of this fact, fabricated words (some will look like typos or misspellings!) are used for flavoring throughout to remind the reader that a different—or greatly modified—language is being spoken by people living in, or originating in, the future. (This of course will not be true of the present-day characters who appear in the final chapters of the book!)

In the "future" language:

Day, days are rendered as *Dae, daez.*

Night, nights are *niot, niots.*

These words hold in combinations: *middae, midniot, daelight, overniot.*

Sike is used for year; *tenite,* meaning ten nights, is the unit of temporal measurement used instead of "week." *Mont* is used instead of month.

Lens and *lenses* become *len* and *lens.*

Some changes in common punctuation practices are also employed to contribute to that future "flavoring."

—Lloyd Biggle, Jr.

1

BERNAL

Bernal awakened suddenly to the drumming of horses' hoofs on a forest road. "Some idiot peerlings on a drunken frolic," he told himself indifferently. He had spent more than half of his life deep in this enemy Peerdom of Lant, and he was fond of telling young scouts he survived only because he was most alert when he was sound asleep.

He raised up briefly to determine where the horses were and what direction they were going. Then he lay back, stretched his arms and legs luxuriously, and considered the one serious problem he faced at that moment, whether his beard needed trimming. The niot was only half advanced, the weather mildly warm, and his bed, fashioned of a chance accumulation of leaves in the shelter of an enormous, drooping prickle bush, the most comfortable he had experienced in more than a tenite. He loved the forest's pungent scents, loved living in the open. For the second time that niot, he composed himself for sleep.

The distant horses rumbled across a bridge and left the main road for a little-used branch that led to a long-abandoned lumber camp. Bernal continued to listen with closed eyes. An experienced scout in a thick forest was in no danger from a rackety enemy on horseback. Almost subconsciously he analyzed the sounds he heard and pondered the question of whether there were four horses or five. He decided on five.

He had begun to doze off again when his ear caught the yapping of dogs, and *that* brought him tensely to his feet. Dogs meant the riders were Lantiff, the vicious, mounted warriors of Lant, and the yapping meant they were on leash. The Lantiff used dogs for only one purpose, tracking, and they leashed them only when someone wanted a fugitive taken alive—which never happened when the ferocious beasts ran loose.

A runaway worth that much trouble to the Lantiff would be worth the loss of a little sleep to him. If nothing else, the fugitive might have useful information. Bernal gave no thought at all to the odds he faced in taking on five Lantiff with dogs. Everything one did in life involved *some* risk.

He unsheathed one of the two long knives he carried, his only weapons, and moved like a flitting shadow through the dense undergrowth toward the approaching horses. He had the confidence of long experience, but the silent, swift sureness of his movements through a dark and dense forest was purely instinctive. The Easlon scout in Lant who could not move with silent swiftness did not survive to acquire experience.

A full moon, shining brightly in a clear sky, had ruined many a hunt for Bernal, but on this niot it would not be a factor. Only where roads and widely scattered clearings had made rents in the dense overhead canopy could the moonlight penetrate the forest.

The sound of the chase altered abruptly, and he paused for a few seconds to listen. The hunters had dismounted to follow their dogs on foot. The advantage now belonged to Bernal, for the squat, muscular Lantiff were clumsy in foot combat and bunglers in a dismounted chase. They crashed through undergrowth, got caught up in vines and bushes, and soon were adding their curses to the dogs' yapping.

The dogs' killing instinct rivaled that of their masters, and both knew that a panicky, exhausted fugitive could not outdistance them for long. The Lantiff's course shouts became frenzied; so did the dogs' yapping, and they snapped at their leashes as they hauled their masters forward. The Lantiff were trying to whip them into line for a methodical search.

Listening alertly as he ran, Bernal used an angling approach that would overtake them from behind and downwind. He would attack one Lantiff and dog at a time, beginning with the pair on his right—the man first, before he could sound an alarm. His death grip on the leash should hold the dog long enough for Bernal to deal with it.

Then he would circle and take the pair on the left, leaving the odds tilted in his favor. He had the advantage of surprise and a fight on his own ground and terms, and the dogs, straining as they were to overtake their prey, would be a deadly encumbrance when their masters were attacked from behind in thick undergrowth. On horseback, the Lantiff's most effective weapons were their long-handled, flesh-ripping, multiple pronged and barbed lances. These were left with the horses when they fought dismounted, and their clumsy, curved swords were of no use at all in a dense forest.

Bernal slowed his pace and began stalking his first victim, moving with long, silent strides.

Suddenly a beam of light cut through the darkness, passing over his head with a deafening crash, severing branches, searing the foliage, and leaving in its wake tiny flames that flickered momentarily on the leaves it had touched.

Bernal sank to one knee and froze there. The light stabbed again and again with the same violent clap of sound. A dog screamed, and a man, and Bernal caught the revolting reek of burnt flesh. Then the air was rent thunderously just above his head, leaving him momentarily deafened, and he ducked as flames enveloped a dead bush close behind him. There were more screams. A beam of light bored into the ground almost at Bernal's feet, and the thick forest humus emitted a rancid cloud of smoke.

Keeping low, Bernal began to edge forward.

A clearing opened before him, half illuminated by moonlight and strewn with death. The Lantiff lay crumpled in the semicircle they had formed when they brought their quarry to bay. Nearby, three dogs crouched with fangs bared viciously, still straining on their leashes in death. A fourth had broken away from its dead master and died in the charge. At the far side of the clearing, the moon glimmered on the most horrible sight of all: the one dog that survived was tearing at its victim.

Bernal leaped forward. His knife flashed, and he heaved the dog's massive body aside to bend over a pathetic, moaning figure. It was an elderly man, hideously wrinkled as though wasted by illness. His head was totally bald but with incongruously thick eyebrows. He was of an age rarely attained in those unsettled times, but that was not why Bernal stared at him. This was no ordinary fugitive. For one thing, he was a foreigner. He possessed none of the usual Lantian racial characteristics. He was slight of build and fair-skinned. For another, he had no beard—merely an untidy growth of facial hair. He had shaved—or been shaved—within the last tenite, and beardlessness was the sternly enforced perogative of a peerager. He also wore finely woven, meticulously cut and fitted peerager trousers, but his blue smock was the one-name badge of high office in Lant. These two garments on the same person were a stark impossibility.

A strange black tube some twelve centimeters long and three in diameter lay on the ground beside him; nearby was a clumsily fashioned back pack with flimsy straps that had broken during the struggle with the huge dog. The old man had tried to protect himself with his arm and his pack, but the dog ripped the pack from his grip and made a gory mess of his arm.

Bernal examined him as carefully as the moonlight permitted. The entire forearm resembled shredded meat more than a human limb, but the artery seemed miraculously untouched. Clucking his tongue softly, Bernal went to the Lantiff, one after another, and swiftly sliced pieces of cloth from their clothing. With these he mopped up the blood and skillfully bandaged the arm. While he was working on it, the old man's eyes opened, and he struggled to a sitting position.

"Who are you?" he demanded.

"Bernal."

"You killed the dog!" The old man sounded incredulous. He sat looking about him while his dazed mind groped to understand this miracle. The dog's next lunge would have buried its teeth in his throat, and he had resigned himself to a hideous death.

"You are a one-namer!" he exclaimed, still sounding incredulous. "And you dare to help me?"

"I scout for the Peerdom of Easlon, and I dare many things," Bernal said. He fashioned a sling from the back of a Lantiff's shirt, tied it in place, and then asked, "Can you walk?"

With his help, the old man struggled to his feet. He was taller than Bernal had expected, and there was an amazing resilience his wiry form, for his teeth were clenched with pain and his breath came in shallow sobs. As the shock lessened, that pain would become throbbing agony.

For the moment, his mind was focused on the miracle of his rescue. "The Peer of Easlon must pay you well for taking such risks," he said.

Bernal smiled. "A scout avoids risks as much as possible, and he works for a cause, not for a reward. In Easlon, I am considered a patriot. Come—there will be less danger if we move quickly. Let's see if you can walk."

"My pack!" the old man gasped.

Bernal retrieved the ripped pack and tied its torn straps together. The old man leaned unsteadily against a tree and followed every movement with anxious eyes. When Bernal stooped to pick up the strange tube, the old man exclaimed, "Give it to me!" and extended a trembling hand. He snatched it and tucked it under his blouse.

"Were there more of them?" Bernal asked.

"No. I only kept one. To defend myself."

"It certainly did that," Bernal remarked. If he hadn't arrived on the scene when he did, he wouldn't have believed that one elderly fugitive could have wrought the carnage that lay about them.

Blood was soaking through the bandage on the old man's mangled arm, so Bernal added more layers of cloth. Then he picked up the pack and began to guide him toward the road, gently supporting him with an arm around his back.

"I am Egarn," the old man said suddenly.

Bernal halted. He couldn't contain his astonishment. "You are *who?*"

"Egarn."

Bernal didn't believe him. Egarn was Med of Lant and the peer's most trusted advisor. He was an enigma even to the Lantians, living a solitary life, holding himself apart from palace intrigue and preferring the study of sorcery to the court cycle of hunts and parties. Younger peeragers avoided him out of fear that he might cast spells on them, or so it was said, but the Peer of Lant, the most cynical and cruel tyrant alive, was said to rely on him absolutely. Only a colossal court upheaval could have placed him in disfavor.

No hint of such a thing had reached Bernal, but court gossip was difficult to come by when a peerdom was at war. Certainly there always had been something peculiar about Egarn. He held a high office that was reserved for peeragers, and he enjoyed all of its privileges despite the fact that he had only one name.

Bernal could make up his mind later. The fugitive's importance hardly mattered unless he could be kept alive and gotten out of Lant quickly. They would have to travel fast and cover their trail as well as they could. If this old man really was Med of Lant, the peer's pursuit would be incessant and relentless. Only a great personal affront or the foulest act of treason would so infuriate her that she would send Lantiff with dogs in pursuit of a long-trusted official.

While he guided Egarn back along the trail left by the clumsy Lantiff, he considered what form the pursuit would take next. The peer's commanders would suspect the old man had confederates waiting for him, and once the death scene was discovered, they would be certain of it. One elderly fugitive could not overcome five Lantiff and their dogs without help.

Every one-name village in the peerdom's northwest province would become suspect. An army of searchers would comb the forest and question local inhabitants, who would be uncommonly lucky if they only suffered torture. Bernal wanted Egarn as far away as possible before that search got organized.

The horses were waiting quietly by the road. The Lantiff

had dropped the reins when they dismounted for their dash to death, and these massive, superbly trained black beasts from the peer's own stables would not move as long as the reins trailed.

The dense forest had hidden the moon the moment they left the clearing, but the road was illuminated brightly. Bernal looked about him with a scowl. The niot was dangerously bright for fugitives who might have an army on their heels before the darkness faded. The officer who considered five Lantiff, with dogs, an adequate force for tracking down one feeble old man would taste the whip himself before morning, and a hundred Lantiff would follow the first five—or a thousand, with all of the armed might of the peerdom in support.

Egarn could not ride unassisted. One of these magnificent steeds could easily carry both of them, but if Bernal took one and left the others, the pursuing Lantiff would deduce more than he wanted them to know. He had to take all five.

The first problem was to delay the discovery of the carnage in the clearing. The peer's commanders would be less energetic about sending reinforcements if they thought the original pursuers were still on the fugitive's heels.

Egarn sank to the ground the moment Bernal released him. The short walk had exhausted him, and his mangled arm had to be throbbing more intensely with each halting footstep. He was whimpering with pain.

"I must cover our tracks before we leave," Bernal told him.

First he cut an armful of branches from a pungent stink bush. He spread them along the road and went back for another armful, which he distributed carefully over the trampled trail for a short distance into the forest. He crushed the leaves underfoot and swept the road with them where the old man's tracks had veered aside when he heard the pursuit close behind him.

"Dogs won't try to follow your scent through that," he told Egarn cheerfully. "Especially if your trail continues along the road. You will have to walk about a kilometer. Can you do it?"

"If I have to, I can," Egarn said grimly.

Bernal busied himself with the horses. The lances were a nuisance, but there was no time to find a secure hiding place for them. He tied the horses in tandem and helped Egarn struggle to his feet. Then he mounted the lead horse. Egarn staggered along feebly, clinging to Bernal's leg with his good arm, and Bernal bent low to help him as much as he could. They made slow but steady progress. Bernal watched admiringly as the old man set his teeth against the steadily worsening pain and plodded forward without complaint.

Finally they reached their goal—a tiny, unbridged stream. It was an insignificant ribbon of water trickling off through the forest, but tonight it might save a man's life. Egarn waded into it, and then Bernal hoisted him onto the horse he was riding. Egarn lost consciousness almost at once, but he had accomplished as much as Bernal had hoped for and far more than he had expected. If dogs tracked him to the stream, the Lantiff would waste hours searching it from source to mouth for the place he left it again.

Bernal made Egarn as comfortable as he could and let the horses run while he pondered the opportunity fate had given him.

The swolen armies of the Peer of Lant were everywhere invincible. The war in the north had long been finished. That in the east was in its final stages of plunder, destruction, and slaughter of noncombatants. The southern invasion was rolling relentlessly. Now the peer was looking westward. She had dedicated her life to war, and she had no other neighbors left to conquer.

To the west lay the Ten Peerdoms, protected throughout their independent existence by a formidable mountain range. The only passes known to the Lantians were blocked in winter and difficult even for intrepid explorers the remainder of the year. The scouts of Easlon, the easternmost of the Ten Peerdoms, regularly crossed the frontier on trails known only to them, but the Lantians would have considered these hazardous routes impassable. No sane Peer of Lant would attempt to march an army westward.

So the rulers of the Ten Peerdoms had always believed—while neglecting their defenses and failing to train even token armies. Clouds of war had hung over Easlon's mountainous frontier all of Bernal's lifetime, and Easlon's scouts had skirmished regularly with scouts from Lant, but no army appeared. Unfortunately, those mountain passes were no obstacle for a determined commander, and the present Peer of Lant was a military genius. She could attack whenever she chose, and Easlon had only its few hundreds of scouts to oppose an army of thousands. The Ten Peerdoms were about to be devastated in an orgy of blood and fire.

In a desperate attempt to stave off disaster, the League of One-namers, a secret Ten Peerdoms organization, had attempted to make contact with the one-namers of Lant. The League wistfully hoped independent crafters everywhere could band together and constitute a force for peace and reason. Arne, their leader, had not subscribed to this silliness, but he was the designated emissary. Bernal had recently completed the most important mission of his life: guiding Arne to a series of secret meetings in Lant and bringing him back safely.

The noble errand was foredoomed to failure. The Peer of Lant was outstanding in her viciousness even in a world where evil tyrannies were the rule. All of Lant's one-namers had been cowed by the brutality they suffered daily. They feared the sun and were terrified by darkness. There were no genuinely independent subjects left in Lant.

Arne himself had been an agreeable surprise. Son of a legendary father, already a legend himself, he was only twenty years old. Those few people who were still concerned with civilized values in a torn world could ill afford to lose him, and yet the idiotic council had sent him deep into enemy territory where capture meant instant death. He had been uncommonly lucky that the frightened Lantian one-namers had not betrayed him.

The mission failed utterly, and Bernal guided Arne back through the mountains with nothing accomplished. Now he was in Lant again with several new assignments, but he would willingly abandon all of them in order to lead Egarn to safety. The Med of Lant—with his strange weapon—would more than compensate for the failure of Arne's risky mission.

Their niot-long dash through the thick forest was uneventful except for a few tense moments when the road took them close to a lumber camp. One-name foresters had felled select hardwoods the previous summer and trimmed them. Now a work crew of no-namers was hauling the logs to a near-by river. Bernal couldn't risk having one of their lashers remember hearing horses pass, so he slowed their pace to a walk as they approached the camp. They were clearly visible on the moon-lit road if anyone chanced to look in their direction, but apparently no one did. As they moved quietly past the camp, Bernal could see the flickering torches and hear the cracks of the lashers' whips and the grunts of the laboring no-namers straining to drag the logs. Not until they had placed the scene far behind them did he let the horses resume their frenzied flight.

The road led westward and upward as they passed through forested hills that anticipated the mountains beyond. Shortly before dawn, they encountered a rushing stream that was wide enough and deep enough to require bridging. Bernal turned aside and rode down a dip in the bank where travelers were accustomed to water their horses. There he dismounted. While all five of the huge animals drank and then waited patiently, knee-deep in water, he left Egarn balanced precariously in the broad saddle and went back to erase the tracks they had left on the river bank. No experienced scout would have been fooled by the hasty brushing he gave the ground with a tree branch, but there were no experienced scouts among the Lantiff.

Remounting, he turned the horses upstream and walked them in shallow water for more than two kilometers. His objective was a sketchy forest trail so overgrown that he had difficulty in finding it. When they finally left the water, he dismounted again to conceal their tracks before he hurried the horses forward.

The one-name foresters of Lant had carved this narrow path for their own use. It led from nowhere to nowhere, and since they hadn't worked that sector for several years, the forest had almost reclaimed it. Probably the Lantiff were unaware of its existence. Even so, Bernal would have moved more cautiously if he hadn't feared that Egarn would be dead before they reached a refuge. The going was arduous, and he had to struggle to keep encroaching branches from raking the old man as they passed, but he pressed on recklessly.

Egarn had become delirious. Bernal kept murmuring, "Just a little farther, old fellow," but the old man's feverish mind was beyond the reach of encouraging words. Finally they emerged in a small forest clearing, and Bernal began to whistle the lilting, tremulous call of the spotter, a bird rare in Lant but common beyond the mountains.

The song was answered faintly. Several minutes later, two unusually tall, gaunt men dressed in the rough leather clothing of Easlon scouts stepped into the clearing. Bernal was easing Egarn down from the horse, and they hurried forward to help him.

"Dog," Bernal said, indicating the bandage. "He needs nursing. Probably he will die anyway. Do we have anything to feed the horses?"

Kaynor, the elder of the newcomers, answered, "A bit. But why five? Did you catch the Lantiff sound asleep?"

Bernal said indifferently, "I caught them dead. They and their dogs."

"You took an unnecessary risk," Kaynor said reproachfully. "The Lantiff might overlook one horse but certainly not five. They will turn out every dog in Lant to track you. Is the old man worth it?"

"They will turn out every dog in Lant to track the old man," Bernal said. "Whether he is worth the risk depends on whether he lives. I am going to look after him myself. One of you will have to go south toniot."

Roszt, the younger of the newcomers, said eagerly, "Give me a horse, and I will do it. Those bundles I stole last week had server clothing in them. I can go as a peer's messenger."

"Right now you can backtrack and cover my trail," Bernal said. "If the pursuit comes this far, it will be hot. When you have done that, look after the horses."

The younger man hurried away. Bernal and Kaynor picked up Egarn's limp body and headed into the forest with it.

Kaynor had been scrutinizing Egarn perplexedly. "He is beardless, and he is wearing peerager's trousers with a one-name smock. What is he?"

"I don't know. He may be a peerager, but he has only one name."

Kaynor was silent while they maneuvered Egarn's light body through some dense undergrowth. Then he asked, "Don't the rules forbid intervening in the peer's private affairs? Inskor made it very clear we are to keep our hands off court doings unless it is something really important, and even then we are to make certain the result is worth the risk *and* the aftermath. This poor old crock probably did nothing more serious than sneeze in the peer's presence, but there will be an army beating the forest tomorrow. When they find the bodies of those Lantiff and their dogs, only the evil gods of Lant know what will happen next. That was quite a deed, taking on all ten of them, but what have you gained?"

"I killed one of the dogs," Bernal said. "He killed the rest. He is more important than all of the peer's generals together—or he will be if he lives."

"Be serious! An old crock like this? Probably he is the peer's third assistant gardener wearing cast-off clothing."

"He says his name is Egarn. I *think* he is the Med of Lant."

The other nearly dropped the old man's feet. When he spoke again, it was in tones that blended awe and skepticism. "The Med of Lant with five Lantiff and their dogs after him? What do you suppose he did?"

"I hope he lives long enough to tell us," Bernal said soberly.

By the time the old man regained consciousness, he had been placed on a comfortable bed in a safe refuge. His arm had been bathed, treated with herbs, and rebandaged; and Bernal had a bowl of hot broth ready for him. Egarn ate slowly with Bernal assisting him. By the time he finished, he had revived sufficiently to take an interest in his surroundings.

He gazed about the small room wonderingly. It was lit by a flickering torch, and the smoke was sucked into a crack in the ceiling. There was a charcoal fire to take the edge off the cool, damp air, and skins were hung in two large openings. Comfortable chairs and beds had been improvised from branches and straw.

"Where are we?" he asked.

"In a cave," Bernal answered.

"Are we safe here?"

"As safe as a fugitive can be in the Peerdom of Lant," Bernal said gravely. "As soon as you are able to travel, we well take you to Easlon."

"Across the mountains?"

"Of course."

Egarn sank back comfortably. "I was hungry. They starved me. Is there more broth?"

"Better not overdo the eating for a few daez. You would make yourself sick."

Bernal began to lay out rough garb that matched his own: leather jacket, pants, and mocs, with shirt and undergarments of wool. "When you feel up to it, I will bathe you and change your clothes. We need the things you are wearing. We also want your pack. I will give you another, and you can keep anything you think you absolutely must have. Just make certain you leave enough personal effects to identify you."

Egarn gazed at him perplexedly.

"I am sending a scout south toniot," Bernal said. "He will find a corpse in the Peerdom of Wymeff who resembles you as closely as possible. Fortunately for you—but not for Wymeff— there will be plenty of corpses to chose from. We are assuming the peer will order a massive search for you. If, in the middle of it, she receives word that your over-ripe body has been found in Wymeff, it will confuse the situation very satisfactorily."

"I did it," Egarn muttered.

"You did what?"

"The corpses. I did it. I made the weapons. To defend Lant, I thought, but the peer used them to destroy her neighbors. As if the len hadn't tortured humanity enough." He brightened. "But I got them back. I told her the lens would wear out if they weren't replaced, and then I hid one and destroyed the rest. When I refused to make more, the peer stopped my food and then my water. When I got hungry and thirsty enough, I killed my guards with the weapon I had saved and escaped."

"That was well done," Bernal said. He knew, now, that he couldn't rest until this old man was safely in Easlon.

"Some of the guards were my friends," Egarn said despondently. "But I was afraid I would weaken if I got any hungrier. I had to escape or let her have the weapon."

"It was well done," Bernal said again. "Don't look back, old fellow. Look ahead. The important thing now is to get well. Then maybe you can help us think of a few ways to have back at the Peer of Lant."

Egarn grinned bitterly.

"What about your personal effects?" Bernal asked.

Egarn took a ring from his finger, surrendered a tooled leather belt that he wore, and then—with obviously reluctance—took a strange object from his pack. A blade snapped into view, and it was a knife.

"Jackknife," Egarn said sadly. "And take this, it is called a coin. Anyone who knew me well will recognize them. They are the only things I have left from the place I came from, but they don't matter now. Nothing matters."

Bernal accepted them with a nod of approval. Next Egarn handed him a thin piece of wood with strange figures carved on it in orderly rows.

"Calculator I invented," Egarn said. He added, when

Bernal gave it a puzzled glance, "It is too complicated to explain, but my assistants will recognize it. Take it all. Take everything except the weapon. I wish you could take my memories, too—I no longer need them, either."

One of the skins was pushed back, and Bernal's two companions came into the room. Bernal gravely pronounced introductions: Roszt and Kaynor.

"They are so tall!" Egarn blurted. "Are they from Easlon, too?"

"They are from the Peerdom of Slorn. Their families were killed in the Lantian invasion, and now they scout for Easlon."

"I have met people from Slorn, but they weren't so tall and skinny. One doesn't often meet tall people in this land." Egarn returned his attention to Bernal. "Their families were—killed?"

Bernal nodded.

Egarn bowed his head. "All those corpses," he muttered. "And I did it. I made the weapons."

"Is it true that the Peer of Lant is getting ready to invade Easlon?" Bernal asked.

Egarn nodded miserably. Then he brightened. "But now she can't! I destroyed all of her weapons except the one I brought with me!"

"She doesn't need your weapons to invade Easlon, my friend. She has conquered all of her neighbors and added their lashers to her armies. If the Ten Peerdoms suddenly got energetic and formed a combined army of their own—which she knows their peers would never consent to do—she still would outnumber them twenty to one. Or fifty. Or a hundred. Probably she doesn't know herself how large her armies are."

Egarn covered his face with his good arm. "I suppose I must give the weapon to the Ten Peerdoms," he muttered. "But after they have defeated Lant, they will use it on each other. Everything I do is cursed."

"It needn't happen that way," Bernal said. "Don't give it to the peers. Don't trust any peerager. That was your mistake.

Give it to us—to the one-namers. We are trying to live in peace and keep civilization going."

"One-namers?" Egarn was incredulous. "But every one of them is servile to one peer or another!"

"Things are different beyond the mountains. Our first loyalty is to our own kind, and we have a League of One-Namers that extends through all of the Ten Peerdoms. The hope of the future lies with us, not with the rotten peeragers and certainly not with the no-namers and lashers. We one-namers don't want to conquer anyone. We just want to protect our homes." He added thoughtfully, "There is a rumor about a peerdom somewhere in the west that destroys its enemies with beams of light. Maybe someone already has your weapon."

"A peerdom in the west is using a weapon like mine?"

"So it is rumored."

"Any med server could make it if he knew how. If one of them has stumbled on the right combination of lens, the world is doomed. There is only one way to save humanity. I can't do it alone—I would need help."

"Tell Arne about it," Bernal said. "He is first server of the Peer of Midlow and also of the League of One-Namers. He will see that you get all the help you need. What is the one way left to save humanity?"

Egarn's gaze did not waiver. "By destroying it," he said.

2

EGARN (1)

Egarn remembered little about the first daez in hiding. His fever worsened, and Bernal told him later he had been circling much of the time, which meant deranged or out of his head. His dim awareness of the cave—of Bernal anxiously changing the dressing on his mangled arm and brewing herbal poultices for it; of the two scouts from Slorn just as anxiously discussing the gathering fury of the peer's search—was less vivid than his nightmarish recollections of the distant past.

During those first confused days, when he easily could have been spirited to safety beyond the mountains, he lay in helpless delirium and could not be moved. While the worried scouts watched over him, and he ranted wildly, sometimes in words incomprehensible to them, his feverish mind passed a lifetime in review.

His name was Vladislav Kuznetsov, and he had been a twenty-one-year-old student at Mount Harwell College in Mount Harwell, Ohio. On a Friday afternoon, March 24, 2001, he succumbed to a sudden attack of spring fever and cut his classes for a stroll in a public park near the campus. Even after fifty years and several hundred centuries, he remembered it as vividly as though it had happened an hour before.

It was a warm, fresh day with a promise of spring—the first really pleasant day of the year after the usual vagaries of a midwest winter. He strolled leisurely through the park, thinking with shameless delight of the stuffy classrooms he was avoiding. Eventually he seated himself on a patch of greening grass with a convenient tree to lean against and enjoyed the soft breeze and the peaceful surroundings while he absently whittled on a twig he had picked up. He felt sleepy. Probably he dozed off.

For decades afterward he relived that afternoon again and

again with retrospective editing: What if he had not cut classes, what if he had turned in the opposite direction and avoided the park, what if he had not sat down to rest, what if he had not fallen asleep?

He was awakened by a violently squealing and squirming young pig that had landed in his lap. The pig's fore and hind legs were tied together with strips of leather. Kuznetsov knew at once he was on the receiving end of a heavy-handed practical joke, and he also knew the ones responsible. He had been the victim of their pranks often enough. Before looking about for the culprits, he good-naturedly set about freeing the pig. His open jackknife was still in his hand, and he quickly sliced the leather restraints. He hoped the pranksters would have to spend the afternoon trying to catch it, which would deftly turn the joke on them.

The pig scurried for cover. Kuznetsov looked after it in puzzlement, wondering what unlikely porcine species it belonged to. He had never seen a pig with long hair before. Perhaps he had unfairly maligned his practical-joking friends. The animal looked peculiar enough to have come straight out of another dimension. So many odd things had happened to him in his short lifetime that he would have felt more resigned than surprised to find himself the target for a materializing pig.

As a child, he had blamed all of his misfortunes on his name. It had blighted his life in so many ways. Not even a boy's best friend could be expected to call him Vladislav Kuznetsov, and the changes rung on it varied from the humiliating to the obscene. As he grew older, some of his friends began to call him Wally Kuznet, which seemed like a substantial improvement but failed to alter his life an iota.

He finally accepted the fact that his luck was going to be bad no matter what people called him. A snowball thrown into a crowd unerringly sought out his nose, which was broken three times before he finished grammar school. A bully always acquired a yen for beating up a smaller boy a moment before Kuznetsov innocently walked into view. Teachers invariably scheduled surprise quizes on the one day of the term he failed to prepare an assignment. If, after timidly admiring a girl for months, he finally nerved himself to ask her for a date, it always turned out she had agreed only the day before to go steady with a star halfback. Every job he applied for had three relatives of the employer in line just ahead of him. Nothing overwhelmingly bad ever happened to him, but he found life a long succession of increasingly intolerable frustrations and petty failures.

He'd had a single-minded passion for space engineering. By the time he reached college, the space program had been curtailed, and he'd had to face the bitter fact that with so many experienced engineers out of work, a brand new degree in space engineering wouldn't even qualify him for a job as bus driver at Cape Canaveral. Reluctantly he switched to something solid, conservative, and perpetually reliable: automotive engineering. It would not surprise him in the least, now that he was about to graduate, if the auto industry suddenly collapsed and his brand new degree would not even qualify him to drive a bus in Detroit.

He was a good-looking blond youth, popular with those who knew him well. Though all of his disappointments, he learned to persist and face life with an attitude of calm resignation and determination. Bullies quickly learned to avoid him when he began judo lessons, and he worked hard until he became an expert. In college he was an excellent student, but his deeply ingrained inferiority complex meant that success in his studies failed utterly to compensate for his sense of failure in life. Deep in his subconscious, he probably expected that sooner or later fate would dump a hairy pig into his lap.

The pig ran off with deep grunts of piggish satisfaction, and—after glancing about for sniggering practical jokers and seeing none—Kuznetsov decided he had better get back to the dorm and study. Then came a tremendous jerk, like having a chair pulled from under him at the same instant that a truck hit him, and he almost lost consciousness. He landed with a painful bump and skidded for a short distance along a very rough wood floor. He still held his open jackknife in his hand.

For a moment he sat gazing about him dazedly. He had been abruptly translated from his seat on the ground in a pleasant park on a lovely spring day to a seat on a wood floor in a large, dim room with a thunderstorm raging outside. He had a distinct impression that the two scenes had been linked by an earthquake. He tried hard to focus his thoughts, staring first at a table where a candle burned brightly and then at an animal tied to one of the table's legs by a short leash. It was another hairy pig. He raised his eyes to the room's two small, water-streaked windows and saw nothing beyond but branches swaying in a strong wind.

There was only one other person in the room, and he was staring at Kuznetsov with profound astonishment. He was elderly and wizened, with a deeply wrinkled face and amusing tufts of hair scattered about his overly large head. His skin had a mildly oriental, or perhaps a southern European, tinge. He wore white clothing and a white apron, and he smoothed the apron with nervous fingers while his mouth worked soundlessly.

Finally he produced words. He mouthed them strangely and ran them together, and Kuznetsov's impression was of a wholly alien language.

"Where am I?" Kuznetsov demanded.

Again the man spoke unintelligible sounds. Kuznetsov struggled unsuccessfully to make a meaningful arrangement of them. Another repetition, and the sounds began to suggest a blurred question. "Who are you?"

Kuznetsov looked about him perplexedly. He knew who he was, and he also knew his identity would mean nothing to this character. He wanted to know *where* he was, and how he had got there, and why. He had been sitting on the grass in the park, and a hairy pig landed in his lap, and immediately after he released it, the jerk hit him. Now he was somewhere else.

He didn't want to believe it. He started the thought again

and went through the sequence slowly, wondering whether any part of it could have been cause and effect. Then he went through it a third time. He had been sitting on the grass in the park, and the next thing he knew . . .

His mind seized on the strangely placid animal that was tied to the table leg. An identical hairy pig had landed in his lap. That could only mean it had come from here, after which—perhaps in an attempt to recover it—this old villain had snatched Kuznetsov instead. He didn't want to believe that, either, but surely the pig tied to the table was the spitting piggish image of the strangely hairy one Kuznetsov had released in the park.

He got to his feet. He towered over the stooped old man, holding his open jackknife like a weapon. The forceful anger he displayed was genuine. "Send me back!" he demanded sternly.

The old man's features continued to register astonishment.

"Your pig landed in my lap," Kuznetsov said accusingly.

"Peeg?"

Kuznetsov pointed. "Pig. That's a pig. One just like it landed in my lap. The next thing I knew, I was here. Send me back."

The old man suddenly became articulate. His jabbered response engulfed Kuznetsov like an rampaging Niagara. Any meaning his words carried was swept along on the same current, and both words and meaning washed over Kuznetsov unintelligibly. Finally Kuznetsov put an end to the torrent by shouting at the top of his voice. He didn't know where he was, or why, but he had already decided he didn't like it.

"Send me back!" he demanded again. "Back. Where I came from." Then, as he began to grasp the full implications of his predicament, he modified his tone. "Please send me back."

The old man seemed to understand. He walked to the far corner of the room. Staring after him into the dim light, Kuznetsov made out something that looked like an enormous, crudely built photographic enlarger. On the floor, a series of concentric circles had been burned into the wood, and these were divided into segments by chalk lines, some of which had been partially obliterated by Kuznetsov's sliding entrance. The old man stood Kuznetsov in the central circle. Then he brought a short wood stepladder, climbed up to his apparatus, and began fussing with it. Kuznetsov had the sensation of having landed in a perverted Hollywood hodgepodge that blended *Frankenstein* and *The Wizard of Oz,* and it wouldn't have surprised him if the old man had next handed him a bottle labeled, "Drink me," but he stood waiting patiently.

The old man climbed down again, pushed the ladder aside, and took a dangling cord in his hand. He looked preposterously like an old-time photographer about to take a picture with an overhead, sadly obsolescent camera. He pulled the cord.

Kuznetsov screamed. His instinctive leap as the wave of torment swept over him probably saved his life. He collapsed on the floor a short distance away, writhing in unendurable agony. The intense pain quickly swept him into unconsciousness.

The agony persisted for days. He floated in a delirium of pain. His bones ached, his head throbbed, his ears rang, and his vision seemed blurred and distorted. He felt as though he had been flayed, and any hand, any finger that touched his flesh was a dagger stabbing him viciously. A woman came and went, and her hideously misshapen face gave Kuznetsov nightmares about being condemned to live forever in a world of grotesque distortions. Then the old man came, and his face was as Kuznetsov remembered it. Kuznetsov's vision was normal. The old woman's face really was hideously deformed.

Words were spoken to him, or spoken in his presence, and as time passed, some of them began to make sense. Even as he struggled out of the all-enveloping fog of pain, his mind was subconsciously learning or adapting to a language. There were familiar words pronounced differently and unfamiliar words that sounded confusingly familiar, and gradually he got them sorted out. Kuznetsov wasn't good at languages, and the ease with which he assimilated this one seemed proof enough that it was somehow related to English.

His systematic study began with his quest for a date. It had been March 24, 2001 when he went to the park. When he began to recover, he wanted to know how long he had been delirious.

"Month" should have been an easy place to start, but the old man failed to recognize the word. Neither could Kuznetsov discover an equivalent for "March," or "April" or any other month, or for "year," or "week."

Learning words for table and chair, for clothing, for food was easy. Kuznetsov pointed; the old man said the word. It was his attempt to relate the calendar he was familiar with to whatever system the old man used that tantalized and frustrated him. Winter, spring, summer, fall or autumn apparently had no analogies. Not until he accidentally happened on the word for "season," which was "esun," did he begin to make progress.

The calendar in this strange civilization was closely tied to the agricultural year. There were seasons of planting, of growing, of harvesting, and of resting, named Plao, Gero, Haro, and Reso. With that beginning, he was able to form an outline, and the old man quickly filled in the blanks once he understood what Kuznetsov wanted.

The year began—or ended—with a five day holiday, six days every fourth year, that undoubtedly had originated as a period of supplication to the gods for prosperity in the year to come. Kuznetsov was in no way surprised to discover that the original religious basis for the festival had been all but forgotten, and it had degenerated into five or six days of dissipation. Then came the first season, Plao, the season of planting, starting early in the March of Kuznetsov's time reference. Each season was divided into three unnamed months of thirty days, called monts. They were designated Plao 1, Plao 2, Plao 3. "Days" were daez, "nights" niots, but weeks did not exist. Instead, each mont was divided into three tenites. Second Plao 2 referred to the second tenite of the second mont of planting.

Years were called sikes, and once Kuznetsov learned that, he quickly found out what year it was—A.T. 301, meaning "301 sikes after the troubles," which told him nothing at all.

Gradually he acquired a vocabulary and became able to converse.

As soon as he could walk again, he began helping the old man with his experiments, and he made an astonishing discovery. This wrinkled, comic-opera looking gaffer possessed a spectacular scientific genius. He worked without electricity, without engineering—instruments and tools were fashioned with pathetic crudeness—without chemistry, without physics except for an unaccountable precision in lens grinding, and he accomplished miracles.

Kuznetsov also learned that the old man was a person of transcendent importance in this strange land, which was called Lant. He was Med of Lant, and visitors to his laboratory bowed to him as though he were a high nobleman, which he actually turned out to be. Everyone called him the Old Med, an astonishing license with a person of his rank. It indicated at the same time affection, awe, and reverence.

While Kuznetsov's education went forward slowly, the Old Med was making an astonishing discovery of his own. This young stranger was an ideal research assistant. He was a college-trained engineer, and despite the lack of almost everything to work with, he could build instruments and tools with a precision the old man had not even imagined. Further, in a land where very little was known about anything, the knowledge of even a college undergraduate was beyond price.

The old man quickly gave Kuznetsov honored status as his principal assistant, and, when difficulties arose over what to call him—Kuznetsov naturally didn't want the same name blighting his existence in this new incarnation—the Med shared a name of his own with him. He called him Egarn.

One fact had been burned into Kuznetsov's consciousness indelibly. He could never go back. The attempt to return had come within an eyelash of killing him. Wherever he was, and however he had got here, it had been a one-way trip.

He savored his new name—Egarn, he liked the sound of it—and gradually he began to grasp the possibility of a career in this strangely primitive Peerdom of Lant. It was already evident that the Old Med wanted him to continue his research after he died. The newly christened Egarn resolved to accept that legacy as a sacred trust. He would devote his life to advancing the Old Med's discoveries. Genuine scientific and technological achievement would be impossible with such limited resources, but there were many simple inventions and discoveries he could make that would transform his newly adopted land. Just for a beginning, he intended to give its people the germ theory of disease. If he could find anything to use for wire, he might even invent electricity.

His techniques would be as crude as those of a medieval alchemist, but *his* alchemy would work. There would be no meaningless dissolving and crystallizing and coagulating such as occupied the old alchemists for entire lifetimes. His discoveries would have genuine value, and his inventions would be aimed at specific needs.

In return, he confidently expected distinctions far beyond anything he had dreamed of at Mount Harwell College. Already he was accorded enormous respect as the Med of Lant's assistant. As his successor, the highest material rewards a primitive land could offer would be his for the asking or—he had quickly grasped the role of the elite in this Peerdom of Lant—for the taking. He could marry whenever he found a girl he liked. Any daughter of commoners would be eager to mate with the Med of Lant's assistant. He would pass his days in the Old Med's comfortable workroom, a rambling log building in a delightfully rustic setting. When he wanted a vacation from work, there would be tramps in the woods with a fascinating, strangely distorted botany and biology to study, rides about the countryside—the Peer of Lant's own stables provided a horse whenever he wanted one—or an occasional wild porkley hunt with lance or bow and arrow. He never could have achieved such serenity in the frenzy of twenty-first century America. Gradually Kuznetsov—now comfortably answering to the name Egarn—began to look forward to it.

Of course no society, no social structure, offered Elysium, and this one had some ominous imperfections. The old woman with the disfigured face had been mercilessly whipped. Kuznetsov never learned why or by whom, but very early he grasped the fact that Lant's was a slave economy, and both slaves and commoners could be—and often were—treated with unbelievable harshness.

But the only commoners Kuznetsov came in contact with were the Old Med's trusted servants. They received not only kindness and consideration but even affection, and they gave a full measure of devotion in return. What happened elsewhere had nothing whatsoever to do with him.

3

EGARN (2)

The Old Med remained the central figure in Egarn's life as long as he lived, and they came to love each other dearly. The gift to Egarn of one of the Med's names actually signified a type of informal adoption. The Old Med would have gladly bestowed both of his names on him, but the society's rigid class distinctions made that impossible. No one but a born aristocrat could bear two names.

Time passed, and Egarn learned to live and survive in a primitive society where technology and scientific thought had reverted to their medieval infancies—with one puzzling exception. The Old Med's knowledge of optics vastly exceeded the college physics Egarn had mastered. Lenses, which were called len, singular, and lens, plural, were ground with a skill far beyond anything Egarn had imagined. Lant's prentice len grinders had to invest years of hard work to master the rudiments and much longer to become expert.

The most important len was called the Honsun Len. It had a wavy surface that required consummate grinding skill to produce, and it had peculiar scientific properties that were beyond the scope of Egarn's undergraduate knowledge of physics to describe. This len was the principal component in the odd contraption that had sucked Vladislav Kuznetsov out of the park.

The Old Med had been experimenting with the Honsun Len for years, grinding different shapes and sizes of len on the Honsun Len principle and putting them together in combinations that produced very strange effects indeed, and he conducted experiment after experiment for no other reason than to find out what would happen. One arrangement of lens started fires that almost destroyed his workroom. Another shattered fragile objects. Light flickered from one when it was suspended in darkness—an illumination as fleeting as the flash of a firefly but far more mysterious. The Old Med kept trying different combinations until finally one of them made small objects disappear.

He repeated that experiment numerous times over a period of sikes, but he failed utterly in his attempts to find out where the things went. As he increased the size of his apparatus, he could make larger and larger objects disappear. Then it occurred to him to reverse the lens. This time the opposite happened. Things began to appear out of nowhere—ordinary things, such as rocks and debris, and utterly strange things the med had never seen before. Once an unusual bird materialized before his astonished eyes. It flew about the laboratory until a server accidentally let it escape.

That gave him the idea for the great experiment of his life. He decided to make something vanish and then bring it back. First he tried a young porkley. It vanished, but when the lens were reversed, nothing happened. The Old Med deduced that it had run off when it got to wherever the lens sent it. He tried the experiment again and tied the porkley's legs together.

This was the pig that landed in Vladislav Kuznetsov's lap. It also ran off—because Kuznetsov released it—and when the lens were reversed, the strange power they controlled snatched Kuznetsov.

As Egarn, Kuznetsov helped the Old Med continue these experiments. One day he inadvertently brought a mongrel dog out of the unknown. When he attempted to send it back, it died in agony—confirmation he hadn't really needed that he was marooned where he was. But where was he?

Down the relentless procession of sikes, Egarn and the Old Med worked together on two questions that tantilized them. Egarn was obsessed with finding out where he was; the Old Med, a truly scientific personality in a barbarous age, was equally engrossed with the problem of where Egarn had come from. They finally accepted the incredible truth only because they had eliminated everything else—at which point they began trying to determine *when* Egarn was and *when* he had come

34

from, because he had traveled through time. Apparently the len focused temporal energy. This primitive Peerdom of Lant existed in Vladislov Kuznetsov's future—but exactly where in his future? The two of them were determined to find out.

In the Old Med's youth he had accumulated a large collection of antique books, ransacking ruins and even traveling to neighboring peerdoms in search of them. Egarn examined that library diligently. Some of the books were in English, and their dates, scattered through the first four decades of the 21st century, offered further proof that he had traveled through time.

He next became an archeologist and began to study artifacts that had been accidently discovered in Lant and its neighboring peerdoms. Two shattering truths forced themselves on him: He had traveled at least two hundred years into the future and probably more than three hundred; and some horrendous catastrophe had struck the planet Earth in the first half of the twenty-first century. None of the books had been published after the year 2039.

While he worked, and studied, and experimented, he paid little attention to the Peerdom of Lant and its people. Their lives had nothing whatsoever to do with his, which centered on the Old Med and the workroom. Egarn's admiration and affection for the old scientist continued to grow.

Then the Prince of Lant, the peer's eldest daughter and heir, a spiteful young lady of sixteen whom Egarn had quickly learned to avoid, inexplicably decided she was in love with him. She chose him as her consort in the casual kind of marriage that peeragers affected. In the Peerdom of Lant, only a recklessly headstrong prince would have insisted on mating with an unknown commoner; only a ruthless one could have gotten away with it.

The Old Med advised Egarn to consent. "If you refuse, you will make a permanent enemy," he said. "A stranger like yourself can't afford to offend the future peer. Accept her, treat her kindly, and indulge all of her whims. It won't last long. If you can make her your friend, you will have an invaluable patron."

The marriage lasted two years, which was far longer than peeragers' matings usually endured. There was one child, a daughter, who died young. They parted amicably, and when Egarn returned to the Old Med's workrooms, he had made a lifelong friend.

So involved did he and the Old Med become with problems of history and with their Honsun Len experiments that Egarn gave no further thought to social or political matters until the old med died at an advanced age. Then the prince, who now was the peer, appointed him Med of Lant. This was more astonishing than her choice of him as consort. The med was the peerdom's public health officer with responsibilities Egarn knew nothing about despite his long association with the Old Med. The appointment carried with it the lofty rank of Warden of the Peerdom, and only a peerager, a nobleman, could hold the position. But the Old Med had recommended him, and the peer appointed him, and no one dared object.

Egarn suddenly found himself administrator of a governmental bureaucracy that was, next to the army, the peerdom's largest. He had a complexity of duties and a huge staff of med servers to perform them for him. Since Egarn's arrival, the Old Med had ignored those duties. Many expected Egarn to do the same, but he wrenched himself away from his studies and doggedly set to work. He had long been the accidental guest of these people of Lant. They had treated him generously and given him high honors, and he had ignored them and their problems completely even though he knew from the beginning that his life was linked with theirs until death. Now he undertook to become a conscientious and competent Med of Lant.

What he learned on his first day in office horrified him.

This primitive society of the future was made up of rigid social classes, as he already knew. There were the peeragers, the age's aristocrats. They had two names, in which they took overweening pride, and they guarded their class lineage with vehemence. Even as consort to the prince and father of a daughter who would have become peer if she had lived, Egarn, a one-namer, was not allowed to acquire a second name.

The one-namers were the peerdom's crafters and skilled workers. They operated the mills, they wove, they baked, they engineered the roads, they built, they repaired, they kept the civilization functioning and its pathetically scant learning alive. As servers to those peeragers who headed the various governmental departments, they formed a type of civil service and actually ran the government. They also worked as personal servants to the peeragers and looked after their households. The few things they had no connection with were agriculture, any form of rough, heavy labor, and the military.

Rough labor was the responsibility of the work-humans, the no-namers, mentally deficient brutes who performed the most rigorous and exhausting labor under the lash without whimpering.

The no-namers' supervisors were called lashers. They, too, were no-namers, but at least they were given numbers. No-name males who had slightly more mental capacity than others of their kind became lashers, and forever afterward their cruelly flicking whips peeled flesh from the backs of their fathers and brothers and cousins—and, ultimately, sons. The military drafted its soldiers from the ranks of the lashers.

Egarn watched the brutal way the lashers drove the no-name laborers and felt revolted. He was even more horrified when he discovered the abominable basis for these class distinctions.

The Honsun Len.

And he, as Med of Lant, was responsible for its use.

Not only was the Honsun Len the foundation of the grossly superstitious medicine practiced in this civilization, but it also was used to numb the minds of no-namers and lashers and keep them subjugated. The treatments started in infancy. All babies born to no-name females received their first Honsun Len exposure shortly after birth. The mothers trustingly took their newborn babies to the med servers for what they thought were beneficial medical treatments—if the mentally impaired no-name females were able to think at all. The babies' still un-formed minds were partially destroyed by rays from the Honsun Len, which focused energy out of nowhere. Such treat-ments were repeated throughout the no-namers' lives. As a re-sult, a class of mindless humans was condemned to a lifetime of uncomplaining, totally submissive, slave labor.

The lashers received a different course of treatments. Their minds were left more alert but still sadly impaired. This proba-bly had nothing to do with their revolting characters. The fact that their entire lives were devoted to inflicting pain on others hardened them into unfeeling monsters.

The system had originated in the aftermath of the holo-caust, Egarn reasoned. One petty state managed to subjugate another and then, with fiendish cleverness, used the len on its people, thus eliminating any possibility of revolt and at the same time originating the most loathsome form of slavery ever devised. From babyhood, the minds of the slaves were bound in shackles that could never be loosened.

As the system became entrenched, work-humans were bred to achieve the stature best suited to a human draft animal. The system had functioned so efficiently that human slaves now were far less costly to breed and maintain than horses would have been.

A baby's schedule of treatments was predetermined by its alertness and stature. No-name females were left with suffi-cient mentality to enable them to rear children. Husky, more aggressive males became sub-moronic lashers and soldiers. The remaining no-name males were condemned to a lifetime of in-cessant labor that ended only when work or sickness killed them.

This shambles of a civilization was totally dependent on the system of slavery brought into being and maintained by the Honsun Len. But where had the Honsun Len come from? Egarn returned to his studies and eventually pieced isolated scraps of information into a staggering discovery. The Honsun Len had been invented at the end of the twentieth century by a man named Johnson, who had lived in Rochester, New York. Probably he had been a specialist in optics who worked in the photographic industry there. During his lifetime, the peculiar properties of his len made it an innocent curiosity, and only a few uses were found for it in children's toys or household gadgets. It was not a subject of serious scientific research until certain military applications were discovered.

When that happened, civilization was doomed. The Honsun Len, adapted to war, unleashed the primal energy of the universe on the planet Earth. It devastated a world and annihilated much of its population. Mounted in artificial satellites, huge Honsun Lens wiped out armies, destroyed cities, cut enormous chasms across plains, leveled hills, piled up new mountains. Coastlines and the courses of rivers were altered. The Honsun Len changed the face of the planet and almost obliterated it.

Now it was about to destroy civilization a second time—thanks, in part, to Egarn, who rediscovered the military potential of the len and unthinkingly gave a few copies of a weapon to the Peer of Lant when she convinced him her peerdom was threatened by its neighbors. In between, it had destroyed the minds of two thirds of the surviving human race.

"A great pity," Egarn mused, "that the Johnson who inflicted this curse on humanity didn't die young."

It was then that the great idea took possession of him: He could save humanity by destroying it. He had once read a story that posed a similar problem: Is it possible to change the present by journeying through time and altering the past? In the story, the quest failed. Egarn went over his plan again and again, trying to analyze it with cold logic, and he convinced himself it could succeed.

If the Honsun Len had never been invented, the destruction of Earth in the twenty-first century could not have happened, and the hideous aftermath that produced this civilization of brain-damaged slaves would not have occurred. If Egarn could retroactively eliminate the len, what would replace it? Something better, surely. He couldn't imagine anything worse. He had only to return to his own time, seek out this Johnson, and prevent him from inventing his insidious len or at least from giving it to the world. If it took murder to do that, so be it. It was the one way this barbaric future could be prevented: by destroying it before it happened.

He was the only person in the world who had the requisite knowledge to do that—to travel through time to a past where he knew the language, knew how to behave and function effectively, knew exactly how to commit a murder if there had to be one. He alone had sufficient knowledge, and he couldn't use it. The mere attempt to return to the past would kill him.

He would have to train someone else to do it.

The technical problems were mind-twisting in their complexity. It was one thing to speak of sending someone into the past; it was quite another thing to send that someone to a precise year, month, day, and time of day, and even that would not be sufficient. He also would have to be sent to a precise place. If the emissary landed in New York's Times Square at noon, his effectiveness would be severely impaired.

Egarn dedicated the remainder of his life to solving these problems. Metals were so scarce and so difficult to work that he had to fashion gears of wood, and for a long time no carver could make them with sufficient precision to produce the fine adjustments he required. He had been close to success, or so he thought, when the Peer of Lant came to him with her panicky story about Lant being invaded. Probably he had given her the weapon as much to keep his work from being interrupted as to save Lant. That error in judgment destroyed more than Lant's neighbors. It also destroyed his last chance to save Earth—or so he had thought when he heard the Lantiff's dogs on his trail.

Thanks to Bernal, fate had spun the wheel one more time, but where in this ghastly future could he find another time traveler, a martyr willing to immolate himself to save humanity? Because a trip through time was a one-way trip. Egarn's own experience proved that. Not only would the emissary be marooned in what would seem like an appallingly complex civilization, but he might be imprisoned or executed for murder.

As Egarn's delirium lessened, and the scouts came and went and worriedly discussed the intense search that was going on over their heads, he lay quietly on his bed of branches and thought about his great idea.

He not only had to find an emissary, but he had to give him a comprehensive survival course. He had to teach him what to say and do in every circumstance: instruct him about automobiles—driving one, buying one, insuring one, renting one; instruct him about auto repairs, anti-freeze, oil, lubricants; instruct him about traffic lights, pedestrian walkways, drivers' licences; instruct him about IDs and credit cards; about tall buildings and elevators; about airplanes, trains, busses, and taxis; about fast food, motels, and self-service gas stations; about money, tipping, shopping, and supermarket checkouts; about newspapers, radio and TV; about libraries, city directories, and telephones; about advertising, shopping malls, salesmen, sizes of clothing and shoes. The emissary would have to know the rudiments of investigation—how to track down one Johnson among the hundreds to be found in any major city—and he had to know how to survive while he did it, perhaps for months. Merely understanding money wouldn't be enough. He had to be able to acquire money when he needed it. He had to know about law and the police. He would even need coaching in breaking and entering.

The task of teaching someone from a primitive society about the complex wonders of the Twentieth Century was so enormous that Egarn hesitated even to make a beginning. He was much too old and much too tired. He had waited too long.

But he was the only man alive who could do it, and so he had to try. He would work while there was any life in him, and do his best, and pray that for once in his life he would be lucky.

"No," he muttered. "I will need a lot more than that. Luck wouldn't be enough. It will take a miracle."

4

EGARN (3)

The Peerdom of Lant was at war, but its campaigns had been little more than organized pillage. The peer began her invasions with a tiny force. Opposing generals invariably reacted to this insolent gesture by flinging every available lasher into a massive counterattack in the hope of overwhelming the Lantiff and ending the war quickly.

Strokes of lightning tore that counterattack to shreds, and claps of thunder routed the terrified survivors. Formal resistance in a newly invaded peerdom ended before battle was joined. The defending forces had neither the bravery nor the fanaticism to stand and fight against a foe that could invoke the terror of the elements. The peer's army, which had been waiting in concealment, then moved forward to rape and loot and vandalize at leisure.

The moment it became known that Egarn had escaped, the peer called off two of her wars to turn long ranks of Lantiff toward the western mountains. She had begun her southern invasion only recently, and she was reluctant to interfere with it; but she snatched entire armies from the north and east, leaving token forces to occupy the conquered peerdoms there. By the time Egarn's fever abated, the opportunity for flight that had existed during the first days of his escape had vanished.

His conscience-stricken gesture of destroying his weapons may have come too late—as Bernal pointed out, Lant's swollen armies no longer needed them for their conquests—but that fact did nothing to mitigate the peer's rage. She reacted with mindless fury and threw every available force into her search for the traitor. Now the Lantiff had sealed off all approaches to the border and were diligently combing the forested mountain slopes.

"Never mind," Bernal told Egarn. "We still have the advantage. If the dead Lantiff have been found, the peer knows you have horses, and she is lying awake nights wondering which way you went. North, south, east, west, you could have covered a lot of ground while the hunt was getting organized. No matter what oaths her border guards may swear, she will fear you slipped through one of the passes before word of your escape reached them. In that case, you are already in Easlon, and her massive hunt is a farce."

"If one-name foresters found the dead Lantiff, the peer will never find out what happened to them," Roszt said. "The foresters know from bitter experience that the nearest villages would be pillaged on principle if they left the bodies for the peer's army to find."

"Whether they were found or not, the peer won't rest until she catches me," Egarn said resignedly. "She will use torture to make me restore the weapons to her, and then she will have me killed in the most painful way she can think of. She will do the same with you three, of course."

"She will have to catch us first," Bernal said cheerfully.

"You know how to take care of yourselves. She wouldn't be able to catch you if you didn't have me to look after."

"Nonsense. There is nothing wrong with your legs, and anyway, we have the horses. As soon as you get your strength back, we will run for it."

Egarn stretched out languidly on his rough bed and remained silent for a time. Then he said, speaking slowly and hesitantly, "I wish I were able to tell you things—and show you things—just in case you escape and I don't. If I die without telling anyone, my life has been wasted."

Bernal waited silently.

"It is difficult to explain," Egarn said. "Can you grind a Honsun Len?"

Bernal chuckled. "I wouldn't know how to begin."

Egarn's voice took on a note of puzzlement. "I thought all one-name boys learned len grinding. They do in Lant, and med servers take the most talented as prentices. This civilization couldn't survive without Honsun Len grinders. There is an oddity about the len I have never been able to figure out. Whether it is used or not, in time it loses its effectiveness. Medical lens have to be replaced every sike and sometimes oftener—which is why med servers must become expert len grinders. That is also why the peer believed me when I told her the weapons needed new lens. They didn't, but eventually they would have. Lant's med servers are always looking for prentices. Are things different in the Ten Peerdoms?"

"No different," Bernal assured him. "My schooler taught len grinding to the younger boys, and a med server looked in on the classes and gave special lessons to those who had ability. He didn't include me. Probably the talents that made me a successful scout also made it impossible for me to sit for long hours grinding meaningless ripples in glass."

Egarn said regretfully, "Then you have never ground even one Honsun Len."

"According to my schooler, the mutilated objects I produced didn't bear the faintest resemblance to one. Those ripples required a precision that seemed inhuman to me. Only a few boys had both the patience and the ability, and they were sent to a special school. When we next saw them, they were wearing their prentice smocks and bragging about their futures as high servers of the peer. I wonder what they think of those futures now."

"Don't Easlon crafters have confidence in the future?"

"Perhaps len grinders do. We scouts know Lant will turn westward as soon as it conquers its other neighbors."

"So it will," Egarn agreed. There was a note of bitter sadness in his voice. He was silent for a moment, and then he returned to the subject of len grinding. "Did your schooler tell you anything about the Honsun Len?"

"That was for the students who became prentices."

"He should have told you as much as he knew. It has shaped your entire life. It will shape the lives—and deaths—of your children. It made your civilization what it is, and it will also destroy it."

"We scouts aren't much given to deep thinking," Bernal said cheerfully. "We have to be able to do the right thing quickly without thinking at all. But perhaps if you would explain what you mean—"

"I am sorry," Egarn said. "I would like to, but I wouldn't know how to begin if you don't know anything about the Honsun Len. Perhaps Roszt or Kaynor—"

"They are as ignorant as I am, but don't worry yourself about it. If we were expert len grinders, you might be able to make us understand, but we wouldn't have the slightest notion of how to get you out of Lant. What you need right now are expert scouts, and you have them. When you are safely across the mountains, you will find plenty of len grinders to talk with."

Egarn's arm was healing. He would never be able to use his hand again, but he was much more fortunate than most victims of the Lantiff's dogs. As he became stronger, the three scouts began planning their next move. It promised to be very dangerous indeed—so risky, in fact, that Bernal brought up the subject of Egarn's strange weapon.

"I don't want you to use it," he told Egarn soberly. "If you do, and there is a survivor, the peer will know exactly where we are. Her armies will stop chasing all over western Lant and start looking where they are likely to find us. On the other hand, the Lantiff have filled the forests with traps, and we haven't time to scout out all of them. It would be far better to use the weapon in order to escape than to not use it and be captured or killed."

"I will give it to you," Egarn said. "You can use it when you think it is necessary."

"But I don't know how," Bernal objected.

"It is easily learned. The Lantiff had no trouble with it, and what the Lantiff can learn in a week, any one-namer can master in an hour. It takes a bit of practice be accurate with it, and I don't suppose we can risk that, but even without practice you will be at least as good as I was. If I had aimed better, that last dog wouldn't have got to me."

The weapon did indeed seem easy to use. One pointed the correct end at the enemy and moved a small lever back and forth—an astonishingly simple manipulation for such an overwhelming result. Bernal tried it once, inside the cave, and marveled at the smoking hole it bored through solid rock.

When Egarn was finally ready to travel, Roszt and Kaynor went to search out a safe escape route. They reported that Lantiff were building encampments all along the frontier.

"I am sorry to hear that," Bernal said. "I was hoping the peer would have a message from the south by now about a corpse found with Egarn's clothing and pack."

Roszt shook his head. "I told you at the time—there were far too many corpses and far too many human vultures plundering the dead. Only an incredible stroke of luck would have got that body identified as Egarn's before the looters stripped it completely."

"I thought there was a fair chance," Bernal said. "These encampments mean the peer is combining the search for Egarn with preparations to invade Easlon, and that doubles our problems. We must get out of Lant quickly."

A trek through the mountains would have been difficult for an elderly cripple even in the best of circumstances, and they would travel in darkness, on rugged, little-used tracks known only to the scouts, and under a constant threat of ambush or attack. Egarn resigned himself to a nightmarish journey that would tax his strength to the utmost.

When they finally started, the going seemed so easy that he had a bewildered feeling of disappointment. The Lantiff had blocked all the roads, but he rode a horse at a leisurely pace half of the night, from one of the scouts' way stations to another, without seeing a single soldier.

"Where are they?" he blurted during one of their brief rests.

"You will see more than enough of them before we are finished," Bernal said. "The Lantiff have concentrated to protect

46

the passes. The further west we go, the more of them we will encounter. Enjoy your ride while you can."

Roszt and Kaynor rode ahead. Then came Egarn, with Bernal bringing up the rear. The two scouts from Slorn cheerfully accepted the fact that they were expendable. If the little party rode into an ambush, their task was to keep Egarn from becoming involved. Even if they were disastrously outnumbered, they had to somehow occupy the Lantiff until Egarn and Bernal slipped away. Bernal carried Egarn's weapon inside his shirt; he would use it only as a last resort.

The moon, which had been full the night of Egarn's escape, was now only a sliver in the sky, but so thick was the forest that they rarely saw it. They followed paths that the forest floor did not hint of—ways known only to the scouts of Easlon. They threaded along hillsides and took unexpected loops to avoid roads and habitations.

On the first night they came abruptly on a place where a landslide had peeled away the forest and left a sweeping view of a broad valley. It was a cove, a rare area of cultivated land in the Lantian hills, and they paused for a moment to look down on the community there: the long sheds where the no-name males slept; the brood buildings where no-name females conceived and bore their children; the nursery; the lashers' dormitory; the cook shed and storage buildings; the inevitable neat med cottage where a med server gave the community's population its Honsun Len treatments. Day and night had no meaning for the no-namers, the work-humans. They were laboring in torch-lined fields, long hair and beards drooping as their muscular bodies bent low to strain at the ropes that drew the heavy cultivating sledges. The lashers were shouting orders and wielding their whips. The scene looked small and very far away, and the coarse shouts were only faintly audible, but the *whups* of whips striking the no-namers' bare backs could be heard clearly. Of course the upwelling blood that appeared as each stroke peeled away living flesh could not be seen from such a distance.

Egarn knew the blood was there. He had witnessed such scenes often enough during his long lifetime in Lant. He jerked sharply on his reins and sat looking down into the valley until Bernal overtook him.

"'Man's inhumanity to man,'" he muttered. "How can anyone look at that without sickening? Poor, mindless brutes laboring their lives away while other brutes trained to sadism systematically torture them. In the med cottage, we practice a different form of viciousness on them from the moment of their birth. I have done it myself. I am as responsible as anyone. These are the foul dregs of a humanity that once sought the stars. Perhaps it is no longer possible to save the human race, but if I have time—if I live long enough—"

Bernal had been listening quietly. "When we get to Easlon, we will send for Arne. This is his kind of problem. You mentioned once that the way to save humanity is by destroying it. What would that accomplish?"

"Maybe nothing," Egarn said.

They spent their days in hiding places well-known to the scouts, and they had the carefully contrived good fortune to slip past the Lantiff's watchposts without incident. It was evident by the third night, however, that they couldn't go much farther. The mere presence of so many Lantiff clogged not only the roads but even the trailways leading west, and though they deftly avoided these routes, they still had to cross one occasionally. That became increasingly difficult, and finally Bernal decided to turn north.

They moved laterally across the mountain trails, slipping between Lantiff encampments, and eventually they gained the high mountains far north of the heavily guarded passes. Then they turned south. It was a journey perilous beyond Egarn's imagining, but his strength was returning rapidly, and he throve on it. Frequently he had to dismount—because a misstep might send both horse and rider plunging into an abyss—and lead his blindfolded steed along ledges that looked far too narrow for any animal larger than the short-eared mountain rabbits. They traveled high, lonely valleys, riding recklessly at night but not daring to expose themselves by day. In that barren country, one could see for many kilometers. Finally they left their horses with Easlon scouts they met at a secret way station near the border, and they performed a final, tortuous climb on foot. In this way they reached Low Pass, one of the two gateways to the west the Lantiff were guarding so zealously.

They looked down on it from a thousand meters above.

"This is one of *our* passes," Bernal said grimly. "The Lantiff would consider it impassable—which is why they have never been able to figure out how Easlon scouts come and go so easily."

"Easily?" Egarn muttered.

But their tribulations were not over. Once they were safely across the high divide, they discovered that Lantiff had already pushed beyond the pass into Easlon, and they had to turn north again. For a time they feared the long expected invasion was upon them, but the Lantiff contented themselves with patrolling a few lateral valleys. Finally, after several nerve-wracking near encounters, they left the forces of Lant behind them.

They pressed onward until, in the deepest hours of an overcast night, they saw flares ahead of them. It was a lumber camp where no-name laborers strained at ropes to haul logs to a rushing river while the lashers' whips wrote new chapters in agony on their bare backs—but these were Easlon lashers and no-namers working in an Easlon camp. Bernal halted their march long before dawn. He authorized a campfire and announced that they could rest until the following middae and then travel by daelight. He would try to find a horse somewhere and get to headquarters as quickly as possible to warn Inskor, the chief scout, that the Lantian invasion was imminent. Then he would meet them somewhere down the line with horses.

"You are safe, now," Bernal told Egarn. "You are as safe as anyone can be in these troubled times. That doesn't mean there is no longer any hurry. It is too early to say whether Lant is planning a full-scale invasion or only a reconnaissance, but we must prepare for the worst. We will need some of your weapons as quickly as we can make them. Inskor will send for the best len grinders in Easlon, and they will do whatever you want."

"Will he send for the Med of Easlon?" Egarn asked.

"Certainly not. What help would he be? One-namers will make your weapons for you. One-name scouts will use them. We won't let Easlon's peeragers know anything about them. Otherwise, you would quickly find yourself in the same kind of trouble we just rescued you from."

Roszt and Kaynor were nodding their agreement.

"What we absolutely must do is crush the Lantiff," Bernal went on. "If we don't, we won't have any future to plan for. A victory will buy time for us and give you a chance to tell your ideas to Arne and the League of One-Namers. They are the ones concerned with saving humanity."

He spoke his farewell and vanished into the night.

Egarn watched him go with a feeling of emptiness. He had become fast friends with Roszt and Kaynor. The tall, gaunt scouts from the ravished Peerdom of Slorn were rootless exiles like himself and victims of the same tyranny he was fleeing from. There was a strong empathy between them; but Bernal was their leader. He had made the decisions, sternly kept them on the move, and finally led them to safety.

Now they could relax for the first time in more than a tenite. The scouts from Slorn were far better company than the dour Bernal, who had become increasingly tense and irritable as they faced one delay after another. Even Kaynor, who liked to complain, also liked to joke. Before sleeping, they sat by the fire and ate hot food—a rare treat—and Egarn listened contentedly while the other two discussed the lore of the trail and hazards faced alone in the land of an inexorable enemy. The tales fascinated him. So did the scouts. In his long years at the court of Lant, he had come to know many people well, but he had never met anyone like these refugees from Slorn.

"In my childhood, there were legends told of a Med of Lant who was a sorcerer," Roszt said suddenly. "I suppose he was long before your time."

Egarn said quietly, "I was his student."

Roszt nodded understandingly. "Every med trains his successor from boyhood, or so it is said. I thought perhaps you were an exception because you don't look like a Lantian. The sorcerer med traveled through all the neighboring peerdoms ransacking old ruins for books. He had a reputation for acquiring forgotten wisdom that extended far beyond Lant."

"He was a great man," Egarn said. "He not only acquired wisdom, but he was also wise enough to know when not to use it."

Both Roszt and Kaynor seemed interested, so Egarn told them about the Old Med and his experiments. When he reached the point where things began to disappear or appear out of nowhere, he expected them to turn away with polite skepticism. Instead, they were fascinated.

"Where did the things come from?" Roszt asked.

Egarn described the Old Med's experiment with the porkley and its astonishing result.

"Were you the man?" Kaynor asked.

Egarn changed the subject. "The Old Med made many discoveries. It was he who invented the weapon. Then—when we understood a little about what it would do—he destroyed it. He said, 'This is far too dangerous for anyone to know about, even us.' He was far wiser than I."

Roszt's mind was still fixed on the disappearances and appearances. "But where *did* you come from?"

"It took us many sikes to find out," Egarn said with a wistful smile. "We worked on it together, experiment after experiment. Each of us knew half the answer, but there was no way either of us could explain his half so the other could understand. We experimented, and we searched through book after book of the Old Med's collection. Finally the combination of my past and his present gave us the answer."

"Gave you—what answer?" Kaynor asked blankly.

"I had traveled through time. That meant—"

He broke off. There was so little chance of their under-standing him that he might as well have been talking to him-self.

"Too bad you didn't bring the Old Med's machine with you when you escaped," Roszt said. "You could have sent the four of us to Easlon without the trek across the mountains."

"Could you have done that?" Kaynor asked.

"Yes. With time to experiment, I suppose I could have."

"Could you send scouts into Lant from here and bring them back when they are ready to come? That would save tenites of weary travel each trip."

"If he could send a few scouts, he could send an army," Roszt observed. "That would give the Peer of Lant something to think about—an army that appeared out of nowhere, attacked her in the rear, and then vanished. It might even convince her to keep her own armies at home. What else can this machine do?"

"It can save humanity," Egarn said.

"That's what you were telling Bernal. How could it save hu-manity?"

Egarn looked at them uncertainly across the dying camp-fire. Their ugly faces were weathered like ancient rocks that had been exposed to the elements for eons, and their lank bod-ies were preposterously thin despite their hearty appetites. Their rough, leather clothing was worn and soiled from their long days and nights of travel. They seemed like the most un-likely audience possible for speculation about time travel, but Egarn had had no one to talk with for sikes—not since the Old Med died.

"If they start looking bored," he thought, "I will plead ex-haustion and totter off to bed. Either way, they will forget about it by morning."

He told them of his plan to send someone more than three hundred years into the past to prevent a certain Johnson from inventing the Honsun Len. He was convinced, now, that the only sure way to accomplish this was to murder him, but he carefully avoiding mentioning that.

They listened attentively. They may have been simple men, but their perceptions were sharpened by the dangers they faced constantly, and they hated the Peer of Lant and her infamous deeds as much as he did.

When he finished, the two scouts were silent for a time. Then Kaynor said, "If someone traveled through time and kept this Johnson from inventing his len, what would happen to Lant, and the Ten Peerdoms, and everyone who lives here?" His gesture delineated the world as it was known to him. "What would happen to everything that is all around us right now? You say that without the Honsun Len, something decent would take its place. Where would it come from, and where would this go?"

"I don't know," Egarn said soberly. "Perhaps nothing at all would happen. Perhaps time has a momentum that would prevent wrenching it aside into some other path. Or we might change the past, and give humanity another chance, without affecting this doomed present at all. Perhaps every past has many possible futures and this is only one of them. I simply don't know." He paused. "Or perhaps 'here and now' might vanish the way the flame on a candle vanishes when it's blown out."

"And all the people with it?"

Egarn nodded. "It is the future of the human race that must concern us, not our own futures."

Kaynor turned to Roszt. "It sounds like a job for for scouts," he said.

"A job for us," Roszt agreed. "It will be much more interesting than snooping about the court of Lant. When you are ready to send someone, let us know."

"You couldn't go—just like that," Egarn protested. "It would take work and study to prepare yourselves. Hard work and hard study. Maybe for sikes. And if you do go, you can't come back. It also will be extremely dangerous, and you may be risking your lives for nothing. I can't even promise you will accomplish anything if you succeed. Maybe the whole idea is impossible."

"We don't mind danger as long as there is a worthwhile purpose," Kaynor said. "If there is any chance at all of blowing out the Peer of Lant and her armies, I want to help."

Egarn had spent daes worrying about the difficulty of finding a willing emissary, and he was astonished that this was happening so easily.

It was happening too easily. The scouts from Slorn were were superbly qualified as scouts—as spies and saboteurs in enemy territory. If courage and resourcefulness were the only necessary qualifications, they would be an ideal choice, but when he tried to visualize them in any twentieth century social situation, such as ordering food in a restaurant or doing research in a library reading room, he failed. They would look clumsily out-of-place wherever they went. Probably they would attract attention to themselves with every move they made—he could imagine them bumping into people, stumbling over things, spilling their drinks, dropping their forks, and destroying their mission out of sheer clumsiness.

He said slowly, "You will be exiles forever in a place that will be terrifyingly strange to you. You will have to face dangers of a kind you can't even imagine."

"One place is as good as another to us—or as bad," Roszt said. "We no longer have homes anyway. As for the dangers, we have no fear at all of death—only of a wasted death. We welcome a cause to die for."

Kaynor added, "When we first heard you talk about saving humanity by destroying it, we thought it was some silliness brought on by your fever. Now we understand, and we want to help you."

"If your plan doesn't work, humanity is going to destroy itself anyway and leave nothing," Roszt said.

That was Egarn's thought exactly, but he had wanted an emissary who would appear completely ordinary in every respect; one who would never stand out in a crowd—who could carry out the mission almost unnoticed.

But perhaps it was a job for scouts—for what would they be

when they reached the twentieth century but saboteurs in enemy territory? Perhaps courage and resourcefulness were more important than a commonplace appearance. "Very well," Egarn said. "If you are able to learn what you have to know, you can go together."

"We will find this Johnson," Roszt said, "but it won't be enough to destroy his len. As soon as we left him, he would make another."

Kaynor nodded. "That is obvious. We will have to kill him."

5

THE PEER OF LANT

The Med of Lant was missing.

The rumor spread through the court like one of the preposterous diseases the old man was so fond of warning peeragers about, carrying with it a rash of unlikely symptoms—fits of temper, seizures of indigestion, irritating itches, swollen gums, even a plague of hangnails. These maladies in combination dampened an entire tenite of the traditional Plao Fest and forced the cancellation of several hunts.

The disorders were much talked about, symptoms were compared, elixirs were exchanged. No one mentioned the Med of Lant aloud. No one dared to—and yet the rumor spread, and spread.

One-name servers and servants, always inexhaustible sources of court gossip, turned inexplicably reticent when asked about the Med. No one-namer in the entire court complex would admit to knowing anything at all, not even that the old man was missing. Court officials watched the peer for a sign. There could be no public comment on the Med's absence until she herself officially acknowledged it and indicated the attitude she favored.

The Peer of Lant said nothing. She acted as though totally oblivious of the old man's existence. When she passed the vanished Med's quarters and workroom on her morning ride, she seemed not to notice the guard placed there. She even attempted to keep secret the far-ranging search she was conducting, but in that she failed spectacularly. The whispered rumors that seeped through the court carried descriptions of the rage with which she received her harassed officers' reports of failure.

The routine work of the Med's office suffered no disruption. His servers were highly competent, and—since he had devoted much of his time to private matters—they certainly didn't need him to tell them what to do. Even so, it was remarkable for the peer to leave a high office vacant, and with each passing dae, uneasiness and uncertainly increased among the med servers and those with tasks linked to theirs.

"All this fuss about someone I don't even *know!*" a pouting peerling, a younger daughter of the nobility, complained guardedly when told that yet another hunt had been cancelled. Peerists and peerlings, the younger aristocrats, were only vaguely aware of the Med's existence. He had hovered dimly in the court's background, a slightly comical, shadowy figure who preferred fussing in his dusty workroom to taking part in the richly varied cycle of fests and hunts. Some had never seen him at all. It was said that early each morning he walked in his garden, where strange and unpalatable fruits and vegetables like plums and strawberries and tomatoes were cultivated, but even if the garden had not been enclosed, no peerager would have been up at that hour to catch a glimpse of him.

Older peeragers could remember a time when he was very much a part of the court scene—an advisor, even a confident of the peer. Elderly peeragers his own age, of whom very few survived, could have told a great deal more about him, but they wisely made a virtue of their failing memories and said nothing.

Only in the peerdom's one-name villages was the Med's disappearance discussed openly. One-namers who lived away from the court did not have to rely on rumors for their information. Forest workers had seen the growing army of searchers beating the undergrowth. One-namers whose duties required travel had been harassed by road patrols and questioned at frequent watchposts. Outlying work camps had been searched. The Lantiff turned out every resident of one small village and tore their dwellings apart. Accounts of these experiences were passed from village to village until one-namers from one end of Lant to the other were watching and waiting apprehensively and sifting every scrap of news for portents of catastrophies to come, and their forebodings crossed the borders to one-namers of the conquered peerdoms.

Egarn's predecessor in office, still referred to as the Old Med, had been a legend in his own time, an awesome figure venerated by all, a sorcerer who dealt with forces of darkness better left unmentioned. By comparison, Egarn—a one-namer, a commoner in a high office that tradition reserved for peeragers—had been a nonentity, and few had been aware of his power and influence. Elderly one-namers remembered him as a kindly man willing to speak out against an injustice when no one else dared. Elderly peeragers considered him an aberration because he worked hard. Not only had he accepted the responsibilities of his office, but he actually attempted to carry them out. A peerager would have considered it a solemn obligation to perform as little work as possible.

Egarn had concerned himself with everyone's health, even that of the no-namers, and he made the peerdom a far healthier place by emphasizing the need for sanitation, for pure water, for carefully prepared food, for skillful nursing of the sick, and for the isolation of those with certain kinds of diseases. He held the respect of all of his contemporaries, including the peer, because he avoided court intrigue and disdained the sordid maneuvering for personal advantage that was the foremost concern of peeragers and their one-name high servers.

Now he was missing, and even those who thought they knew him well were discovering how little was known about him. He was a man of mystery in a land and an age where there should have been no mystery about anyone, and the peer's incomprehensible conduct underscored his strangeness. Every member of her court savored the latest rumors and watched alertly to see what she would say and do.

She said and did nothing.

The Peer of Lant had attained the age of sixty-five in robust good health, and she fully expected to enjoy a remarkable longevity. She attributed this good fortune to her austere habits, and—conveniently forgetting the multifold indulgences of her youth—she was constantly taxing her fellow peeragers with their excesses.

Food, drink, fests, hunts, and love affairs circumscribed the peerager's life, not only in Lant, but in every peerdom she was familiar with. She was determined to do something about that—not with her surviving contemporaries or their children, whom she scornfully considered beyond redemption, but with their children's children. She redeemed those young peerlings and peerists whenever she could, snatching them out of their indolence and working them hard, especially at military command and organization, and they responded creditably. Already some were performing well in responsible positions.

The Peer of Lant meant to conquer the known world. One of her uncles had been fond of ancient military legends, and he retold these tales to her when she was a child. They fired her imagination and engendered a vision that never left her of warriors, and conquest, and the purification of a decadent human race by battle. She spent much of her youth playing at war games with troops recruited from among the children of servants, and she had followed her vision steadfastly throughout her life with very few deviations.

One of those deviations had been Egarn. She vividly remembered the day the Old Med her uncle brought him to court for the first time. She had been fourteen or fifteen—beautiful, she thought, and flushed with triumph from a mock battle in which her youthful warriors had soundly outmaneuvered a similar troop blunderingly led by a male cousin.

She came dashing along on her horse followed by an elite mounted escort of hulking lashers she had chosen herself for their ferocity in practice duels. Her uncle was approaching the palace from his workroom accompanied by the strangest-looking male she had ever seen. He was tall in stature but, compared with her lashers, preposterously slender. His hair was cut short enough to look silly, but it was the purest, most glimmering blond hair she had ever seen. Despite his outlandish clothing, he seemed handsome to her. She dismounted, as did her escort. Her uncle knelt; Egarn, who had been walking a pace ahead of him, failed to notice. He strolled past her, the Prince of Lant, as though she didn't exist and without a hint of obeisance.

Any spirited prince would have reacted as she did. She used her whip on him. What followed was in every way astonishing. Egarn, speaking words that were incomprehensible to her, turned and with unbelievable quickness calmly caught her wrist, twisted it, took the whip from her, and tossed it aside. Her escort sprang forward to avenge this treasonable insult, and she, with becoming fury, signaled she wanted the miscreant dead. Moments later, all five members of her escort were trying to pick themselves up from the ground. Two had broken limbs and did not succeed. The other three abandoned their intention of tearing Egarn apart with their bare hands. They drew their swords. He stood waiting calmly for their next move. That was when the peer her mother arrived and demanded an explanation for this mayhem that was disturbing the peace of her court.

The Old Med presented the stranger to peer and prince as his personal guest. He was called Egarn—his real name was difficult to say, so the med had given him one of his own names to use—and he was a traveler from a far place. He had special knowledge and skills of great value that were unknown in the Peerdom of Lant. The Old Med hoped to persuade him to remain as his assistant. Unfortunately, Egarn hadn't yet learned their customs, and therefore he didn't know that everyone in Lant was required to kneel to prince and peer.

The Old Med then turned to Egarn and explained, speaking slowly and with simple words, that a single knee must touch the ground in greeting the prince, after which the subject could rise but with eyes downcast unless spoken to. Both knees must touch the ground in greeting the peer, and the subject was not permitted to rise until the peer had passed by unless the peer granted permission. The Old Med demonstrated.

Egarn watched and listened with obvious indignation.

When the Old Med finished, he turned his gaze on the prince. She had never experienced one like it. It expressed contempt as well as a fierce desire to retrieve her whip and use it on her. No other inhabitant of Lant or any other peerdom would have dared to look at a prince in that fashion.

Egarn announced proudly, "An American Citizen kneels to no one," and there was no mistaking his meaning even if the words were incomprehensible.

Since kneeling was contrary to the practices of the stranger's own land, the peer ruled him exempt until he'd had time to familiarize himself with the customs of Lant and decide whether he wished to remain there.

He never did kneel. He contented himself with bending forward slightly at the waist. The peer her mother, who developed a liking for him, was content with that; the prince was not. For an entire sike she venomously plotted his death. Then it suddenly occurred to her that Egarn was by far the bravest person she had ever met, and she idolized bravery. Five oversized lashers had assaulted him simultaneously, and he met them without a flicker of fear and casually tossed one after another to the ground. When three of them came at him with drawn swords—himself unarmed—he had faced them just as calmly. His was a different sort of bravery, a bravery of skill and courage rather than the brutal force with which lashers met danger and dealt out death. Once she understood that, she fell madly in love with him and made him her first consort.

In Lant, it was unheard of for a peerager to openly mate with a one-namer. Even a willful prince such as herself wouldn't have dared to do so if he hadn't been a stranger. When several of her uncles objected, she told them what Egarn himself had said—in his own land, no one held a rank that was higher than his—and they had to be content with that.

Egarn was the father of her first child, a beautiful, gentle daughter who looked remarkably like him. Fortunately for the Peerdom of Lant, the girl died young. With her shy inwardness, she would have made a deplorable prince and peer, but she *was* a lovely child. Even when the prince tired of Egarn's quiet ways and found other consorts, for many, many years—in fact, until she began her wars of conquest—they had remained friends, and when she needed advice, she had gone to him without hesitation and with the certainty that he would speak honestly and unselfishly. She appointed him Med of Lant when the Old Med her uncle died, and she had never regretted it.

She did not regret it now. Not only had he made Lant a healthier place for everyone, but none of her military conquests would have been possible without him.

The lashers of Lant, who guarded and supervised the no-namers and filled the ranks of the peer's armies, were a race apart—a squat, muscular people possessed of a fearless recklessness that could, with proper training, make them invincible warriors. She saw that even when she was young. As soon as she became peer, she began organizing and training her Lantiff, elite troops of lasher horsemen whose frenzied charges, flashing, curved swords, and vicious lances were calculated to inflict terror on their opponents. She tested her ideas with occasional raids into neighboring peerdoms, and the results were gratifying.

Unfortunately, she miscalculated. She alarmed her neighbors before she was ready for war, and they responded by developing armies of their own. Worse, as the army of Lant became stronger and its incursions more frequent, the neighboring peerdoms began to band together for mutual assistance against the marauding Lantiff. Over the years a stand-off developed, but the Peerdom of Lant was badly outnumbered, and that disparity increased yearly. Finally the neighboring peers decided to put an end to Lant's perpetual belligerency. A combined invasion was planned; Lant was to be partitioned amongst its neighbors and its peeragers exterminated.

In deep despair, the peer turned to Egarn. He promised to devise a weapon that would protect the peerdom against any combination of enemies, and he had done so, to her delight and astonishment. The amount of destruction a mere handful of trained Lantiff could do with the strange tubes Egarn fashioned strained the powers of belief. Suddenly she possessed a force powerful beyond her wildest imaginings.

The lesson of a near defeat had taught her to plan her moves with care. She launched a lightning campaign, triumphantly concluded before her enemies could react in concert, and toppled the first of her neighbors. Before she she struck again, she paused long enough to assimilate the conquered army into her own, fortify her new borders, and set up an administration that could exploit the subjected territory's war potential.

She had conquered all her northern and eastern neighbors, began a long-planned southern invasion, and was turning her thoughts beyond the western mountains to the Ten Peerdoms when Egarn committed his appalling treachery. He came to her with a tale about renewing the weapons. She had believed him. Why not? She knew med servers had to replace their lens from time to time. Further, Egarn had given the weapons to her freely as a gift and asked nothing for himself. He never asked anything for himself except the freedom to pursue his studies.

Then he informed her he had destroyed the weapons—every one of them, he said—and he refused to make more. When she inflicted privations on him and threatened torture, he killed his guards with a weapon he somehow had kept hidden and escaped.

She had thought him the most selfless, the most totally loyal individual in her peerdom. When he turned against her, she discovered she hadn't known him at all. In her fury she taxed him with treason, and he answered, "I have repaid my indebtedness to Lant and to you many times over. I have kept your peerdom healthy through both of our lifetimes, and I gave you weapons to defend it against invaders. When you used those weapons for conquest, you also used them against me."

Now he had vanished utterly. So had the Lantiff sent to capture him, along with their dogs and horses, leaving her wondering uneasily about other miraculous weapons he might have.

She was consumed by apprehension that he might escape over the mountains and bestow his weapons, his knowledge, and his counsel—she well knew the value of all three—on the decadent rulers of the Ten Peerdoms. She took the only course open to her. She hurriedly concentrated her Lantiff, blocked all routes to the west, and began a massive search.

Then a totally unexpected report arrived out of the south. She refused to believe it, but she sent Com Gerna, the young commander of her guard, to investigate. He returned after eight daez of frenzied riding and silently offered her a shabby bundle. The peer opened it with her own hands.

She recognized Egarn's clothing. The combination of peerager trousers and one-name smock defied both custom and common sense, but Egarn had worn it because he thought it comfortable.

The peer sniffed distastefully. The clothing reeked of death.

"I had the garments washed carefully, Majesty," Com Gerna said. "The odor clings to anything it touches."

She pushed the clothing aside and examined the small bag of oddments that accompanied it. The belt she recognized at once. There was a package of dried leaves of a kind Egarn had been fond of munching; a quill sharpener; the thin, flat piece of wood with patterns of figures used by Egarn in making calculations; an ordinary pocket len that had assisted his failing eyesight; a few trinkets. Most of it was mere pocket debris, but the trinkets brought back memories.

She fingered them thoughtfully. Egarn had worn the disk of metal on a thong as a neck ornament. A coin, he called it, and claimed it held a mysterious significance in the land of his origin. Where that land was she never understood. Perhaps the Old Med her uncle had known. Egarn never talked about it to anyone else. Certainly he had been a strange man.

"No weapon," she said suddenly. "But we know he had at

64

least one weapon when he escaped." She looked at Com Gerna narrowly. "Are you positive the dead man was Egarn?"

"Yes, Majesty. There can be no doubt at all that it was he. These are personal things his servers know well. Another might have come into the possession of one or two, perhaps, but who else would have been carrying all of them, both the valuable and the trivial? The body was advanced in decay by the time I saw it, but the recognizable features were those of the Med of Lant—the tallness of stature, the slender build, the bald, beardless head. Of course the face—"

The peer shuddered. "But there was no weapon?" she persisted.

Com Gerna squirmed uneasily. "Majesty, I searched as carefully as the conditions permitted. The battlefield had been plundered twice—once by Wymeffian one-namers and once by local lashers from a nearby compound. There were many bodies, and scavengers would not waste time on trifles as long as there was a possibility of richer loot on the other dead. That is why these things were left. We can't know what they took. It was sheer luck that a commander who formerly served your majesty at court chanced to see the body."

"Then you think plunderers took his weapon?"

"I think it was taken by a one-namer or common lasher who thought it might prove valuable. When he couldn't discover a use for it, he threw it away. Believe me, Majesty, if such a one had started using it, we would have heard."

"And—there is nothing else?"

"I organized a careful search of a large area around the place where the med's body lay. We discovered only one thing of interest, and that was found a considerable distance away. A plunderer could have taken it and then tossed it aside as worthless. It may have no connection with the med. Certainly he made no regular use of it—his servants and assistants don't recognize it—but because it is so strange, I immediately thought it might be his."

He placed the object before the peer.

She inhaled sharply. "His folding knife," she murmured. "That was clever of you, Com Gerna, to search the area so widely. It was indeed his. It belonged to his past, and he valued it enormously. He never would have parted with it while he was alive."

She took another deep breath. "So—Egarn is dead." She felt triumphant and at the same time regretful. "I will make the announcement at once. Thank you, Com Gerna. You have exceeded my expectations."

"Majesty," the young commander murmured and knelt.

She sat motionless for a long time, thinking about Egarn. Perhaps—just perhaps—she had made a serious mistake. Egarn had been an old man, and the minds of elderly males were subject to strange aberrations. If she had been patient, treated him with kindness, and appealed to his friendship, perhaps she could have coaxed him back to normality. She had acted as a peer when she should have approached him as an old friend who needed his help.

"If I had been able to consult Egarn," she reflected pensively, "he would have advised me to use patience and kindness." At the time she had needed his counsel the most, she could not ask him for it. Now he was dead. He had escaped her. He also had defeated her. His miraculous weapon was lost— perhaps forever.

But this was no time for vain regrets. She wanted to look ahead, not backward. She conferred at once with Com Welsif, her first general. He was her cousin, the one who so frequently lost war games to her in their youth, but he had developed into her best commander. He handled an army with ease, and he had refused to panic over the flight of one elderly med.

"We know for certain, now, that a party of Easlon scouts slipped through our cordon many daez ago," he said.

"They seem to have a knack for that," the peer observed frostily.

The first general scowled. "They were riding black horses, Majesty. Four, perhaps five."

The peer raised her eyebrows.

"They seem to have circled far to the north," the first general went on. "They may have a secret pass there."

"What does it mean?" the peer asked.

"It was silly to send a single squad of Lantiff after Egarn. We know he possessed strange knowledge, and we shouldn't be surprised that he fooled his pursuers so easily. The puzzling thing is that he fooled their dogs as well. Could he have worked some kind of sorcery with his scent?"

"I hadn't thought of that," the peer mused. "Certainly it is possible. Maybe it is even likely. As you said, he possessed much strange knowledge."

"However it happened, he eluded the pursuit and turned south. The Lantiff, thinking they were still close behind him, continued westward. Lantiff and dogs are much alike—once they fix their minds on a chase, they never hesitate. They went charging into wild country, and Easlon scouts managed to ambush them."

"How many scouts would it take to dispose of five Lantiff and their dogs?" the peer asked.

"Fewer than you would believe," the first general said grimly. "They are resourceful and capable men. Take it that it was done. It was the horses they wanted, of course. Easlon has long envied us our horses. They must have hid the Lantiff's bodies, but they were in a hurry to get away, so probably they did it in haste. Sooner or later someone will find them. The horses went north and west. Egarn went south and got caught up in the battle there. His weapon wouldn't be of much use to him in the middle of a battlefield with enemies on all sides. Probably he had it in his hand when he fell, and it was the first thing looted—if it wasn't covered by the debris of battle."

The peer nodded thoughtfully. "Yes. That explains everything. The death of Egarn is the worst defeat Lant has suffered in my lifetime because I gave him my complete trust and he gave much in return and could have given more. But in the end he ranted at me—soft-livered male that he was—about the slaughter of peaceful populations, as though neighbors who train large armies and conspire against Lant are to be considered peaceful until the moment they strike. Now Lant's army is large enough to be irresistible with or without Egarn's weapon. We should be planning our next move. Isn't it time to turn west?"

The first general said cautiously, "It is time to *look* west, perhaps."

The peer understood what he meant. Lant had not made a successful border raid into Easlon for sikes. The mountains, gouged and twisted almost to the point of impassability—by great wars of the past, Egarn had said—were an invaluable defensive barrier but an enormous disadvantage to a peer intent on conquering her neighbors. They were as easily defended by Easlon as by Lant, and when Lant's depredations among its neighbors increased, the Peerdom of Easlon greatly augmented its squadrons of scouts. Not only did they make the Lantian scouts pay dearly for every attempted incursion, but they so completely suppressed all efforts to obtain information that the peer's generals did not even know whether any of the Ten Peerdoms maintained an army.

Certainly it was time to look west. The Peer of Lant reflected, with the darkly ominous scowl that had brought death and destruction crashing down on many a distant, peaceful village, that the lands beyond her other frontiers were no longer worth despoiling. Peerdoms that fancied themselves to be the next victims of Lant were hiding food and valuables and avoiding the accumulation of goods that could easily be wrested from them. They were even removing their commoners from the border regions. An army traveling in any of those directions would have to carry its own provisions.

The Ten Peerdoms, rich with wealth accumulated during sikes of peace and indolence, were ripe for plundering, but she reluctantly conceded that her cousin was right. Before exposing an army to unknown hazards, they first must take a careful look and gather information.

"A surprise raid?" she suggested. "A reconnaissance in sufficient strength to brush aside the curstuff Easlon scouts but small enough to withdraw quickly when it chooses?"

The first general agreed. A reconnaissance in force could map Easlon's eastern province while gathering information and prisoners. If the force were large enough to crush local resistance and still small enough to travel lightly and quickly and live off the country, it could test the defenses and pick up invaluable intelligence at negligible risk.

"The Ten Peerdoms have been hiding their prosperity long enough," the peer said. "Let's do it."

Half the peeragers of her court petitioned for permission to lead the raid. The peer scornfully rejected them. Her strategy for years to come would be determined by the outcome, and nothing could be permitted to go wrong. The first general would command in person. Her only concession to court clamor was to assign three of her own sons to his staff on the off chance that the dolts might learn something. After Egarn, she'd had a series of alliances with weak consorts able to beget only sons. She was in her late thirties when she finally bore the two daughters she wanted. These she had brought up in her own image, and she assigned the elder, her prince, to be the first general's second in command.

The first general himself hand-picked the other commanders, and they hand-picked their troops. There would be a hundred Lantiff, ten scouts, a mapper and his two assistants, and a full contingent of officers.

Once the force was complete, the first general moved quickly. He sent it westward by niot in groups small enough to pass unnoticed among the armies that congregated along the entire western border. He knew Easlon's scouts were watching the frontier alertly—perhaps even watching from within Lant—and if they became aware of the existence of such an elete force, they might suspect a raid. He would wait for an afternoon of misty fog to move through High Pass. Once his force gained the far side, it could disappear into the thick forest that covered the mountains' western approaches.

Even if these precautions failed, the Easlon scouts certainly wouldn't expect a reconnaissance in force to debouch from the High Pass. No one had ever succeeded in taking a horse through that hazardous gap. There had been only two known attempts to do so. In both of them, animals terrified at the treacherous footing and the pounding roar and spray of High Pass Falls had plunged to their deaths and taken their riders with them.

But the raiding party rode horses from the peer's own stables. These beasts were superbly trained and conditioned to hardship and battle and to the discipline that both required. Med servers had rendered them mute by incising their throats. No horse's whinny would betray this raid. Their hoofs were muffled with wrappings of cloth, a trick the prince suggested and her mother the peer proudly ordered. Finally, the horses had several days of training at being led in blinders.

They moved through the pass on foot in a heavy mist, guiding their blinded mounts along treacherous ledges, up and down steep inclines, and finally through the thundering, foaming spray of the falls. Abruptly the trail began to tilt downward. Gradually it widened. One by one they remounted, removed their horses' blinders, and moved on at a slow walk. By the time darkness fell, all had cleared the pass. By morning the force was deep within Easlon's eastern forest.

It moved at a leisurely pace, but its every action was severely disciplined. This was no frenzied charge at the enemy, but a stealthy, coldly calculated attack with all of its objectives carefully delineated in advance. It sheltered by dae in the dense mountain forest without so much as a sound or a wisp of smoke to betray its presence while its scouts searched surrounding hills and valleys in an attempt to capture any lurking Easlon scout before he could give an invasion alarm. They found none.

They encountered no defenses of any kind. The Peerdom of Easlon had not merely been caught napping but sound asleep.

The Lantian force continued to travel by niot and shelter by dae. On the fourth niot it moved forward swiftly, and at dawn it fell upon Easlon's most eastern community, a flourishing town called Eas.

Eas was deserted. Its granaries were empty. Even its most valuable and cumbersome object, the mill's irreplaceable, enormous steel circular saw, had been removed and spirited off or hidden.

"The curstuff Easlon scouts saw us at least two days ago and gave warning," the prince informed the first general. "The one-namers took their prized possessions with them."

Even so, the loot that remained was enormously valuable. During the sikes of peace, Eas had transformed itself from a frontier village to a wealthy town. Every abode had pottery in graceful designs and colors that were wholly alien to the rough civilization across the mountains. The wall hangings were richly illustrated. Furniture in the humblest home was of a quality and style not even affected by peeragers in Lant.

They despoiled the town at their leisure and scoured the countryside for wagons that could be piled high with loot. Then they set fires and began a well-laden withdrawal toward Low Pass, the only route the wagons could negotiate.

To reach it they had to cross the foaming Stony River, and at that treacherous ford the Easlon scouts sprang their ambush. Beams of light ripped the invaders, and terrifying claps of sound crashed about them. The Lantiff knew those horrors only too well. They had used them with delight on the foes of Lant; now the same forces of death and destruction were unexpectedly turned on them, and they succumbed to a frenzy of terror. The reek of burned flesh filled the peaceful valley and terrified the horses. Easlon scouts plied Egarn's weapon with an accuracy the armies of Lant had not even imagined, and they destroyed the entire raiding force—scouts, mappers, peeragers, officers, and Lantiff—to the last man and woman and captured unharmed nearly eighty of the horses.

6

INSKOR

Sheer happenstance had given the the Ten Peerdoms' critical mountain border to the peer most capable of defending it. The Peer of Easlon was a rotund little woman with sharp eyes and a plain but kind face. Her eldest daughter, the prince, was as unlike her mother as possible in appearance, being tall, slender, and handsome; and as much like her as possible in intelligence and ability.

An equally fortunate twist of fate had given Easlon a genius for a chief scout at the precise moment when he was most needed. Inskor was a grizzled veteran of conflict on Easlon's eastern border and the survivor of more hazardous missions into Lant than he could recall. His effectiveness was enhanced enormously by his relationship with his peer, which was one of respectful admiration and also of mutual affection—emotions rarely found in contacts between different social classes. They worked together in perfect rapport. Inskor was of course a one-namer. The job of scout—full of danger and severe hardship with small reward—held no appeal for peeragers.

When word reached Easlon Court that raiders from Lant had crossed the frontier, the peer sent no orders to Inskor. None were necessary. The event had long been considered inevitable, and plans for dealing with it had been formulated sikes before. In principle, Inskor's task was to make the raid as costly as possible for the Lantiff with the smallest possible loss to Easlon. He was not to offer battle. Instead, his scouts were to hang on the flanks of the raiding force, picking off stragglers and restricting the activity of the Lantian scouts but without risk to themselves.

If time permitted, he was to evacuate everything of value in the path of the raid. He was to ambush the raiders whenever the opportunity occurred—but only if this could be done without endangering his own force—and repeat the ambushes until the invaders were wiped out or driven out of Easlon.

The plan had worked to perfection, but Inskor had no time to savor his victory. He hurried his scouts back to the frontier to await Lant's next move while he set about disposing of the Lantian dead and their possessions. He also had to decide what should be done with Egarn. He was still pondering that perplexing question two daez later when Arne finally arrived.

Inskor greeted him with mingled affection and relief. Arne's father, Arjov, had been the old scout's lifelong friend. They got to know each other well because Arjov, as first server for the Peer of Midlow, often performed errands for her throughout the Ten Peerdoms, and they had become friends in a way that was unusual for one-namers who were subjects of different peers.

Inskor had known Arne since he was a grave-eyed boy of six accompanying his father. Whereas others were astonished to see a child with so much intelligence and maturity, Inskor perceived the truth: Even at six, Arne was no child. He was a childish-looking adult who matter-of-factly accepted adult responsibilities and made decisions that would have frightened men many times his age. As illness incapacitated Arjov, Arne gradually assumed his duties. When the Peer of Midlow appointed him first server after his father's death, she was merely confirming him in a post he already held.

At twenty, Arne still looked like a mere boy despite his sturdy build. His short facial hair had scarcely attained the status of a beard, but when there was anything to be discussed, when there was a decision to be made, everyone waited for Arne to speak—and then did what he suggested. He had ample opportunity to meet marriageable girls throughout the Ten Peerdoms, and girls everywhere thought him handsome despite his short stature, but he was still unwived. The girls may have been put off by his overwhelming seriousness of manner and total devotion to his duties; or perhaps girls his own age

73

seemed frivolous to one who bore the cares of ten peerdoms on his shoulders.

"You have finally come!" Inskor exclaimed, grasping his hands. "Did you have trouble getting away?"

"Some. You know I can't absent myself without a reason."

"Have you heard what happened?"

"I heard your scouts wiped out two Lantian armies, burned Lant Court, and captured the peer. If it is true, I will apologize for not believing it."

"You will find the truth just as unbelieveable."

They talked for the remainder of the dae. Inskor described the rescue of Egarn, the strange weapon he carried, and the copies of it made under Egarn's direction for the scouts. Then he called for horses, and they rode to the ford where the ambush had occurred. Inskor showed Arne where each scout had been hidden, described the Lantiff's disarray in crossing the river—evidence of deplorable discipline, it had played into the scouts' hands—and spoke with awe of the carnage the weapon had wrought. He pointed out the places where each peerager had fallen: The first general here; the prince over there; one of the peer's sons by that tree; two high officers in a clump of bushes where they thought to hide; another of the peer's sons while crossing the river, his body was recovered later; the third son . . .

Arne listened quietly and had few questions except when Inskor tried to describe Egarn's weapon. Arne knew len grinding well. Arne knew everything well—that was part of his job. Inskor was unable to explain how or why the weapon worked, but he had no difficulty in describing its effects and discussing the most effective tactics for its use.

They returned to Inskor's headquarters, and Arne was given one of the weapons to examine and a porkley to try it on. That niot Egarn and the two scouts from Slorn, Roszt and Kaynor, joined them. First they feasted on roast porkley—the porkley being the one Arne had killed with Egarn's weapon—eating it with critical interest and trying to determine whether the strange beam of fire had tainted the meat. It tasted delicious. Then Egarn described his plan and the role Roszt and Kaynor were to play in it. Arne said little, but he was willing to listen as long as Egarn was willing to talk, and they sat late over the remains of the porkley and heard Egarn's tales of his own country and a time he called the past.

Early the next morning, Arne and Inskor rode to a high bluff and sat on a log looking at the sweep of forested hills that marched in diminishing order into Easlon. Beyond the horizon were the other nine peerdoms—safe for the time being from the ravages of Lant because of Egarn's weapon and the valiance of the Easlon scouts. The grizzled old scout wore leather scouting garb; Arne, the wool jacket and trousers of a one-name crafter, much stained by travel. As first server of the Peer of Midlow, he was entitled to a uniform appropriate to that high office, but he disdained it. Two more nondescript-looking men had ever held the fate of a world in their hands—if they actually did. That was what they were trying to decide.

"All of this is beyond me," Inskor said. "I can't believe it is possible to travel through time and kill someone. We both know the past is over and done with, but if what Egarn says is true, while you and I are sitting here talking, I also am sitting somewhere else and talking with your father as we often did many sikes ago."

Arne's gray eyes were fixed on more remote horizons. "What Egarn said about the past—the wars and the destroyed civilization—explains much we have wondered about."

"Maybe," Inskor said doubtfully, "but talking about the past and traveling there are two different things. This Johnson must have been a monstrously evil man if the len he invented really did destroy the world and kill off most of the human race. If that could be prevented by murdering him, there is no doubt someone should do it. But who would believe such a thing is possible? Even if it could be done, Easlon has dozens of len grinders who can make a Honsun Len with ease. So does Midlow. So does every other peerdom. Why does Egarn think killing one man would make the len disappear? Surely someone else would have made it if this Johnson hadn't."

"A complicated thing like the Honsun Len can't be made until it has been thought of," Arne said. "It is the *idea* of the len that must be destroyed. If our own len grinders had neither seen nor heard of a Honsun Len, none of them could make one. This Johnson must be killed before he tells anyone else about it, or writes a description, or draws plans. Better yet, before he even thinks of it. Egarn made that clear enough. Has he said what will happen to us if he succeeds in changing human history?"

"He doesn't know," Inskor said. "He hopes the past will be set on a new path toward a future without war and catastrophe. If many futures can exist at the same time, whatever that means, then we may not notice anything different. If the past has only one future, then the world we know would simply stop existing. We might vanish like the flame when you blow out a candle. Obviously he doesn't know—he is simply guessing. He says if we do disappear into nothing, we would be sacrificing ourselves for the welfare of humanity. This is the one chance humanity has to keep most of the people of Earth from living out their lives in mindless slavery."

"It *is* difficult to believe." Arne turned and looked thoughtfully at Inskor. "But if Egarn hadn't brought the weapon with him, would you have believed him when he told you what it would do?"

"No. Not a word of it. I would have asked him to make one and show me."

"We are in the same position with this talk about time travel, so we will ask Egarn to build his machine and show us. He may not be able to. Some of the things he needs are so rare they may no longer exist, and without them he can't even make a beginning. Even if he builds his machine, it may not do what he expects it to, and I have my doubts that Roszt and Kaynor can learn the past's ways well enough to carry out his mission. If a total stranger who talked and behaved oddly suddenly appeared in Midd Village, people would keep an eye on him and stop him if he tried to kill someone. The past shouldn't be much different in that respect."

"That is true," Inskor agreed. "Egarn says there were guardians who did nothing but try to prevent serious crimes like murder."

"In any case, it may be sikes before Egarn's machine is ready, and we can stop the the project any time we choose—if it doesn't stop itself because of difficulties that can't be overcome. There are only two decisions that must be made now. The first is whether to let Egarn start—because if he is to do this thing, he must start at once. He is elderly, and the future for the Ten Peerdoms looks bleak. The longer we wait, the more likely it is that events beyond our control will decide this for us."

"I hate having to make decisions about things I don't understand."

Arne smiled at the old scout. "You have already made several important decisions about this, my friend, and all of them have been correct. The most vital was deciding not tell your peer about the weapon. I would trust my own peer with my life. I already have, several times. I feel the same way about the Peer of Easlon. Among the ten peers, they alone merit any kind of trust, as you well know, but I wouldn't trust either of them with Egarn's weapon."

Inskor glumly agreed.

"Do your scouts know how totally secret all of this must be?" Arne asked.

"Only Bernal, Roszt, Kaynor, and one len grinder know about Egarn. The len grinder is Inskel."

Arne nodded approvingly. Inskel was Inskor's son, now middle-aged himself and highly skilled.

"The moment they were safely within Easlon, Bernal came on ahead to tell me what had happened, and I made certain no one else saw Egarn. Roszt and Kaynor have been with him ever since. Egarn showed Inskel how to make the weapon. Inskel divided the labor among the best len grinders in the peerdom. No one of them did enough work to understand what it was Inskel was making, and none of them knew that anyone else was helping him. Each was sworn to secrecy, of course. That was as much care as we could contrive when copies of the weapon were needed so urgently. The scouts who used them also were sworn to secrecy, but except for Bernal, none of them knows anything about Egarn. Are you really going ahead with this?"

"I will decide before I leave here. There are so many uncertainties in Egarn's plan that it will probably come to nothing anyway, but the decision to start must be made at once. If we delay, we may find that it can't be done at all. We will have ample time later to decide whether we really want him to send assassins into the past."

"Will you confide in the League of One-Namers?"

"Not even the League can be trusted with this. I have to guard against spies in everything I do. There are always a few one-namers who will sell their birthrights for favors and advancement. Where Egarn is concerned, we can't afford a single act of treachery. No one is to know this secret who doesn't need to know it."

"Where will Egarn work?"

"That is the second thing to be decided," Arne said with a smile.

"I suggest Easlon. The Prince of Midlow will turn that peerdom into another Lant within a tenite of her mother's death."

"Some of us doubt that she will wait a tenite."

"Yes. A pity. It is Midlow's tragedy, but it is bound to affect all of us. I haven't seen her since she was a child. They say she is a beautiful woman."

"The most beautiful in the Ten Peerdoms. And the most vicious."

Inskor leaped to his feet. A horseman was approaching in the valley far below them. "Messenger," he said. "We had better meet him."

They mounted and rode back down the slope. The messenger brought his galloping horse to a halt when he saw them approaching.

"The peer is coming!" he gasped.

Inskor turned to Arne. "I must be there to greet her." He rode off at a furious pace with Arne and the messenger trailing after him.

Inskor's command post was a large stone building artfully concealed in a mountain forest. It served as his residence and also as a supply depot for his scouts. Usually there were several of them resting there between missions. He was waiting at the entrance when the Peer of Easlon rode up at a smart canter.

She rode superbly despite her short, plump stature. Her daughter the prince was with her, only eighteen sikes old but already a radiantly beautiful woman. Their only escort consisted of two elderly servers, one of whom had been sent on ahead to announce her coming.

Inskor greeted them warmly and assisted them in dismounting. Then he sank to both knees and told the peer quietly, "Majesty, you should not have come here. You should never travel anywhere without a strong escort. You should never come this far east no matter how many servers accompany you. You and the prince should never travel together. These are perilous times."

"Perilous for an invader, certainly," the peer said. "But surely not for a peer traveling in her own domain." She signaled Inskor to rise.

He did so, and then he committed an unthinkable breach of decorum by speaking while looking the peer squarely in the face. "Majesty, we know how easily our scouts penetrate the Peerdom of Lant. The Lantian scouts only require practice to become as skilled as we are. It would be a rare coup for them to carry the Peer of Easlon to Lant as a prisoner. It would be a disaster for Easlon and the Ten Peerdoms if peer and prince were lost together. You must not travel without a strong escort. You must never travel together. Neither of you should venture so close to the frontier."

His intensity disconcerted them. They followed in silence when he turned and led them into the building. Plao 3 mornings were chill at that altitude, and a fire crackled in the enormous stone fireplace. The furniture was roughly fashioned—the chief scout of Easlon did not maintain his home as a place of ease—but Inskor made them as comfortable as possible.

When they had seated themselves, Inskor again sank to his knees. "Your bidding, Majesty."

"My bidding is that you bring a chair and sit with us," the peer said impatiently. "We need to talk."

Inskor obediently brought a chair and composed himself to listen. When a peer told a one-namer, "We need to talk," she usually meant she had much to say to him.

She was deeply disturbed. When, years earlier, she had approved Inskor's plan for defending Easlon against raids—with the provision about annihilating the invaders if possible—she had been thinking of small parties of scouts, not a raid of a hundred warriors led by notables from the Peer of Lant's own family, the prince among them.

She was not surprised to learn that Inskor and his scouts had attacked and defeated a vastly superior force. They were expert night fighters. They could choose the time and place of their attack, and they were fighting for their own peerdom in territory where they knew every twig. The enemy had been far from home and fighting blind. She fully expected Inskor to send even such a large raiding force as this one reeling back over the mountains in bloody defeat. It was essential that he do so—essential that the raid be made a cautionary example for the Peer of Lant.

She had not expected him to launch a daytime attack with a mere twenty-five scouts and kill more than a hundred of Lant's best warriors and all of their officers at the cost of two scouts slightly wounded.

Peer and prince had ridden to the scene of the carnage before they called on Inskor, but they quickly withdrew. The sickening sweet odor of death hung over the river valley, blended with the stench of burning flesh, for Inskor had decreed the complete destruction of the corpses and all of their equipment. One of his scouts was in charge, and a force of no-namers—supervised by lashers—was dealing with the battle's debris. All of the metal had been hammered into unrecognizable shapes to be hauled away for salvage. Everything else was being burned or pulverized. If a dedicated Lantian scout somehow managed to penetrate that deeply into Easlon, there would be no shred of bone, no splinter of tooth remaining to mutely proclaim the fate of his prince. The captured horses had been taken west to places of concealment. Along the border, Inskor's scouts were already poised to turn back Lant's inevitable probes for news of the lost raiding party.

The peer said soberly, "I am sorry the Prince of Lant and her brothers were killed. Couldn't they have been made prisoners?"

Inskor kept his gaze on an opposite window while he spoke. "In battle, Majesty, it is often difficult to know who is present until it is over."

"Yes, yes, I understand that. You were only carrying out a plan long agreed upon, but I really didn't think it possible to totally destroy such a large force. Now I am wondering whether it was necessary and whether it wouldn't have been wiser to take prisoners."

"Majesty, our plan was not devised merely to be vindictive. It was based on a sound military premise. In her insolence, the Peer of Lant thought to demonstrate that all the massed might of Easlon was not strong enough to interfere with a mere hundred Lantian warriors. She thought us far weaker than we are. Now that her force has disappeared without a trace, her sleep will be troubled with imaginings about how powerful we are. She may even suspect we use sorcery. Already our scouts have begun planting rumors across the border, and we will harvest a goodly crop from them. The next Lantiff raiding party that comes west will do so reluctantly, and it will be better prepared to flee than to give battle."

"The Peer of Lant is not one to be influenced by rumors," the peer said.

Inskor kept his eyes on the window. "Majesty, the Peer of Lant will not require assistance from anyone to see the truth in this matter: What Easlon has done once, it can do again, and unless she learns what befell the first force, a second force may commit the same errors and disappear in the same way. She will send scouts—many scouts. If she is the military genius her victories suggest, she won't raid Easlon again until it has been successfully scouted, and she won't send an army until it has been successfully raided. We have bought ourselves something beyond price, Majesty. Time."

The peer was still troubled. "I know we had to strike as hard as possible. Still—the prince and her brothers would have made valuable hostages."

"Dangerous hostages, Majesty. The peer would have spared nothing to rescue them."

"But now she will spare nothing to avenge them," the peer objected.

"You can't have it both ways, Majesty," the prince said impatiently. "They invaded us. They plundered and burned Eas, and if Inskor hadn't evacuated it, they would have brutalized and murdered our one-namers. If the Peer of Lant sends her children into a neighboring peerdom to loot and kill, the deaths that result are her own doing."

The peer murmured sadly, "I wish there were a better way."

"Majesty, all of us wish the Peer of Lant would leave her neighbors in peace," Inskor said dryly. "That would solve so many problems. But she won't. If we hadn't given battle, if we had let the Lantiff raid unopposed, the peer would have taken that as a sign of weakness and followed the raid with her army. If we had merely defeated the raiders and chased them back into Lant, she would have tested our strength by sending a stronger force. Now she will be uneasy. She will suffer many troubled nights when all of her dreams end in unanswered questions. Very soon she will have to accept that her Lantiff have been wiped from the Earth like the vermin they are. She will be enraged, but she is too good a general to rush west with another force that may vanish in the same way. We have bought time, Majesty. How well we use it depends on us."

The peer sighed. "On us and on the other nine peerdoms—which means it will be used badly. I will do what I can, of course. Inskor, I want you to speak frankly. If the Peer of Lant seeks revenge with her army this year, what chance do we have?"

Inskor smiled. The outlook had been dismal before Egarn's arrival. Now, for the first time in years, he could look eastward with confidence. He would soon have all of his scouts armed with the miraculous weapon—all except those who ventured into Lant. He could not risk having the weapon recaptured; but for a time, until Lant produced something to counter this astonishing force or managed to overwhelm it with sheer numbers, the scouts defending the border would be invincible. He wished he could tell the peer about that, but of course he could not.

"When the Peer of Lant looks toward Easlon, Majesty, she sees nothing. For sikes, every scout she has sent out has disappeared. If she strikes—with another raiding force or with an army—it will be a blow launched in the dark without knowing what or where the target is. We will fight her at a time and place of our own choosing. We will win the first battle, Majesty, and also the second."

"Will you defeat her severely?"

Inskor nodded slowly and spoke in measured tones. "We will defeat her horribly. We will fill the valleys with dead Lantiff. If she finally attacks in a blind rage, throws in every reinforcement from her conquered lands, and pursues her revenge to the bitter end, she will outnumber us tens of thousands to one. Only the peer and her generals know how large the armies of Lant really are. In the end, she may crush us with the sheer weight of numbers, but in doing so she will destroy herself. She knows that danger. She is surrounded by defeated enemies who will seek their own revenge the moment she weakens herself. For that reason, she must prepare her moves with care. If we use our bought time well, we will be ready for her. If we don't, we will be in the position of sitting and waiting until she discovers a sure method of destroying us."

The peer gestured helplessly. "I know. You have been telling me for sikes that the Ten Peerdoms need an army."

"If not the Ten Peerdoms, then Easlon. We should have formed our own army long ago."

"My neighbors would have thought I was plotting against them—as you well know. Perhaps now that Lant has actually invaded us, one or two of them will listen to me and a beginning can be made."

"It may be too late for beginnings, Majesty," Inskor said. "The war will be over before the Ten Peerdoms can field an army competent to do battle with Lant. Armies aren't assembled in a day, and even if one were, who in the Ten Peerdoms knows how to train and command one? Not I, and the Peer of Lant is unlikely to give us time to learn. But such an army is impossible while the peers fear each other more than they fear Lant. They will still be trying to cut each others' throats when the Lantiff arrive to do it for them."

The peer got to her feet. "The blunt truth is that we are doomed."

Inskor slipped from his chair and sank his knees. "We at the eastern gates have always been doomed, Majesty. I offer you no pledge of a long life, but this I can guarantee: If the Peer of Lant leads her army through the mountains this year, the Peer of Easlon will survive her."

"Thank you, Inskor. I would like to thank your scouts personally, but I understand that most of them have returned to their posts."

"Victory over a few raiders doesn't end a war, Majesty. It only begins one. There is much to do."

"Please give them my thanks when you are able."

There were six scouts resting at his headquarters, and Inskor ordered them to escort the peer all the way to Easlon

Court. He saw the riders off. Then he returned to the house and sank into his chair. Talking with a peer was exhausting—especially when that peer was the Peer of Easlon.

Arne entered the room and took the chair the peer had just vacated. Inskor asked, "Were you able to hear?"

Arne nodded. "Your peer has a shining goodness. The Peer of Midlow has it in almost the same degree. The two of them are far too gentle and righteous for these troubled times."

"That is why I think Egarn should work in Easlon. The only places worth considering are Easlon and Midlow, and only Easlon has a prince."

"It is true that the Prince of Midlow will turn that peerdom into another Lant the moment she becomes peer," Arne said. "If that were the only consideration, I would choose Easlon without hesitation. But how long will the scouts of Easlon be able to hold off the massed armies of Lant, even with Egarn's miraculous weapon?"

"Who knows? If the Peer of Lant is able to practice patience, and if her generals are capable of learning new tactics, we won't last long. But I don't think either of those things will happen."

"I have heard refugees describe a Lantian invasion. 'Lantiff like the trees of a mountain forest,' one said. You told your peer you would be outnumbered tens of thousands to one. While your few hundred scouts are massacring the Lantiff facing them, the other thousands upon thousands will simply flow around them. If you block the passes, there are other passes far to the south from which the Lantiff can turn north to attack you. They may find a way unknown to us through the mountains far to the north and attack from that direction. If the Peer of Easlon relents and lets you have an army, will it make any difference?"

"Not at any time soon. Lashers learn too slowly. If the war lasts long enough—and I intend to make it last as long as possible—then an Easlon army could become important. Peeragers know almost nothing about history, and it is tragic that the one event they do remember has prevented all of us from defending ourselves."

In the dim past, at a time almost beyond memory, the army of one of the Ten Peerdoms had revolted. Peeragers were slaughtered, and the rebel officers tried to set themselves up as the peerdom's rulers. The remaining peers had been horrified. They massed their own armies and hunted down the rebel officers and lashers without mercy. Then they resolved never to trust their armies again. They gradually replaced them with elite guards of lashers owned by individual peeragers—none of them large enough to cause trouble. These guards provided escorts for their masters and took turns patroling the roads and harassing the peerdom's innocent, hard-working one-namers. Even with the armies of Lant on the march, the peeragers of the Ten Peerdoms were still too frightened by that spector out of the past to establish their own army.

"In any case, Easlon is too close to Lant," Arne said. "We don't want Egarn recaptured. The peer wouldn't allow him to escape a second time. And then—Easlon has no ruins of the kind Egarn described. He said he must scavenge them for the materials he needs, and that would be difficult if he settled in Easlon. It also would be difficult to find a place for him to work here and people to help him. He must have his own little self-contained community of guards and crafters. They should be refugees from the wars—fugitive one-namers who have lost their homes and no longer have positions and responsibilities. They can dedicate themselves to assisting Egarn without being missed and causing questions to be asked."

"That is almost a village you are describing."

"Exactly. And it must be as secure as we can make it. We can't expect Egarn to pack everything periodically and cart it into hiding. The machine he described will be too large to be moved, and it would be catastrophic to have to abandon it. The materials he needs are so scarce it might not be possible to build it more than once."

"Then you will take Egarn to Midlow?"

"Midlow has the ruins Egarn needs. It is far from Lant, and as long as the peer lives, it is the safest place in the Ten Peerdoms."

"But how long will that be? It's rumored her health is poor. What will happen when the prince becomes peer?"

Arne smiled. "It is precisely because Easlon has an admirable prince that I choose Midlow. The Peers of Easlon and Midlow are both intelligent. Both are kind. Both have wisdom. If the direct support of the peer became essential, both would sacrifice much for the future of humanity. But the Peer of Easlon has the hope of a brilliant daughter. She would sacrifice herself, but she would never deny the prince her own opportunity to heal humanity's hurts. The Peer of Midlow knows her daughter only too well. She has no such hope. Therefore Egarn's plan to save humanity by sacrificing ourselves should not be based in Easlon."

"Can humanity's hurts be healed?"

"I fear not. We one-namers could take Egarn's weapon and eliminate the rotten peeragers in all ten peerdoms, but we would still need no-namers to produce our food and repair our roads. We would need lashers to supervise them and to fight for us when the invasion comes, whether from east, west, north or south, as it certainly will. We would end by replacing the peeragers with a new group of rotten peeragers—ourselves. Our revolution would have changed nothing."

Inskor said, "I still feel troubled about Egarn working in Midlow. I accept your decision for only one reason." He smiled. "*You* will be there. My instinct tells me this project will require all of your skill to keep it going."

"There is one thing I can do for Egarn that no one else could do—in Midlow or anywhere else. The crafters who assist and guard him must be fed and clothed. I can apportion food and other supplies so they won't be missed. It is a problem that will last as long as Egarn's work lasts."

"I hadn't thought of that. Of course—you run the peerdom. Your father did it before you, and now you are doing it. That is why Midlow has the Ten Peerdoms' most efficient government."

Arne shrugged and got to his feet. "We have made the two decisions we had to make. Egarn will start work immediately, and he will work in Midlow. We will leave tonight. Later, I may send for Inskel. He is the best len grinder in the Ten Peerdoms, and the large lens Egarn needs may cause problems. But keep Inskel here for now. I want him to make enough of Egarn's weapons to arm one-namers throughout the Ten Peerdoms."

Rapid hoofbeats brought Inskor to his feet. The door was flung open, and a scout burst into the room. Behind him, his lathery horse stood snorting and panting.

"The Lantiff," the scout gasped. "They are coming through Low Pass."

"Another reconaissance group?" Inskor asked calmly.

"Bigger than the last. Bernal thinks two hundred, at least."

"Very well. I will come at once. Everyone knows what to do. Look to your horse."

Inskor turned to Arne. "You are right about the danger of leaving Egarn too close to Lant. The peer has allowed her personal feelings to override her military judgment. She is impatient to know what has happened to her sons and her prince. I suppose she will probe with heavier and heavier forces until the losses become too costly. The sooner you take Egarn out of Easlon, the better."

"She may already suspect that we have Egarn's weapon—or something like it," Arne said. "I wonder what she will do when she is certain."

They paused just inside the door. Beyond it lay the future with all of its enormous uncertainty. Both were accustomed to exercising responsibility and authority, to making far-reaching decisions, but they felt totally unprepared for this reckless plunge into the unknown. Egarn's quest pointed beyond their vision and even beyond their imagining. The two of them—young first server and old chief scout—only knew that humanity was in desperate straights and a venture aimed at saving it was worth setting out on.

7

ARNE

Lashers raided Midd Village at dawn.

Arne heard shouts and the neighing of horses long before the winding dirt road took the final, downward curve that would bring the village into view. He turned abruptly and fought his way through thick undergrowth to the top of the wooded hill, leaving old Marof gaping after him bewilderedly.

At the crest, an ancient lookout gave him a sweeping view of Midd Valley. The rushing river that cleft it was lined with stone buildings where it passed the village: saw mill, flour mill, tannery, various craft factories. The village lay directly below him at the valley's edge—three long cobbled streets of neat stone houses of two or three stories built on the terraced hillside. Scattered among the dark roofs were several new thatches that gleamed yellow in the early sunlight. The badly cracked and weathered red tiles that roofed a small shed stood out starkly. Farlon the potter had been trying for sikes to fire durable roof tiles.

The mills were already in operation, and a sudden, rasping whine announced the saw mill's first cut of the day. All was normal there. The workers were unaware of what was happening to the homes they had left only moments before.

The village was a turmoil, and Arne studied the scene unfolding there with sickening apprehension. The Great Secret had been in his trust for more than three sikes without a breach of any kind, and he found it difficult to believe this was happening. It meant the collapse of all their plans. He had known from the beginning that a mere whiff of suspicion might be ruinous. All of Egarn's equipment would have to be moved and his machines taken apart and rebuilt in new quarters, and that might set his work back fatally. And where could a secure workroom be found for him if the present one failed?

Stirring events had occurred on the Ten Peerdoms' frontiers since Egarn's arrival. The Peer of Lant sent force after force into Easlon, increasing the size of the invasion each time. All had been annihilated, though of course it was impossible to say whether every last Lantiff had been killed. A few might have escaped. If any did, what they told their peer had no affect on her tactics. After a series of defeats, she should have known—or at least suspected—that Easlon had Egarn's weapon. Either she refused to believe, or she thought the weight of numbers must ultimately triumph.

Finally Easlon scouts sent back word that the peer had lost patience and was about to invade Easlon with two armies, moving one through High Pass and the other through Low Pass. Inskor led his scouts on a bold raid that pushed the Lantiff back from the passes, and Egarn's weapon was applied in a new way: rocks, dirt, trees, entire mountain sides were sliced off to pour down into those critically important gaps. The water that had fed High Pass Falls was diverted westward into Easlon—whose dry eastern province needed it—and both passes were blocked permanently. Enterprising Lantian scouts might find high, hazardous ways through the mountains like those the Easlon scouts used, but no army could make the crossing until time or the weapon cut a passage for it.

The Peer of Lant accepted the inevitable and turned her armies southward. Their onslaught had long been expected there, and they no longer had Egarn's weapon to terrorize their victims. The southern peerdoms were making the invasion a costly one, and it seemed likely to occupy Lant for sikes to come.

On the opposite frontier, the Peerdom of Weslon had been overrun by marauding lashers out of the far west, and its rotten nobility fled in panic—as did the cowardly peeragers of neighboring peerdoms. Fortunately Arne and Inskor had prepared for such an emergency. With the help of the League of One-Namers, they had formed a one-name defense force with Arne as the commander. A select group of one-namers from all of the Ten Peerdoms, both men and women, secretly trained as scouts and received lessons in warfare. From time to time a few one-namers who could absent themselves for a few monts without being missed went east to train with the scouts of Easlon or west to train with the scouts of Weslon, who likewise had a long border to guard.

This small army numbered only two hundred at the time of the Weslon crisis. It was pathetic force compared with the hordes of Lant but a respectable one for dealing with renegade lashers—especially since half the volunteer warriors were armed with Egarn's weapon. Arne led his tiny force to battle and quickly cut the invaders to pieces.

The peeragers returned, Arne received commendations from all ten peers—who of course had no notion of how such a resounding victory had been accomplished—and with the critical eastern frontier sealed off and the western threat dispelled, an attitude of complacency, even somnolence, settled on the Ten Peerdoms—so much so that the Peer of Easlon gave up her agitation for a common army.

Through all of the turmoil, Egarn's work had quietly gone forward, protected against every contingency except one—treachery by someone they trusted. Now it had happened.

The raid was meticulously organized. Lasher captains had taken up central positions on the three village streets, and their lieutenants patrolled on foot, looking into the houses and calling orders. Squads of lashers were searching each dwelling systematically and reporting to the lieutenants when they finished. Even the waiting horses had a role. They were held in readiness outside the houses their riders were searching in case there was a need to remount quickly.

The lashers wore uniforms Arne had not seen before: black cloaks with a slash of white, leather jackets, high boots, and red overs. For generations, Midd Village had made uniforms for the peeragers' servers, whether for ceremonial or common use. This clothing, too, should have been designed and sewn by the village's crafters from cloth woven in the mill below and leather from the tannery, but no part of that absurd dress had come from Midd.

Arne grimly turned this riddle over in his mind as he watched. The answer probably involved several loads of grain that were mysteriously unaccounted for and prentices the prince insisted on sending to the Prince of Chang in an exchange she worked out herself. The prentices she received in return vanished like the grain—probably into the prince's own household. If they were seamster and leatherer prentices, that accounted for the uniforms. The vanished grain had gone to Chang to pay for the cloth and leather.

The Prince of Midlow suddenly rode into the center of High Street, the village's topmost street, and halted there, sitting sternly erect on a creamy white horse that stood with its nose pointed at the largest house in the village, Arne's dwelling. The polished leather of her boots and jacket and the flaming red of her overs gleamed in the early sunlight. Her long, golden hair tumbled in careless disarray on her shoulders. Only peerager females had the perogative of long hair, and they guarded it jealously—as peerager males defended their distinction of being clean-shaven—but most of the women piled their hair into elaborate structures dictated by the latest fad. The Prince of Lant scorned fashion and allowed her hair to fall freely.

Even from a distance, she was awesomely beautiful. Arne had admired her since they were children, but that did not prevent him from holding her in utter comtempt. He might have been hopelessly infatuated with her—liasons between peeragers and one-namers were unheard of in Midlow except for an occasional scandal involving a one-name server who lived at the court—if he had found it possible to love a woman he despised. The Prince of Midlow's fellow peeragers were notable for sexual excesses and fits of selfishness and cruelty, but even they considered her flagrant misconduct shocking.

Old Marof took his place at Arne's side. He had approached without a sound, and he stood motionless for a moment, staring down at the village, before he began muttering curses.

"Let's burn 'em," he said scornfully. "Let's get the weapons and burn 'em. The prince, too. It will be easy. They aren't expecting a thing. We can cut 'em to pieces and dump their bodies in the quarry."

Arne said soberly, "We can't. The entire village would know, and an entire village can't be trusted with a secret like that." He paused. "There is nothing we can do. We don't dare offer any kind of resistance to the next Peer of Midlow."

"Her mother must be told at once," Marof said. "We can do that."

"The lashers are members of the prince's new guard. Has there been any gossip at court about those uniforms?"

Marof shook his head.

"The Prince of Chang has a personal guard of uniformed lashers," Arne said. "When our prince visited Chang Court last Haro, she saw the prince's guard and wanted one for herself. The peer her mother said no. The prince must have recruited one without the peer's knowledge, which is why she has been so secretive about it. I would like to know where she got the uniforms."

He was anxiously scrutinizing the activity around his dwelling. As he watched, a lasher emerged from it, strode up to the prince, saluted, and handed something to her.

Marof cursed again. "He don't even kneel. A lasher, and he don't kneel to his prince. Let me tell the peer."

Arne spoke slowly, keeping his eyes on the drama being enacted in the street below. "You came to me last night to report a rotten plank in the bridge below the east pasture."

Marof chuckled. "Aya. Bad plank, that. If you say so, that's what I did. Is there really a rotten plank there?"

"There is one that looks rotten. I have been saving it for an emergency like this. We went out before dawn to have a look at it. Then I sent you on a watchwalk along the South Wood Road to see whether the other bridges show signs of rot."

"Aya. We parted at the fork. Do you want me to give the alarm at the ruins?"

"Tell them what is happening. Someone has talked, and the prince is looking for something—if she hasn't already found it. Roszt and Kaynor were staying at my house."

Marof turned in alarm. "Aya. That sounds bad. I'll give the alarm."

"Circle around by the swamp road and inspect the bridges there. Then head back and approach the court from the south. If anyone asks, tell him you have been inspecting bridges all day, and you have come to tell the land warden about that rotten plank."

"Aya."

"The prince's guard may may bar the road to keep news of this from reaching the peer, but I don't think they will stop one-namers arriving from the south. If they do, come back and tell me, but don't enter Midd Village unless the lashers are gone."

"Aya."

"If you are able to talk with the land warden, tell him what you saw here. He will decide whether the peer should be told—or when."

"Aya. This wouldn't have happened if the peer weren't so sick." Marof nodded at the village. "Are you going down?"

"Of course."

"You will get a lashing."

"I must do what I can."

They returned to the road. Old Marof, giving Arne a grim nod and an absent gesture of farewell, started back the way they had come. Arne turned in the opposite direction.

As the road approached the village, it passed through a barrier wall that Arne had designed himself. A tall, sod-covered mound of dirt with steep sides ran from river to hill and back to the river. Dwellings on High Street, at the top of the village, had walled gardens. Thus the entire village was enclosed, including the mills and a large garden common that was used as a sheepfold in winter. In other peerdoms, drunken or bored lashers had slipped their restraints and rampaged through the one-name villages, vandalizing, raping, and looting, and Arne used these incidents as an excuse for fortifying Midlow's one-name villages.

Midd Road, which became Midd Street as it passed through the village, was supposed to be blocked from dusk to dawn by logs slid into place between stone pillars where the road passed through the barrier on either side of the village. Further, Arne had ordered a niot watch kept on barriers and foot paths and a dae watch by village children. Unexpected though the raid was, there would have been ample warning if Arne's orders had been followed.

This was no blundering assault by drunken lashers. It was a carefully calculated military operation by a peerager's personal guard, and nothing like it had happened in Midlow within living memory. It seemed all the more sinister because Roszt and Kaynor had moved from the ruins to the village only two daez before. They wanted to be closer to Wiltzon, the elderly schooler, who was drilling them in studies Egarn had prescribed.

Arne never wasted time looking for scapegoats when something went wrong. He accepted the responsibility himself and set about salvaging what he could, even if—as in this case—he had to take a lashing. He approached the village boldly as though nothing unusual were happening.

Two hulking lashers were posted at the barrier opening. They stood like grotesque statues with whips poised and black capes flapping in a brisk breeze. Their horses were munching grass in the nearby drainage ditch. Arne walked past them without a glance, and a blow from a heavy whip sent him sprawling. The lashers roared with laughter; Arne calmly got to his feet and walked on. They made no further attempt to interfere with him, which meant they knew who he was.

He strode along Midd Street for some distance before another lasher noticed him. This one charged from a dwelling bellowing angrily. "Inside! You heard the orders!"

For a lasher to speak unbidden to the peer's first server, let alone attempt to order him about, was a flagrant breach of custom. If the peer had been present, she would have ordered the man lashed severely. Merely to take notice of him was beneath Arne's dignity. He walked on, and another vicious snap of a whip hurled him to the cobble stones. He was seized and marched away with one arm brutally twisted behind his back. At the first crossing, he was jerked to the right and rushed up the slope to High Street where the prince still sat on her horse. By the time he reached her, he was stumbling badly, and only the excruciating grip on his arm kept him from falling. He was flung casually to the ground in front of her.

As calmly as he could he got to his feet, performed the obeisance of touching one knee to the ground, and rose.

The prince spoke with chilling sarcasm. "Does the peer's first server care so little for the responsibilities of his office that he can't be on hand to greet his peer's heir?"

Arne sensed her rage, but he kept his eyes averted and spoke calmly, quietly, firmly. "Word of your intended visit failed to arrive, Highness."

"Where have you been?"

For the first time Arne looked at her directly. Her windswept hair caught the sun like gold. Anger had distorted her face, and she seemed the more beautiful for it.

"Inspecting a bridge, Highness."

When she spoke again, her fury made her almost inarticulate, but she also sounded triumphant. "You were asked to report the appearance of strangers immediately—any strangers. Not only have you not reported them, but you are caught in the act of harboring them in your own dwelling." She added scornfully, "Such is the faith of the one-named."

The sensation of despair that swept over Arne was more painful than his bleeding back, but he managed to keep his voice steady. "I harbor no strangers, Highness."

"Then what do you call this?" A bundle of garments landed beside him. "Discovered this morning when your dwelling was searched—along with the unmade beds their owners had slept in."

Arne knelt and spread the contents of the bundle on the cobblestones. Time remained suspended while he sifted through the paltry assortment of garments and personal oddments with the prince glaring down at him.

Then he stood up and met her eyes boldly. "These garments, Highness, and these other possessions, belong to two of the new sawyer prentices from South Province."

The prince said blankly, "Sawyer prentices—living in the first server's dwelling?"

Arne continued to meet her gaze. "Midd Village has been assigned more prentices than it can accommodate, Highness. The sawyer prentices you sent to the Prince of Chang had to be replaced. Because I have more room than I need, two of them are living with me. We didn't consider them strangers because they arrived with credentials signed by the dom warden's high server. I apologize for not reporting them, Highness. The error was mine."

The prince stared down at him. Arne met her eyes unwaveringly.

Abruptly she turned her horse and rode away. The lasher cast a last, perplexed glance at his late captive and shuffled after her. At the cross street, the prince called an order. A lasher captain turned and blew a piercing blast on his whistle. In a matter of moments the lashers remounted, formed up, and collected the sentries left at the barriers. They flashed along Midd Street with a sustained rumble of hoofs and were gone.

Even before the last of them had disappeared, villagers poured into the streets. Many of the crafters worked at home, and the raid had come so early that children were not yet at their tasks or studies. Arne was quickly surrounded by a sympathetic crowd.

"Never mind," he said as a woman tugged worriedly at his ripped and bloody shirt. He gathered the prentices' belongings into a bundle and handed it to her. "Would you take charge of this, Erinor? It must be returned to the owners with our apologies. The clothing is soiled, and small objects may have been lost." He turned to another woman. "Margaya, I want a full report in writing describing what the lashers did in every dwelling in the village. I want a list of anything that was taken or damaged and the names of anyone who was injured or mistreated in any way. Would you see that this is done?"

He hurried up the rough stone walk to the schooler's house and burst in without knocking. Old Wiltzon, massively gray, rugged like a granite boulder, irrepressibly good humored in most situations, was ruefully surveying a room littered with books. Those precious objects had been ripped from their shelves; several had lost their covers.

But the schooler smiled delightedly when he saw Arne. "The prince was hunting blind," he said. "She knew nothing, and she got nothing."

"Roszt and Kaynor?"

"I moved them over here after you left yesterday. I was worried that one of those nosey prentices might have noticed something. One of my students brought the alarm the moment the lashers entered the village, and I had them bundled away, nary a trace, long before the search reached this street. The lashers vented their spite on my books. They have an instinctive hatred for books." He sadly picked up a detached cover and placed it lovingly around a bundle of loose pages. "Sit down. Rest. Have a little wine—you look as though you need it. Let me take care of your back. It is still bleeding. Don't worry about the raid. The prince got nothing."

"You would have had more time if the barriers had been up and a watch kept."

"The barriers weren't up?" Wiltzon asked wonderingly.

"We were lucky. We were extremely lucky. The prince was *not* hunting blind. She knew exactly what to look for. She wouldn't brave the peer's wrath without good reason. I need to think about this."

Tiredly he dropped into a chair. He sat there, turning the

events over in his mind, stirring them, rearranging them, while Wiltzon, clucking his tongue with concern, washed the blood from Arne's back and applied a dressing. When the old schooler had finished, he righted a chair the lashers had knocked over and sat down to wait.

Arne gingerly leaned his sore back against his own chair. Now that the suspense was over, he felt exhausted. He said finally, "While the prince was getting nothing, she gave us something. Two things."

"Aha!"

"For one, she gave us a lever. To her mother, she pretends she is still a child amusing herself with war games, but this raid can't be called a game. The guard *and* the prince must be disciplined severely, or the peer will lose her authority."

Wiltzon nodded excitedly. "Yes. Of course. It wasn't merely her mother's orders that the prince violated. It was years of tradition. What is the other thing?"

"We have a traitor among us. We ought to thank the prince for letting us know."

"A traitor? Are you sure?"

"The prince wouldn't have raided Midd Village unless she had good reason to believe there was something here. She wouldn't have dared. When I arrived, she was triumphant. She had caught me violating the rule about reporting strangers— she thought—and that would have justified her own violations. It was my house the lashers concentrated their search on. The prince must have known two strangers were staying there. Thanks to your foresight in getting Roszt and Kaynor hidden, the only evidence they found belonged to the sawyer prentices. Now she has no justification at all for her raid, and she will be extremely worried about the peer's reaction."

Wiltzon's gentle face suddenly became flushed with anger. "You are right. There must be a traitor. What can we do? We have a long road to travel yet. Not even Egarn knows how long. If the prince has any kind of suspicion about the Secret—"

"The Secret is safe, and this is one spy she will never believe again, but I wonder why she suddenly became so obsessed with the notion there are strangers about." He thought for a moment, and then he said slowly, "When she visited Chang, she may have heard rumors about the League of One-Namers. The League is in difficulty there. Chang viciously mistreats its one-namers, as you know, and during the prince's visit, a local officer of the League was questioned under torture. He recited a lot of nonsense, but he also let slip some truth. Peeragers are suspicious of crafts and learning because they know so little about either, and many of them fear a one-name revolt. Also, the idea of an organization that reaches through all of the Ten Peerdoms and transcends peerdom loyalties is frightening to them. That was the reason for the order to report the arrival of strangers. The League couldn't exist without a system of messengers, and the peeragers know that. When the prince's spy informed her I was harboring unknown persons, she hoped to capture a pair of League officials. She intended to use torture to strip their secrets from them."

"We were lucky," Wiltzon agreed. "We must be more alert in the future. Did they really fail to put the logs in place? That is frightening." He dropped his voice to a whisper. "But what happened? In all of this confusion, I forgot why you were away. Did the thing work?"

"It worked perfectly. The first flare went out during passage, and that worried us. I fastened the others to stones to keep them upright, and they kept burning."

"The rabbits?"

"As far as we could tell, they went precisely where we intended them to go and arrived in excellent condition. There is quite a jolt to the landing, and some of them seemed momentarily stunned, but they got over it quickly and hopped away. The sending has never been a problem. It is the sending to a precise place and a precise time that is difficult. Now Egarn has identified two places and two times, and that gives him a basis for calibrations."

"What did Egarn say?"

"He was pleased, of course, but he said little. He is extremely tired. He has been working too long without a break. I wish we could make him rest occasionally."

"Did you remind him about the money?"

Arne shook his head. "We were much too preoccupied with the experiment. But he will remember. He will scan again today, I'm sure. Perhaps he will be able to suck some up for you."

"The money is important. Roszt and Kaynor are having trouble understanding it. Don't go—you are hurt, and you have been up all night. Rest yourself and take some food."

Arne shook his head impatiently. "I must see about replacing a rotten bridge plank."

"Surely it can't be that urgent!"

"It must be done at once. I will tell you about it later. Everyone deserves a rest, especially Egarn, but he won't take one, either. It was an eventful night. Tell Roszt and Kaynor, will you?"

"I will tell them," Wiltzon promised. "It has been an eventful morning, too. Don't try to do more than you have to."

Arne nodded and went out. In his anxiety about the prince and her lashers, he had forgotten just how eventful the night had been. When Inskor first mentioned Egarn's plan to him, he thought it an old man's senile fantasy. Now each incredible step forward seemed no more remarkable than reaching the next kilometer stone on a well-marked road.

And the Great Secret was still safe. The villagers he came in contact with on this day might notice that he seemed more tired than usual, but none of them would suspect that he had just spent a night looking some three hundred sikes into the past and transposing objects through time.

8

EGARN

Old Marof, moving his creaky bones with determined steadiness, took twice as long to reach the ruins as he would have normally, but on this day there could be no mistake. He followed the most devious route possible, using paths and dim forest trails known only to local one-namers, and he paused repeatedly to make certain he hadn't aroused the curiosity of a lasher patrol.

Finally he arrived at one of three locations called "checkpoints"—one of Egarn's strange words that Marof always meditated while he waited. This "checkpoint" was located in an overgrown hollow, so why was it a point? Marof seated himself on a log, leaned back comfortably against a tree, and relaxed. Eventually, when the sentries were positive he hadn't been followed, one of them would come for him. Egarn called the watchers above ground "sentries" and those below ground "guards," which gave Marof more words to meditate.

Egarn also called everyone living and working there—sentries, guards, helpers, and crafters—his "team"—another strange word. Marof occasionally acted as sentry when one of the regulars was sick or had another job to do. He admired Egarn, but he preferred to work for Arne. Arne always let a helper know what was happening. Few of those on Egarn's "team" seemed to understand what he was doing except that it was something important to all of them.

Local people had a superstitious dread of the ruins and avoided them. Marof could understand why. From his position in the hollow, he could see the mysterious tower looming above the overgrown remains of collapsed buildings like a petrified monster about to feed on them. As a sentry, on days when absolutely nothing was happening, he relieved the monotony by contemplating the tower's graceful, curved shape and wondering how it came to be there and what purpose it could have served. Egarn knew, of course, and Wiltzon, but their answers to his questions never made sense to Marof. From his position in the hollow, the tower seemed to be intact; from the opposite side, it looked as though a larger monster had taken a bite out of it. Around its base, the ruins that cluttered the forest floor reared up from deeply delved concrete roots to flaunt their strangeness. An enigmatic people of the past had lavished long forgotten skills on them and then, for inscrutable reasons of their own, left them for time to erode.

The sentry approached soundlessly. He was Havler, a middle-aged man with a crippled leg. Like most of the members of Egarn's team, he was a one-name refugee who had lost his family in the wars. He was an excellent sentry. He moved slowly, but he saw and heard everything.

Marof delivered his message in a whisper, made certain Havler understood it, and then left immediately. He had his own work to perform, and the sooner he reached South Wood Road and began inspecting bridges, the better.

Marof vanished into the trees; Havler turned in the opposite direction and chirped a bird call before he limped soundlessly toward the ruins. Just outside the concealed mouth of a tunnel, he whispered Marof's message to Connol, who was serving as head sentry for the day.

Connol gestured at the ground. "I suppose they should be told."

"Aya," Havler agreed. "They certainly should."

"I'll go," Connol said. Havler's lame leg made him a slow messenger on stairs, and there were multitudes of stairs between them and the first of the guards stationed below. "Hold the post for me."

Havler drew back into the trees and seated himself. He would act as head sentry until Connol returned. Arne had issued a stern order: the post could not be left unattended unless a raid were in progress—in which case the head sentry himself was to pull the alarm wire, make certain that the alarm actually sounded, and then withdraw with the other sentries, trying to distract the raiders' attention from the ruins. The alarm wire sent a large basket of stones and scrap metal cascading down those endless flights of metal stairs, and if the racket this made was not quite loud enough to raise the dead, as the old saying went, it certainly would attract the attention of anyone below who was still living. Havler had heard the alarm tested.

The tunnel's entrance was concealed by a layer of sod attached to a base woven of sticks. Connol pulled it open just far enough to admit him and closed it after him. There was barely enough room inside for him to crawl through the darkness on hands and knees. He made his way blindly around several obstructions, followed a sharp turning, and saw, far ahead of him, jagged patches of light that marked rents in the tunnel's roof. The tunnel seemed to curve into infinity; actually, it went nowhere. When Connol reached a bulging rock, he scraped dirt from its edges and pressed on it until it pivoted to reveal an opening. The rock was a hollow shell fashioned of clay and fired to simulate a real rock. Connol entered and pivoted the fake rock into place behind him. On his return, he would replace the dirt.

He emerged at top of the first flight of stairs, paused to make certain the alarm system's basket of debris was in position, and then started down at a run. An enemy would try to creep down silently, so members of the team always made as much noise as possible.

The stairwell was roofless. At middae, under a clear sky, it received enough sunlight to sketch shadows on the upper levels. By niot it was a black pit with an occasional star glimpsed directly overhead. Connol quickly descended into nether regions that were dim even by day.

Down, down he went, one flight after another. Each time he made that descent into darkness, the depth seemed more immense to him. At the bottom, a metal door stood a few inches ajar. When it was opened further, it emitted a resounding, grinding screech of protest. Beyond it was a room that must have been enormous before the upper levels collapsed into it. It was totally dark, but Connol had seen it by torchlight. Massive columns that once had supported the building protruded from the rubble like scattered sticks of firewood, and projecting from the walls were monstrous, broken pipes that showed gaping, jagged ends. Egarn had explained why such gigantic pipes had been necessary, but no one understood him.

On the other side of the room, Connol entered a broad corridor that ended far ahead of him at a barrier of light. The illumination was produced by a single dim candle in an overhead niche, but it looked blinding to one who had been fumbling through darkness. When the sun reached a certain position overhead, a small, strangely shaped patch of illumination appeared in the corridor at that point. An unlikely juxtaposition of fissures in the floors above permitted that one tiny splinter of brightness to momentarily penetrate the depths of the ruin, and this was Arne's inspiration for an underground "checkpoint." Every time Connol passed it, he tried to imagine light collecting somewhere far above, from tiny drippings, the way a pool of water collects, and then seeping through the ruins to reappear here as a fleeting reminder of the sun.

Connol performed the ritual required of anyone visiting Egarn's workroom. He stood under the light, slowly counted to twenty, and then moved on. If he hadn't done so, the exit from the corridor would have remained closed to him, and a guard would have set several silent alarms in operation. Connol moved on and stopped beside a pile of rubble. The rubble swung open; it was a concealed door.

Connol did not enter. He spoke tersely to the guard, relaying the message he had received. He made the guard repeat it twice. Then the rubble swung shut, and he heard a clunk as a bar was shoved into place. He returned to the stairs and began the long, tiring climb back to the surface.

The guard, whose name was Lanklin, made certain the bar was secure before he turned and crawled along a dark tunnel.

As he approached the end, he called, "Message." A voice demanded, "Who?"

"Red," Lanklin replied. The color was changed daily.

A panel slid open—not at the end, as an invader might have expected, but at the side. Lanklin entered a large, torch-lit room where two more guards, Dayla and Ellar, waited.

The far end of the room was filled with strange objects. One of them, an oddly-shaped shell of wood built by Ellar, a former carpenter, was called a mock auto by Egarn, and when Lanklin was on duty in this room, he often watched Egarn instructing Roszt and Kaynor in its use. They sat on a low seat with a wheel fashioned of wood in front of one of them, and Egarn leaned in from a side that had been left open and spoke words that seemed more like a magical incantation than speech while he drilled the two scouts from Slorn in incomprehensible movements.

The mock auto represented a carriage that propelled itself, Egarn said. Real ones were in common use in the land Roszt and Kaynor would visit on their mission, and they carried people and loads without horses to pull them. Lanklin wondered what was gained by it, since the management of the thing was obviously far more complicated than driving a horse. Egarn rehearsed Roszt and Kaynor tirelessly, over and over, and never seemed satisfied.

Dayla went back up the tunnel to take Lanklin's place at the rubbish pile. Ellar pivoted a section of brick wall to reveal yet another tunnel. This one led to the corridors and rooms used as living quarters by Egarn's team and to a door of steel that was kept barred except to a select few.

Lanklin's responsibility ended there, outside the door of the workroom. He removed a rag from the protruding end of a broken pipe, tapped a code, received a reply, and spoke the message into the pipe. Such was the tortuous labyrinth of defenses Arne had devised. Lanklin waited only long enough to hear the message repeated correctly. Then he turned away.

The news was alarming, but Lanklin welcomed the interruption. His "dae" consisted of sitting in total darkness waiting for intruders who never came. The rare message, the basket of supplies, the much rarer visitor brightened the gloom that enveloped him like a burst of sunlight. All of the guards working below envied the outside sentries who could enjoy the sun and rain and perform their signals with bird calls instead of clanging knocks. Assignments were rotated to give everyone an occasional breath of fresh air.

Of course Egarn and his close assistants labored tirelessly one mont after another without getting to the surface at all.

Beyond the steel door, a len grinder named Garzot, a refugee from Wymeff, immediately took the message to Inskel, Inskor's son, who had been first len grinder at the Court of Easlon before Arne brought him to Midlow to be Egarn's assistant. Inskel had to feign death in order to absent himself from his post, and he'd had the interesting experience of watching his own burying—from a distance—before he left.

Inskel was huddled near a large, rectangular cabinet fashioned of wood. Its supports raised it a meter above the floor. It was roughly built—Egarn had no concern at all for the exterior appearance of an apparatus as long as its functional parts were fashioned as meticulously as possible—and at one end was an enormous Honsun Len, a meter square, upon which shadowy figures and objects moved. While Inskel watched the len, Gevis, Wiltzon's young assistant schooler, stood by the cabinet ready to make any necessary adjustments.

The len was a window on time that looked a staggering distance into the past. That distance could be approximated with involved calibrations, but Egarn had devised another method using guidelines he evolved himself. The length of a woman's skirt, the shape of the odd horseless carriages, even the kind of buildings being erected held enormous significance for him. The others found this highly confusing, and the fact that the images were so indistinct added to their difficulties. Egarn hoped eventually to design a len that would show them the past more clearly.

Inskel's position was slightly to one side of the len. This was Egarn's order. There were many oddities about it no one understood, and one of them was the occasional surge of energy it released. Egarn feared this could be harmful, and he wanted no one watching a len from directly in front of it.

Garzot waited respectfully until Inskel became aware of his presence. Then he delivered the message: Midd Village raided by lashers—Roszt and Kaynor probably captured—no lashers anywhere near the ruins as yet—Arne at the village dealing with the raid as best he could. Marof had witnessed part of the raid himself, and he said the lashers were behaving viciously and pulling the village apart. Arne probably would be lashed for his efforts, and that was the worst news of all. Anyone punished when the lashers were in that mood might not survive.

Marof had cautioned the sentries to remain alert.

Sentries at the ruins were always alert, but those who heard the message were too disturbed by it to take offense. The news that Roszt and Kaynor—and possibly Arne—were in the hands of the prince's guard staggered everyone.

Inskel heard the message incredulously, his face tense with sudden apprehension. He had to decide whether Egarn should be told. The old man was asleep in the room next door, which served as their living quarters, and he needed every moment of rest he could get. Since no lashers had approached the ruins, Inskel decided to tell him after he awoke.

But Egarn was not asleep. He was lying on his bed comfortably swathed in a mound of blankets—the cold, damp, underground air made his bones ache—and petting a large black dog that lay at this side.

The dog's career in the ruins had begun with an unfortunate mistake. It was a child's pet, and Egarn sucked it up accidentally when he was trying to steal clothing from a backyard clothesline. He wanted to outfit Roszt and Kaynor completely before they left. Unfortunately, the attempt hadn't worked, and the dog jumped into the time vortex. Egarn was grateful it hadn't been a child—a moment later a little boy was running about looking for his dog—and he resolved not to try that again.

Of course they couldn't send the dog back. He seemed to be an intelligent creature, and he quickly made himself at home in the underground rooms. He answered to the name of Val. Actually, he answered to almost anything, but Roszt and Kaynor made a special pet of him, and they called him Val. When he heard that name, he wagged his tail with pleasure.

None of the members of Egarn's team had ever had a pet before. Egarn had often wondered where all the domestic animals vanished to. The vicious hunting dogs of Lant were the only survivors he had seen. In the hard times following the wars, when there wasn't enough food for people, he supposed no one could afford the luxury of feeding an animal. Probably all the dogs were eaten—and cats, too, and Guinea pigs and canaries and anything else that could serve as nourishment.

He heard the faint flurry of excitement in the next room, but he ignored it—they would tell him at once if it concerned him—and continued his reverie.

He was thinking about the Honsun Len. A lifetime of trying to understand it had convinced him he lacked a scientific mentality. He was an empiricist of some resourcefulness, an opportunist whose luck ran in streaks, but he certainly was no scientist. He tried things, building on what the Old Med had taught him and concentrating his efforts wherever a glimmer of promise appeared. Even so, the work of an abnormally long life—as lives were measured in this cursed future—had carried his knowledge a pathetically short distance beyond the legacy the Old Med had bestowed on him.

The len was made of a special glass produced by a select group of one-namers trained to that task only. They kept their guild's secrets to themselves, rightfully feeling that their privileged position depended on this. In an earlier economic system, this would have been called job security. The little they were willing to impart to Egarn told him almost nothing. From other sources he heard vague references to the various treatments the glass was subjected to, and he suspected that important trace elements were added. Even if he'd had proper equipment for a chemical analysis, both his chemistry and his knowledge of glass were so rudimentary the results probably would have told him nothing. From the scant records that survived, he thought the len's original inventor probably had stumbled upon some unlikely combination of ingredients by accident. That combination was now the glassmakers' trade secret.

The glass they sent to the len grinders was black and opaque with a shiny surface. The grinders, working with unbelieveable precision for that primitive technology, formed the ripples that various types of Honsun Len called for. Egarn deeply regretted not being able to run simple laboratory tests involving standard forms of radiation on one of the lens. He had tried numerous experiments while the Old Med was still alive to advise him, but none of them were successful because he lacked basic laboratory equipment.

It had taken him years to conclude that the len emitted energy and more years to decide where it came from. It was temporal energy, the basic force of the universe. The Honsun Len absorbed and focused energy from time. No other explanation accounted for its peculiar effects. Again and again Egarn had drawn upon all of the scientific rudiments he could remember from his distant youth in an attempt to understand this, but each time they failed him.

The len emitted temporal energy. The genius of the Old Med had found a way to store that energy and release it in bursts—though he certainly hadn't understood what he was doing. The strange, massive apparatus that looked like a photographic enlarger had a device faced with a thick, unpolished slab of Honsun Len glass that functioned like a camera shutter. Egarn reasoned that temporal energy backed up on one side of it or the other, depending on the arrangement of the lens, and rushed through when it was opened. That burst of force could push an object through time. Or, if the lens were reversed, it could suck an object from time.

It was impossible to test such a complicated device without

proper laboratory equipment. He could only try different things and observe what happened. He had spent nightmarish months—monts, in this frustrating future—just trying to position his lens with the precision he knew was essential if he were to repeat experiments accurately. He searched tirelessly for ways to calibrate differences so he could make measurable adjustments. Nothing had worked satisfactorily until Arne asked the most expert wood carver in Midlow to make a system of gears for him. With these, he finally was able to move his lens accurately through small gradations.

Now he had refined the settings sufficiently to give him two identified places and two identified times in the past. He needed dozens, but from this point the experiments should proceed quickly. His present worry now was that Roszt and Kaynor would not be ready when he was. He had learned very early that he had neither the time nor the patience to teach them properly. They seemed to learn so slowly, perhaps because much they had to learn was incomprehensible to them. Wiltzon, the old schooler, had a passionate interest in history, and he suggested that Egarn teach him and let him drill the scouts. The schooler was able to assimilate information much more quickly than Roszt and Kaynor did, and he relieved Egarn of the tedium of repeating lessons over and over. But now this system had become cumbersome, and the scouts simply were not progressing rapidly enough. Egarn feared he would soon have to resume their training himself.

Wiltzon had asked him for examples of money from the past. Roszt and Kaynor were having difficulty in understanding twentieth century economics. The notion of exchanging pieces of paper or bits of metal for the goods and services they needed seemed outlandish to them. Wiltzon wanted real money for them to practice with so they could recognize different denominations of bills and coins easily and handle them without looking like befuddled aliens from another time and place.

Although the len sometimes accidently picked up objects, it was undependable in capturing items Egarn wanted for Roszt and Kaynor's training, and he had failed utterly in his attempts to scoop out the contents of an open cash register drawer. It had been difficult enough merely to find an open drawer to practice on because he didn't dare make the attempt when a cashier was nearby and risk abducting another human into the future. He was wondering whether he could focus on a bedroom and suck up someone's wallet or purse. That might also provide examples of important documents for Roszt and Kaynor to familiarize themselves with—driver's license, checkbook, credit cards, various ID cards. They had to know about all those things even though their own transactions would be on a strictly cash basis.

He hadn't yet faced the serious problem of how they were to finance their mission. They would need a fortune by the standards Egarn remembered—thousands of dollars. It would be too cruel a fate to have them fail for the want of money after long sikes of work and preparation. He would stress the importance of their living frugally—extravagance would attract attention to them, and attention was one thing they absolutely had to avoid—but they must be able to buy anything they really needed. That included an automobile—or maybe a series of automobiles—and even if they shopped for bargains in used cars, they had to have access to a large amount of money and know how to handle it and safeguard it.

Egarn could think of only one way for them to quickly acquire the amount of money they required. They would have to rob a bank.

That would be no problem. He could teach them how to do it, easily. A miniature version of his weapon would drill a lock from any door or safe and melt a burglar alarm before it could go off. He was much more worried about their learning to drive a car. They couldn't track down the mysterious Johnson in a large American city without their own means of transportation, but how was he to teach them with only a rough mockup for them to practice on and a knowledge of cars that came from the flickering images the Honsun Len showed them? His one attempt to describe the workings of a gasoline engine had been a fiasco. It would be far easier if he could snatch an automobile through time, but grinding lens large enough for that would pose horrendous technical problems.

He would have to figure out something.

Finally he dozed off.

By the time he awakened, a second message had been received. Roszt and Kaynor were safe; Arne had a badly cut back but otherwise was unharmed. The Prince of Midlow had been chasing a rumor that had nothing to do with them; even so, she had come dangerously close to capturing Roszt and Kaynor.

The news that she had a spy in Midd shocked and frightened them. The Secret was safe, but new precautions had to be taken at once. Roszt and Kaynor would return to the ruins that night, and other arrangements would be made about their education.

Every resident of Midd had to be scrutinized in an attempt to identify the prince's spy.

Egarn listened quietly. "Arne will take care of everything," he said confidently.

Arne always did. Inskor had been right in letting Egarn settle in Midlow so Arne could look after him. Without Arne, he couldn't have found half of the scarce materials he needed. Without Arne, he couldn't have contrived a safe place to work, and where in this brutal society could he have found reliable people to help him? He wouldn't have known how to begin.

Arne had taken care of everything, and he would solve these new problems.

Egarn said to Inskel, "We absolutely must find some money for Roszt and Kaynor. This is what I would like to try."

While he talked, he continued to think about Arne. The young first server's presence here seemed like divine intervention. Nothing had gone right for Egarn until he met Arne; since then, every difficulty had been overcome as though by magic. No matter what the problem was, Arne could take care of it—and did. If humanity was to be saved, this clearly was the time and place to do it.

9

ARNE (1)

There were many who confidently relied on Arne to take care of everything—not only in Midlow but throughout the Ten Peerdoms. One-namers everywhere were acquainted with him; peeragers, even those who had never seen him, were aware of his importance.

Only a few people—such as Inskor or Wiltzon—knew him well and had an inkling of how he had become what he was.

He had been a celebrity before he was born. The peer herself came to his naming and chose his name, which she formed by combining the names of Arjov, his father, and Lonne, his mother. Lonne was only seventeen—young for a one-name mother in Midlow. Arjov was beyond the usual age for fatherhood. He had lost his family in a fire when he was still a young man, and he had never been wived again nor wanted to be; but the peer said to him, "Arjov, I won't command you, but I implore it. My peerdom has need of a son of yours."

Arjov protested he had no idea how to court a wife at his age, so the peer did it for him, choosing Lonne, already a master weaver despite her youth, a pretty, intelligent girl who was liked by everyone. The son of Arjov, the peer's first server, was the most favored one-name child in the Ten Peerdoms, just as his father was the most favored and highest ranking one-name adult. The position of first server had been invented for Arjov. The office was unknown elsewhere because no other peerdom had a one-namer capable of filling it.

Other children envied Arne—and Arne envied them their freedom to be children. One of the earliest lessons his father taught him concerned the high price that must be paid for favoritism and rank. These might be given freely, sometimes even ceremoniously, but after that they had to be earned, over and over.

From infancy, Arne was trained and educated to succeed his father. While other children were still at play, he was sternly put to his lessons by Wiltzon the schooler. Later he worked among the prentices of all of the crafters in turn.

He was only four years old when he learned the transcendent importance of his name—his one-name. West Road was being extended to the peerdom border to link up with a road the Peer of Weslon was building. In Weslon this road was called East Road, a contradiction the four-year-old boy found delightful. His father went to inspect the work force and took Arne along. It was the boy's first close look at no-namers and their lashers.

To a four-year-old boy, the lashers looked enormous. When his father questioned crew chiefs about the work or gave them instructions, his slender frame looked so fragile beside their hefty bodies that Arne feared for his safety. But the lashers treated Arjov with immense respect, answered his questions, listened to what he said, and then, if it concerned something that needed doing, took their no-namers and did it. The no-namers plodded about their work, never tiring, never hurrying, and carved a road through the forest with brute strength and the few tools they knew how to use.

At frequent intervals, often for no apparent reason, the no-namers were lashed. A flick of the wrist, and the multistranded tips of the lashers' strange whips raked a no-namer's back, leaving a tangled network of fine lines that oozed blood. All of their backs had the viciousness of a brutal age delineated on them in scar tissue. They paid so little attention to this cruelty that Arne wondered whether they actually felt the whip at all. They certainly were incapable of thought.

Arne, who delighted in his own ability to think, was both perplexed and bewildered by this sudden encounter with non-thinking. Set to clearing tree sprouts, a no-namer would impassively jerk up one after the other until he chanced to grip a young tree too large to be pulled up by hand. He would haul on it futilely until a lasher came and, with strokes of a whip, redirected his attention to the sprouts. Then he would work until another young tree stood in his way, to be hauled at brainlessly. One no-namer attempted to pull up a tree with a trunk twelve centimeters in diameter.

The alert four-year-old wanted to know why.

"They have no minds," Arjov said. "They can't think for themselves, so someone must impress thoughts on them with whips."

Arne stared up at his father with immense puzzlement. "Why do they have no minds?" he asked.

His father grinned down at him and ruffled his hair. "Aha. Do they have no minds because they are slaves, or are they slaves because they have no minds? Once long ago people worried about questions like that. Wiltzon can tell you about it. Now we struggle to keep the little knowledge we have left, and we can't afford the time to play games with words."

Arne's face puckered with concern over these humans who had no minds. He wanted to know who and what and why they were and where they came from.

"They are the nameless ones." Arjov said. "The work-humans. To the peeragers, they are just another species of animal—to be bred and trained and made use of in the most effective way possible. I suspect their life fire is the same as ours, but for some reason it doesn't burn purely. Lashers are the numbered ones. They also are nameless, but every lasher has his own number, and they are different in other ways. They have minds of a sort, but I have always considered them far more bestial than the no-namers. Lashers practice cruelty as a workcraft. They exult in it. No animal does such a thing, and no man's humanity can long survive that. We one-namers never speak to a lasher unless we have to."

After that first journey, Arne frequently accompanied his father on travels about the peerdom. Wherever they went, he saw no-namers laboriously plodding through the sike with lashers expertly inscribing each day's history on their bare backs. In Plao, the season of planting, they worked the peerdom's farms, pulling plow and cultivation frames. In Gero, the warm season of growth, the cultivation continued, but they also worked on roads and cleared new land for farming. In Haro, the season of harvesting, they helped to gather crops. During Reso, the cold season when the land rested, the no-namers did not. Whatever rough work was needed, whenever it was needed, they did it. They dug drainage ditches, built roads, and cleared fields. They hauled rock and leveled ground. They cut ice and hauled it to deep storage where it would be available for peeragers' hot weather refreshment. Throughout the sike they did everything that brute strength and a dead mind could handle, always with lashers standing by and flicking their whips.

The sight of them affected Arne strangely. In the Peerdom of Midlow, no-namers and lashers came from the same racial stock as the one-namers. They possessed taller, more robust bodies—the result of generations of selective breeding over the same period of time that one-namers were developing their minds and dexterity—but their appearances were similar. A no-namer seemed to feel nothing at all when a lash flecked his back, but Arne did. Arne felt the pain intensely.

The no-namers, men and women, were slaves; the lashers were their masters, and lashers also furnished peeragers with their guards and the peerdom with its army if it had one. Both lashers and no-namers were fathered on no-name women by lashers. All of the female no-namers were breeding stock. They were bred at the earliest possible age and kept pregnant throughout their short adult lives. They tended to die young, usually in childbirth. Med servers selected the larger, healthier, stronger male children to be brought up as lashers; the other males began their lives of slavery as soon as they were able to do useful work.

Arne experienced a lashing himself at a young age, and that intensified his concern for the no-namers. It happened the same year his father began to take him traveling. They went together to visit the peer. Arne had seen her before as a lofty, inaccessible figure surrounded by one-name servers and other peeragers. On this day his father's visit was informal, and the peer received them in her private lodge with only her own family present.

It was a revelation to Arne. The peer, her consort, and her children looked no different from his father and himself except for fancy clothing that even he could see was unsuitable for any kind of work—but of course he had never seen a peerager working. He wondered if their clothing could be the reason. The only other differences he could discover were that peeragers lived in ornate dwellings surrounded by gardens and had servers standing by anxiously to wait on them. Arne's mind gave another turn to the riddle his father had posed concerning no-namers: Were peeragers elevated above ordinary humans like his father and himself because they were somehow special, or were they special only because they were peeragers?

It was the peer's second daughter who introduced Arne to the lash. She was far, far prettier than her older sister, the prince. He thought her a marvelous creature, so soft-looking in her long, frothy dress, so unlike the little one-name girls he knew who wore plain, practical clothing and had hands already roughened by work. She floated over the ground in a way that reminded him of the tales elderly persons told about angels that flew through the air. He wondered whether this second daughter of the peer was an angel.

While he sat waiting for his father, she invited him to play with her. He trailed after her in mute ecstasy, and she led him across the palace grounds to a small, secluded glade. His euphoria vanished when she produced a whip. "You are a no-namer," she announced. "I am going to whip you."

"I am not!" Arne protested indignantly.

"You are because I said so, and I am a peerling. If you don't let me, my mother will send a lasher to do it."

She began to lash him. Fortunately it was not a real whip but only one she had fashioned for herself with pieces of string. Even so, its strokes stung severely when his bare arms and face were touched, and Arne didn't know what to do about it. He could only stand, smouldering with anger, and receive the blows, for a one-namer could not lift a hand against a peerager.

There was no telling how it might have ended had not the peer's eldest daughter chanced to see what was happening. She ran for her mother, and the peer herself administered a different kind of lashing to her second daughter—with the flat of her bare hand. Arne was permitted to watch, and the girl glared venomously at him all the time the punishment was being inflicted.

"Too bad," Arne's father said afterward. "I am afraid the peer has made you a lifelong enemy. Never mind, it wasn't your fault. There was nothing else you could have done. That second daughter has a vicious temperament, and she seems fated to be everyone's enemy. Probably it doesn't matter. Second daughters of peers aren't very important."

But a few years later the eldest daughter, an intelligent girl very like her mother, died of an illness, and the second daughter became Prince of Midlow and its future peer. The fact that she hated all one-namers and had spent her childhood pretending they were no-namers began to matter a great deal.

Arne never again mistook her identity. She definitely was not an angel; she much more closely resembled another strange being from the tales of the elderly, a devil.

Arne continued to work with the prentices of one crafter after another. When he had a solid grounding in every craft practiced in Midlow, he went through the entire cycle again. He was not expected to perform any of the crafts well, though his father urged him to become as proficient as possible. His object was to learn as much as he could about their problems and techniques. Evenings he continued his studies with Wiltzon. He also traveled with his father whenever Arjov thought the experience would be useful to him.

He puzzled over his father's "work." Arjov never seemed to do anything, but he always knew what had to be done, and how to do it, and he was able to tell others. Arne gradually came to realize his father was as unique as the peer, and that it was Arjov's own unusual abilities that made the position of first server possible.

Suddenly his father grew old. Overniot, or so it seemed to Arne, Arjov's hair turned white and he was unable to move about easily. More and more frequently, Arne was sent to perform his father's work. He inspected buildings or bridges or roads requiring repairs and decided what must be done, and how to do it, and what tools or supplies were needed. Then he requisitioned crews of no-namers, or he appointed eligible one-namers to tasks that no-namers could not perform, carefully entering their names and work credits in his father's ledger. Every adult one-namer owed a sikely debt in work credits to the peer.

One-namers were permitted to drive a wagon when their work required it, but they were forbidden to ride a horse or travel in a carriage without a special pass signed by every peerager on the peer's council. The peer pooh-poohed that and sent his father a two-wheeled carriage and a team of horses. For a time Arjov traveled freely wherever the roads could take him, and Arne went with him; but soon the old man became too weak to ride in the carriage. Arne was the peer's first server in all but the title before he was fifteen, with his father—now an invalid—advising him when he was able.

Arne had known about the hiding places from infancy because there was one in his own home. From time to time strangers visited Midd Village, arriving and leaving by darkness and sometimes resting there for a few daez. Several of the dwellings on High Street, the street at the top of the village, had secret rooms designed to accommodate such visitors. The dwellings were connected by underground passages, and concealed doors in their garden walls provided escape routes into the thick forest that grew just above the village.

Arne didn't learn about the League of One-Namers until he began to act as his father's assistant and had to meet with these mysterious visitors himself. Most of them were League messen-

gers, and he knew without being told that the momentous secret they represented must be guarded with his life and never
mentioned.

Visitors of a different sort passed through the village once
or twice a sike. Sometimes there were families among them
with young children. When they left, the villagers gave what
they could from their surpluses to replenish the travelers' supplies. Sometimes one or two families from Arne's village—inconspicuous families that were unlikely to be missed—left with
them. They were never mentioned again.

Arne's father died when he was sixteen. The peer and all of
her wardens attended his burying, and the following day she invited Arne to Midlow Court. In a lengthy, impressive ceremony,
she invested him as peer's first server. He felt far too young for
such a responsibility, but the peer gave him her full confidence
and promise of support, and the other peeragers—all except the
prince—seemed friendly. The prince looked more beautiful
than ever with her long, flowing blond hair, but throughout the
ceremony she glowered at him as spitefully as she had on that
fateful day when she lashed him.

Arne returned to the village, to the one dwelling that could
ever seem like home to him, and found it empty. His father was
dead; his mother had moved out. It was her simple but decisive
way of informing him that he was now a man, with a man's responsibilities, and even though he was young for it, it was time
for him to be wived, to chose a mate and rear his own family. As
for her, she was still young enough to make a new life for herself. Within a few monts she was wiving Kellan, a woodworker
whose wife had died of an illness, and though she continued to
visit Arne almost daily, she soon had another child to occupy
her.

Arne buried his sorrow and loneliness in work. The responsibilities were overwhelming despite his thorough prenticeship,
and his workload was staggering. He had to know where everyone was, and what everyone was doing, and why. He had to
know what needed to be done today, and tomorrow, and a tenite

hence, and—planning ahead—next esun, next sike, and the one after that. He had to know what to do in emergencies.

That was only the beginning. He had to tell people what to do and when to do it, and often he had to explain how to do it and why. Then he had to see that it was done. Without his father to remind him, he had to know that planking must be sawed now and put in the kiln for next Reso's bridge repairs, or that the growing herd of cattle would require an increase in silage capacity, or that it was time for the annual inspection of window panes at the palace, or that servers of the no-name warden, the peerager in charge of no-namers, should be reminded to send work crews to plow the village garden plots for planting.

The villagers were slow to extend to Arne the trust in which they had held his father. Many refused to believe he deserved his high position. Some felt he had been favored because of his father; others, that the peer appointed him because he had promised to place the interests of peeragers above those of his own kind. Arne knew his career might depend on how he handled the first crisis he had to face. In the meantime, he tried to be himself and do his work as well as he could.

The test came early. A long-standing dream of adult one-namers throughout the Ten Peerdoms became known to Arne only when it ended in catastrophe. The families that left the village in the dead of niot were headed westward to a new peerdom beyond the reach of peers and lashers—a peerdom of one-namers, a peerdom where they could manage their own affairs, educate their children, and guarantee a full measure of freedom to all.

Weslon scouts, one-namers themselves, sometimes ranged far into the wilds beyond the Weslon frontier. On one such trek they found an easily defended, fertile valley, and over the years one-namers who could slip away without being missed made the secret journey westward, a few couples, a few families at a time with whatever they could take with them. The community seemed to be thriving. It held the promise of a place of refuge for all one-namers, and a strong one-name peerdom could have imposed a measure of control on those peers given to periodic persecutions of their one-name subjects.

That dream of a more secure future was shattered by an exhausted messenger who awakened Arne in the dead of night and sobbed out his dreadful news. A marauding band of lashers had caught the new community by surprise and inflicted an orgy of rape, arson, murder and pillage on it. The survivors were starving.

Arne took charge of the rescue efforts. He juggled his accounts to make food available, and he invented errands to cover the absence of those he sent westward to assist the fugitives. The new settlement's survivors were brought back to the Ten Peerdoms and distributed among one-name villages from Weslon to Easlon. By the time they were settled in their new homes, one-namers of all ten peerdoms knew they could rely on Arne as they had on his father, but their dreams of security in the west were gone forever.

Arne handled problem of Egarn with the same tireless efficiency. He brought Egarn, Roszt, and Kaynor to Midlow, found a secure place for Egarn to work, helped him scrounge through Midlow's ancient ruins for materials he needed, and took complete charge of supplying him and his helpers with food, clothing, and outside support.

He selected Egarn's guards and assistants from one-name refugees who were drifting into the Ten Peerdoms in increasing numbers. All of them had been crafters, and between them they possessed the skills to do or make almost anything Egarn needed. Arne preferred them to the local one-namers. No one was likely to miss them, and they were happy to have a place to stay and a meaningful occupation. They didn't understand what Egarn was doing, but they knew that he, like them, was a refugee, and that he was working for the mysterious destruction of the Peer of Lant and her armies. Assisting him gave them an opportunity to strike a blow of their own, however small and indirect, at the evil force that had wrecked their lives.

The group was so self-contained that apart from Arne, no more than three residents of Midd Villager knew the secret workroom existed. One of them was Marof, who who had been Arjov's personal server and now served Arne in the same way. Because he was accountable to no one but Arne, he was available for outside errands or whatever additional help was needed at the ruins. Another was Wiltzon the schooler, who visited the workroom as often as he could and helped as much as he could. He was as fascinated as any historian would have been with the opportunity to watch history while it was happening. The third was Gevis, Wiltzon's young assistant schooler.

One-namers had a strongly ingrained ethic concerning the secrecy of one-name affairs. They grew up knowing that the stranger occasionally glimpsed in their midst was never to be mentioned. Those who chanced to see Roszt or Kaynor on a visit to the schooler, or one of Egarn's helpers sent to Arne with a message, forgot about it without really noticing it. No one had ever spoken to anyone about such a thing until now. That was why the presence of a spy in the village was so alarming.

Egarn's revelations about the Honsun Len had troubled Arne severely. Obviously something should be done to prevent the cruel brain damage to no-namers, but he had no idea what it might be. It would take sikes to rear a generation of no-name babies with normal brains, and a tremendous program of deception to keep the project secret, and Arne feared the Ten Peerdoms' time was running out.

Time was running even faster in the Peerdom of Midlow. Shortly after Egarn's arrival, the peer had been stricken. Her health grew steadily worse, and for days at a time she was incapacitated both physically and mentally. This made no difference to Egarn's work. The peer would not have been told the Great Secret in any case, and Arne obtained more by craft than she could have bestowed on them even if she had favored Egarn's project.

The peer's failing health diminished the significance of distant events in Lant and even those closer at hand in Weslon.

While she lay dying, the prince hovered in the background like a storm about to happen. One-namers had long been aware of her intention to reduce them to slavery and transform Midlow into a tyranny. It was not merely their independence as free crafters that was threatened but their survival.

Now the storm had arrived—sooner than anyone anticipated and with the peer still living. The prince was behaving as though the power of the peerage was already hers. She hadn't merely disobeyed her mother; she had defied her, and the peer's own power to rule trembled in the balance. If she failed to act quickly, the prince might depose her.

Whatever the peer decided to do, the peerdom's one-namers would lose. The prince would exact full retribution from them the moment her mother died. A revolt seemed inevitable to Arne—but so was an outside invasion, either by Lant or by some unknown force. An invasion might make the prince an ally of her one-namers while it lasted. Temporarily they would need each other. Arne wondered which would come first. Either way, the future held nothing but conflict and bloodshed.

Arne hadn't yet made up his mind about Egarn's plan—whether it would work, whether it would be a wise thing to do in any case. It was difficult to calmly review human history and make decisions about it when one's own fragile world was about to crash in ruin, but he continued to support Egarn because he could think of no alternative.

To the young Arne, as to the old Egarn, it seemed that there had never been a better time and place for a conspiracy to save humanity.

10

ARNE (2)

Once the one-namers recovered from the shock of the lasher raid, the village buzzed with anger. Word quickly reached the mills and workrooms. All work halted. Men and women gathered in the streets, and each incident of the raid was discussed wrathfully while the children raced about making the most of this impromptu holiday.

Arne found himself an embarrassed object of admiration and sympathy. The villagers were ecstatic over the way he had faced the prince and brought the raid to an end with a few quiet words. Half the adults of the village sought him out and volunteered to dress his cut back with poultices made from cherished family recipes.

He urged them to put their experiences in writing while the details were still vivid, to clean up any mess the lashers had made, to return to work. He knew this would be another test for him. He had stopped the raid, which was wonderful. He had asked for written descriptions of what happened, which certainly was wise. Now the village wanted to know what he intended to do about it.

By evening, apprehension developed that he intended to do nothing, and the village council, which villagers called the Three, marched to his home on High Street to demand a hearing. These elderly crafters constituted the only local government the village had. Usually they were far more government than it needed, and on this occasion they were determined to do something if Arne did not. Their anger had been festering since morning. Arne greeted them with grave courtesy, and Ravla, the elderly woman who acted as housekeeper for both him and the schooler, brought chairs for them.

Nonen, the miller, acted as spokesman. He was a sturdy, blunt individual who had never been known to waste a word.

"The peer must be informed as soon as possible," he blurted. "I intend to petition for a hearing. Every adult in the village is willing to sign a formal accusation against the prince's guard. We will insist upon severe punishment."

"The guard certainly merits punishment," Arne agreed. "Much property was damaged, things were stolen, several people were injured—one of them seriously—and two women were raped. But the guard was only carrying out the orders of the prince. Will you also demand that the prince be punished?"

Nonen sputtered into his beard. "Surely those who commit outrages must be held accountable for them!"

"Nevertheless, the prince was responsible. Her guard wouldn't dare to enter a one-name village unless she ordered it. Are you certain you want to do this? The prince has a long memory, and she will be peer herself sooner than any of us would like to believe. If she retaliates then, there will be no one to appeal to."

Toboz, the portly old sawyer, tugged at his own beard. One-name males did not wear their beards long—that was for lashers and no-namers—but Toboz's beard was exceptionally thick, and he took inordinate pride in it. He growled, "Do we have to bow down and accept this outrage? Our persons and homes will never be safe again if the guard goes unpunished."

"The prince expects us to file some kind of complaint—with the wardens if not with the peer—and she is doing everything in her power to prevent it. This morning, not long after she and her guard left, I sent two carpenter prentices to replace a plank on the bridge below the sheepfold. Lashers from the prince's guard had already set up a watchpost on the road. They stopped the prentices and demanded to know their errand. Then one of the lashers went with them, watched them work, and escorted them back to the village when they had finished. The prince has every route between Midd Village and Midlow Court posted. She is determined that no word of the raid shall reach the court until she has given the peer own version of what happened."

There was a stunned silence. Then Toboz said indignantly, "Are you saying we can't even tell the peer about it? That the prince won't let us? Surely she can't isolate Midd Village for long without questions being asked. The court couldn't exist for a tenite without us. It would run out of everything, starting with food. We have cloth, shoes, harnesses, crocks, lace, flour, and I don't know what all in our warehouse right now waiting for the next scheduled delivery. Repairs and building will stop if one-namers can't get to the court. The prince's watchposts won't be there long. Anyway, we don't need roads to send a messenge to the peer."

"Of course we don't," Arne agreed. "We can petition the peer any time we choose. The question is whether we should. She is so desperately ill that her servers may refuse to bother her with such a difficult problem. She may be helpless to deal with it in any case."

"What do you suggest?" asked Margaya, an elderly master weaver.

"I already have sent Marof to tell the land warden what happened. I did it while the raid was still in progress. He was to make a wide detour and approach the court this evening from the south. The prince probably won't think to block that route. Even if she does, her guard won't dare stop a messenger who has official business with one of the wardens. The land warden understands our problem, and the peer has given him authority to act for her during her illness. He will investigate the raid himself and make sure the prince doesn't know how he found out about it. She will be less inclined to retaliate if she thinks the information came from another peerager."

"And the land warden will tell the peer?"

"When her health permits."

Margaya said bluntly, "*If* her health permits, but it isn't going to. I hear her only thoughts are of death. You are right—she is much too sick to be told anything at all."

"In that case, a formal petition would accomplish nothing except to antagonize the prince. Let's let the land warden handle this for us and hope the peer won't be too sick to act when she is finally told. Only the peer has authority over the prince. Only she can decide what should be done. We one-namers have a problem of our own to deal with."

All three of them regarded him uneasily. Nonen asked, "What problem do you refer to?"

"The prince ordered the raid because she thought the peer's first server was harboring strangers."

Their uneasiness changed to alarm. This touched on matters they preferred not to know about. Like all one-namers, they had learned from childhood to look the other way and say nothing if they chanced to see strangers in their midst.

"She wouldn't have thought that if someone hadn't told her," Arne went on. "It means she has a spy in the village."

Now they were incredulous. Margaya exclaimed, "Surely none of our people would actually tell the prince—"

Arne said earnestly, "As all of you know, no peerager, not even the wisest and kindest—which our peer is—can be trusted with information that concerns only one-namers. Those of us with responsibilities never speak openly of these things, not even in a private meeting such as this one. The only secrets that can remain secret are those that are unspoken. Any one-namer—in Midd Village or elsewhere in the peerdom—may glimpse something from time to time that he has no need to know. We live close together, and our lives are linked in so many ways it would be impossible to prevent that—which is why the presence of a spy in our village is far more serious than the raid. A one-namer loyal to his own kind would pretend to see nothing and forget at once. Only a traitor would remember and tell."

They exchanged frightened glances. To have a friend, a neighbor, or even a relative eagerly retailing their harmless gossip, their petty complaints and disagreements, their every deed to an agent of the prince seemed too horrible to contemplate.

"If this is true, we must find out who it is as quickly as possible," Nonen said. "I suppose his guilt will become obvious in time—there will be unmistakable signs of the prince's favor—but that might happen too late to help us. We must identify him him at once."

"Aya." Margaya nodded grimly. "He won't receive his full reward until the prince becomes peer. Then I suppose she will make him her first server."

Arne had long expected to lose his office the same day the peer died, but he made no comment. "The traitor is my responsibility," he said. "Mine—and the League's." They shuffled their feet uneasily. "There is one thing you can do," he went on. "Find out why the log barricades weren't in place and a watch kept on them. It wouldn't have kept the guard out of the village, but everyone would have had more time to prepare."

"The logs weren't in place?" Nonen asked wonderingly. "Maybe there is more than one traitor."

"Or maybe someone was lazy. Whatever the cause, it is important to find out who was responsible and make certain it doesn't happen again. The barricades are your very proper concern, and an inquiry about them can be made publicly."

Arne promised to press his own search for the traitor, and the three left immediately, pleased to have something to do. Arne thought it best not to tell them—he had decided not to tell anyone—he already had identified the prince's spy.

He knew it would be a young person. The loyalty of the older crafters to their own kind was deeply ingrained, and all of them had good reason to resent the privileges of pampered peeragers.

Arne's garden was surrounded by high walls. It was further shielded by his house, which was wider and much deeper than others on the street. The only windows the garden was exposed to were those of the lesson room on the upper story of the schooler's house.

So the traitor had to be one of Wiltzon's students, Arne reasoned—a youngster of limited ability, an inept prentice making no progress at all in his craft, one who had received very little praise in his life. He would know he could never rise far above prentice status, and he would prefer the promise of a fine future as a fawning court server to a life of drudgery in Midd. Such a one would be only too susceptible to the prince's flattery.

Backward students sometimes were required to return to Wiltzon in the evening for extra lessons. This one must have caught a glimpse of Roszt and Kaynor—either when they arrived by way of Arne's garden or later when they carelessly went out for a breath of fresh air before it was quite dark. The scouts from Slorn knew Wiltzon lived alone and anyway was to be trusted. It wouldn't occur to them that the schooler might be giving a late lesson.

Under the pretense of reviewing the progress of Wiltzon's students—a legitimate concern of his—he asked which of them had required extra attention lately. The worst offender was Barlin, Wiltzon said—a thoroughly inept carpenter's prentice. Wiltzon described Barlin's problems disgustedly.

"He has difficulty with everything, but it is numbers I have been drilling him on. Imagine—a carpenter's prentice who can't remember something he will need all his life. Other students his age learned their numbers sikes ago. He didn't, so I have to give him extra lessons."

Arne quickly established that Barlin had been standing near the windows to recite about the time Roszt and Kaynor arrived. "That is, he was trying to recite," Wiltzon said. "All he did was look out of a window and stammer."

"It is time Barlin was given a different vocation," Arne said thoughtfully. "I will see to it at once."

Arne sent for Barlin, an ungainly youth of sixteen or seventeen who was already terrified. He broke down and confessed at once. The raid had shaken him; he had seen his mother in tears over the damage the prince's guard had done to their home. The prince herself had flattered him and coaxed him until he agreed to help her. She promised unspecified rewards, but he hadn't done it with the thought being paid. No one had ever needed his help before, and he simply couldn't refuse his beautiful prince. He hadn't realized what the result would be.

It was an enormous tragedy, heightened by the fact that his father and mother were worthy people. If the Three were permitted to judge him, he would be ostracized for life. No village would receive him; no one-namer would work with him. He would have to become a herder, a solitary occupation that few one-namers cared for.

But Arne could temper judgment with mercy. He wrote Barlin's release from the carpenter prenticeship and sent him off at once to the husbandman of another village who needed help with his cattle.

"No one-namer mentions a one-name secret to anyone," Arne told him sternly. "If ever again you have the urge to do so, promise you will tell me before you tell anyone else."

The grateful Barlin solemnly promised. Unfortunately, there was nothing to keep the prince from quickly buying herself another traitor or trying to. Arne would have to be eternally vigilant.

Old Marof returned early the next morning. No one had interfered with him when he approached Midlow Court from the south. He had seen the land warden at once and described the lasher raid to him, and that worthy official promised to tell the peer about it the next time he was able to talk with her.

The lashers at the watchposts had paid no attention to Marof when he returned to Midd Village, but for two days no one was permitted to leave—not even Arne, who protested that the peer's first server had orders from the peer herself to carry out. The village was so completely cut off from Midlow Court that Arne's daily instructions from the wardens failed to arrive. He was left wondering whether none had been sent or whether the lashers had dared to interfere with an official messenger. Finally he told Hutter, his student surveyor, to walk to the court, avoiding roads and keeping to the forest as much as possible, and see what was going on there. Hutter reported no sign of activity at all. Meadow and forest near the court, where the peeragers rode and played, were empty. If the one-namers were confined to their village, every peerager in Midlow seemed to be confined to the court, and the court itself was wrapped in an ominous silence. Everyone knew the peer was in the final throes of a fatal illness. Perhaps the prince already had seized power.

Or perhaps the peer was dead. One or the other must have happened. Hutter's description was of a court gripped by fear or already in mourning.

Then the peer's heavy four-wheeled coach rolled into the village, drawn by her favorite team of white horses. This time Arne's watch system worked perfectly. Everyone was alert, and the coach's approach was reported when it was still a kilometer away. The warning set the entire village aflutter and emptied mills and factories. By the time the coach climbed the steep slope to High Street and halted before Arne's dwelling, the street there was crowded with suspensefully-waiting villagers. They knelt around the carriage in a circle as soon as it came to a stop.

The oddity was that it had no escort. There was no mistaking the peer's ornately carved, fully enclosed coach, but the peer *never* traveled without her own mounted guard of lashers. On this day she seemed to be accompanied only by her coachman. No one knew what to make of that.

Arne had been at work in the sawmill, in a pit beneath the machinery where a shaft had broken, and he was one of the last to hear of the coach's arrival. With sawyers and prentices trailing after him, he hurried up the slope to High Street, picked his way through the kneeling villagers, and, brushing sawdust from his clothing, sank to his knees before the coach's door.

Everyone watched breathlessly as the door slowly opened—but it was only the peer's elder brother, the old land warden, who clambered out. He was a small, elderly man, comfortably rotund but surprisingly energetic and one of the few peeragers who did any work. His office was responsible for roads, forests, pastures, and agriculture. He had run it competently when he was younger, but as he advanced in years and afflictions, Arne assumed many of his duties, for which the old peerager expressed his gratitude with surprising friendliness. Their relationship was more like that between a fussy but affectionate uncle and favorite nephew than peerager and commoner.

They met often to discuss the peerdom's problems, but always at court at the land warden's garden lodge where he preferred to work. A visit to the village by a peerager was an extraordinary occasion—as unusual as the prince's raid—and Arne knew the land warden would not make the journey merely because he had a message to deliver. In that case, a one-name server would have brought a message board or recited something carefully memorized. But perhaps the old warden had come to announce the peer's death.

Creakily he signaled Arne to rise.

"Your service, Master," Arne said.

"The peer regrets her illness has long kept her from visiting her subjects," the land warden announced in his thin, high-pitched voice. "She has appointed me her deputy and asked me to hold open audience today. Anyone in the village who has information that should be brought to the peer's attention is invited to impart it to me. I also will hear complaints of injustice, and I will see that everything told to me has her full consideration."

So he had come as the peer's emissary. Even in her desperate illness, she was capable of acting with wisdom and firmness, and this was the most effective way she could learn about the raid without turning the prince's ire against the one-namers.

Arne told Ravla to prepare a room for the audience, and he appointed three men and three women to act as the land warden's servers. Margaya presented the written discriptions of the raid that Arne had asked her to collect, and other villagers waited patiently in line while one after another described the conduct of the prince's lashers and answered questions.

It was dark when the land warden finally left. Arne escorted him to the coach and opened its door for him. As the old man started to mount, he placed his hand gently on Arne's back and asked in a whisper, "Were you injured badly?"

"A few cuts, Master. They will heal."

The land warden shook his head. "I fear the prince has inflicted wounds on herself that are beyond heeling. I have never seen the peer so angry. She has enormous power when she chooses to wield it. Midlow's peeragers have forgotten that because she has used it so rarely. They are about to be reminded."

He gripped Arne's arm in friendly fashion and boarded the carriage. It made a rapid descent to Midd Street, turned, and left the village at a sharp clip. Behind it, villagers were describing their interviews to each other, and rumors were already circulating.

Two more days passed. Then Arne received a terse order. He, the Three, and six other villagers chosen by him were to be present at court at middae on the morrow for a happening. Every one-name village in the peerdom was being ordered to send representatives. They were to observe the happening carefully so they could describe it to other villagers when they returned.

Arne gave the messenger his acknowledgement and immediately went to see Wiltzon.

"What is a happening?" he asked.

The old schooler was perplexed. "I have never heard of such a thing."

"I want you to be one of the six," Arne said. "I will order a horse and wagon for those who have difficulty walking."

Wiltzon grinned. "That is against the rules."

"Not when we are using it to carry out the peer's orders."

Arne called on Katin, the oldest one-namer in the peerdom. She was blind, but she was still a skilled seamster. She worked all of her waking hours, and her old fingers moved as nimbly as those of seamsters half her age.

She welcomed Arne warmly. She had made swaddling clothes for Arjov's father as well as for Arjov and Arne.

"Katin, what is a happening?" Arne asked.

"Happening?" Katin frowned. "It is just a word, isn't it? It means when something happens."

"The peer's servers use it as a word for a special event. I need to know what it is."

Katin thought long with her head tilted back and her sightless eyes fixed on the ceiling. "Happening," she muttered. "Now I remember. It is some kind of court fuss. I haven't heard of one since I was young. It has nothing to do with us."

"It does now," Arne said. He told her about the message. His concern was that he, as the peer's first server, might be expected to perform some role in it.

Katin shook her head. "No. It is something for peeragers. One-namers weren't allowed at those I remember. It has nothing to do with us."

With that Arne had to be content.

He left for Midlow Court early the next morning, walking slowly and allowing himself plenty of time. This was his practice whenever he traveled. Along the way, he checked the condition of the roads, noted which drainage ditches needed clearing, inspected bridges, and turned aside to see whether buildings at the no-name compounds he passed needed repairs.

Midlow Court loomed on the horizon long before he reached it. The old walled castle pointed its high stone tower skyward from the top of a tall, knobby hill that stood isolated in a broad, flower-flecked meadow. A splendid old forest, which on most days—and nights, too—echoed with the cries of peerager hunters, ringed the meadow. The forest was broken only by the court's network of roads and by a slow-moving river—the same stream that rushed past Midd Village. Just below the castle and almost invisible behind another high wall was the present palace, a sprawling structure of wood and stone surrounded by its gardens and the buildings where the peer's household staff lived. Crowded tiers of buildings descended in steps to the bottom of the hill, each rank secure behind another high wall. The lowest, where the court spilled out into the meadow, contained stables and storage buildings as well as accommodation for one-namers who worked and lived at the court.

The castle had the same sturdy stone construction as the dwellings of Midd Village. The remainder of the court had evolved around it, creeping slowly but steadily down the hill in successive layers of peeragers' dwellings. With the passage of time, wood had become more popular than stone, and the houses of each descending level were flimsier than those above but far more comfortable and more easily built. They also were more lavishly ornamented, it being easier to fashion intricate designs in wood than in stone. In contrast, the outer stone walls became thicker and higher, reflecting an increasing nervousness on the part of the peeragers. Some were apprehensive about the distant wars. Some feared a lasher revolt. Many were highly suspicious of the peerdom's one-namers.

Peeragers ventured from behind their walls only for play and amusement. The meadow was the site of games; the river, of bathing and water sports; the forest, of hunts and romantic trysts. One-namers learned to keep to the road and look straight ahead when approaching the court.

The court was enveloped in the same uncanny silence Hutter had described. There were no creaking carts climbing or descending the steep roadway that spiraled from level to level all the way up to the castle. The sharp clicks of horses hoofs on the cobblestones, the clatter of one-name carpenters making repairs—the court required prodigious amounts of maintenance—the buzzing clamor of one-namers at work, the excited shouts and furious arguments of peeragers at play—all of that was missing. There was no one in sight, not even the gate guards.

There was *nothing* in sight. Even the paddock where horses were exercised was empty.

Arne wondered again whether the peer had died. The mysterious quiet was of a community dedicated to death.

Guards stepped into view as Arne approached the gate. They saluted him as though he were a peerager, which he found disconcerting. One of the peer's servers was waiting there. He directed Arne to the parade by the river where the peeragers held their outdoor ceremonies and riding contests.

"What is a happening?" Arne asked him.

"I don't know," the server said.

Arne circled the hill, and soon he was able to see a small cluster of one-namers waiting at the distant end of the parade, looking awkward and uncomfortable in their holiday garb. They had been shunted aside even before the happening began. Their wagons and carts were parked just beyond, surrounded by tethered horses.

Katin had been right: A happening was for peeragers. In some way it had to do with the welfare of one-namers, or they wouldn't have been invited, but they were not a part of it. They were spectators.

Resignedly they sat down to wait. Time passed, and the day became hotter and increasingly uncomfortable.

From the castle tower high above them, a drum began to beat with mournful monotony. Arne waited for the sound of trumps to echo across the valley—an impressive feature of every peerager ceremony. The trumps were ancient, magical devices of metal that survived only in the Peerdom of Midlow. Their one-name performers were members of a single family, and they jealously guarded the secret of producing trump sounds. No one, not even the peer herself, was permitted near them when they were trumping.

But the trumps remained silent. The drum beat continued. Peeragers began to file from the court gate, all of them dressed in black. For monts they had been making frantic demands for black cloth so they could have ceremonial clothing made for the peer's funeral. That clothing was proving useful in a way no one had anticipated.

The peeragers seemed as puzzled as the one-namers—as though they neither knew what to expect nor what might be expected of them. One of the wardens led the way, and another marched beside the column and spoke sharply to anyone who got out of line or dawdled. Commanders from the peer's own guard kept a watchful eye on the procession and occasionally snapped an order. The peeragers were unaccustomed to such treatment. They glowered but said nothing.

Arne and his one-namers got to their feet and waited respectfully. Never before had he seen *all* of the peeragers assembled at one time and place, but obviously all of them were going to be present at this happening—even children and babies in arms carried by their one-name nurses. The elderly were assisted or carried in chairs. The procession seemed endless.

It was a silent procession. Anyone who spoke was reprimanded sharply.

Finally the peeragers formed an enormously long line that extended the entire length of the parade from the one-namers waiting suspensefully at the far end to the main road that led to the court gate. Only the peer, her family, and a few of her high advisors were missing.

The court's one-name servers followed, and they took their places behind the long row of peeragers. The drum continued its solemn, monotonous beat.

Then lashers filed down from the court: the personal guards of various important peeragers, the court guard, a large group of lasher officers from the no-name compounds, and members of the peer's own guard. They formed a line facing the peeragers.

The peer arrived, carried in a chair and accompanied by her wardens and her younger daughter. The drummer followed, still thumping a solemn rhythm. Behind him came servers carrying a platform in box-like sections. They assembled it in front of the row of lashers, and the peer's chair was placed on it, facing the line of peeragers. The land warden stood beside her. The other members of her party gathered around the platform.

The land warden silenced the drum with a gesture and began to speak. His thin, high-pitched voice was barely audible where the little group of one-name spectators stood, and Arne had to lean forward and cup an ear to follow what was said.

"At dawn six daez ago . . ."

He was describing the lasher raid on Midd Village. He recounted it in enormous detail, reciting the items of property damaged or stolen, the villagers injured, the high iniquity of actually lashing the peer's first server. This heinous conduct, he said, which was performed at the order of the Prince of Midlow, was in defiance of long-established custom, in defiance of common sense and decency, and in flagrant defiance of the peer's explicit commands. It could neither be tolerated nor forgiven. The peer had ordered this happening so all of them could witness the punishment of those who perpetrated such monstrous acts.

The drum began to sound again. The lashers of the prince's guard were marched down from the court. They were still wearing their fancy uniforms, but not for long. The peer's own guardsmen stripped them down to a single, scant undergarment, after which they were severely lashed. The twenty strokes that each received peeled away strips of flesh and left the patch of meadow where they stood stained red with blood. The drum halted, and they were brought, one at a time, to face the peer.

The land warden told the first, "You were 792. Now you are naught." He was dragged away whimpering with fright, and the second was brought forward. "You were 1473. Now you are naught." And so it went with each of them.

The peer had taken away their numbers. It was an awesome, a terrifying fate. No more horrible punishment could be imagined. Death would have been far kinder. They had lost their identities. They were no longer lashers; they were no-namers, work humans, and they would be relegated to the work pools of the no-name compounds where len treatments would burn away the little intelligence that remained to them and they would spend their waking hours in incessant labor while their former cohorts peeled more flesh from their backs with expert whip strokes. No lasher who witnessed this happening or even heard it rumored would ever again dare to raise his whip to a one-namer.

The last of them was led away. The drum sounded again. Peeragers at the end of the line stirred. A murmur arose and was quickly silenced. The Prince of Midlow was brought forward. She also wore the new uniform she had devised. The peeragers watched incredulously as the peer's guard led her slowly along the line and turned her to face the slumped figure of her mother the peer.

"Terril Deline," the high-pitched voice announced. "You have defied the traditions of the peerdom. You have defied the commands of your peer. You are unworthy of your family, unworthy of your status, unworthy of your rank. Therefore rank, status, and family are stripped from you."

Members of the peer's guard stepped forward and roughly tore off her garments and boots, leaving her in a knee-length undergarment and with her feet bare. At first she resisted furiously, but they quickly overpowered her. When it was over, she stood with head bowed in quiet resignation.

"You are no longer Terril Deline," the shrill voice announced. "Now and forever after you will be known as Deline, and you are cast out from the place you have occupied."

The guards stepped forward again, seized her firmly, and cropped off her long golden hair close to the back of her head. The hair was handed to the Land Warden, who in turn handed it to the peer.

The prince had lost one of her two names. She was no longer Prince of Midlow. She could no longer wear her hair long because she was not even a peerager. She was a one-namer.

11

DELINE (1)

As the peer's guard led the former prince away, Wiltzon, who was standing beside Arne, whispered incredulously, "Is it possible? I have never heard of such a thing—anywhere. Can the peer really do that?"

"She has done it," Arne said.

In a peerdom like Lant, where the peer was a ruthless tyrant exercising absolute power over everyone and everything, no one would have been surprised. In the Ten Peerdoms, where other traditions had evolved, the power was still there for any peer who cared to use it, and both peeragers and commoners had to be reminded of that.

"What will the prince do now?" Wiltzon asked.

"She is no longer the prince," Arne said. "I don't know what she will do. There isn't much she can do."

Nowhere in the peerdom was there an occupation for a deposed and denamed prince, a wilfull female accustomed to having her own way about everything. She had no craft; she had never worked at anything. She was now a one-namer, but one-namers would have no place for her—in this peerdom or any other. She couldn't remain at Midlow Court in any capacity without becoming a focus of unrest and a problem for the new prince.

A peerager who had fallen from favor often sojourned for a time at the court of a neighboring peer. Perhaps the prince could find haven with her friend the Prince of Chang.

"Can a deposed prince succeed?" Wiltzon demanded.

"Certainly not," Arne said. "She isn't even a peerager."

The happening wasn't finished. Elone Jermile, the peer's younger daughter, a shy, plump girl of fifteen, was invested as Prince of Midlow. In appearance and manner she was totally unlike her sister. Her long hair was brown, as were her eyes, and she was introspective and contemplative where her sister was outgoing and domineering. As far as Arne knew, she had not yet taken a consort. Little attention was paid to the second daughter of a peer, and Elone Jermile had moved about the court like a shadow, almost unnoticed, always ignored. Arne couldn't recall that she had ever spoken to him.

The ceremony droned on. Finally those present were brought forward, a few at a time, to swear fealty to the new prince. The peeragers seemed dazed. Probably they had never heard of a denaming, either. They took their oaths mechanically and returned to their places in silence.

After them came the one-namers attached to the court. Then all of the lashers present were sworn as a group.

Arne and the other spectators were overlooked until one of the officials suddenly remembered the peer's first server had not yet been sworn. Then his little group of one-namers was hurried forward.

Arne came last of all. He touched his knee to the ground, the land warden recited the formula in a voice now cracking with fatigue, and Arne firmly repeated it. As he got to his feet, the old man leaned forward and whispered to him. "The peer wants to see you. The prince does, too. Meet me at my lodge, and I will take you to the palace."

Arne murmured, "Certainly, Master."

He wondered how the peer would be able to conduct audiences after the prolonged, exhausting ceremony. She seemed to have lost consciousness.

The drum sounded. Surrounded by her guard, the peer was carried away. The wardens and the new prince followed. After them came the remainder of the court in the order of its arrival: Peeragers, the court one-namers, and then the various guards.

Again the spectators were left until last. They drifted toward their horses and wagons, leaving Arne alone. He had much to think about. He waited, a solitary figure in the broad meadow, until everyone else had vanished from sight, and then he slowly made his way to the court entrance.

As he plodded up the steep, spiraling road that rose to the castle, he was saluted by every lasher posted along the way. The land warden's house and garden, and the lodge in which he worked, were on the level just below the palace, and the crusty old official was waiting for him at the turning.

He greeted Arne with a sigh. "It has been a tiring day."

"A bewildering day," Arne said. "A day of strange events. I understood very little of what was happening. Why are the lashers saluting me?"

"The peer ordered it. I told you how angry she was. She is determined no first server of the Peer of Midlow will ever be lashed again. As a reminder of today's ceremony, every lasher in the peerdom has to salute you."

Arne thought it would be achievement enough for the lashers just to remember the salute. They would quickly forget the deed that prompted it. "How is the peer?" he asked.

"Exhausted. I was afraid the strain would be too much for her, but she insisted she had to do it. She was right, of course. She did have to do it."

"She looked awfully weak."

"She is awfully weak, but she insists on seeing you. Determination is all that keeps her going. She is determined to see the end of this—to see that Midlow is ready for whatever comes—before she dies."

They walked to the next level and took the long avenue to the low, sprawling palace. The guards posted there saluted both of them, giving Arne's salute a special flourish. Inside, the hushed atmosphere was deathlike.

A group of servers had gathered near the entrance. They looked stricken. They were the former prince's personal servants, and the denaming of the prince had cost them their places. Down through the sikes, they had inflicted an unending series of cruel discourtesies on the prince's totally unimportant younger sister. Now that object of their disdain would be choosing her own servers, and none of them would be included.

In the days of the peer's good health, she had received Arne in a small room near the entrance where she worked at an old, ornately carved desk that her mother had salvaged from a ruin. When her health began to worsen, she transacted business from a bedside chair. Later, as she became still weaker, she reclined on the bed propped up by pillows. Now she lay corpselike, as though the effort to turn her head toward Arne was more than she could manage. Delor, the one-name server who had been her close companion from childhood, stood nearby and watched over her anxiously.

Each time Arne saw the peer, the ravages of disease had written new chapters of pain and suffering on her face, but always the steely determination had been there. She refused to succumb.

Now even her determination seemed exhausted. As he knelt beside her bed, she tiredly stretched out her hand to him. "Arne," she murmured. Her eyes remained closed; her voice was no more than a whisper, weak, tired. "I am sorry for Terril Deline. The fault was mine as much as hers. She was a beautiful child and such a beautiful prince—but I overlooked what she did too long and too often." The tired voice broke. "I have done what I could to make amends. I do hope things will go well for Elone Jermile."

Suddenly she opened her eyes and stared at him. "Twice your father saved the peerdom, Arne. He and the one-namers. He saved it once for my mother and once for me. Did you know that? When he was as close to death as I am now, he told me you would make a better first server than he had been. You are still little more than a boy, but already you have saved the peerdom and more. You have saved the Ten Peerdoms. I don't know how you did it. The Peer of Weslon said there was no way to stop the wild lashers, and most of the peeragers ran off like the cowards they are, but you took your one-namers and destroyed the lashers utterly. Those who saw the battlefield said there were dead lashers lying everywhere and no one ever won a more overwhelming victory. The other peers wanted to give you a second name and make you a peerager, but I told them you were invaluable to all of us just as you are—as a one-namer and my first server. You saved the peerdom—the Ten Peerdoms—and the prince's guard lashed you."

She was exhausted and fighting for breath, but for the moment her indignation had aroused her. "Each of my subjects, peerager, one-namer, no-namer, and lasher, has a responsibility to the peerdom, and the peerdom bears a responsibility to each of them. One-namers know that. Too many peeragers don't. I have made certain that the new prince knows. I don't have to ask you to give her the same loyalty you have given to me. I know you will."

Her eyes closed again. Her breath was coming in a whistling wheeze. Her lips moved again. "Have you any favor to ask of me, Arne?" She didn't say "last favor" but Arne knew what she meant.

Arne thought for a moment. "There is one thing, Majesty. The prince's guard acted on the prince's orders in raiding Midd Village. Its conduct during the raid was inexcusable, and the lashings were deserved, but not the loss of numbers. Give the guard to me, Majesty, and I will use it to start the army we have long needed. Further delay might be fatal."

The peer raised up for a moment and looked at Arne intently. Then she turned her gaze on the land warden, nodded, and sank back.

The land warden touched Arne's arm. As he got to his feet, the peer's eyes opened again. "Arne—did I do the right thing? About the prince?"

Arne clasped her hand and spoke firmly. "Majesty, you did the right thing. You did what had to be done. If Terril Deline had become peer, Midlow would have been torn apart in less than a mont."

She whispered, "Thank you."

The Land Warden led Arne away.

In an adjoining room, the new prince was waiting. Arne and the land warden dropped to one knee and then got to their feet again. The prince said to her uncle, "How is she?"

"Tired," the land warden said. "Terribly tired, but still fighting. She has a fierce determination."

The prince turned to Arne. The astonishing upheaval in her status seemed to have matured her. Her poise surprised him. She said, "The peer has made it clear to me that the success of my reign will depend upon you. I already knew that. All of my life, whenever anything needed to be done or whenever anything went wrong, the first server was sent for. When I was a child, it was Arjov, your father. Now it is you. We are both still young. My hope is that we will grow old together and I will always have you to turn to. I make you one solemn promise. In this peerdom, no lasher will ever again raise his whip to a one-namer, and the first server is to be accorded all of the respect due a peerager—by everyone in the peerdom, including the peeragers."

Arne thanked her.

"I will send for you soon," she said. "I have much to learn, and there is an enormous amount of work to be done."

He and the land warden knelt, and the prince took her leave of them.

The land warden said, "The peer asks one more thing of you. She wants you to take an assistant. Not only would this lessen the burden you carry, but the peerdom needs someone who can stand in your place when you travel."

"The peer and I have discussed this," Arne said. "Neither of us could think of a suitable person. The more capable one-namers are already skilled crafters, and Midlow never has enough of them. Their work is needed. The less skilled are less capable in other ways, also."

His assistant had to be a one-namer. No peerager would consent to serve under a commoner, and a lasher could not be put in the position of giving orders to one-namers even if one had been capable of it. "Did her majesty suggest anyone?"

"Yes. She has already made the appointment. Your new assistant is waiting to meet you."

Arne was astonished. It was unlike the peer to take such an action without discussing or even mentioning her choice. "Is it a court server?"

"Yes. From the peer's own household. The peer thinks her capable of learning quickly and assuming responsibility, which are essential qualities for your assistant."

Arne nodded resignedly. "If the peer requests it—"

"She does. She knows training an assistant will be one more burden on you, and the fact that you didn't choose her yourself may make it especially difficult, but she asks that you do the best you can."

Arne wondered if the peer was using his need for an assistant as an excuse for choosing a wife for him as she had done for his father. There were several conspiracies underway to get him wived, and he received broad hints in that direction almost daely. The most recent, firmly put forward by his mother, Lonne, was an attractive village girl named Selta, a talented seamster. Lonne had long considered Arne's household poorly managed, and Selta was her candidate to correct that—the fourth she had advanced since Arne's father died. She persistently recounted each girl's virtues to him until the girl lost patience and accepted another man's offer.

All of Arne's lovers had thought him the most desirable suitor in the peerdom at first—he owned the best and largest house in Midd Village, he had the highest earning credits of any one-namer, and the wife of the first server would instantly become the first woman of the peerdom among commoners—but they quickly learned that a man who worked enormously long hours, who had to travel frequently, who could be called away at any moment, who always had his thoughts on some crisis that had to be resolved immediately and several others that might happen, made a poor lover and would make a worse husband. Lonne didn't know it yet, but Selta already had taken another lover.

Until now, the peer had been more subtle. She frequently asked Arne about the village girls, but their discussions always concerned work skills.

The land warden led him to the room where his new assistant was waiting. She was looking out of the window when they entered, a tall, slender woman with blond hair cut short in the manner of court servers. The land warden spoke to her, and she turned to them with obvious reluctance.

Arne didn't recognize her until she flashed a look of undisguised hatred at him. It was Deline, the deposed prince.

He was too startled and disconcerted to speak. More than that—he was flabbergasted, but even as his mind struggled to grasp this strange turn of events, he could not help admiring the dying peer's wisdom. She had a mother's concern for her elder daughter. She knew there was no place in the peerdom for a former prince, so she had created a place. The peer also knew Arne would have to look after Deline if she were his assistant.

The land warden introduced her with awkward formality and then left them. Arne seated himself—which he could not have done without permission a few hours earlier—and signaled Deline to sit down. "Did the peer offer you any choices?" he asked.

Deline shook her head dully. "She ordered me. This is my punishment."

Arne frowned. If Deline thought of her new job as punishment, she would be a thoroughly inept assistant. In order to succeed, she must see it as an opportunity for redemption.

"Your life will be entirely different," he said slowly. "If you come to Midd Village with the idea of continuing the leisure you enjoyed as a peerager, you will be useless to me and to yourself. One-namers work. If they didn't, the Peerdom of Midlow and Midlow Court couldn't exist."

"I know that—now."

"The first server's job is to plan their work, make certain they have whatever it is they need to work with, and then see that the work is done and done well. I was trained to it from childhood—almost from infancy. I served a prenticeship with every kind of crafter in Midd so I could learn the techniques and requirements of all of the crafts. You will have to do the same. While you are doing it, you also will have to train yourself to know what is happening everywhere in the peerdom, and what has to be done, and when, and how. The position of assistant to the first server is both an honor and a responsibility. In order to deserve the honor, you must fulfill the responsibility. My father taught me that honors must be paid for, over and over. Do you understand?"

She shrugged. Then she nodded dully.

He wondered how long it would take to teach her how to work. This was something she knew nothing about. She was accustomed to physical exertion, she was an excellent rider, and the way she controlled a horse showed that she had strong hands and arms, but Arne couldn't even guess how she would react to unending, monotonous labor.

She also had to learn to walk. She was accustomed to riding her horse everywhere, and one-namers traveled on their feet. The walk to Midd Village would be the longest she had ever taken.

"You made yourself my enemy when we were children," Arne said. "You probably aren't aware that I have never been yours. Now you need help, and I am prepared to give you as much as I can—but you must earn it. You must work hard and well. You must want to succeed, or no one can help you."

"I know the peer my mother won't order you to keep an assistant you don't want," she said. "Both she and my uncle the land warden made that very clear."

Arne didn't want to begin their relationship with a threat, so he made no comment. "Your life is in your own hands, now," he told her. "It will be whatever you make it. If you hate your neighbors and those who work with you, don't be surprised if they hate you. If you share your joy with them, they will share theirs with you."

"What joy?" the former prince demanded.

Arne got to his feet. "The peer asks this of both of us, and she expects us to do our best. We will go to Midd Village now, and find a dwelling place for you, and get you settled there."

He began demonstrating the first server's responsibilities on the walk to Midd Village. They took West Valley Road, which had not been repaired that sike, and even though dusk was approaching and the light was poor, he showed her places where soil erosion was about to undermine the road and told her the procedure for ordering repairs and seeing that they were done. He showed her how to inspect beams and planks in the bridges they passed, how to spot a defective roof in a no-name compound, how to quick-survey a wooded plot to determine the number of trees ready for cutting. He turned aside to speak sharply to the lashers in charge of a group of no-namers whose cultivation sledge was not cutting deeply enough.

She watched and listened sullenly without the slightest spark of interest. It seemed like a most unpromising beginning, and while he talked, he was pondering another problem that had to be faced: How would Midd Village receive his new assistant?

He feared it would be horrified. Since the lasher raid, everyone had become spy conscious. Neighbors and fellow crafters who had lived and worked together amicably for a lifetime suddenly suspected each other of betraying the village to the wicked prince, and now that same wicked prince, disguised as a one-namer, would be living among them and doing her own spying.

Perhaps Deline sensed the irony of her returning as a one-namer to the village she had arrogantly raided as prince. By the time they arrived, she seemed to be in a state of shock and incapable of speech. Arne arranged lodging for her in a boarding commons, a house where unattached women lived. Her room was on the ground floor with its own private entrance, an important convenience. The first server's assistant would have to work odd hours, and she could come and go without disturbing the other lodgers. For a one-namer's quarters, the room was comfortably sized and adquately furnished.

He left her there, telling her he had other arrangements to make for her, and he would look in on her again when he had finished with them.

He first had a long talk with Gretley, the common's manager. Then he went to see one of the Three, old Toboz the sawyer. Toboz and his wife Midrez were aflutter with news of the happening. Arne told them the peer had chosen an assistant for him, a young woman, and they excitedly wanted to know all about her. When they learned who it was, they were outraged.

"Why couldn't the peer send her out of the peerdom—to Chang, or Easlon, or anywhere a long way off?" Midrez demanded.

"Deline has great ability. That is why the peer tolerated her for so long. If she had been able to think of the peerdom rather than herself, she had the potential to become a great peer. Her mother doesn't want that ability wasted. She is counting on us."

"Will she make a good assistant?"

"She will make an excellent assistant—if she can reconcile herself to being an assistant
.""And if she is willing to work," Toboz said with a scowl. "I suppose she doesn't even know how."

"All her life she has never done anything except what she wanted to do. She will need help with the simplest things. She is even accustomed to having a server help her dress. She won't know how to clean her room, or her clothing, or maybe not even herself. She won't know how to cook. Until now, everything has been done for her."

"She won't get waited on here," Toboz said. "She won't get to do what she wants to do, either. We will help her just as much as she is willing to be helped but not a jot more."

"She can't expect more than that."

"If she tries to boss people around, there will be trouble even if she is your assistant. Does the peer plan to get rid of you and make her first server after you train her?"

Arne shook his head. Such deviousness was not part of the peer's nature—nor of the new prince's, either. "The peer had to decide quickly what to do with Deline, and I have long needed an assistant."

"Learning all the things the first server's assistant has to know will be a slow process. What if she gets impatient?"

"She will. She will also get bored, and edgy, and weary, and everything else that discontented people feel. Remember—until today, whenever she felt any of those things she could call for her horse and go for a wild ride, or a hunt, or jump obstacles, or spear a porkley that someone else would have to haul back to court and prepare for dinner, or order her guard to race with her. Or she could change lovers. Or she could order her servers—and the peeragers, too—to play whatever game appealed to her. Now she will sit at a workbench doing one dull task after another until she is told to go home to a meager supper. Her sanity may be tested severely, but she will do her best to control it. She knows this is the only opportunity she will ever have to redeem herself, and a single complaint from me will end it. The peer her mother very much wants her to succeed, but the peer will never again listen to her excuses. If I tell her Deline is making a nuisance of herself, she will remove the nuisance."

"If the peer lives. What about the new prince?"

"She may be an agreeable surprise to all of us. If she is willing to work, and learn, and accept advice, the Peerdom of Midlow might have a future none of us would have expected. She will have to grow up quickly, though. Would you tell the other villagers about Deline? It will take time for her to become accustomed to life as a one-namer, and it will take time for us to get used to her. Ask people to treat her politely even if she is rude. Ask them to keep offering friendship to her even if it is spurned."

He talked with Wiltzon and several others before he returned to Deline. He found her standing by the window with tears in her eyes looking out at the cold gloom of the village's garden common and the dark mills beyond.

She turned on him with fierce resentment because he had surprised her in a moment of weakness. He pretended not to notice. "You know where the first server resides. Report to me there at dawn. We will discuss the day's work and plan your schedule."

She nodded resignedly.

"Gretley will bring you some supper and help you decide how you want to take your meals. There is community dining for single people and those who aren't householders. If you decide to join, the community kitchen will draw your rations, but everyone who eats there takes turns preparing the food and helping with the cleaning and chores. If you don't care for community dining, you can arrange to eat with a hospitable family—Toboz the sawyer and Midrez his wife are willing to have you on a trial basis. If you eat with them, Midrez will draw your rations for you—but you still would be expected to help prepare the meals and clean up afterward. That is the rule among one-namers, and it is the only way you can learn to do things for yourself, so you should offer to assist people at every opportunity.

"Suppose I decide to draw my rations myself?" she asked defiantly.

"You can whenever you like, but then you will have to do all the work of preparing the food and cooking it yourself. It would be best to wait until you have learned how. And even when you think you know how, it would be wise to wait until you have your own kitchen or can arrange to use someone else's."

"I see." Deline turned to the window and looked again at the cold gloom of the common. "There doesn't seem to be much happening here."

"A great deal," Arne said with a smile, "but one-namers keep their happenings private. Come to my house first thing in the morning, and we will plan your schedule."

Arne slept lightly, as usual. While he slept, his mind sorted through his responsibilities for a long procession of tomorrows and busily arranged and rearranged the multitide of details he had to keep track of.

He awakened suddenly. There was someone in his bedroom—an astonishing occurence. No one barred doors in Midd

Village, but neither did anyone prowl about at night. A server with an urgent message would have called his errand from the street door.

A cold hand touched his face. Then the blanket was pulled aside and the weight of another body settled into the bed.

Deline's voice said, as her arms encircled him, "It is time to plan my schedule."

12

DELINE (2)

They floated from darkness into the brightly dawning new dae, Deline the imperious, demanding princess, he the obedient subject; and then, in a dazzling reversal, he the lordly conqueror, she the humbly submissive slave. They remained long abed—remained there until a court server arrived to demand Arne's attention.

Arne told himself Deline was friendless and lonely, she had desperately needed to forget her shattered her life for a few hours, and the incident really meant nothing at all. Her passion seemed genuine and limitless, but of course she'd had many lovers. That was the custom with peeragers. Most one-namers quickly settled on a life-long partner; few peeragers ever did. There were other differences. No village girl had ever made love to Arne the way Deline did, but in their most enraptured transports, when he murmured every tenderness at his command, she remained silent.

The court server brought a bundle of messages and requests that had accumulated during the days of upheaval. He also brought a verbal message from the new prince. She wanted to see the first server that afternoon if he could spare the time. The phrasing was so unusual that it took Arne a moment to recognize it as a command.

He sent his customary formal assent and sat down to deal with the other business, going over each request carefully with Deline. Most concerned items that were in short supply at the court because there had been no recent deliveries. A train of wagons would be needed to correct the deficiencies. Wagons and drivers had to be assembled from all of the one-name villages. He showed Deline how to write the requisitions and explained what was supposed to happen at their destinations.

When this work was completed, they ate a late meal at

Arne's dining common, ignoring the curious stares of the atten-
dants, and then he took Deline to Farlon the potter. Farlon gave
her a workplace beside those of the two prentices he was training, and he began a lengthy discourse about clay. Deline fingered the samples gingerly, holding them as though she feared
to soil her fingers. Her attention had been caught by a pot that
was miraculously arising from a prentice's wheel.

It was the ideal place for her to begin. She could fashion
simple things at once, and the complexities of the craft could be
left until she became interested. The pot so fascinated her that
she didn't notice when Arne left.

He busied himself with a number of petty chores. He
checked the maintenance at the mills—all of the machinery
was old, and it broke down frequently if it wasn't properly cared
for. He also made certain the orders from the court were being
handled properly and supplies of meat and flour were being distributed again throughout the peerdom. Food reserves had
been depleted while the lashers were guarding the village. He
saw that his own private food cache was well stocked. By artfully juggling records, he kept a secret store of food in a stone
shed at the rear of his garden. Old Marof, working quietly in the
dead of night, wheeled bags of grain and an occasional haunch
of beef or mutton to the shed in his barrow. An increasing
amount of food had gone that route in recent years, but few villagers knew this. Those who did neither asked nor wanted to
know what became of it. As in the past, some found its way into
secret reserves the League of One-Namers maintained all
across the Ten Peerdoms, but most went to Egarn's team—his
helpers took whatever supplies were needed, entering Arne's
garden at night through the concealed door in the wall.

It was late morning when he finished his chores, and he left
at once for Midlow Court. The twenty-four members of the former prince's guard were waiting in orderly ranks just outside
the court gate. The land warden had formally restored their
numbers, telling them Arne requested it. Now they were the
first server's guard. Whatever he told them to do they were to

do instantly, or the peer would condemn them to a worse punishment.

They had been fanatically loyal to the prince. That loyalty
now belonged to Arne, reinforced by an emotion lashers rarely
experienced—gratitude. They were embarrassingly worshipful
and eager to please him.

Here, thanks to Deline's disgrace, was the beginning of an
army, something he and Inskor had long advocated in vain.
What it became depended on him, and he hadn't the faintest notion of what he should do with it. His vague intention was to
train these lashers as officers for the troops he would obtain
later, but how did one train an army officer, and what did one
train him to do? The lashers had lost their horses and their
whips. The horses could be returned to them, but they had to be
armed differently. A whip, however skillfully wielded, would
count for little in battle.

With the land warden's assent, he sent a message to
Inskor, asking for an Easlon scout to train the new army. The
Ten Peerdoms would never have a force large enough to stand
up to the mounted hordes of Lant. Their army would have to
conserve its strength and substitute skill for might, doing battle only under conditions of its own choosing and trying to inflict maximum destruction with minimum loss. It would be an
army of scouts.

Arne first examined the lashers' cruelly cut backs and saw
that they were dressed properly. Then he took them on a walk
through the forest. The ground was uneven. The path rose and
fell steeply, and by the time they returned to Midlow Court, the
lashers were exhausted and visibly wilting. Probably none of
them had ever walked so far.

He placed their former commander in charge and instructed him to begin a regimen of physical conditioning with
several long walks each dae. He wanted them away from the cor-
rupting influence of the court, so he asked one of the peer's servers to find housing for them at a remote no-name compound.
Then he went to the Land Warden with another request.

As soon as the former guardsmen were adequately trained, he wanted to begin drafting lashers from the no-name compounds for his new army. He also wanted no-namers who could be formed into military labor platoons. He had already discussed the necessity of this with Inskor. The Ten Peerdoms needed a defensive barrier along their entire southern frontier, and that would require enormous amounts of labor.

The land warden referred the question to the peer's council, which consisted of the prince, the wardens, and other advisors. None of them objected, not even the no-name warden, who had the responsibility for the peerdom's lashers and no-namers. All of these stuffy officials had just seen the former prince lose one of her names, and at this juncture none of them were inclined to oppose the peer's first server.

The new prince listened attentively, but she said little. Afterward, she conferred with Arne privately. "Have you any advice for me?" she asked.

"These are times of conflict, Highness," Arne said. "We defeated a threat from the west. There may be others, but the real danger lies in the south. Eventually the Peer of Lant will cross the mountains and turn north, and there is no other barrier to stop her. We should have begun our preparations long ago. When the Lantiff come, we must fight—and win—or those of us who survive will be the slaves of Lant."

"I have heard Lant has thousands and thousands of mounted lashers, and they sweep over the land like plague and fire combined." She walked to the window and looked out. "It is hard to imagine that happening here. Do you think it could?"

"It could and will if we don't prepare to stop it. Perhaps we will fail and it will come anyway. But we must do our best."

She turned. "You stopped the wild lashers in the west," she said. "I don't understand battles. You must tell me what to do."

"The peerdom is home to all of us, Highness. One-namers are willing to fight and die for that home. That is why they fought the wild lashers so fiercely, but they would be helpless before the armies of Lant. There are too few of them. We can't begin to defend ourselves against Lant unless each of the Ten Peerdoms contributes as much as possible—not only one-namers, but also lashers and no-namers. All must be trained with care and determination so they know what they have to do and how to do it."

The prince listened with a frown. Her sister had been ruled by impulses, but Elone Jermile would consider every move carefully and try to understand what was involved before she made up her mind. She would make few wrong decisions, but she might be unable to act quickly.

She summoned her uncle the land warden, who was waiting in the next room, and asked him, "How can we make the other peerdoms help? Should we send an emissary to them?"

"That would be the way to begin," the land warden said.

They discussed the different peers and how they were likely to react.

"Could Arne be the emissary?" the prince asked finally.

"Of course he could," the land warden said. "But with the peer dying and your sister deposed, he is needed here."

"Then we must find someone else." She looked to Arne for suggestions.

Things were happening with an ease Arne found difficult to believe. "Perhaps we should wait until the scout from Easlon arrives," he said. "If each peerdom sent us a hundred lashers to-morrow—which wouldn't make much of an army—I would have no idea what to do with them. I could arrange to feed and house them, but their training must be left to someone who knows how."

They agreed to wait until the Easlon scout arrived before they asked the other peerdoms for help.

The prince's final question concerned the new one-namer, Deline.

"I won't know about her for at least a tenite," Arne said with a smile. "By then, she will have made a beginning—if she is going to make one."

He was curious himself as to how Deline was doing. When

he returned to Midd Village, his first stop was Farlon's pottery. He found the potter highly pleased with his new prentice. Deline learned quickly, she had deft fingers, and she produced common crockery with ease. Now he was letting her experiment with different kinds of clay. She had modeled an oddly shaped object of curved surfaces and fragile loops, and she sat looking at it intently. Arne was pleased she had found something to interest her even though she seemed thoughtful rather than enthusiastic.

She remained so in the days that followed. She did everything expected of her and did it well. She was cooperative, she was polite to her fellow workers and the villagers she came in contact with, but she shared nothing of herself. It was as though her real self were imprisoned beyond their reach.

She worked with the prentices and quickly learned the rudiments of the more important crafts. She traveled about with Arne, learning to walk long distances; learning to look for damage or wear in anything from roads to machines; learning the procedure for arranging repairs when she found the need for them. Arne showed her how to check inventories and order new supplies when stocks on hand dropped below an acceptable level.

Together they helped one-name foresters survey stands of timber and mark trees for cutting, fell them, saw them into logs. Then they watched no-namers haul the logs to a stream so they could be floated down to the river, which carried them to the mill. The mill cut them according to need, and Arne determined the need himself—whether for rough planks, finished lumber for building, or carefully finished boards of selected rare woods for use at the court. The wood was placed in a drying kiln if it was needed quickly or air dried if it was not.

Deline continued to share his bed each night. She waited until darkness fell, and then, a lithe shadow, she flitted to the top of the town and slipped into the First Server's dwelling.

The daez became tenites; the tenites a mont. Arne gave as much time as he could spare to his two new responsibilities—his tiny army and his assistant. The army responded with eager enthusiasm. Deline worried him because she continued to hold herself apart from this new life that was happening around her.

But she did her work well, and she soon learned the customs of the village. She managed her love affair with Arne so deftly that no rumor of it circulated. Probably some villagers suspected it—love affairs were always suspected—but the villagers practiced discretion in their own lives and respected it in the lives of others. The only things gossiped about were those that were done openly.

When Deline had finished the most important prentice assignments, she was able to spend more time with Arne during the day. They became co-workers and colleagues, and Arne marveled at how quickly she learned and how well she worked with him.

Late one afternoon they went out together in response to a report of road damage. Walking back in the gathering dusk, Arne discussed the repairs and how they should be made. He would go at once, he said, and requisition a crew of no-namers so work could begin early the next morning.

Deline said suddenly, "The land warden told me you ran the peerdom. I thought he was joking. Now I understand what he meant. I was a fool to think anyone who works as hard as you do—as hard as all the one-namers do—could be plotting treason. When would any of you have the time?"

"Plotters find the time," Arne said. "I suppose no one bothered to tell you treason is an important concern of mine."

She turned and stared at him.

"I am responsible for one-namers' loyalty throughout the peerdom," Arne said. "I also am expected to keep an eye on no-namers and lashers. As you know, it can be extremely easy to corrupt a naive prentice."

"You mean—you found out—"

"Of course. I found out at once. He was a clumsy spy, but he illustrates why we must be constantly on the lookout for traitors. From time to time one of the other peerdoms sends an agent to Midlow—ostensibly on a legitimate errand but actually to recruit spies when no one is looking. His peer suspects Midlow is conspiring against her, or perhaps his peerdom has some plot of its own to advance. We also suspect the Peer of Lant of recruiting spies in all of the Ten Peerdoms, and that is much more serious. We must watch for treason constantly."

"We are a long way from Lant. Why would its peer want spies here?"

"The Peer of Lant wants to conquer the world—which includes Midlow."

She was silent for a time. Then she said, "With all of that going on, I accused you, the person responsible for preventing treason—"

"Even when I find someone behaving suspiciously, I find it dangerous to take action in such matters without first investigating carefully. It is so easy to accuse an innocent person—and so difficult to make amends."

"Yes." She nodded. "It is dangerous."

The realization that she would remain an outsider for sikes pained him. One-namers accepted her, but they wouldn't trust her until she had been tested by time. Arne, too, though his love for her gradually became a certainty, was unable to trust her completely. He couldn't tell her about the secret rooms in the houses at the top of the village, for example, or about the cache of food in his garden. In that respect, she remained a renegade peerager.

He would never be able to share the Great Secret with her, the work in the ruins. Not even his most trusted one-name friends were aware of that.

The Easlon scout finally arrived. It was Bernal, whom Arne already knew. Inskor sent his apologies for the delay. Bernal was the scout best qualified to train an army, but he had been far to the south when Arne's request came.

The two of them talked through the night. Arne had been trying to learn how the Peer of Lant organized her armies.

Egarn knew something about military theory and could tell him how armies had been organized in the past—he'd had officer training himself as a young man—but he had paid no attention at all to Lant's military establishment.

Bernal knew all about the Lantiff. Together they compared the system Egarn had described with the one Lant was using and considered what should be done to build an army quickly and efficiently.

"The Peer of Lant's conquests have come more slowly since Egarn tricked her," Bernal said, "but they are none the less certain, and her army keeps growing. She simply overwhelms her opponents. She never hurries. Each victory makes her stronger, and she has long hoped that her len grinders would eventually devise a weapon to take the place of the one she lost."

He turned and met Arne's inquiring gaze firmly. "Now they have done so. She has a weapon of her own."

The fragile hope of Arne's little army vanished in the sudden chill that he felt. "That alters all of our strategy," he said slowly.

"Ah—but Lant doesn't have *Egarn's* weapon. It has something like it but different. Lant's weapon produces a force but not a fire—it strikes without burning. It stuns, but it doesn't destroy. Also, it doesn't strike from as great a distance. The tube looks the same, but the kinds of lens and their arrangement are very different."

"Then we still have an advantage."

"For the present. No doubt her servers will try to improve this new weapon, and they may succeed. They may even produce one more devastating than Egarn's, but the one they have is more valuable for the battles they are fighting now. It doesn't kill. When the defeated lashers recover, they find themselves in the army of Lant. The peer's army is growing faster than ever. I brought two of her new weapons for Egarn to see."

He passed two small tubes to Arne.

"How did you get them?" Arne asked.

Bernal smiled. "Lant made the mistake of attacking the

Peerdom of Ramor. Ramor has an unusual peer—she is willing to learn and able to take advice. We set a trap and annihilated most of an army. The Peer of Lant hadn't encountered Egarn's weapon since we closed the passes. She had got careless. Now she will proceed with extreme caution for a time. In the past, time gained from her caution hasn't meant very much, but if the Ten Peerdoms can actually make use of it to build their own army, the future suddenly begins to look brighter."

"What do we need to do?" Arne asked.

"You are doing it. You are doing everything that needs to be done—everything except one, persuade the other peerdoms to help, and Inskor thinks you will do that, too. Inskor is especially pleased that you are adding no-namers to your army. Lines of defense require huge amounts of work, and we need several of them so we can inflict a series of losses on the Lantiff before they reach our border."

"Is the attack certain?"

"The Peer of Lant is elderly. She may not be menacing the world for many more sikes, but while she lives, her wars will continue. We have been trying to assassinate her. We killed two of Lant's top generals, but thus far the peer has managed to protect herself. I am looking forward to seeing Egarn again."

"I will take you to him now," Arne said. "Then I will introduce you to your army."

Suddenly everything was on a dizzying upswing. Arne had a brief interview with the dying peer and a longer one with the prince and the land warden. Things had returned to normal in Midlow, and he could be spared for a mission to the other peerdoms. Deline had done so well that he could temporarily leave his routine duties to her. As a buffer against one-namers who might still be resentful of her, he gave her an assistant, Hutter, his young prentice surveyor.

He knew he would miss her desperately. Perhaps it shouldn't have surprised him that they were still lovers; unlike the village girls, she had no reason to resent the long, uncertain hours he worked and his frequent absences. She shared his work with him and traveled about the peerdom with him, and they were able to steal delicious moments from the cares and humdrum routine of running a peerdom.

But he had always expected to lose her eventually. He had long been resigned to the fact that he was a poor lover, and he knew he couldn't hold a passionate woman like her.

Unless—was it possible that she loved him?

On their last night together, he asked her to wive him.

She drew back in astonishment, her moon-lit blond hair in alluring disarray, her body an enticing, bright contrast to the dark bed. She said slowly, "You mean—live here with you, bear children, be a village wife—"

The first server's wife would be the foremost one-name woman in the peerdom, but the distinction between that and any village wife hardly mattered to the former prince. "Share my life," Arne said, "and let me share yours."

"A one-name life in a one-name village," she mused.

"But *you* are a one-namer," he said.

She winced as though he had struck her. "Yes. Yes, I am. Sometimes I forget." She put her arms around him. "You love me, and I love you, but that becomes so complicated when one is a one-namer. Do you really want to share the rest of your life with me?"

"I do."

"I see. I must think. I must think about being a one-namer. By the time you return, I will have decided."

The prince provided a horse for Arne, and he went first to a hero's welcome in the Peerdom of Weslon. The wild lashers had burned and plundered Weslon Court before Arne defeated them. The court was being rebuilt, but the charred ruins that remained were a sobering reminder of what had happened. The peer, a tall, slender young woman, had inherited her title shortly before the lashers arrived, and she had thought it lost forever until Arne led his one-namers to her rescue. She greeted him warmly, proudly displayed her baby daughter, Weslon's new prince, and ordered a feast for him. She gave him an immediate interview with her advisors in attendance.

Arne had several requests for her in the name of the Peer of Midlow. The first was that she permit Weslon's scouts to train one-namers from all of the Ten Peerdoms. They had been secretly training a limited number for sikes, but an enormous force of scouts was needed to keep watch on the Ten Peerdoms' frontiers. The scouts of Easlon could not train so many.

"We must send our scouts far into the wilds so they can give an early warning when trouble approaches," Arne said. "The wild lashers were almost within your borders before they were noticed."

The peer agreed immediately.

Arne's second request was that Weslon contribute lashers and no-namers to a common army that would defend all of the Ten Peerdoms—one that could move instantly wherever it was needed. "We already have started such a force in Midlow, and an Easlon scout is training it," Arne said. "I invite you to send us a hundred lashers and a hundred no-namers now and as many as you can spare later. When the army has been trained, parts of it will be stationed along all the frontiers, including Weslon's, and if danger threatens anywhere, the entire army will respond."

This request was received with hesitation and doubtful muttering. The memory of the rebel army was as green in Weslon as elsewhere. Finally Arne appealed directly to the peer. "Majesty, the Ten Peerdoms cannot survive without an army. If there had been additional scouts when the wild lashers came, and a common army you could call upon, there would be no charred wreckage in Weslon Court."

She promised to send a hundred lashers and a hundred no-namers to Bernal immediately. He next took his story to West Southly, which was already apprehensive that Lant's army might suddenly burst upon its unprotected southern frontier. The peerdom had long neglected its defenses simply because nothing ever seemed to happen beyond its borders, and it agreed at once to send the requested hundred lashers and hundred no-namers to Bernal and fifty one-namers to Weslon to train as scouts.

By the time Arne reached the Peerdom of Chang, he had made a discovery. Success engenders success. The fact that Weslon, Midlow, and West Southly were already contributing to a common army overrode all of the arguments the Chang peeragers could muster. He continued his circuit of the Ten Peerdoms, leaving Easlon for last—but the Peer of Easlon learned of his mission before he arrived, and Easlon's quota of a hundred lashers and a hundred no-namers had already started for Midlow. When all of the promised lashers and no-namers arrived, there would be a thousand of each, and five-hundred one-namers were gathering in Weslon and Easlon for scout training. Inskor had sent six more scouts to Midlow to help Bernal. It all happened so easily Arne was left wondering why they had waited so long.

He spent several daez with Inskor before he turned homeward, discussing the uses that might be made of the new army. His success elated him, but it had been a grueling trip, and he was exhausted when he reached Midd Village. He found riding more tiring than walking.

Deline came shortly after he arrived and threw herself into his arms. It was the homecoming he had thought about through all of the long daez of travel; but when he gathered her to him, she drew back.

"Have you decided?" he asked.

"Yes. But we need time to ourselves to talk about that. Your duty comes first."

"All right," he said with a weary smile. "Tell me."

He expected her to recite the list of petty problems accumulated during his absence, but she said, "There are none."

"None at all?"

"Everything has been taken care of." She was actually functioning as the first server's assistant, and doing it well, and she couldn't conceal the pride she felt. "There are no problems, but the land warden has sent a message for you. He wants to see you as soon as possible."

"Tonight?" Arne asked in dismay.

"The message said the moment you arrived."

"Did the message say what he wants?"

She looked away. "No. But the peer's death is expected at any time."

"Very well. I'll go at once."

He kissed her again and left. At least he still had the horse to ride. He rode it into the court and all the way up the spiraling road to the land warden's level, a privilege normally reserved for peeragers. No one challenged him, and all of the guards saluted. The land warden was at the palace and had to be sent for. Arne settled himself to wait and fell asleep in his chair.

The land warden awakened him—happy to see him but humbly apologetic for the abrupt summons. "It could have waited for morning," he said, "But as long as you are here—"

He tersely summarized what had happened since Arne left. It finally had dawned on the other peers that Lant was more than a remote threat, and the wild lasher attack on Weslon was something that could happen to any of them. All had sent messages pledging cooperation. Lashers and no-namers had begun to arrive from the other peerdoms, and Bernal was elated.

As for the peer—she was dying, of course. She had been dying for a long time, but she still possessed determination. She wanted to live until she was assured Midlow was prepared for the future. The prince?

"The prince is why I sent for you," the land warden said. "The prince feels it is time she took a consort."

Arne was astonished. This was social matter that concerned only peeragers. Never before had anyone bothered to mention such a thing to him, let alone consult him. "She is young, but if that is her desire—is there a problem?"

"A possible problem," the land warden said. "There may be serious complications, and it is well to consider them in advance and be prepared to meet them. You see—the man she has chosen is you."

13

ARNE (1)

"She won't have anyone else," the land warden said. "She has admired you ever since she was a child, but she was too shy even to speak to you. She still is, which is why she asked me to do it."

"I see," Arne said dazedly. He had the sensation of having a deep pit suddenly open under him, and his mind was scrambling frantically to find an escape. There was none.

"She had always hoped you would be free to be her consort when she became older. She thought it wouldn't matter that you were a one-namer—no one cared what the peer's second daughter did. Now she is the prince, and this is certain to cause an uproar. It would have been wiser for her to wait another sike or two, but she is worried you might get yourself wived in the village and no longer be available." The land warden added anxiously, "I hope you don't find the idea distasteful."

Arne found it staggering. He had never thought of Elone Jermile in any connection at all except as the new prince. His mind continued to search desperately for a way out. He said slowly, "I know that now and then a peerager mates with a one-name server, but it isn't even considered respectable. For the prince to do it—"

"It will cause a commotion," the land warden said regretfully, "but there may be a way around that. There was all that talk among the peers about giving you a second name. If they had done so, you would be a peerager yourself, now, and there wouldn't be any problem. You weren't even consulted—about the second name, I mean. It still could be done."

"No," Arne said. "The peer was entirely right—if she gave me a second name, she would have to find another first server. A peerager couldn't associate with one-namers as I must do."

"You know best about that. Maybe it will help that you

have been offered a second name. After all, you are the highest one-namer in the peerdom. The prince is waiting for your answer. What do you want me to tell her?"

Arne suddenly remembered that he *had* heard of a prince taking a one-namer as consort. Egarn had been consort to the Peer of Lant when she was prince. Perhaps Egarn could help him find a way out.

The land warden hadn't given a thought to how the one-namers would react. Arne would have to consult with the Three and other leaders. He wanted Egarn's reaction. Perhaps if enough people objected . . .

First of all, he must talk with Deline. The happiness that had seemed within his grasp had suddenly been jerked away.

"Please give the prince my thanks for the high honor she has shown me," he said slowly. "Both of us have important responsibilities, as she knows, and for that reason we are not free to do exactly as we like. First we must consider what would be best for Midlow. The prince should confer with the peer, and the peer's advisors, and other peeragers whose opinion she values. I must do the same with the Three and with other one-namers."

"I entirely agree," the land warden said. Then he added, with a shy smile, "Even if everyone's reaction is favorable, don't forget that in the end you must also confer with each other."

Arne left his borrowed horse at the court stables and returned to Midd Village on foot, meditating worriedly as he walked. How would Deline react? Even though peerager matings were notoriously short-lived, he couldn't say to her, "I want you to wive me, but you will have to wait until your sister has finished with me." That described the situation perfectly, but she would have a right to be furious with him.

He had to think about his responsibilities. He couldn't take the prince to his dwelling in the village. He would have to live at the court, which would disrupt both his work and his life. Midd Village was the largest—and, with its mills, by far the most important—settlement of one-namers, and Arne was accustomed to starting and ending his day by dealing with the villagers' immediate problems and the small daily crises that arose in their lives. That would no longer be possible. He would quickly become a remote figure, unavailable for routine matters. He also would be unavailable to Egarn's team in a crisis, and neither Deline nor anyone else could be trusted with that responsibility.

He decided to visit the Three and then talk with Egarn. In the end, the decision would be his, but he wondered whether he really had a choice.

Deline was waiting for him with the same joyous greeting she'd given him earlier. She sensed at once that something was wrong. "What is the matter?" she asked. "What has happened?"

"The prince has asked me to be her consort," he said.

She stared at him incredulously. Then she laughed. "From the expression on your face, I thought perhaps the peer had taken your name." She went to a window that looked out on the darkened garden. "My little sister," she said. "I keep thinking of her as little. But she is grown, now, and I never noticed when it happened. I never paid any attention to her at all, but she managed to grow up anyway, and now she is the prince and paying no attention to me. Probably it is time she took a consort."

She laughed again, harshly. "My sister wants you for a consort? If you agree, where is the problem?"

"She is a peerager, and more—she is the prince. And I am—"

"So what does that matter to anyone except you two?"

"The other peeragers may object."

Deline shrugged. "There is no reason why they should take notice at all. They never paid any attention to my consorts. A consort never lasts long anyway. If Elone Jermile's first is a one-namer, that doesn't mean she is going to make a habit of it, and you are an exceptional one-namer. It isn't as though she were taking one of the mill hands." Again she laughed harshly. "You one-namers are much too serious about these things. Imagine keeping the same mate for years and years! Why be so glum about it?"

"I don't know what to do."

She laughed again and turned away. At the door, she paused. "Surely you aren't thinking of refusing! She is the prince!"

He wanted to call her back, to tell her again that he loved her, but he could not. It would only complicate things further. He couldn't speak to her until he had decided what to do, but first he had to find out whether he had a choice.

He sent for the Three at once, and they did indeed take his problem seriously. Nonen, the miller, said bluntly, "Now why would you want to do a thing like that? There are much prettier girls in the village, as you would know if you bothered to look at them, and any of them would jump at the chance to wive you and turn your big, drafty house into a home for you. I'll guarantee you won't get much wiving from the prince."

"Just a moment," Margaya said. "It isn't that simple. It wasn't Arne's idea. The prince asked him. What happens if he refuses?"

"That is what I am thinking," old Toboz said. "We had problems enough when Deline was prince. This would be a bad time for any of us to make an enemy of her sister. The peer doesn't have any more daughters."

"Peerager matings aren't like ours," Margaya said. "If you think you can put up with the prince for a little while, it would be best to accept."

"My first concern is my work," Arne said. "There is no way I could become the prince's consort without neglecting it."

"That is true," Nonen said. "You would have to spend some time with her—live at the court, I suppose. You might have to spend quite a lot of time with her until she begins to tire of you. Deline can manage routine things, but if a real emergency came up, we would have to send to the court for you. On the other hand, you have always traveled a lot, and we manage to get along without you then, so I think we could cope with this. There is no way you could mate with anyone without neglecting something."

"The closer your connections with the court, and the more highly the peer and the prince regard you, the more you can accomplish for all of us," Margaya said. "I am sure everyone realizes that. I think you should do it."

In the end, they decided it would be a considerable advantage to one-namers everywhere, even those in other peerdoms, if the first server were the prince's consort. They also were in agreement that Arne shouldn't accept for that reason. "If you want to do it, then do it," Nonen said. "If you don't want to, then don't."

But they didn't really believe that. They knew he had no choice.

As soon as they left, Arne left also, through his garden, and strode off into the dark forest. The cool night air helped him to shrug off his exhaustion. He wanted Egarn's advice at once; he also wanted to know how Egarn's work was going, and he had a project of his own to discuss.

Finding the ruins by night was an ordeal, and when he finally arrived, it was almost impossible to locate a checkpoint. The identification procedure was equally difficult. Even though Arne's voice was known to all of the guards, his own orders permitted no exceptions. He had to crawl into a tiny shelter so a sentry could light the stub of candle and visually identify him.

·Then came the ordeal of creeping through the totally black tunnel, followed by the torturous descent. Even in dim light the stairway seemed impossibly long; in darkness, it went on forever. At the bottom checkpoints, flashes of light were used to identify him.

When finally he reached Egarn's workroom, he turned aside to visit the kitchen and storeroom where a refugee one-namer named Fornzt ruled with absolute authority. Fornzt was from Slorn, the peerdom Roszt and Kaynor came from, and he served as Egarn's housekeeper. He had managed a boarding common in Slorn, no doubt with the same firmness he used now. He supervised the supplies and tried to keep on hand anything that might be needed. He prepared the meals and busily concerned himself with everyone's health and happiness. Rain water that dripped down through the ruins was hoarded for baths. He kept track of the weather outside, saw that the sentries were properly dressed for it, and gave them hot food in cold weather and cold food when the weather was warm. He took Egarn's meals to him and, if the old man was too preoccupied to eat, Fornzt coaxed them into him while he worked.

He had already gone to bed—he got up early to begin the day's cooking—but he had a pot of stew simmering on his charcoal burner for those who came off duty late. When Arne called to him, he awoke instantly and came waddling out with a grin on his face. He was a short, tubby, round-faced man, as unlike Roszt and Kaynor as could be imagined. He had been emaciated from the ordeal of his escape over the mountains when Arne first met him, but regular meals cooked by himself agreed with him. He was unlike the lank, intense scouts in another way—he saw the bright side of everything. Egarn's helpers tended to be grimly serious men, and Arne found Fornzt's touches of humor a welcome relief in the gloomy depths of the ruins.

Because it had been so long since Arne's last visit, they went together to inspect the stocks of food and other supplies, and Arne made notes of shortages. Two of the sentries had worn out their shoes in their escape from the Peer of Lant's armies. It was true they did little walking now, but the steel mesh of the stairway was painful for them to negotiate. Arne promised new shoes and also noted the need for more blankets. The cold dampness of the underground rooms was distressing to the older men.

Arne next described a problem he had long been meditating. From the beginning, he'd had a nagging concern about what might happen if all else failed—if the massive armies of Lant arrived sooner than anyone wanted to believe and somehow discovered what the ruins concealed. Despite the optimism engendered by the sudden cooperation of the ten peers, Arne's common sense told him that if war came soon, his sketchy little army would quickly be overwhelmed in spite of Egarn's weapon. Arne could envision the Lantiff swarming over the ruins, torturing a sentry until he talked, and then pouring down the long stairway in a cascade of military might. Those who lived and worked underground had an escape route, of course. The guards should be able to hold off the Lantiff with Egarn's weapon long enough for everyone to get away, but Arne wanted more than this. If they were forced to flee, Egarn's great project would be ruined. There was no way he could take his machines with him. He seemed more aged and enfeebled each time Arne saw him, and even if a secure place could be found, with sufficient food and other supplies for him to start over, Arne doubted that Egarn had the strength and will to do it.

Fornzt had more free time than anyone else on Egarn's team, and he used it to explore the ruins. He found passageways where none were thought to exist, he tunneled through collapsed rooms, he made astonishing discoveries of materials that would have been valuable salvage if Egarn hadn't already scrounged everything he needed.

"Egarn should have a hidden workroom with a secret escape route to it and a reserve supply of food and water," Arne told him. "He should duplicate all of his machines there. Then his project wouldn't have to fail if the Lantiff captured this place. He could escape to the secret room with Inskel, Roszt, Kaynor, and a few others and finish his plan. I want you to work on this yourself and tell no one. Only Egarn and Inskel should know about it."

Fornzt nodded excitedly. "Of course. I've thought about it myself. If everything else fails, Egarn should have some place to go. I'll start work right away."

"Remember—except for Egarn and Inskel, you aren't to say anything about this to anyone, not even under torture."

"I've had a bit of that," Fornzt said. He smiled as though it were a pleasant recollection, but Arne knew his satisfaction came from having escaped. Now he had the privilege of helping Egarn strike back at the Peer of Lant. He didn't understand what form the blow was to take, but it gave him enormous satisfaction to have a part in it.

Arne left him and went to see Egarn.

In the main workroom, an audience was seated before the cabinet and its enormous len: Egarn; Wiltzon the schooler; the scouts Roszt and Kaynor; and Garzot, one of the len grinders. Gevis, the young assistant schooler, was operating the controls; the others were so intent on the flickering picture the len showed them that for some time they were unaware of Arne's presence.

Gevis had become one of the most valued members of Egarn's team. Because he was resposible only to Wiltzon, he could absent himself from the village for a few daez whenever Wiltzon thought of an excuse. He had assumed almost the whole responsibility for training Roszt and Kaynor in ways of the 20th century. He had an excellent memory and a genuine affinity for life in the past, or so Egarn said. He grasped things far more easily than Wiltzon did, and he instructed the scouts from Slorn with infinite patience. He also assisted Inskel whenever possible, and he was becoming highly competent in what Egarn called the technology of time travel.

His appearance belied his capabilities. He was slight of build, boyish looking, sallow-faced. He was still impatiently anticipating a beard. When he was not underground with Egarn, he was in the classroom drilling students or in his quarters in Wiltzon's house, reading. Villagers joked that he had never seen the sun. They also joked that he had never done any work in his life, but that was only because they refused to consider a schooler's duties as work. Gevis worked extremely hard.

The dog Val padded over to Arne, sniffed his fingers, and then returned to his place between his favorites, Roszt and Kaynor. Arne stood behind the others and stared at the len. It showed a street lined with buildings, wonderful buildings such as he had never imagined. Some of them extended upward far beyond the len's reach. The people on the walkways along the street wore strange and dazzlingly colored clothing. Their behavior was even stranger. They hurried swiftly until they came to a cross street. Then they gathered in groups and stood motionless. Arne was familiar with the mock car that Ellar had built for Egarn—he had even sat in it while Egarn tried to explain how it worked—but this had not prepared him for the sight of numerous cars in a variety of colors moving magically along the street in both directions. Suddenly they came to an an orderly stop, and the waiting people rushed across the street and resumed their frenzied walking. Arne found it totally bewildering.

Egarn became aware of his presence and welcomed him with a smile. "Finally I have succeeded!" he exclaimed. "Now I can choose a time and a place and see it clearly. I can send Roszt and Kaynor exactly where I want them to go, and I can watch them after they arrive there. Maybe I can even send them messages—if we write in this language and use code words, no one there will be able to read them if they miscarry. The picture is clear enough to show Roszt and Kaynor what life is like where they are going, and that means they will be much better prepared. I think we have an excellent chance for success. A few more experiments—"

He broke off. It suddenly occurred to him that Arne, the busiest person in the peerdom, wouldn't make the laborious descent to his workroom merely to exchange greetings. He asked anxiously, "Is anything wrong?"

Wiltzon had kept Egarn informed about the dramatic events at Midlow Court. Now Arne described what had occurred recently and told them about his journey and the creation of an army. The others were enthralled, but Egarn listened impatiently. "It is a turn for the better, I suppose," he said when Arne had finished. "The only problem with Midlow all along has been its prince. Now there is a different prince. We can relax a bit."

"We can't relax, ever," Arne said. He dropped his voice. "There are things we need to discuss privately."

"Is the former prince making trouble?"

The question surprised Arne until he remembered that everyone, including himself, had expected Deline to make trouble. He told Egarn she was becoming an excellent assistant.

"I suppose she is a considerable nuisance to you personally," Egarn said. "You have her living in Midd Village, and you have to work with her and train her, but you will handle things. You always do."

Arne led Egarn to the room's most remote corner and quietly asked him what he thought about a one-namer becoming the prince's consort. "The only advice I have is what the Old Med gave me," Egarn said. "If you refuse, you will make an enemy. If you accept, if you establish a real friendship with the prince, you will have an invaluable connection with the court and a lifelong patron. Of course you should do it." He added, with a gesture of finality, "You have no choice."

The trap had closed; there was no way out. Arne protested feebly, "I would have to neglect my work at a critical times."

"You'll manage," Egarn said. "Anyway, it won't last long. Peerager matings never do. I didn't have any choice, and neither do you." He dismissed the subject with a shrug. "Look—I want to show you something."

He hurried Arne back to the large len's flickering picture. Gevis stepped aside so Egarn could take the controls, and with practiced precision the old man turned knobs that moved the meticulously carved wood gears.

The picture changed to a different street with fewer cars and much smaller buildings.

"These places mean nothing to you, of course," Egarn said. "What you saw before was downtown Rochester, New York. This is a small town in Ohio. I have been there—I recognized it immediately when I chanced on it. It helped me with my calibrations, and it is the place I am going to send Roszt and Kaynor. It has a bank that should be easy to rob. They can buy a car there and be in another state before morning. Then they can settle somewhere and learn something about living in the 20th century before they go to Rochester."

"When will this happen?" Arne asked.

Egarn raised his hands wearily. "There is so much for them to learn, and they are still having serious problems with the language. They will have only one chance, and they must be as carefully prepared as possible. With everything going so well, I have to resist the temptation to rush things."

"Certainly you shouldn't send them before they are ready," Arne agreed.

Later, Arne took Egarn and Inskel to the sleeping room, where they could talk undisturbed, and told them of his conversation with Fornzt.

"It wouldn't have been possible to do this earlier because we didn't have the materials," Inskel said. "Now we can do it easily, thanks to Fornzt's explorations. My work here is almost finished. There isn't anything I can contribute to Roszt and Kaynor's education. I easily can make the necessary duplicates."

Egarn nodded. "It is well thought of. Inskel can begin with the smaller parts. The larger ones can be made in the new workroom when it is ready. Will it be located somewhere else in the ruins?"

"Yes, but somewhere remote from here. You and Inskel can escape to it if everything else fails."

"Roszt and Kaynor, also," Egarn said. "From this time on, they will be more important than we are. But why do you suddenly bring this up now? Do you sense some kind of danger?"

Arne smiled. "You must remember I was trained from childhood to consider not only what will happen but also what might happen. So I keep looking ahead, and I plan for the bad as well as the good."

"Fortunately for us," Inskel said, and Egarn nodded.

Egarn returned to workroom, but Arne held Inskel back for a few private words. "The attitude of the new prince, and the fact that the ten peers have finally been persuaded to cooperate, may make it possible to write the history of these times far differently than we anticipated."

"It is almost the first cheerful news I have heard in my lifetime," Inskel said. "But we mustn't forget the Peerdom of Lant and its enormous army. Unless Lant can be defeated, this land has no future."

"Exactly. But I don't want Egarn to launch his mission until we find out what is going to happen."

"Yes. Yes, I see what you mean. We have no obligation to save some other civilization by destroying ours. If we are capable of achieving our own bright future, that is what we must fight for. Egarn looks at this differently. The other civilization he wants to save is his own. I agree with you completely. Nothing need be said now, but if Egarn tries to rush things, I will insist that Roszt and Kaynor aren't to be sent anywhere without your consent."

Arne took his leave of them and hurried away. The walk back to Midd Village always seemed much longer in the dark, and this one seemed longer than usual, but at the end of it he finally was able to go to bed.

He spent the next day catching up on his work and talking with various villagers whose opinions mattered to him. He wanted to talk with Deline again, to tell her—but there was nothing he tell her except that he still wanted her to wive him and he hoped she would wait until her sister had tired of him. A passionate woman like her could find a mate easily. He wished—but what he wished didn't matter. Egarn and the others were right. He had no choice.

When he returned to Midlow Court, he told the land warden, "Now I am ready to take your advice. I would like to confer with the prince."

The land warden smiled happily. "I will bring her here. If you come to an understanding, the palace will be no place for a newly-mated couple. The peer is unconscious much of the time. Servers tiptoe and whisper, and happiness would seem like treason. You can use my lodge as long as you like."

To Arne's suprise, the days, and tenites, and monts that followed were reasonably happy ones. He was intensely lonely for Deline—the more so because he spent so much time with her. She remained the capable assistant, was politely cooperative in everything—and as distant as she could be under the circumstances. Probably she had already taken another lover. If she had, she continued to practice discretion. The village gossip never mentioned her.

The prince was a sympathetic and understanding companion who listened intelligently to everything Arne could tell her about the peerdom's affairs and whose concern for them matched his own. In public, Arne addressed his new mate as "Highness" and knelt to her like everyone else. In private, he called her "Ely"—from her first name, Elone—but he could not bring himself to use the terms of endearment that he had lavished on Deline. The prince responded with a wholly unexpected passion, and probably it was unfair of him to compare her daily with his memories of her sister, but he could not help it. She was ecstatically happy, and he had to seek his own happiness in that.

They visited the peer whenever she was alert enough to talk with them. She delighted in seeing them together, and she clung to Arne as the one person capable of guiding her peerdom through dangers most peeragers were incapable of imagining. Arne had been the prince's consort for three monts when Elone Jermile announced joyfully that she was pregnant. It was cause for celebration at court because the peeragers were always apprehensive of the turmoil that would follow if a peer died with no one to succeed her.

Lashers and no-namers continued to arrive from the other peerdoms. Working with Arne, Bernal imposed an organization on the army and a rigorous conditioning on the troops. His optimism grew daily.

Then a message arrived from Inskor, brought by a scout who had ridden his lathery horse all the way from Easlon without stopping. The armies of Lant had broken through.

14

ARNE (2)

Beyond the southern border of the Ten Peerdoms, chains of steeply sloping, wooded hills marched southward on either side of long, narrow valleys. The trees often spilled down the hillsides to crowd the banks of the small streams that ran below.

"The Lantiff are on horseback," Inskor's message to Arne said. "They will follow the low ground. We need cover, so we will keep to the hills. Our object is to set trap after trap, lose battle after battle—and make each of the Lantiff's victories so expensive it will seem like a defeat. They will keep trying to encircle us. We must make them think our army is much larger than it is."

The Lantiff's formula for victory was a simple one. Their charging vanguard bristled with multi-pronged lances and flashed with gleaming, slashing, curved swords. Every thirtieth Lantiff was an officer, apparently unarmed, and it was these officers who wielded the deadliest weapon, the tube of lens that some unsung Lantian len grinder had invented. Its beam knocked the defenders senseless, after which the Lantiff surged forward to overwhelm an unconscious enemy.

It was an ideal tactic for troops with minimal intelligence. The Lantiff never had to think at all. They never sent out scouts; never varied their scheme of attack an iota. They had no need to; they were invincible. They tasted victory after victory, and no one bothered to tell them about the occasional defeats Lant suffered. They attacked with deliberation; they conquered even before they made contact with the enemy; and then they occupied themselves with more important matters such as pillaging undefended towns and villages. What the opposing army did or tried to do was no concern of theirs.

These were the invading hordes that came riding up the narrow valleys that pointed toward the Ten Peerdoms. The terrain forced them into awkward formations—long, narrow columns of mounted warriors with patches of woods to contend with—and Inskor, delighted that he could attack fingers rather than a clenched fist, was spreading his own army as thin as he dared in an effort to convert each of those valleys into a death trap.

The partly trained army of the Ten Peerdoms now numbered almost five thousand lashers with another two thousand no-namers organized into labor platoons. It was by far the largest army the Ten Peerdoms had ever assembled. Arne's personal force of one-namers, the one that had defeated the wild lashers, had been expanded to more than five hundred men and women, and one-namers who had been hurriedly trained as scouts added five hundred more. There were another five hundred regular scouts from Weslon. The total seemed astonishing to Arne, who had to find a way to feed this swollen force, but it paled to insignificance beside the massed armies of Lant.

Arne's original plan had had been to garrison these troops at strategic points along the southern frontiers. Now he would march them to war instead. He summoned his scattered one-namers, telling them to overtake him as quickly as possible; took a poignant leave of the prince; and set out. He left Deline to make arrangements with all of the Ten Peerdoms for the supplies that must be kept moving after them.

The army of Lant was moving north at its own deliberate pace. Surprise had never been a Lantian tactic—the peer had long-since learned that the more warning a victim had, the longer it had to wait, the more frightened it became. Many of Lant's victories were no more than triumphant marches in the wake of a fleeing enemy.

Arne's fear was that the Lantiff would arrive before he joined his force with Inskor's. He left a squad of scouts, a small company of lashers, and a platoon of no-namers in each valley with instructions to build a series of barriers of upright logs, using them to link wooded areas or natural obstacles. When the Lantiff came, the lashers would feign a defense of each barrier, fleeing in pretended terror from one to another to entice the

Lantiff to follow them. When the Lantiff were deeply committed to this trap, one-namers hidden on the wooded hillsides would cut them to pieces with Egarn's weapon.

They moved east, and Arne's army shrank dramatically as he left behind one defense force after another. He was becoming extremely worried that he would run out of troops when finally he made contact with Inskor and his Easlon defenders, who were extending westward.

Inskor greeted him warmly, listened with delight to what Arne had accomplished, and then told him to take the remainder of his force west again, along with a reserve of Easlon lashers and one-namers that had not yet been committed, and extend the defenses as far as possible.

"The Lantiff will keep moving west," he said. "When we defeat them in one place, we will have to withdraw as much strength as we can and hurry it westward to meet their next attack."

Arne obediently turned back with the Ten Peerdoms' uncommitted strength. The next day he met a lone rider. He had heard nothing from Midlow Court since he left, and he had been waiting for a peer's messenger.

But this rider brought no messages. It was Deline.

"I have come to fight," she said.

Arne said sternly, "Your job is to keep food moving south. That is more important than any fighting you could do."

"I have already arranged for that," she said. "There will be plenty of food. Hutter will look after it." She added smugly, "I have the peer's consent. I told her I wanted my horse so I could fight for Midlow. I am not going to sit in a safe place and rot while my one-name friends are dying for the peerdom. Anyway, you need an assistant here more than you did at Midd Village, and that is what I am—your assistant. The peer herself appointed me."

"When you asked the peer, what did she say?"

"She didn't say anything. It is painful for her to talk. She nodded, and the land warden gave me my horse."

Arne extended his army as far west as possible, sent scouts far into the wilds to detect any encircling movement, and turned east again. Along the way he conducted training sessions with each valley's defense unit, and this introduced Deline to something she had never seen before or even imagined: Egarn's weapon.

She was astonished. Then, as she began to understand the destructive power of the small tubes, she was elated. "I thought we here helpless against the might of Lant," she said wonderingly. "It is the Lantiff who will be helpless. Does the peer know about this?"

"No peerager knows," Arne said shortly. "Peeragers would use the weapon on each other."

Deline was silent for a time. "You are right," she said finally. "No peerager should know. I'm glad I didn't know. I would have been worse than the others."

When they passed south of the Peerdom of Chang, Deline volunteered to persuade peer and prince—former friends of hers—to furnish more lashers and no-namers so Arne and Inskor could hold a few units in reserve. Chang gave her everything that could be spared, and she trained this force on the march. It arrived in fine fettle and eager to fight the Lantiff.

So was she. The Prince of Chang had presented her with a uniform designed for the prince's private guard—the same she had modeled her own guard's uniforms on—and she arrived resplendent in black and white. She looked magnificent. Unfortunately, this was the wrong war for the heroics that went with her costume, and Arne quietly pointed out to her how a conspicuous dress could give away a battle plan.

"I didn't come here to hide," she said. "I'm going to fight."

The long, narrow columns of Lantiff continued to seep northward. Finally one of them encountered the defenses Arne had planned so carefully and erected with so much labor. A barricade of upright logs completely spanned the valley. At intervals there were other barricades where Arne's lashers waited.

The Lantiff paused while their officers rode forward a few

yards to study these obstacles. Then they aimed their weapons, the weapons of Lant. The logs of each barricade were sent flying. Huge gaps opened up, Arne's lashers fled, and the Lantiff pressed forward, still moving in leisurely fashion.

A defense that Inskor had devised proved more effective. A wide stripe of burnooze, a black substance found in the mountains where severe land upheaval had taken place, had been laid down across the valley. When ignited, it burned furiously, and it could be touched off from a distance with Egarn's weapon. When the Lantiff's vanguard was almost upon one of these strips, the ground at their horses' feet erupted in flame. The head of column halted; the Lantiff behind continued to press forward until the valley was crammed with them. Then a scout on the hillside touched off another wall of flame behind them, and Egarn's weapon systematically cut the Lantiff to pieces. The valley was piled thickly with corpses and with pathetically screaming wounded men and horses, but still the Lantiff tried to surge forward.

It was Arne's first close view of the Lantiff. Squat, muscular, with dark faces and misshapen eyes, their appearance was completely different from that of the Ten Peerdoms lashers. They had no conception of defeat, and their attacks ceased only when there were no more of them to be killed. Fire might stop them momentarily, but when the leaders shouted their shrill commands, they charged through the wall of flames. The crashing lightning of Egarn's weapon gave them pause, but the next command sent them blindly forward, crushing their own dead under foot, and they kept charging until they were annihilated. Inskor had expected them to flee in panic the moment the crashing beams of Egarn's weapon stabbed among them, but they were superbly disciplined—or too stupid to understand what was happening.

Day after day Arne's forces decimated the Lantiff in battle after battle in westward succeeding valleys. Finally the Lantiff happened onto a valley that was broader than the others, and their commanders mounted a massive attack. This time they kept charging until Egarn's weapons exhausted their stored energy. The weapons recharged automatically, but they had to be rested for a short time, and while they were silent, the Lantiff suddenly spurred their horses forward and burst through the last of the defenses into gently rolling terrain where there was little cover for Inskor's scouts.

Suddenly a lone rider appeared in their path, a rider clothed in black and white who galloped directly toward the menacing line of lances and swords. The Lantiff reined in their horses and watched this apparent suicide attempt with puzzlement. As the rider drew nearer, it proved to be a woman with blonde hair flying, which magnified their confusion.

Grooming was difficult in an army fighting one battle after another. All of Arne's one-name women had been letting their hair grow, and the men were becoming shaggy. Now Deline's blond hair streamed behind her as she rode recklessly toward the waiting Lantiff.

Arne, too far away to come to her assistance, could only watch with horror. She seemed intent on a suicidal collision with the leveled lances, but suddenly, at the last moment, she swerved and rode down the long line of Lantiff, turning one of Egarn's weapons on them.

They were too astonished to retaliate. The awesome power sliced their front ranks to pieces and terrified and mutilated those behind. The lantiff that survived wheeled and fled without firing back. Deline's magnificent audacity had saved both herself and the battle.

"Don't do that again," Arne said severely when he had overtaken her.

"Why not? It worked!"

"It worked once. Next time they won't hold their fire—and I need you."

That night Deline came to his bed—as audacious in love as she had been in battle. She was still caught up in the exuberance of her wild ride, and her passion seemed unquenchable. Their love affair resumed as though there had been no interruption. Each night they lay together on Arne's narrow sleeping pad—on hard ground or a bed of leaves, sheltered or in the open, wherever the vagaries of war took them.

Deline felt no compunction at all about sleeping with her sister's consort. For a time Arne's conscience bothered him, and that amused her. She pointed out that the other one-namers who had come to war with Arne, both men and women, also had mates at home, but they hadn't hesitated to take lovers.

"What do the stay-at-homes matter?" she asked derisively. "We are all going to die—we will fall in battle and they will be slaughtered in their beds when the Lantiff break through, so why worry about them? We can't possibly win. I thought the weapon would make a difference, but now I can see that it doesn't. The Lantiff are being sacrificed in hundreds and thousands to keep us occupied. When their generals find a weak place, they will pour more thousands through it. Let's enjoy what life remains to us. We haven't lived until we have lived dangerously. I never realized that."

Arne was stubbornly committed to fighting cautious battles that killed as many Lantiff as possible. As soon as one was finished, he left a token force to guard that valley and rushed everyone else westward in an attempt keep ahead of the encircling enemy. He still hoped to win, hoped that eventually the attacks would become too costly to be pursued, but it gradually became evident that Deline understood war far better than he did.

She exulted in combat; Arne quickly came to hate it. He loathed performing meaningless butchery on brain-damaged lashers who probably had only a dim awareness of where they were and what they did. Deline laughed at his scruples. "Maybe they don't know what they are doing," she said, "but if we don't kill them, they will kill us just as thoroughly as if they knew."

With Inskor's approval, Arne devoted more and more of his time to feeding the army and moving reinforcements where they were needed. This quickly became as important as winning battles. Without it, there soon would have been no battles.

Deline assumed more and more of Arne's command responsibilities. She continued to revel in battle, but when the Lantiff
began knocking horses from under her, she learned to restrain
her most rampagant urges. She would halt a charge just beyond
the range of their weapon—but well within the range of
Egarn's—and decimate them. They came to fear her. Their
front ranks would have fled when she approached if the ranks
behind them had permitted it.

Inskor overtook Arne's westward push with a small army
of his own. The old scout agreed with Deline on the nature of the
war, and he had decided to rush west with all the troops that
could be spared.

"My scouts have lost touch with Lant's main army," he
said. "It is circling more widely than I had thought possible.
Gather as large a force as you can and follow me."

His insight came too late. While the Lantiff were making
their trivial feints, their main army remained far to the south,
wheeling to attack the Weslon frontier from the west. Hutter
arrived in a panic to report disaster. Everyone had been caught
by surprise, and both the Weslon and the Midlow courts had
been overrun as Lantiff poured into the middle peerdoms.

Chang was making a defense and needed all the help available. Arne numbly sent out orders to withdraw his forces from
the various valleys they were guarding, assemble them, start
them north. Then he placed Deline in charge and rode westward as fast as his horse could take him. He had to see for himself what had happened to Midlow Court and who might have
survived.

He found a burned-out ruin encircling the once picturesque
hill, and on the parade was the strangest scene he could have
imagined: orderly rows of corpses covered by clouds of insects.
He tried to ride up the spiraling road to the hilltop on the for-
lorn chance that survivors might have found refuge in the castle ruins, but the way was blocked by fallen and charred walls
and roofs. The intense heat of the conflagration had even
brought down the castle's old stone walls. Anyone who sought

shelter there would have been crushed or burned, but apparently no one had.

He returned to the parade and tried to imagine what had impelled the entire population of the court, peeragers, servers, and guards, to arrange itself in orderly ranks as though awaiting execution.

He dismounted and picked his way through the dead. A platform stood in the center of the parade, and the prince, the land warden, and several of the peer's advisors had been standing before it when they were struck down. On the platform was a coffin containing the peer's body.

So the peer had died, and her funeral had been in progress at the moment the Lantiff arrived. No other event would have left the court so totally helpless. The abrupt appearance of fierce horsemen had frozen everyone in terror. At least the peer had not lived long enough to see her world collapse.

The prince's body had been hacked cruelly, but her face was untouched. Arne smoothed back her hair and straightened her clothing. She had the same serious look in death that she'd had in life. He stood for a long time, looking down at her. Finally he turned away. There was nothing left for him to do but rejoin the war and kill Lantiff, and kill, and kill while his own life lasted.

Suddenly he noticed an oddity, probably because his thoughts were on his own unborn child. There were no bodies of young children among the dead. The peeragers certainly would have brought them to the peer's funeral. Contrary to all expectations, perhaps the Lantiff did have a streak of mercy in their brutal natures—but what had been done with them?

A chilling premonition about Midd Village seized him, and he hurried back to his horse. He had taken everyone to war who had been trained to fight, leaving Midlow virtually defenseless, but probably it didn't matter. Even if he had kept his little army at home, the hordes of Lantiff would have quickly overwhelmed it in spite of Egarn's weapon. In military matters, everyone in the Ten Peerdoms, even Inskor, was a fumbling beginner. The Peer of Lant had taught them a severe lesson.

Unfortunately, those defeated by Lant had no opportunity to learn from the experience.

A short distance from the court, he met several lashers leading a full company of no-namers carrying picks and shovels. He sought out the leader. "Where are you going?" he demanded.

"To the court," the lasher said. "To bury the dead." He recognized Arne, and he added defiantly, "The Lantiff ordered it."

"Do that," Arne said. "Bury all of the dead."

He rode on. At Midd Village, nothing but smouldering debris remained. Houses and mills lay in ruins. The no-namers had been at work there, and the garden common was marked with freshly turned dirt where trenches had been dug to dispose of the bodies. Arne was about to turn away when he saw a man approaching on foot.

It was old Marof. Arne dismounted; the old man threw his arms around him and wept unashamedly.

"What has happened to Egarn?" Arne demanded.

"The Lantiff never went near the ruins," Marof said. "No reason why they should. No one except us knows what is there. So everyone is safe."

"Wiltzon?"

"Dead. He was at home. Everyone in the village died. A few may have been away on chores, but I don't know who or what's happened to them."

"Does Egarn know what happened?"

"Aya. I took word to him myself."

"What happened to the children?"

"Lantiff took them to the no-name compounds," Marof said. "I got close enough to hear them talking. Their orders were to kill all adult peeragers and one-namers—peeragers in revenge for the Peer of Lant's children, one-namers because the Ten Peerdoms never taught its one-namers to be properly submissive and obedient. Also, the peer already has all the one-namers she needs except med servers. Med servers at the no-name compounds were spared. Peerager and one-namer children were taken to them for len treatments. Now all of them are no-namers. The peer always has a need for more no-namers, they said."

"I want you to take a message to Egarn," Arne said tonelessly. "You are to deliver it to him in person and make certain he understands it, and when you have done that, come back here and tell me. First, there will be no more support for him. He should send a few men immediately, before the Lantiff return, to pick through the village's debris and maybe the court's, too, in case there is anything left worth salvaging. That will be the end of it. There are concealed storage bins in all of the villages and at the court, but I haven't time now to see whether they were damaged. Whatever food Egarn has may have to last until his mission is completed unless his sentries can scrounge something or do a little hunting. Second, Roszt and Kaynor must start immediately so he can give them as much help as possible before his supplies run out—or before the Lantiff return and find him. They represent our last chance for any kind of victory over Lant. Do you understand? They must leave at once."

"Why don't you tell him yourself?"

"I am not finished here. Take the message now—hurry!"

"Aya. What are you going to do next?"

"I'm going to Chang. There will be a battle there. Maybe a whole series of battles that will keep the Lantiff's attention away from here for a time. That is the only way left to help Egarn."

"It won't do any good," Marof said. "You will get yourself killed."

"That hardly matters now. A devastated peerdom has no further need for a first server. If the Peer of Lant can revenge her dead children, I can—in a small way—revenge my dead prince and unborn child. Now take the message. Come back as soon as you have delivered it."

He prowled through the ruins, smoothing the village's dead embers over a lifetime of memories and the ashes of friends he had known from childhood. Finally Marof returned to tell him Roszt and Kaynor were ready and eager to leave and would be on their way by nightfall.

Arne embraced the old man again and took his leave of him. Then he rode east to a raging war already lost.

15

ROSZT AND KAYNOR

The off-duty members of Egarn's team gathered in is work-room. Roszt and Kaynor had taken their leave of the guards and sentries earlier, and now they embraced the other members of the team in turn, listened to a few last words of advice, and paused to rub the dog Val's silky ears.

At the far end of the room, a contraption very like the strange machine that had snatched Egarn out of the past stood waiting for them. Nearby, the cabinet with the large len showed a night scene with an expanse of grass and dim shadows of trees in the background. It was the park Egarn had chosen for their landing.

Egarn called, "Fornzt?"

The housekeeper came forward carrying a small crock.

"It is the last of the wine," Egarn said sadly. "We have missed Arne badly from the moment he went to war. Now when we use the last of something, we know there won't be any more."

The others were silent. The wanton destruction and slaughter of the towns and people of Midlow had left all of them stunned.

Egarn took the crock and raised it to Roszt and Kaynor. The long sikes of intense work had aged and enfeebled him, and the final preparations had left him exhausted, but at this moment his eyes flashed with triumph. "The hearts of all of us all go with you," he said. "If there is a benevolent spirit anywhere who watches over the tribulations of men, may she grant you courage and wisdom and bless you with the success you deserve."

He tilted the crock and took a swallow of wine. Then he passed it to Inskel and turned away. The others drank in turn, Roszt and Kaynor last. As the lank scouts followed Egarn, Val uttered a sharp bark and leaped after them. Gevis, the assistant schooler, who now had neither school nor students, grabbed the dog and held him. Egarn made a final check of his controls, and then he stood poised with the cord in his hand. He nodded at Kaynor.

With a cheerful wave at the others, Kaynor positioned himself in the circle Egarn had chalked on the floor. He was fingering his bare chin. Egarn thought beards would attract attention in a society where most men were clean-shaven, so both Kaynor and Roszt had been shaving for monts with a razor of honed glass, but they still missed their beards.

Egarn pulled the cord; Kaynor vanished. All eyes turned to the grassy setting shown on the large len. Kaynor's shadowy figure had just made a perfect landing. He performed a series of exultant skips, and then he turned in a complete circle, arms extended—the signal that everything was all right.

Egarn mounted a small ladder to reset his apparatus. Then he took his position again, cord in hand. Roszt stepped into the circle. As Egarn stretched the cord taut, Val uttered a sharp bark, wrenched free from Gevis, and leaped after Roszt. Hands snatched at the dog—too late. There was a chorus of cries as dog and man vanished together. The same instant, the len showed the dog gamboling beside Roszt and Kaynor. The scouts from Slorn seemed as overjoyed to have Val with them as he was to be there. All three of them skipped with delight as they walked away.

Inskel spoke wonderingly. "The dog lived!"

He turned to Egarn for an explanation, but the old man had just received a tremendous revelation, and for long moments he could not speak.

"When one travels through time, one can't return immediately," he said finally. "I almost died trying. But the danger must diminish with time, and the dog had been here long enough to have it wear off completely." He added wearily, "I could have returned to the past anytime after a sike or two. When I found out about the Honsun Len, I could have gone back myself and made certain it couldn't be invented. Maybe I should go now and help them."

Inskel looked at him worriedly. "You can help more by staying here."

On the len, three diminishing figures—the two scouts and the dog—danced merrily into the distance. Gevis made adjustments to follow them. The expanse of grass ended at a road that led to the park's main gate. The sign above it read, *Alomia City Park.*

Roszt and Kaynor had spent monts studying Alomia's "downtown." They knew every business establishment facing Main Street and what its function was. They knew how frequently the police patrolled the area at night and what the officer did. They had laid out a route from the park to the business section by way of the town's alleys, and they followed it without incident. Once there, they paused by the rear entrance of Frylon's Clothing Store while Roszt inspected the lock. Frylon's was to be their second stop. The first was the Alomia National Bank, whose rear entrance was next door.

Egarn had invented several tools for them. He called the first a lock pick. The small tube produced a temporal force field, he said, which opened a lock just like a key if the beam was fixed on it while the tiny tube was rotated. Roszt and Kaynor didn't pretend to understand that, but Fornzt had located several doors in the depths of the ruins that had locks, and Egarn had cleaned and oiled them and made them work, and they practiced until Egarn was convinced they had the skill to open most locks they would encounter. Those that refused to cooperate could be melted away with a second tool, a miniature version of Egarn's weapon.

The third was an anti-burglar alarm device. When operated near a wiring system, it produced surges of power guaranteed to burn out everything connected to it. Egarn had instructed them carefully in its use. He didn't want them to cause a catastrophe at the local telephone company or even interfere with the bank's night lights, but the burglar alarm had to be knocked out. They wouldn't know for certain whether this tool worked until they tried it.

The last was a small hand light powered by the energy of time. It was tiny enough to be enclosed in a fist, but its illumination could be adjusted from a trickle to a flood. On this night Roszt and Kaynor would need no more than a trickle—their eyes easily adjusted to darkness because of their sikes of scouting and living underground.

Each of them carried two of Egarn's weapons for ultimate emergencies. He hoped they would never have to use them except perhaps at the climax of their adventure when they had identified the Honsun Len Johnson beyond any doubt.

Roszt traced the outline of the bank's door with the anti-burglar alarm tool. They paused to listen for alarms before Kaynor applied the lock pick. He turned the tube, and the door opened. They slipped inside with Val at their heels. At a gesture from Kaynor, the dog obediently seated himself by the door. Roszt ranged about tracing the bank's alarm system while Kaynor locked them in. Then they went directly to the safe and went to work.

Steve Sterovitz, one of the two Alomia police officers on night patrol, had been delayed by a complaint about prowlers. The prowlers of course had vanished by the time he reached the scene. Now he was performing his nightly check to make certain doors of business establishments were properly locked. He strolled along nonchalantly. In his opinion, nothing exciting had happened in Alomia, Ohio, since about about 1920 when the town experienced its last runaway horse, and his thoughts were not exclusively on his work.

At Frylon's Clothing Store, he paused to look at the window display. A sign in screaming red letters proclaimed, "THE LONG AND THE SHORT OF IT—50% OFF ON ODD SIZES!" The odd sizes on display were outlandishly-patterned suits with equally silly, broad-brimmed hats. There was a luggage sale, too, and the two manikins wearing the suits were carrying suitcases, while other cases and bags had been left about their feet for them to stumble over. Sterovitz tried to imagine anyone actually wearing clothes like that and failed.

As he was trying the door, the old burglar alarm on the venerable bank building emitted a single "Ding!" Sterovitz abandoned the clothing store and dashed for the bank. Its front door was properly locked and the safe at the rear wasn't visible from the door or from the high Main Street windows. Sterovitz ran at top speed to the corner, circled around to the alley, and arrived at the bank's rear door. It was locked. He placed his ear against it, heard nothing. Running as fast as he could, he returned to Main Street and his parked patrol car, where he panted his message into the radio's microphone.

Inside the bank, Roszt had carefully explored the vault's door to fuse the alarm system. Then Kaynor applied the lock pick. As Egarn had predicted, it didn't work. Kaynor set about melting the lock.

At the same moment, Sterovitz was arguing with his sergeant. "Look, I'm trying to tell you," he panted. "The bank's burglar alarm just went off."

The fat desk sergeant, whose environment was cluttered with empty coffee cups, overflowing ashtrays, and crushed beer cans, liked to spend his duty hours studying confiscated pornography. He resented the interruption. He said sarcastically, "What d'ya mean, the burglar alarm went off? If it'd went off there, it'd a went off here, too, and it didn't."

"I was checking Frylon's door, and I heard it. Clearly. It went 'Ding.'"

The sergeant said incredulously, "It went 'Ding?'"

"That's what I said."

The sergeant exploded. "You idiot! Burglar alarms don't go 'Ding!' They go 'Ding ding ding ding ding ding ding ding.' Didn't anyone ever tell you that?"

"I don't remember ever hearing it mentioned."

"I'm telling you now. Next time, you'll have to think of a different excuse. Now you tell me. How do burglar alarms go?"

"Ding ding ding ding ding ding ding ding," Sterovitz said with profound resignation.

"Right. Remember that. Now get a move on. You were due out at the hospital twenty minutes ago."

Sterovitz, no longer sauntering, resumed his door check. As he passed the burglar alarm, he looked up at it and said disgustedly, "Ding ding ding ding ding ding ding ding."

At the same moment, Roszt and Kaynor were carefully relocking the bank's rear door behind them. When they moved off, each was carrying two large cloth bags bulging with money. At the clothing store, Roszt fused the burglar alarm and Kaynor deftly opened the locked door. Two dim figures moved about in the dim store while Val waited patiently. The window manikins were snatched from view and reappeared a short time later stripped of their clothing. Four large suitcases that had been displayed with them vanished permanently.

When Roszt and Kaynor left the store a short time later, they were dressed in the outlandishly styled suits and hats from the front window and wearing, with agonized discomfort, shoes hurriedly selected at the rear of the store. Each of them carried two of the suitcases. One of these contained the clothing they had worn from Midlow and also a selection of items from the shopping—or shop-lifting—list Egarn had prepared for them: undergarments, socks, shirts. The other three suitcases contained the money. The dog sensed their seriousness, and he followed silently at their heels as they quickly walked away. Egarn, watching them on the flickering len, was elated. The mission could not have begun better.

Twenty minutes later, Officer Sterovitz, cruising rapidly along Main Street on his way from the hospital to the country club, brought his patrol car to a sudden, screeching halt. He had caught a glimpse of Frylon's front window as he passed. He leaped out and charged over to it.

The manikins that had displayed the outrageous suits now faced the world in their underwear. Some of the luggage had disappeared. Sterovitz stood there for several minutes, one hand on his hip, the other scratching his head. He knew damned well something extremely screwy was going on. He also knew he wasn't going to make an ass of himself a second time. He could imagine the sergeant's reaction if he radioed a report that manikins were appearing in a Main Street store window in their underwear. "What are you, some kind of sex freak? What does it matter what manikins wear?"

He shrugged and turned away, muttering, "Ding ding ding ding ding ding ding ding."

Near the edge of town, under the last street light on a quiet residential street, a venerable Oldsmobile with no license plate was parked on the lawn of a large, shabby-looking house. In the window of the car was a sign: "FOR SALE—$400."

Roszt and Kaynor came walking silently along the sidewalk with Val at their heels. When they reached the car, they set the suitcases down. Roszt remained there with the dog; Kaynor went up the walk to the house. He rang the bell for a long time before there was any response. Finally the porch light came on, and a boy of nineteen or twenty, wearing pajamas and a robe, opened the door. He stared with astonishment at the lanky Kaynor. In his flamboyant new apparel, the scout from Slorn was an arresting sight.

Kaynor said, "You have car for sale?"

It took a moment for the question to register. Then the boy exclaimed, "Yes, yes! It's for sale. I've been asking four hundred, but—"

Kaynor's gloved hand thrust money at him. The boy stared, stared at Kaynor again, and then snatched the money. He counted it disbelievingly. "I'll get the keys and the title!" he said and dashed away excitedly, leaving Kaynor waiting at the door.

He was back a moment later. "I need your name and address."

Kaynor handed him a slip of paper that carried a fictitious name and a nonexistent address in Cleveland, Ohio. The boy hurried away again.

Finally he returned to hand over the car keys and a package of papers.

"I signed the title for you, and here is a receipt. The title has got to be notarized. If you will stop by tomorrow evening, I'll take you to see Ed Wheeler—he lives around the corner, he's a realtor—and he'll fix it for you. I hate to bother him this late. It's a real good car, and it runs swell, and it's got a hot motor. If it didn't burn so much oil—I mean, you got yourself a real good buy, mister."

Kaynor said carefully, "Thank you," accenting the "you" despite Egarn's patient drilling. He turned and walked out to the car. The boy stood in the door, watching. Roszt and Kaynor put their luggage in the back seat, along with the dog, and took their places in front with Kaynor at the steering wheel. He had trouble finding the ignition switch, trouble inserting the key, trouble getting the motor to start. The starter ground, and ground, until the boy was about to go out and help him. Finally it caught with a roar. Racing the motor and pumping the clutch, Kaynor drove off with a preposterous series of jerks. The car moved like a wounded jack rabbit. Half a block down the street he killed the motor and had to start it again.

Egarn, nervously watching the scene on the len, thought with resignation that he was doing about as well as could be expected for one to whom the automobile and the gasoline motor were the ultimate mysteries of the universe. The boy, still watching from his front door, belatedly remembered something. He shouted after the car, "Hey—you're not supposed to drive without a—"

The car turned the corner. ". . . license plate," the boy finished weakly. Suddenly he turned in alarm and held his money up to the porch light. There seemed to be nothing wrong with that, so he shrugged, pocketed it, went back into the house, and turned off the light.

Before they left town, Roszt and Kaynor found a parked car that looked as though it hadn't been used recently and stole its license plate. They drove south and then east. Kaynor quickly learned to control the car's speed—he meticulously kept it under the speed limit—and point it where he wanted to go, but they had trouble with highway signs, trouble working the pump at a self-service gas station, trouble adding oil, trouble ordering food at a drive-in restaurant, and finally, in West Virginia, trouble finding a motel that looked sufficiently shoddy so the owners wouldn't fuss about their lack of identification.

They quickly noticed that their clothing attracted attention. Attention was the one thing they did not want. They abandoned their hats and suit coats almost at once. The next day they stopped at a shopping mall, where they bought sweaters and jackets and shoes that fit them and work trousers that almost fit.

That night they bought another used car from its owner and abandoned their first car in the parking lot of a large motel where it might go unnoticed for daes. Traveling through Maryland and Pennsylvania, they repeated this procedure twice before they reached the state of New York. They had much less trouble the second night. After that, they had none at all.

In Buffalo they found themselves a shabby rooming house in an area that even they could sense was a high-crime district. Because they didn't want the nuisance of having to rob another bank, one of them guarded their money while the other exercised the dog and attempted to accustom himself to twentieth century civilization.

Then they had a stroke of luck. Their next-door neighbor noticed their awkward behavior and stiffly incorrect English and deduced that they were aliens—though of course he had no idea where they were aliens from. Aliens were his livlihood, and he cultivated their acquaintance diligently.

He was a forger. He offered them complete sets of documents, guaranteed to appear authentic to anyone but a expert with scientific instruments. Their birth certificates, for example, would list birthplaces in a southern community whose records had been destroyed in a fire. To Roszt and Kaynor this was an incredible stroke of luck, but they managed to handle it with nonchalance. They remembered Egarn's stricture that they must never act as though they had money, so they haggled about the price—but only a little.

Their new friend was willing to perform as many services for them as they were willing to pay for. He disposed of their Pennsylvania car at a junk yard. He wouldn't attempt to forge drivers' licenses, but with their other documents for identification, they were able to obtain them legally. He helped them study for the test. He found them a used car of more recent vintage and showed them how to get it insured. He also showed them how to apply for social security numbers. He even licensed Val for them. An illegal alien, he told them soberly, couldn't afford to slip up in anything.

While he was doing that, he helped them with their English, found them a dictionary that was easy to use, and patiently explained the more perplexing aspects of life in Buffalo, New York at the end of the twentieth century.

With a properly licensed and insured car, with complete sets of documents, with inconspicuous clothing their friend helped them select, their confidence grew daily. They would have remained there for monts, learning from their friend, but they remembered that Egarn and his team would be watching anxiously and perhaps eating the last of their food while the Lantiff prowled overhead, so they bade their friend farewell and drove to Rochester.

They stopped first at the Howard Johnson Motel in Henrietta, a Rochester suburb, where the desk clerk thought their carefully worded query about Mr. Johnson was a scream. They stayed there for a tenite, driving about and trying to become familiar with the city. They already had a sketchy knowledge of Buffalo, and they were disconcerted to find so many differences.

They drove slowly along the Genesee River that wound its way through the city, passing parks and the University of Rochester. They explored neighborhoods that caught their fancy, pondering the striking contrasts. They fell in love with Mount Hope Cemetary and the Victorian splendor of its monuments and mausoleums, visiting it by day or—after they found a hole in the fence that someone was using as a shortcut—by night. The cemetery contained magnificent hiding places, and in one of them, an old boarded-up chapel and crematorium, they cached a bundle of supplies for an emergency.

They hadn't visited central Buffalo, and Rochester's tall downtown buildings fascinated them. It took all of their courage to enter a self-service elevator for a claustrophobic ascent—after which the arrangement of buttons so confused them that they had to walk down. They stood staring up at the "Wings of Progress" atop the Times Square Building until they made the embarrassing discovery that they were obstructing pedestrian traffic. They never succeeded in figuring out the function of the strangly shaped "wings."

They wanted a more central location to work from, so they moved to the Sharber Motel off East Avenue close to downtown Rochester. It was an older motel striving to remain respectable. Its restaurant was much patronized at lunch time by people working in the downtown area. The rooms were neat and well looked after; the atmosphere, despite the hectic traffic of the inner city, peaceful; and they were permitted to keep Val with them.

Their Buffalo friend had considered motels much safer than apartment buildings or rooming houses. In these latter establishments, he said, the same neighbors would see them day after day. Any oddities or irregularities in their conduct would arouse curiosity and cause talk, and the things an alien absolutely had to avoid were curiosity and talk. In a motel, they had new neighbors daily or every few days, and travelers were much too preoccupied with their own affairs to worry about two men who left the motel early and returned late, lived quietly, and bothered no one.

They settled at the Sharber Motel for an extended stay. Their room seemed reasonably secure, and Val was there to guard their possessions, but they bought a small safe anyway, fastened it securely to the floor under their bed—where the bed frame, which extended to the floor, concealed it—and hid a reserve of money in it.

Their search for the Honsun Len Johnson began with the telephone directory in their motel room, where the name "Johnson" occupied more than ten columns and filled two and a half pages. "Johnston" and "Johnstone" added two columns more. The task of narrowing that list to the one person who had invented—or was about to invent—the Honsun Len staggered them. Doggedly they visited an office supply store, invested in index cards and a filing box, and went to work.

Then they discovered the telephone directory's yellow pages, which alphabetized names within classifications, and this necesitated a prolonged and tedious search for people doing business under the name of Johnson. Obviously it was an honorable name. Most of the entries told them nothing at all, but a few seemed intriguing. Johnson Cameras, for example; and Johnson Exterminators, which—until they discovered what a professional exterminator did—suggested that someone had already found a use for the Honsun Len.

Except for the few Johnsons who could be linked with specific businesses, their research gave them a long list of people about whom they knew nothing at all. Egarn had briefed them carefully as to their next step. They went to the main Rochester Public Library on South Avenue.

The place seemed infinitely confusing—people coming and going, people reading at tables, books everywhere; but the helpful librarians were accustomed to confused patrons. Roszt and Kaynor were directed to the long, narrow reference room, where they quickly located something they were familiar with—telephone directories from near and far. Some were arranged in carousels, which they spun delightedly until they noticed the puzzled glances they were receiving. Their next discovery was a set of suburban Rochester telephone directories, and these added nine more columns of Johnsons to their collection.

The most essential reference work—the one Egarn had attached the most importance to—was a city directory, which they were unable to find until a reference librarian referred them to the Local History Room on the second floor. There they struck a bonanza: City Directories dating all the way back to 1870 and suburban directories from 1930.

It was the long, uninterrupted run of directories that proved invaluable. In current volumes, few of the entries mentioned a resident's place of employment. Citizens had been less obsessed with privacy and security a decade or two earlier. Those Johnsons who were long-time residents of the area had their employment given in earlier directories even though the more recent ones omitted it.

They worked for two long days compiling a list of most likely subjects—Eastman Kodak Company employees and former employees; employees and former employees of optical companies; and those Johnsons directly connected with a technical product or service that suggested they might have the competence to invent a new form of len. Not until they attempted to make use of their list did they become fully aware of how hopeless their mission was.

On the basis of a few casual questions, they had to decide whether a total stranger had invented, or was about to invent, the most evil device in all of human history. Even if they had the good fortune to locate him, would he be likely to let them know he was the right Johnson? Why should he willingly confide information about his invention to strangers? And what could they do if he lied and professed to know nothing about lens?

It seemed like an impossible task, but of course they had to try.

They began with those Johnsons who had a likely business connection, and one Randell Johnson, listed as the owner of Johnson's Cameras, stood high on their list. They called on him at his place of business and had a polite conversation with him. He was a gaunt, elderly man who would have been almost as tall as Roszt and Kaynor if he hadn't been so stooped. He listened with a half smile to Roszt's short presentation of the material Egarn had taught them for situations like this: They were searching for the descendants of Ebeneser Johnson, who had resided in Portsmouth, Rhode Island, at the time of the American Revolution. There was an inheritance involved—not a huge one but one sufficiently large to justify a diligent search for heirs.

By the time Roszt finished, Randall Johnson was smiling broadly. "What's the catch?" he demanded.

Fortunately this had been a favorite expression of their friend in Buffalo. "There is no catch," Kaynor said carefully. "We only want to learn whether you are a descendant of Ebeneser Johnson."

"If I'm not, you'll go quietly?"

"But of course."

"I've never heard of Ebeneser Johnson. You're shaking the wrong family tree."

"We speak of a time more than two hundred years ago. You could have had eight, or ten, or twelve ancestors since then. Just give us the names and principal places of residence of your Johnson forebears as far back as you can remember. Our genealogist will connect you if he can."

"And what does this cost me?"

"Nothing. The estate pays all expenses."

"In that case, there won't be anything left for the heirs," Johnson said sourly, but he provided names and addresses for his father, his grandfather, and his great-grandfather.

Roszt and Kaynor returned to their car, which was parked around the corner, and discussed Mr. Randell Johnson. He seemed like a most unlikely inventer of the Honsun Len; on the other hand, he owned an obviously successful camera and photographic supply business. He sold lens, and there was nothing to indicate that he didn't make them himself.

Doubtfully they turned to the next name, and as they slowly worked through their "most likely" list—Johnsons whose backgrounds made them immediately suspect—they also began sampling the Johnsons on their general list. Egarn had said many people in this civilization had private pastimes, and unbeknownst to friends and neighbors the Honsun Len Johnson might be an amateur len grinder. This confronted them with the task of discovering not only known occupations but also secret hobbies.

They visited the George Eastman House, the splendid mansion once occupied by the famous photographic inventor and industrialist and now the home of the International Museum of Photography. There they confounded a guard by asking to see the lens invented by Mr. Johnson. After investigating, the guard informed them that the museum had no record of such a lens.

They visited Johnson Center, an enormous old house on Mt. Hope Avenue near the university, which proved to be headquarters for various social services that had no discernable connection with anyone named Johnson. In studying a map of the area, they found a Johnson Road—near the Eastman Kodak Research Laboratory, which was suggestive—but as far as they could determine, no one named Johnson lived on or near it.

When finally it became obvious that their inquiries were leading nowhere, they moved to the next step of their investigation: breaking and entering. They broke into buildings where a Johnson lived or worked and searched for evidence of an interest in lens—instruments or equipment using lens, drawings of lens, devices that could be used for len grinding.

Egarn had feared that their search would come to this, and he instructed them accordingly. They were to spread their activity as widely as possible and make it so varied that the police wouldn't perceive the connection. They also were not to burglarize any Johnson they had called on recently. If they did, someone would be certain to associate the two events.

Thus began the most peculiar series of crimes in the history of the Rochester Police Department. Burglars for whom no lock or alarm system was a deterent broke in wherever and whenever they chose and left the premises as tidily secure as when they entered. Burglar alarms mysteriously malfunctioned in their presence. Surveillance cameras turned out blank photographs. There were no fingerprints because the burglars always wore gloves.

Even more bewildering was the fact that they took nothing. They sometimes made a mess in their search, as though they were looking for something of value, but after checking carefully, the perplexed owners always had to report nothing missing.

They took nothing because they found nothing—nothing, that is, that connected anyone with the Honsun Len. In a very short time they became so proficient at breaking and entering that they could literally do it under the noses of the police without arousing a wiff of suspicion. Each night they crossed more names off their list. The list, unfortunately, was a long one.

Two kinds of places gave them difficulty. With apartment buildings, they first had trouble figuring out addresses—often they were unable to determine the precise apartment the bewildering array of letters and numbers referred to. Next there was the problem of reaching an apartment through a common building entrance and passing numerous doors of other apartments without being seen. Until they discovered the telephone, they had a problem finding out in advance whether anyone was home. Large houses also posed a problem because of the constant presence of servants. There always seemed to be someone home in a mansion.

As they worked, their worry about Egarn and his team grew. They had heard nothing from him. The methods he devised for sending them messages and picking up the messages they left for him hadn't worked. Each morning and night they searched their room, but always there was nothing. The messages they left for him—in an envelope attached to a weight placed at the center of an otherwise bare table where it could be picked up easily—were never disturbed.

Each night before retiring they signalled with a flashlight, using the code Egarn had taught them, but they received no sign at all that he was still watching. As the daez passed, they became tormented by fear that the Lantiff had returned to butcher everyone in the ruins as they had those at court and in the villages, leaving them completely on their own with a world to save.

16

ARNEAND DELINE

One-namers from the western peerdoms were devastated by the news Arne brought, but fate of Midlow Court affected Deline hardly at all. She had resented her mother, she had hardly known her sister, and—she remarked with a toss of her head—most of the peeragers weren't worth bothering about anyway.

Only the ravaging of Midd Village distressed her. Midlow's one-namers had been kind to her, and she wept for them, but her eyes were dry with anger. "The trouble with this war is that we aren't killing enough Lantiff," she said. "Let's get on with it."

It was a different war, now. The little army was no longer defending the Ten Peerdoms. Half of these were gone; others were crumbling. Easlon, with its brilliant peer and prince, still stood, and both peerager and one-namer refugees who'd had the good fortune to escape the Lantiff circled far around the armies of Lant and arrived exhausted and starving. The one-namers, at least, were fiercely determined to sell their lives dearly and take as many Lantiff with them as possible. Like Arne, they joined Inskor's army. Even the lashers of the Ten Peerdoms, impaired though their minds were, dimly perceived that their lives under the Peer of Lant would be far worse than anything they had experienced, and some of them, too, took the long trek around the war to reach Easlon where they could fight for their survival.

The fighting was a brutal repetition of all that Arne had experienced, but in that, too, he quickly noticed differences. For one, the Lantiff had a new weapon. It sent out beams of light that looked similar to those produced by Egarn's weapon but were silent and harmless. They lit up a battlefield spectacularly, but if the object was to frighten the enemy, Inskor's army scorned it.

The Lantiff also began to use new tactics. When their vanguard was ambushed, the following ranks, instead of riding furiously into the same trap, dismounted, left their horses, and took to the wooded hills on foot. Trees provided cover for them and made Egarn's weapon less effective. The Lantiff tried to work close enough to use their weapon, the one that stunned the enemy, and the defenders, always outnumbered, had to withdraw before that could happen. The diminutive army of the Ten Peerdoms continued to kill enormous numbers of Lantiff, but fewer than before, and dae by dae it was forced backward.

Arne's relationship with Deline also was changing. The war had brought them together; now it began to tear them apart.

He already had learned he was no warrior. He was a far more efficient commander than Inskor—he ran a battle the same way he had run the Peerdom of Midlow, methodically mastering every detail, overlooking nothing, anticipating the enemy's moves for that dae, and the next, and for tenites to come—but he had none of Inskor's craftiness, nor did he have Deline's elan. She was still the magnificent warrior, and she quickly became Inskor's valued deputy. There was no battlefield crisis she could not master, and she blunted every Lantian breakthrough, rallying the defenders and terrifying the enemy. The two of them, Inskor and Deline, gradually divided the army's command between them, leaving Arne with no role at all in the fighting.

This did not disturb him. He moved easily into the position of first server to the Peer of Easlon. He organized and managed food supplies, took charge of transport, sent foraging parties into the conquered territories to bring out loads of food from hidden storage bins the Lantiff had overlooked, and ran a scouting system that located refugees, guided them around the army of Lant to safety, and trained them as reserve troops.

It was when the press of work began to keep him from the battlefront that his estrangement from Deline became serious. She expected him to continue the war at her side, fighting as they had before—under her command, now, since he had none of his own. She seemed unable to comprehend that managing an army's supplies and training new troops required the same dedicated efficiency as managing a battle. Arne's talents were uniquely valuable—as the Peer of Easlon remarked, there were many who could fight, and several who could lead an army, but only Arne knew how to keep an army fighting—but Deline had nothing but contempt for one who fought his battles in the rear.

She had formed her own guard of twenty carefully-chosen lashers. They had no distinguishing uniform, but neither did anyone else in this war except the Lantiff. She emphasized severe discipline and bold action, and she pleaded with Arne to organize a similar guard and join her in battle. Their meetings were spent in argument rather than love until she stopped her nightly visits to him and began to denounce him publically as a coward who hid far from the battlefield while pretending to assist with the war.

She also resented the fact that he, a non-fighter, conferred regularly with Inskor and with the peer and prince about tactics and strategy, while she, who fought brilliantly, was allowed no voice at all in the war's planning. She thought the other commanders—most of them grim scouts who had been fighting Lant all of their adult lives—kept her out of a battle until their own stupid plans and leadership went amiss, at which time they came pleading to her to save them. Otherwise, they ignored her suggestions and gave her no credit for her achievements.

Because Arne was in charge of so many things, she began to bring all of these complaints to him, as though every problem she encountered was his responsibility, and he listened patiently and did whatever could be done. Often that was nothing at all. He couldn't furnish special uniforms for her guard. He had difficulties enough finding clothing for the refugees. The food was often as bad as she alleged it to be, but Arne's resourcefulness was taxed to the utmost in ensuring that army, refugees, and the civilian population of Easlon were adequately fed, and in hording sufficient reserves so the war could continue. He couldn't supply the weather-proof shelters she wanted for her troops. There was nothing to build them with and no point in elaborate constructions when their lines of defense had to be abandoned almost as soon as they were occupied. A battle was nothing more than a slow retreat as the Lantiff steadily pushed the war eastward.

He did what he could, resignedly accepted her incessant complaining about things that could not be changed, and tried to keep keep her discontent from affecting the rest of the army. Rumors of it finally reached Inskor, and he came to Arne for suggestions.

"There is nothing that can be done," Arne said.

"I suppose former princes make very poor subordinates," Inskor said resignedly.

Arne shook his head. "No, that can't be the reason. She was an excellent subordinate when she was my assistant in Midlow. Whatever the cause, if we need her—and we do—we must put up with her."

Her private life became a public scandal. It was rumored that young Hutter, who accompanied her everywhere, shared her bed as well. It was also rumored that she had recruited the husky lashers of her personal guard for their sexual prowess and that it required all twenty of them to satisfy her insatiable appetite. All of that may have been true, or none of it, but in the chaos of war, no one except Arne really cared what her private life was. The rumors gave the army something to gossip about.

In battle, she was invaluable. With the faithful Hutter at her side and her ferocious guard following, she appeared where least expected, rallied defenders, put attackers to flight. Her very recklessness inspired terror in the Lantiff. A glimpse of her on the skyline—erect on a tall white horse that the Peer of Easlon had given to her, hair flying, black and white uniform flashing—brought the most relentless Lantian attack to a halt.

Twice she led her guard too close to the enemy and was knocked unconscious by the weapon of Lant. This should have rallied the Lantiff; instead, the fall of the foe they most dreaded seemed to appall them. They waivered; Deline's guard charged with renewed fury, routed the Lantiff, and carried her to safety, where she regained consciousness with a bruised and aching body but no other symptoms of her experience except a burning desire to lead another attack.

Inskor was sufficiently concerned about Deline's conduct to mention it to the peer, and she sent for Arne and received him in the large tent she used when she visited the army. The dumpy little woman was an unlikely-looking ruler, but each time Arne met her he was more deeply impressed with her astuteness. She signaled him to rise and asked her server to bring a chair for him—indication she had much to say to him.

"Inskor told me about the trouble you have been having with Deline," she said with a smile. "He finds it bewildering, but that is to be expected of an old scout who has never had anything to do with court society. He thought perhaps a peerager might better understand what has gone wrong. He is right. I understand Deline perfectly. The problem is that she is in love with you."

"Her behavior seems very strange for one who is in love, Majesty," Arne murmured politely.

"Not for one who is in love and doesn't want to admit it. I have been observing these things all my life. When I was a child, my mother told me kindly that no one would ever think me beautiful or even pretty. Very few men would love me, but a great many would court me because of what I could do for them as prince or peer. If I didn't want to be crassly used by my lovers, I had to understand their motives. She told me to observe all the court romances and study the conduct of women as well as men. The knowledge I gained from this has been invaluable to me." She added, "My mother was right, of course. It took a long time for me to find a consort who was interested in me instead of what he could gain through my position."

Arne said politely, "Majesty, I don't understand what that could have to do with Deline. There is nothing either of us stands to gain from the other."

"It has nothing to do with her," the peer said. "It has to do with me. I am explaining why I understand Deline. I have been studying romances, and broken romances, and love—requited and unrequited—since I was a child. Deline was the most unpleasant prince I have ever met—obsessed with her position and beauty without a thought in her head for her responsibilities. It is a great tragedy. She could have been a brilliant prince and peer." She smiled at Arne's puzzlement. "I had excellent sources of information, you see. The other peers often brought their troubles to me. The peer her mother asked me what she should do about Deline, and I told her—she must take away one of Deline's names and make her second daughter the prince and heir. This was the only possible solution to an impossible situation, but the peer thought it unnecessarily severe. Long afterward, when Deline raided Midd Village with the guard she wasn't supposed to have, her mother had to do what I had suggested. It must have been a wrenching experience for everyone but especially for Deline. How did she react?"

"She was stunned," Arne said. "For a time she seemed to go through the motions of living without feeling anything at all. But she recovered well. She did excellent work, and I know she enjoyed it."

"Of course. She always had the intelligence to accomplish anything she wanted, but she never wanted anything beyond her own pleasure. Now I will tell you what happened. She had lost everything that mattered to her, she was alone among strangers and reduced to performing menial labor, but fate gave her the most capable, the most conscientious and honorable, the most dedicated, the most wholly admirable man in the peerdom to work with."

The peer raised a hand to stop Arne's protest. "Your modesty is as remarkable as your devotion to duty. Never mind. That is how you appeared to her. She had to admire your ability and the way you worked, and admiration is as good a basis as any for love. Unfortunately, the more deeply she fell in love with you, the more she realized you were far more interested in your work than in her and always would be. She finally decided you would never love anyone."

"But I did love her," Arne protested. "I asked her to wive me."

The peer stared at him. "I didn't know that. I wouldn't have suspected it. What did she say?"

"I was about to visit the other peerdoms to ask for help in forming an army. She said she would tell me when I returned."

"And?"

"Before I had a chance to talk with her, the land warden told me the prince her sister wanted me to be her consort."

"But if you loved Deline, surely you weren't compelled to—" She paused. Then she continued slowly, "I see. Now I understand. When a prince invites a one-namer to be her consort, he *is* compelled. Poor Deline. Poor Arne. If that mating with her sister had been a brief one, as peerager matings often are, perhaps you could have resumed your happiness. But you and Elone Jermile were both dedicated to Midlow and got on well, the prince became pregnant, and the mating seemed likely to last a long time. It gradually dawned on Deline that she had lost you.

"Then the Lantiff came, and you fought and loved together, the two being more than twice as exhilarating in combination. Her sister was dead, and she thought she couldn't lose you again, but this time you lost each other—to the war—because she slipped naturally into all of her old ways, and suddenly, without any official notice, she was a prince again. She couldn't possibly consider wiving you after that, but she would have accepted you as her consort if you had been willing to remain her humble subject, follow her about obediently, charge into battle with her, and attend her when it was over. Since you couldn't do any of that, her reaction was to blame you for all of her troubles, real or imagined. Poor Arne. Poor Deline."

"What am I to do?" Arne asked perplexedly.

The peer sighed. "If you had been at Easlon Court when I

was a girl, perhaps you would have been one of the rare ones who could court a homely prince sincerely. How sad that Deline can't appreciate that. There is nothing you can do except what you are doing. Be kind. Be patient. Be loving if she gives you a chance. She will despise you the more for it, but that is all you can do, and eventually she may come to understand that the reason she hates you is also the reason she loves you."

"She is so reckless that she worries me," Arne said.

"She worries a great many people. She has reverted to being the self-centered, completely amoral prince. She will continue to act impetuously, do whatever she likes, and decide afterward that it was the wise thing. There is nothing you can do except what you are doing. Now go fight your war. You are right to be concerned about Deline, but you shouldn't worry about her. You should never worry about things you can't change."

There was much about the war that Arne couldn't change, and these things worried him immensely. The little army of Easlon was losing, but it devastated the Lantiff in every skirmish. It could have held the army of Lant back for sikes, grudgingly yielding ground a few meters at a time, if it'd had unlimited supplies. Defeat loomed inevitably because it could only fight as long as its food lasted.

Every finger of attack the Lantiff extended was shattered and chopped off, but the massive army continued to ooze forward, testing the defenders' flanks, ever extending the battlefield, ever stretching Inskor's army thinner and thinner. But refugee one-namers continued to arrive, and the entire one-name population of Easlon was training for war and planning to join the battle the moment it was needed. Easlon's len grinders continued to produce copies of Egarn's weapon, and new recruits trained with them before they met the enemy.

They were littering the Ten Peerdoms with Lantian dead, and still the army of Lant advanced—across the Peerdom of Chang, across that of Labon, across the tiny Peerdom of Zrum, until one day it stood on Easlon's border. Inskor anxiously kept scouts ranging far to the north and south so he would be fore-warned if the Lantiff attempted another wide encirclement, but they did not. They were constantly making shallow flanking movements, but the main thrust of their attack was straight ahead. Their generals must have known the war would end when Easlon ran out of food, and they were keeping Easlon's defenders occupied until then.

This was a new kind of war for the Lantiff. They were ac-customed to triumphant advances and little fighting. Dim as their intelligence was, they soon perceived that the way to vic-tory in the Ten Peerdoms was being piled with their own dead bodies, and they lost their enthusiasm for it. They responded to orders with a reluctance that hadn't existed earlier. A charge by Deline's elite guard could put their entire vanguard to flight.

But defenders were far too few, their food reserves too scant, and there seemed to be no end to the Lantiff and to the war. The brains of Inskor's one-namers functioned perfectly, and they had no illusions at all about the future. They foresaw how the war would end, and they knew the Peer of Lant would ruthlessly exterminate them. None of them intended to be cap-tured. The problem was that they had nowhere to run. They could survive for a time in the wild mountain terrain, but when their foraging became a nuisance, the Lantiff would systemati-cally track them down. Or they could fight to the end and die fighting. There seemed to be no alternative. The children of Easlon knew the fate of children in the conquered peerdoms, and they were resolved to fight to the death beside their parents rather than become no-namers.

Inskor was forming plans of his own. He didn't intend to wait until his battered army was overwhelmed or routed. If it retreated to the mountains, it would not be in order to hide and starve.

He had two options. One was to invade Lant. He could cut his way through the mountains with Egarn's weapon and inflict the same relentless destruction on the Peer of Lant's realm that she had visited on the Ten Peerdoms.

Or he could escape southward, taking with him refugees from the conquered peerdoms and the entire population of Easlon. There were peerdoms far to the south of Lant that hadn't yet been engulfed in war. These states gained a reprive when the Peer of Lant turned aside to attack the Ten Peerdoms, but their peers knew the war against them would resume as soon as the Ten Peerdoms were subdued. They had learned from the unfortunate experiences of peerdoms further north, and for sikes they had been preparing their defenses with help from Inskor's scouts. Their one-namers were already armed with Egarn's weapon, and several of their commanders had joined the army of Easlon to learn about warfare first hand.

Inskor decided to do both. The best fighting elements would cut through the mountains, close the pass behind them, and take the war deeply into Lant. The Peer of Lant, and her main army, would be trapped on the far side of impassable mountains. Easlon's young, elderly, and those unable to fight would be escorted southward through the mountains. The southern peerdoms would send help and supplies to meet the fugitives. The difficulties to be overcome, the hardships to be endured by those who made the trek, were staggering to contemplate. Many would die, but the survivors had a chance to continue surviving—at least for a time.

Inskor sent scouts to find the best route for the long march south, and Arne began placing caches of food supplies at regular intervals along the way.

Once Inskor make his decision, he and Arne met with the Peer and Prince of Easlon to discuss it. Abandoning their peerdom would be a sad wrench for them, but they accepted the inevitable. The beautiful prince had found herself a worthy mate—he was fighting with Bernal's scouts, one of the few peeragers who had gone to war. She had borne a daughter, a future Prince of Easlon, and now she was pregnant again. She and her mother were grimly determined to survive, to work for the downfall of Lant, and then reclaim and rebuild their peerdom, but they were deeply concerned about the risks involved in the hazardous journey south.

"The food worries me," the peer said. "They can't carry more than a few days supply, and how long will the journey last?"

Inskor shook his head.

"How much food will they be able to find along the way?" the prince wanted to know.

"Not enough to feed so many people," Inskor said. "Part of the problem is that they must keep moving. Scouts will range widely on either side, and Egarn's weapon is invaluable for hunting, but they can only take the game they encounter by chance, and what are they to do with the stag they shoot early in the day? They will have to butcher it on the spot and distribute the meat so it can be carried until there is an opportunity to cook it. Probably it will be necessary to stop the march occasionally—the elderly and the young will need rest—and take time to hunt and smoke meat. But there simply isn't enough game in any one part of the mountains to feed that many people. There must be food caches at regular intervals. Arne is working on this."

The peer turned to Arne. "You are a genius at organizing supplies. Will you be able to keep everyone fed?"

"My talent will count for nothing once the trek starts, Majesty," Arne said. "I can't organize supplies unless there *are* supplies. The army invading Lant should have no problems—it easily can carry enough food to last it through the mountains. After that, it can live on what it captures. Lant hasn't been touched by war, and there will be food reserves everywhere. But I am deeply worried about the food for those going south. Every bit we can spare must be sent ahead of them. This means taking scouts and horses from the war to transport it, which will weaken the army, but it must be done."

The peer smiled. "You'll manage it."

"We must manage it."

"Her Majesty and I have been wondering how Easlon got

along for so many sikes without a first server," the prince said. "Surely we couldn't have waged this war without the two of you, but Arne's great career is ahead of him. When the war is over, and the Ten Peerdoms must be rebuilt, he will be the most important man in the world. For that reason, we want him to come south with us. Of course Inskor must go east and lead the invasion of Lant. He knows Lant better than most Lantians."

"We have discussed this with the surviving peers," the peer said. "We are ready to give second names to both of you any time you want them. I know Arne has already refused one, and circumstances may not be favorable now, but I want you to know how we feel about this."

Inskor said gruffly, "I can't think of an instance in the entire war when an extra name would have helped us, Majesty, and it won't help now."

"It wouldn't make the trek south any easier, either," Arne said. "Leave the honors to the future, Majesty. First we must make certain we have a future."

Peer and prince got to their feet. Arne and Inskor knelt.

The prince placed one hand on the shoulder of each of them. "The war has demonstrated what a farce this fuss about names can be," she said. "By the time it is finished, people will be judged on some other basis, and kneeling will go the way of names. But you are right. This isn't the time to be worrying about things like that."

After they had gone, Arne and Inskor held a conference of their own. Arne had been meditating the course of the war ever since he returned from Midlow. Inskor was aware of this. He said bluntly, "You don't think either plan will work."

"I don't think the Peer of Lant and her generals are as stupid as they would like us to believe."

"How will they stop an invasion of Lant?" Inskor asked.

"They won't. But the peer has left an army at home to defend against that. It will be arranged along the frontier waiting for you. You can count on it. She isn't such a military dunce that she would march off to war and leave her peerdom defenseless."

"Do you think the invasion will fail?"

"No. It will succeed because you won't be an army. You can can break up into small groups and scatter all through Lant fighting like scouts. You can attack towns that aren't defended and be gone before the army learns of it. Her generals have never had to contend with that kind of war. You will succeed, you will do enormous damage—but not as much as you hope, and certainly not as much as you must to deal Lant a genuine defeat. Eventually that waiting army will begin to understand your way of fighting and track you down. From that moment, you won't be invaders. You will be fugitives."

"What about the trek south?" Inskor asked.

"All the Lantiff have to do is set an occasional trap, or attack some part of the column now and then with a patrol. That will disrupt the march, make the scouts form up and fight, scatter the marchers, upset the schedule so they can't reach the food supplies they must have. I greatly fear it will be a horrible trek. If it doesn't reach the south before winter, the disaster will be indescribable—but no more than it was in Midlow and the other peerdoms the Lantiff overran."

"Then you think the war is lost."

"I'm convinced it can't be won. We have killed more Lantiff than anyone could count. We have held back the armies of Lant and upset the peer's schedule for conquest. The only result has been death and suffering for the entire population of the Ten Peerdoms, and Lant is winning anyway. I suspect the Peer of Lant already has launched her southern invasion—at least, she has turned much of her strength south. She knows this war is over, and it will dribble on only as long as our food lasts. Those making the trek south will find an army waiting for them, just as you will find an army waiting for you inside Lant."

He clapped the old man on the shoulder. "This isn't a war, my friend. It is a siege. The Lantiff are simply keeping us occupied until we run out of food and have to surrender."

"Are you going south with the peer?"

"My part in the war is finished. I did everything I could possibly do to help win it, and I failed. In the next phase, once the planning is finished, I won't be needed. Your scouts will handle the march south and the invasion of Lant. I am going west. I must find out what has happened to Egarn and help him if I can. If he has failed, or the Lantiff have taken him, then I will circle back and meet the group traveling south."

Inskor nodded regretfully. "I think you are right. Not about not being needed—you always make yourself invaluable. But I have no doubt that Egarn needs you worse than we do—if he is still alive."

"His supplies will be running low," Arne said. "There are flour, grain, and tubers in hidden storage bins that can keep his little group eating well for sikes, but not even old Marof knows about them."

"Go and see Egarn, then. Return when you can. Things aren't quite as hopeless as you think. If we can persuade the southern peerdoms to attack Lant instead of waiting for Lant to attack them, we may accomplish something yet. Our raid over the mountains might panic the Peer of Lant into rushing home with her army, which would give the southern peerdoms the opportunity to attack it on the march. They just might destroy it."

"The Peer of Lant doesn't panic," Arne said dryly. "Also, there is something about this war that puzzles me mightily. We know the peer has Egarn's weapon again. By my own count, the Lantiff have captured eleven of them. One example is all their len grinders need to make copies. So why don't they use it on us?"

Inskor shrugged. "The peer's generals always have been notoriously slow to change their tactics—the Peer of Lant doesn't encourage resourcefulness in her commanders. She doesn't worry about the lives of her Lantiff because she has so many. She may not want to make changes while she is winning."

Arne shook his head. "I think the peer's generals are shrewd tacticians. They don't use it because they know it wouldn't be effective. Our one-namers fight from cover, and they use the weapon far more accurately than the Lantiff could.

They aren't going to flee in panic the first time it is used on them. So Lant's generals aren't using it. They will change their tactics the moment it will give them an advantage. When you invade Lant, the Lantiff may cut their way through the mountains and follow you. If the southern peerdoms attack the Peer of Lant with a massed army, both sides will use it. They will inflict horrible damage on each other and on whatever land the battle is fought in. Don't you see what this means?"

Inskor looked puzzled.

"The Honsun Len is about to destroy Earth a second time," Arne said sadly. "Egarn told us that would happen if it were put to military use. He has been right all along. His plan is the only way to save humanity, and I want to do what I can to help him."

"I see what you mean. I don't agree that our cause is hopeless, but by pursuing the war and keeping the Lantiff occupied as long as we can, we may be giving Egarn important help. What are you going to tell the Peer of Easlon?"

"There are many refugees still hiding out in the conquered peerdoms. Every village had food reserves stored in underground bins. The League of One-Namers had secret stores of food in each of the peerdoms. I will take one-namers who know local conditions, and we will search for refugees and pick up as much food as can be carried. I also will take a few of your scouts along, and they can guide the refugees and supplies back to meet those going south. I will remain with Egarn—if he is still at work."

"It will be risky."

"What isn't risky these days?"

Inskor nodded. "Very well. The refugees are needed. The food will be critically needed. I will suggest it, and I am sure the peer will approve. There is no need to tell her or anyone about Egarn. What about Deline?"

"Surely she would rather go east," Arne said. "Fighting defensively bores her. She should have a glorious time leading her guard through Lant."

"When do you want to leave?"

"Not until everything is ready. Until then, I have a job to do here."

The war ground on. The Lantiff charged, maneuvered, and died while their army continued to edge forward. Again and again they attempted to fold themselves around the flanks of the elusive defenders, who killed Lantiff and more Lantiff and slowly withdrew. Arne tabulated every bit of food that anyone could find in Easlon, apportioned it, and sent south all that could be spared. The plan—still known only to Arne and Inskor—was to withdraw suddenly in darkness and leave the Lantiff with the puzzling impression that their foe had disappeared. It would take time for them to to collect themselves and begin to move forward. If they had forgotten their lessons in caution, widely scattered scouts firing Egarn's weapon would remind them. These bold individuals could harrass the Lantiff for a dae or two and then withdraw—to repeat the process over and over until the southward trek had traveled too far to be overtaken.

Finally everything was ready. Arne selected the one-namers who were to travel with him. A squad of scouts led by Bernal would accompany them and guide back the refugees and supplies. Far to the rear, those taking the southern trek had already left, and the entire group was safely in the mountains. Inskor had announced another withdrawal to the army. This surprised no one; their entire war had been a war of withdrawals.

Deline came to see Arne and found him strapping a pack to his horse. She stared suspiciously. "Where are you going?"

"West," he said. "To look for fugitives and find food supplies."

"I will come with you. I am tired of this stupid war."

"The trip west will be worse. Hard work, food where we find it—if we find it—lots of hiding from the Lantiff, and no fighting unless we have to."

"Hiding!" She waved her arms disgustedly. "Aren't we ever going to stand up to the Lantiff and fight? We kill some of them—from a distance. Then we withdraw, find a new hiding place, and wait until we can kill more of them—from a distance. Now we are about to withdraw again, but you are not even withdrawing—you are running. I knew all along you were a coward."

Arne smiled patiently. "Hardly that. Cowards almost never run toward the enemy."

"Are you coming back?"

"When I have finished what I am going west for, there will be plenty of work left to do here."

"You would be invaluable to the Peer of Lant. With her huge armies to run, not to mention administering all the peerdoms she has conquered, she needs a first server. Before long, she will be the only peer who does. She needs a general, too. Look at the fumbling way her army attacks. You are going west?"

Arne nodded.

"So am I. West to find the Peer of Lant."

"She will have you executed—if the Lantiff don't kill you first."

Deline tossed her head disdainfully. "The Lantiff wouldn't dare lift a finger to me, and the peer is a warrior. So am I, and she will respect that. Will you come with me?"

Arne shook his head. "I'm fighting tyranny. I would choose death before I joined it."

"Then I will go alone."

As Arne took a step toward her, she sprang for her horse. Hutter had not yet dismounted. Deline reined up and turned to him.

"Hutter, I am going west—to give myself up to the Peer of Lant and fight for her if she will let me. Come with me or not, as you choose." She rode off.

Hutter hesitated—but only for an instant. Then he raced after her. Neither of them looked back.

Bernal and his scouts were waiting nearby. Arne shouted a command, and they ran for their horses. They were off in a thunder of hoofs, but he knew they would be too late.

Inskor came later, listened, shook his head gravely. "She certainly would inspire the Lantiff to a greater effort in battle," he said, "but that hardly matters now. There aren't going to be any more battles—not here. Does she know the plan?"

"I think not. She had heard we were going to withdraw, but she thought it was only another adjustment of the defense line."

"Then she doesn't know anything that would hurt us. She knows where some of our troops are, but they will be gone before morning." He paused. "Unless—does she know about Egarn?"

"No. She knows nothing about the ruins. She has never heard Egarn's name. That is fortunate for us. If the Peer of Lant knew Egarn was there, she would call off all of her wars and set her armies to digging him out."

"Does Hutter know anything?"

"No."

"Maybe the scouts will catch them," Inskor said.

But they didn't. The army of Easlon withdrew that night, according to plan, and divided into two groups that went east and south. Arne, with his little troop of scouts and one-namers, went west.

17

ROSZT AND KAYNOR; EGARN

Everywhere Roszt and Kaynor went, they found themselves confronted by telephones. A motel pretending to any status at all had one of these contrivances in every room. From the beginning, they regarded them with deep suspicion. Their very shape defied logic; and though Egarn had explained telephones thoroughly, they hadn't fully believed what he said. Certainly no telephone they encountered spoke to them, and for a long time they had no inclination whatsoever to speak to a telephone.

What Egarn said also seemed to imply that telephones were able to listen, which at first made them reticent about talking to each other in the presence of one.

Then they began to overhear people discussing all manner of things on public telephones, and eventually they discovered that one could ask anonymous questions by telephone and obtain information that otherwise would have required hours of investigation and kilometers of travel. The telephone became a valuable adjunct to their breaking and entering activities. All they had to do was telephone one of the Johnsons, pretend to have dialed a wrong number—something bafflingly easy to do—and thus find out whether anyone was at home in the house. Or one could telephone a business enterprise and discover, simply by asking, the times that it opened and closed.

This use of the telephone produced such excellent results that they became more venturesome. Factories intrigued them because they were so effectively sealed off from outsiders. A retail concern went out of its way to make strangers feel welcome. Factories, with tall fences topped with barbed-wire, guards on the gates to inspect the identification of anyone wanting to enter, and, remote behind vast parking lots, buildings whose functions were not only indiscernible but unimaginable, seemed specifically designed for a sinister object like making Honsun Lens.

One factory could have hundreds, even thousands, of employees. They knew from their research in city directories that many of them had employees named Johnson. They began to wonder whether all of them did.

Once the name of a factory was known—and usually it was painted on the building or displayed on a prominent sign—it was a simple matter to look up its telephone number in the directory. As an experiment, Kaynor called one and asked for Mr. Johnson. The switchboard operator handled the call cautiously; when Kaynor couldn't identify the Johnson or the department he wanted, she transferred him to personnel. The personnel operator was less diplomatic.

"We've got five Johnsons," she said exasperatedly. "Don't you know which one you want?"

Kaynor preserved his anonymity by hanging up. After that, whenever he and Roszt chanced to pass that factory, they wondered again what was transpiring in those remote buildings, what roles the various Johnsons were performing, and whether any of them were on their lists.

They discovered an entirely new reference source in the student directory of the University of Rochester. This gave them an assortment of Johnsons who weren't mentioned in the telephone directory or the city directory. It also introduced them to the university's world of laboratories, classrooms, and dormitories. Several times they sauntered through its lovely campus along the Genesee River, but these incursions gained them nothing. Dormitories were even more risky than apartment buildings to prowl in, and they could make no sense at all of the multitude of things that seemed to be going on in the laboratories.

Before they had quite decided what to do about the university, they were befuddled by another discovery. Far to the south, but also on the bank of the Genesee River, was the Rochester Institute of Technology, whose directory doubtless would give them a new list of Johnsons if they could find a copy. Probably there were other such institutions. Each additional discovery complicated their task further.

They returned to the University of Rochester Campus, strolling along perplexedly and not knowing what they were looking for or whether they would recognize it if they found it, and quite by chance they overheard one student call to another, "I'll meet you at Wilt Johnson's restaurant."

There was no Wilt Johnson on any of their lists. This mystery occupied them off and on for a tenite before they finally discovered Wilt's Snack Shack, a little diner located in a run-down section of busy West Henrietta Avenue just south of Mt. Holly Cemetery. The place did look dismally like a shack on the outside. The interior was scrupulously clean, but there was a makeshift air about it. The lunch counter and the booths were of rough plywood; tables and chairs were rickety; nothing matched. The elaborate white hat the proprietor wore while he worked over the grill was the diner's one ornate feature. Most of the patrons seemed to be students.

Wilt Johnson was a young man, and he had admirable rapport with his youthful customers. He seemed to know most of them personally. The young waitress who flitted gracefully about the crowded room was his wife.

There was nothing to suggest that this Johnson had the remotest connection with any kind of len; nevertheless, he exemplified the problem they faced. They began to eat breakfast regularly at his Snack Shack. They sat in the most remote corner, enjoyed the largest meal the establishment offered at that time of day, and listened to the other patrons' conversation while they gave the proprietor their puzzled scrutiny and reflected on the fact that all of their laborious research had missed him completely. They wondered how many more anonymous Johnsons this enormous city contained.

The revelation seemed to add an entirely new dimension to their investigation, and they weren't quite sure what they should do about it. Puzzle reposed within puzzle in this baffling civilization. If a "restaurant" could be called a "snack shack," was it possible that Johnsons, too, were sometimes called something else? Roszt and Kaynor had learned—again entirely by accident—that women often changed their names when they married. It was also true that they often didn't. The two men from the future could think of no reason why the Honsun Len couldn't have been invented by a woman—but what if she no longer called herself Johnson?

One morning at the Snack Shack, the conversation took a totally unexpected twist: Roszt and Kaynor suddenly heard themselves talked about. In a booth near the front, four students—two couples—were having their morning coffee. Roszt and Kaynor watched them surreptitiously when they weren't watching the proprietor. The manners of students, particularly their overtly sexual behavior, confounded them.

One male student was reading a newspaper. The others were studying. The couples had arms draped about each other affectionately, but all of them kept their attention on their reading.

The student with the newspaper called to the proprietor, "Hey Wilt—those Johnson burglars get around to you yet?"

"Why would they bother me?" Wilt demanded. "I got nothing worth stealing."

"What *are* they stealing?"

"How would I know? Ask Fred—he's working on it."

The student with the paper called, "Hey, Fred—you the detective on those Johnson burglaries?"

A man of about thirty, wearing an ordinary suit but every inch a policeman, turned and grinned. "Some of them."

"What is being stolen?"

"As far as we can make out, nothing."

The student said incredulously, "Nothing? All those burglaries and nothing taken?"

His girlfriend nudged him. "Wilt's got a problem."

"How do you figure that?" the student with the paper asked.

"He says he's got nothing worth stealing, and that's what's being stolen. Nothing. He's in danger of losing his nothing."

Her boyfriend glared at her. Then he got up and dropped some change on the table. "I've got a class," he said and hurried away.

A student across the room remarked, "Whoever's doing it must be looking for *something*. Do you suppose it's connected with those characters who've been pretending to trace Johnson heirs?"

The detective grinned but said nothing.

"You've got descriptions, haven't you?" the student persisted. "Even the papers have descriptions."

"Descriptions—" the detective shrugged. "We have as many descriptions as there are witnesses. All we know for certain is that there were always two of them."

"How are you going to catch them? Stake out every Johnson residence in Monroe County?"

The detective grinned again and shook his head, and the conversation turned to a subject Roszt and Kaynor found totally bewildering—baseball.

They were shocked and alarmed. They ordered more food and kept themselves as inconspicuous as possible until the students and the detective had left. Then they carefully calculated the tip—giving the waitress too much or too little would fix themselves in her memory, Egarn had said—and left with what they hoped was calm nonchalance.

Not only had they been the subject of casual conversation in a restaurant; they also were the object of a strenuous police search, and that staggered them. They didn't know what "stake out" meant, but it sounded sinister.

Further, someone had connected their innocent queries about Johnson heirs with the burglaries. They would have to stop everything until the clamor died down. While they were waiting, perhaps they could think of an entirely different approach. It was obvious that the one they were using had become dangerous. Also, it hadn't worked.

* * *

Egarn had watched their fumbling search with increasing distress. In the complications of getting them to the right place, and preparing them to live in 20th century America, he hadn't given enough thought to the problem of finding the right Johnson. Their intense activity when they first arrived in Rochester elated him. As time passed, they began to resemble the man who mounted his horse and rode off in all directions. If only he could have talked with them for a couple of minutes—asked them what they thought they were doing and pointed them in the right direction.

Suddenly they dropped everything and did nothing at all. They kept to their motel room except to exercise Val, and they began buying and reading newspapers. He had no idea what had happened, and he was plunged into despair.

He kept trying unsuccessfully to send them messages and to pick up the messages they faithfully left for him on their table each night. The code messages they signaled with a flashlight had long since degenerated into a routine, "Search continuing, no results," and the date. They continued to go through the motions of communicating, but because they had heard nothing from Egarn, they probably thought he was no longer watching. Now their search was at a standstill. Egarn's workroom was shrouded more deeply in gloom each dae.

The loyal team of helpers, most of whom never saw the workroom's interior and had little notion of what went on there, sensed that things were going badly. They connected Egarn's distress with the fact that supplies were running low. The food seemed to get worse with each succeeding meal, and Fornzt was in despair. Every time he used the last of something, he knew he was one step closer to the last of everything. Some of the outside sentries went on regular foraging missions—they thought they weren't needed at the ruins because no outsider had been sighted anywhere in Midlow since the Lantiff left—but they rarely found anything. Old Marof, the one person who could have helped them, had died shortly after the destruction of Midd Village from illness and perhaps a broken heart.

Then Arne arrived, and everyone brightened. Egarn's confidence in Arne was shared by all of them. Arne would take care of everything. First and foremost, he would refill their empty larder. If Egarn's distress had to do with something else, Arne would repair that, too.

He knew where each village had kept its reserves of flour and tubers—or, if he didn't, he knew how to find them. He had been ranging all across the Ten Peerdoms emptying these underground storage bins, many of which were buried under the villages' charred remains, and he had sent a huge pack train east for the use of those still fighting the Lantiff. Now he plundered the reserves of Midlow for Egarn's team and quickly restocked Fornzt's shelves.

He did more than that. The Lantiff, on their murderous swoop through the Ten Peerdoms, appropriated the horses, drove off all the animals they could use for meat, and removed every scrap of food they could find. No-namers of the conquered peerdoms, with their lasher supervisors, were left to fend for themselves. Except for the lack of meat, this was no problem. No-namers were accustomed to producing their own vegetables and tubers and growing grain for the entire peerdom. Now they would have to thresh and grind the grain by hand, but they had plenty of time for it because they no longer had to perform the peerdom's heavy labor.

Egarn's team likewise had long been without meat, but Arne quickly corrected that. He knew where to look for stray animals, and the day after his arrival, beef and mutton returned to Fornzt's menu, and a row of carcasses hung in a room in the depths of the ruins where the temperature was always cool. Arne also found a suitably remote place where meat could be dried and smoked.

With the food problem resolved, Arne next set about tightening the security system—the sentries thought they had the entire peerdom to themselves, and they had become inexcusably lax. Not until that had been taken care of did Arne turned his attention to the workroom—and discover that the Great Secret was a shambles.

"It is Roszt and Kaynor," Egarn said. "They haven't found the Johnson, and they have stopped looking." Neither Egarn nor any of the others could understand why *the* Johnson had proved so elusive or why Roszt and Kaynor had given up. Arne, trained all of his life to apply logic and common sense to any problem that confronted him, inquired about the messages that should have been sent and received. Egarn never cared to dwell on his failures, and he waved the question aside disgustedly.

Later Arne pressed Inskel for the details. In theory, the system should have worked at least occasionally, but it had never worked at all. Even in tests, the instrument rarely sucked up the small objects it was aimed at. Much more frequently it snatched things they didn't want. They had failed to retrieve any of Roszt and Kaynor's messages. The messages they sent went somewhere, but they never arrived at Roszt and Kaynor's motel room. Neither Egarn nor Inskel could understand this.

Arne sat for an entire day alternating his gaze between the non-activity of Roszt and Kaynor on the len and the mammoth contraption that sent or drew people and objects through time. Gevis, the former assistant schooler who was so valuable both as Egarn's assistant on historical matters—he had made himself virtually an authority on life in the 20th century, Egarn said—and as Inskel's assistant with the machines, sat beside Arne, answered his questions, and discussed what he had seen Roszt and Kaynor doing before they suddenly seemed to quit.

Finally Arne went to Egarn. Could it be possible, he asked, that Egarn's machine didn't work accurately with such a small thing as a message because of its enormous size? A smaller machine might be much more precise with small objects.

Egarn and Inskel stared at him. Then they stared at each other.

"The size of the machine shouldn't make any difference," Egarn said slowly. "None at all. On the other hand—"

"It wouldn't be much trouble to build a smaller machine and find out," Inskel said. "I've got nothing else to do."

And so he did. It took several daez, after which the three of them, Inskel, Egarn, and Gevis, had a nightmarish problem in calibrating it and matching its settings to those of the large machine, but finally they succeeded, and when Roszt and Kaynor next left a report on their table, the small machine deftly plucked it out of the past.

The jubilation of those in the workroom was tempered by the soberness with which Egarn read the message. "They couldn't find the right Johnson," he said. "They broke into all those Johnson homes and businesses, and they went everywhere making inquiries about Johnsons, and they failed to find a single clue. I never thought they would have to keep it up for so long. The police aren't fools, and eventually all those Johnson burglaries stopped being a coincidence, and now everyone in Rochester is talking about them and speculating about what they are trying to find. Newspapers all over the state have picked up the story and published artists' drawings of what the burglars are supposed to look like. The pictures aren't much like Roszt and Kaynor, but the publicity has frightened them. They also are afraid that the next time they mention the name Johnson, someone will scream for the police. They are waiting for the uproar to die down and trying to disguise themselves. They have bought new clothes, and they are growing mustaches and combing their hair differently. They want to know if I can suggest anything else."

"Why couldn't they find the right Johnson?" Arne asked.

"They haven't run across any trace at all of a Honsun Len or of a Johnson who has anything to do with lens." Egarn added despairingly, "I must have sent them too far back in time. Of course they wouldn't be able to connect a Johnson with the Honsun Len if no Johnson has thought of it yet. I might try to send them to a later time, but it would be risky. I would have to bring them here again and then send them back."

Arne tenaciously held to the point he thought most important. "But what is the right time?"

"I don't know," Egarn said.

"Before you do anything else, perhaps you should find out," Arne suggested.

"The only way to be certain would be to go there and do the kind of investigation they've been doing."

In the end, it was Gevis who suggested a practical solution. While watching Roszt and Kaynor's fruitless search, he had been wondering if there were anything in that place and time for them to find. The answer seemed simple enough to him. If the Honsun Len inventor hadn't yet arrived in Rochester, Roszt and Kaynor ought to look for him elsewhere. As for identifying him, why couldn't they use Inskel's new machine to suck up a city directory or a telephone directory from some future time?

They first asked Roszt and Kaynor to prepare a list of their Johnsons with a summary of what they'd learned about each. It took the scouts three daes, and it filled an entire notebook. They left it on the table for Inskel to snatch.

The next step was to steal a directory that would give them a list of Johnsons living in Rochester at a future date. Telephone directories often were left lying about where they could be picked up easily. Unfortunately, a telephone directory provided only an unadorned list of names, and sucking up a city directory proved to be a complicated manipulation.

They carefully set their instruments to visit the Local History Room of the Rochester Public Library several sikes after Roszt and Kaynor had been there. The only result was that librarians unaccountably found the floor cluttered with books the next morning. The small machine lacked the power of the large one, and pulling a book from a crammed shelf of books proved difficult. They visited the library again three sikes later and managed to abstract a copy of the 1940 directory. Either the books were shelved out of order or they were searching the wrong stack. Again they leaped forward in time and finally scored a success. Egarn found himself opening—with trembling fingers—a Rochester City Directory ten sikes in Roszt and Kaynor's future.

He hadn't expected a Honsun Len boom to develop in that short time, but he did hope to find some indication that it existed. He found nothing.

After several more failures, they managed to snatch a directory that took them another five sikes into the future, and there they found an interesting reference to an H. H. Johnson. He was not on Roszt and Kaynor's list, so he had arrived on the Rochester scene some time after they made their search. He was president of the Johnson Specialty Company, and the directory gave the addresses of both his home and his business. Egarn asked Roszt and Kaynor to include a map of Rochester with their next message. Gevis, operating the small machine, adroitly captured it, and with the map's help they soon had the large len focused on the factory building, a small, neat, cement block structure. With the large instrument—the miniature one was much too small—they made a series of nighttime passes in the shipping room and finally succeeded in sucking up a case of the company's product.

It was called the Permlight, and the blurb on the case proclaimed it a sensational new self-powered flashlight that worked without batteries. With trembling hands Egarn dissected one of them. Inside he found a tiny Honsun Len.

They had finally located the right Johnson, but they knew nothing about him except that long after the date of Roszt and Kaynor's visit to Rochester he would establish a business called the Johnson Specialty Company and take up residence at 1 DuRosche Court.

Egarn passed the information to Roszt and Kaynor with instructions to find out who owned the 1 DuRosche Court property. He wanted to know whether there was any Johnson associated with the place and whether the Johnson Specialty Company existed yet.

*   *   *

The scouts from Slorn had ranged through the enemy territory of Lant without a qualm, but in this perplexing civilization of the past, they had begun to see traps everywhere. They proceeded with extreme caution, which no doubt was wise after their discovery that all of Rochester was looking for them. A check of the telephone directory, a return to the library to consult the city directory, and they could confidently assert that the Johnson Specialty Company did not yet exist. The investigation of 1 DuRosche Court proved far more complicated.

They separated for it. There had been entirely too much discussion in the papers about the two tall, ungainly men who always worked together. Roszt went first and walked quickly through the neighborhood at dusk. Kaynor did the same on the following night. Then, because neither of them noticed anything of interest, they went together the third night but followed different routes, after which they reported that they had nothing to report.

DuRosche Court was a very short and virtually private street. Number 1 was its only address. It was located south of East Avenue and a few blocks east of Eastman House. The neighborhood was one of lavish homes, each reposing in its own wooded setting. The houses were venerable but in splendid condition, the lawns neatly manicured, the shrubbery trimmed. Urban decay was no more than a future rumor for that haven of wealth.

The area was quiet; despite the nearness of bustling East Avenue, there was very little traffic or even foot traffic, and the mansion at 1 DuRosche Court was set far back in its own extensive, park-like grounds. It seemed invulnerable to snoopers. Little could be seen beyond the tall hedge that enclosed the entire estate except the upper story of a huge brick building that loomed impressively through the trees. In that exclusive neighborhood, Roszt and Kaynor couldn't even walk past DuRosche Court without feeling unduly conspicuous. Venturing into the grounds would be risky during daylight; at night they should be able to get close enough to look into windows, but breaking and entering was out of the question with a house of this size—the owner would be certain to have servants.

The mail box, placed at the foot of the drive, had a name on it: DuRosche. The telephone directory informed them that Calvin DuRosche lived at 1 DuRosche Court. A few tenites earlier, they would have boldly called at the house and asked whether any Johnsons lived there. Now they feared to mention the name Johnson.

Egarn had no suggestions beyond advising caution, but he asked them to find out everything they could about the house and its occupants.

Roszt went before dawn the next morning, hid himself in a thick clump of bushes, and spent the entire dae watching the comings and goings at DuRosche Court. By late afternoon, when a newsboy pedaled his bicycle up the long drive to the mansion, he had several things to think about but very little understanding of what he had seen.

The newsboy, red-headed and chunkily built and whistling shrilly, dismounted, rang the doorbell, and waited politely until someone came to accept the newspaper. Roszt watched this maneuver perplexedly. He had seen newsboys in action before— had marveled, in fact, at their accuracy or sometimes inaccuracy with thrown papers. At the DuRosche mansion, the newspaper was hand delivered. Roszt had acquired some slight understanding of motivation in this society, and he rejected the possibility that this particular newsboy was unduly conscientious. He thought it more likely that the residents at 1 DuRosche Court tipped lavishly.

If a newsboy was willing to alter his natural habits for the sake of a tip, perhaps there were other things he would do for money. As the boy rode back down the drive, Roszt intercepted him.

He had a five-dollar bill in his hand, and he flashed it impressively. "Detective," he said, talking out of the side of his mouth like a detective he had seen on TV. "Can you keep your mouth shut?"

The boy nodded, his eyes on the money.

"What do you know about the people who live here?" Roszt asked.

"Everything," the boy said with a confident grin.

He proved to be an extremely well-informed newsboy. They walked slowly along the sidewalk together, the boy wheeling his bike and halting frequently for Roszt to make notes. When Roszt finished his questions, he substituted a ten-dollar bill for the promised five and considered it a bargain. He now knew who the house's occupants were and what they were. It would have required a tedious, prolonged, and probably risky investigation, with numerous questions asked of strangers, to acquire a fraction of this information elsewhere. He thanked the boy and wrote down his name and phone number in case he needed him again. Then he went back to the motel and drew up a report for Egarn.

One thing was certain. There was no Johnson living at 1 DuRosche Court. The owner and occupant, Calvin DuRosche, was an elderly invalid. He'd had a stroke, and for years he hadn't been able to walk, or talk, or even feed himself. Because he was wealthy, he could afford a private nurse to look after him and servants to look after the house and grounds and fix his meals. The newsboy thought it a shame—all that money being spent to keep an old man in luxury and comfort when he didn't even know what was happening.

The only other permanent residents in that huge house were Mr. and Mrs. Kernley, who had been working for DuRosche for sikes. Mr. Kernley was the caretaker; Mrs. Kernley was the housekeeper. There were two maids—Mrs. Calding, who cleaned and helped the nurse; and Mrs. Jefferson, who cleaned and did the cooking. The house needed a lot of cleaning. There was a handyman whose last name was Hyatt and who mostly answered to the name "Hy." He did a little of this and that when he wasn't off on a drunk. Mrs. Halmer, DuRosche's nurse, came five days a week, and a special nurse, Mrs. Raymond, came weekends. The two maids worked alternate weekends, but they went home evenings, as did the nurses. Mrs. Kernley looked after DuRosche at night, which meant he didn't need much looking after.

It seemed like a huge staff to care for one elderly invalid, but of course it was a big house, and he could afford it. It was a happy household, the newsboy thought—the servants and nurses had worked there for a long time. They got along well, and everyone helped out with anything that needed doing.

It now seemed certain that Roszt and Kaynor had traveled too far back in time. The only thing for them to do was to wait quietly until the right Johnson appeared. If this mansion was where he was going to live, their task was vastly simplified. All they had to do was keep a close watch on it so they could deal with him the moment he showed up.

The information was a cruel disappointment to Egarn, but he agreed that the mansion of an elderly millionaire stroke victim was an unlikely place for the Honsun Len to be invented. No doubt DuRosche would die in a few sikes, the mansion would have a new owner, and eventually the Honsun Len Johnson would acquire it.

It was the notion that Roszt and Kaynor might have to wait an unknown number of sikes for the right Johnson that frightened Egarn. While they were waiting, so many things could happen to make their mission impossible. He wanted to be absolutely certain there was no Johnson connected with the mansion's present residents, so he asked them to make one more try. Perhaps DuRosche had a relative named Johnson who would inherit the house.

Roszt and Kaynor were still trying to avoid being seen together, so when they next visited DuRosche Court, Roszt took his former place in the bushes while Kaynor walked aimlessly around the block, around two blocks, around four blocks. Then he returned to his starting point. They had no idea of how to discover a Johnson connection when they didn't dare mention the name, and Egarn hadn't been able to suggest anything. Even on the flickering len they seemed uneasy. Egarn reluctantly decided they should get out of Rochester for a time and give themselves a vacation. Then, when the uproar about the breaking and entering cases had quieted somewhat, they could resume their watch on the DuRosche mansion.

The afternoon faded; Roszt remained hidden in the bushes while Kaynor continued his uneasy circuits of the neighborhood. The nurse, Mrs. Halmer, who walked with the slow, measured stride of a heavy, middle-aged woman, left for the day. There was a path through the grounds that could be used as a shortcut, thus avoiding the long walk down the drive and out through DuRosche Court. She followed it. Egarn adjusted the len and watched her move sedately through the wooded grounds, looking very trim and neat in her white dress. She turned when she reached the sidewalk and walked toward the bus stop on East Avenue.

Kaynor, returning from one more circuit of the neighborhood, met her at the corner. He didn't speak to her. He hadn't spoken to anyone all afternoon. Egarn reflected sadly that the two men were no longer conducting an investigation. They were simply watching the mansion and its grounds and hoping for a break of some kind.

The haze of dusk was spreading through the grounds; lights had been turned on in the house. Kaynor, starting one more circuit, suddenly turned aside, forced his way through the tall hedge, and moved stealthily toward the house. There was no one outside; probably the residents were at dinner. Kaynor disappeared.

Egarn spoke to Inskel, who tried to adjust the len so they could see what was happening. By the time he succeeded, several minutes had passed. Kaynor had been window peeping; he had already checked the first story windows, and now he was kneeling and looking into a basement window. Finally he got to his feet, reached the cover of shrubbery with long strides, and began a stealthy retreat.

As Kaynor regained the sidewalk, Roszt emerged from his bushes, looked about cautiously, and then joined him. The two men talked for several minutes. Then they followed the side-walk toward East Avenue, walking along the high hedge.

At the same moment, a young woman left the mansion. She turned to wave at someone standing in the doorway before she strolled briskly along the same path the nurse had taken. Because of the hedge, she couldn't see Roszt and Kaynor, nor they her, and the three of them halted in surprise when they met abruptly where the path intersected the sidewalk.

Perhaps one of them spoke to her. She obviously spoke to them. Then, suddenly disturbed about something, she gesticulated wildly and seized Kaynor's arm. A brief struggle followed, a sort of "tug of war," until Roszt stepped forward and gave the woman a firm push. She staggered backward and fell heavily.

Roszt and Kaynor fled—not toward busy East Avenue, but in the opposite direction, along the quiet sidestreet. When they turned a corner, they had the good sense to slow their pace and walk normally.

Behind them, the young woman lay motionless, her head at a grotesque angle, her body partially concealed by the thick hedge.

18

THE STUDENTS;
PROFESSOR MARCUS BROCK

Mount Hope Avenue, with its swarming north-south traffic, formed the eastern boundary of Mount Hope Cemetery. Across from the cemetery were venerable sidestreets of large, old-fashioned houses packed closely together—a tranquil neighborhood despite the volume of traffic flowing past. The streets were lined with tall shade trees; the houses, many with their original wood-railed porches, were carefully maintained. Flowers garnished the tidy yards with splashes of color. Here an old neighborhood grocery store had been converted into a residence; a short distance away the wheel had turned completely, and a residence had been converted into a business. Other houses were remodeled into two family dwellings or apartments. The few small, modern apartment building stood out starkly, bearing no resemblance to the houses that had formerly occupied those plots.

Enterprising developers had further crowded the neighborhood by inserting courts of row houses down the middle of the longer blocks, thus diminishing the backyards of the original buildings. One of these, Mount Hope Court, consisted of narrow, elongated rows of apartments. They were occupied entirely by students, some married, some sharing an apartment for the term.

A party was in progress in one of those apartments. Revelers crowded living room and bedrooms, drapping themselves over furniture or sprawling on the floor, talking, singing, or just listening while digging into a variety of chips and dips or inbibing drinks of varying potency. From the kitchen came tantilizing odors that promised more solid fare to follow.

The doorbell rang, and Alida Brylon hurried to answer it. She was tall, with long, unadorned, dark hair and very little makeup—the rare type who could be attractive with no concession to stylishness. Normally she was poised and completely at ease in any social situation, but on this evening her rush to the door reflected a growing nervousness.

She said, "Hi, Shirley. Hi, Charlie. Come in and join the zoo."

"Sorry we're late," Charlie said. He was a small, dark-complexioned youth who had the air of one who went through life apologizing. "My car—"

Shirley, a hefty blond, cut him off with a vicious nudge. "She knows about your car. Everyone knows about your car."

From the living room, a voice called, "Is it Janie?"

Alida called back, "It's Shirley and Charlie."

"Where's Janie?" Charlie asked.

"She went to see her aunt, but she should have been here an hour ago. I'm worried about her."

Shirley grabbed her hand and held it up to the light. A ring with a large diamond sparkled. "Hey—you got it!" she exclaimed. "How did Jeff manage that on an intern's salary?"

"How does any man get engaged?" Charlie asked sourly. "By mortgaging his future."

Shirley's nudge almost knocked him down. "Is Jeff here?"

Alida nodded happily. "He found someone to cover for him."

Shirley and Charlie inserted themselves into the packed living room—a contortionistic manipulation that required experience and skill. Alida returned to the kitchen.

A guitar twanged. "Let's count the stars!" someone called.

"We can't until Janie gets here."

"Ruth can do it."

"Ruth and Bob, then. Ready?"

The guitar twanged again. Ruth and Bob began the duet between an ardent suitor and a young lady who preferred counting stars to love. At intervals the other students commented in chorus, "No, she can't love anyone...until her work is done...she is counting all the stars in the sky."

The song concluded with laughter and applause, followed by

a lull during which everyone reached for food. In the kitchen, the telephone rang. A moment later, Alida appeared in the living room doorway. Her face was white; she obviously was in shock.

Ruth's voice came. "What is it? What's happened?"

Alida said dully, "She's dead."

"Who's dead?" one of the men called.

"Janie's dead."

Jeff Mardell, Alida's fiance, hurried to her side and put an arm around her. She kept repeating, "Janie's dead. Janie's dead," and trying to make herself believe it; and the stunned students, many of whom had got to their feet, were staring at her in equal disbelief.

*   *   *

They buried Janie in Mount Hope Cemetery, a place she had dearly loved. She had jogged there each morning before she went to class, and she knew every monument. Her friends desperately wanted to give her an elaborate funerary sculpture like those she had so much admired—an enormous angel with spread wings, or perhaps Janie herself, jogging perpetually through Mount Hope in her running shoes, but all of them were struggling for financial survival.

She had not been a pretty girl, but she was a wholly beautiful person. She had no enemies, and all of her friends loved her. There was a crowd of students present in the cemetery when her coffin was lowered, along with Janie's aunt and uncle, Mr. and Mrs. Kernley—who were devastated by grief—and the DuRosche maid, Mrs. Calding. There were no dry faces. A young minister said a final prayer and stepped back. Ed Cranston, the slender, bald guitar player from Alida's party, twanged a few notes, and the students sang a farewell song that Ed had written.

> *"We'll forget the friends we've made,*
> *Last year's loves will quickly fade,*
> *But we'll all remember Janie;*
> *But we'll all remember Janie.*

"Flowers wilt and teardrops dry,
Fondest memories may quickly die,
But we'll all remember Janie;
But we'll all remember Janie.

"We'll forget the wind and rain
The taste of pleasure, the throb of pain,
But we'll all remember Janie;
But we'll all remember Janie."

Alida broke away suddenly. Jeff overtook her and put his arm around her, and the two of them walked off together. They followed a curving, descending road, and the fading conclusion of Ed's song drifted after them.

"Brightest stars will lose their light,
Every sunset will soon be night,
But we'll all remember Janie;
But we'll all remember Janie.

"We'll forget the books we've read,
The songs we've sung and the cause we've led,
But we'll all remember Janie;
But we'll all remember Ja-a-nie."

From its founding in the 1838, Mount Hope Cemetery was considered a park for the living as well as a necropolis for the dead. It offered a lovely, rolling landscape, unusual geological features, and views of the Genesee River Valley, and families found it a delightful setting for picnics and outings. Janie and the students who were fond of jogging there were anticipated by residents of nineteenth century Rochester who thought it an attractive place for a stroll or a carriage ride.

The road Alida and Jeff were following dropped into a delightful dell. Against one of the steep hills surrounding it stood the Gothic chapel, which dated from the time of the Civil War. The smokestack of its crematorium looked excessively tall and charmingly ornate. Neither had been used for many years. The windows of the handsome old building were boarded up, and there was a padlock on the door. Nearby was an unused fountain. To the east, past the Moorish gazebo, was the original entrance gate to the cemetery with its elaborate Romanesque gate house.

The dell offered a picturesque history of fashions in dying. Heavy slabs of stone framed entrances to crypts that had been cut into the hillsides. There were free-standing mausoleums that looked like clumsy sheds except for their ornate stone construction. There were ranks of unadorned grave markers. Elaborate monuments were topped with handsome sculptures whose angels cried petrified tears, whose children were perpetually endowed with sweet innocence, or whose soldiers would never know defeat. Tall pillars and obelesques caught the eye and symbollically pointed the way to heaven. Rows of tombstones looked down from the surrounding hills. All of these memorials were designed to withstand the ravages of time, but some of them had aged badly—the erect slabs were tilted, the more substantial markers had taken on odd alignments, and here and there one had begun to crumble.

It had been a beautiful setting, lovingly fashioned with great care and expense to memorialize the dead. Now it was more than merely beautiful because the patina of age had enhanced each weathered structure and monument and because most of those who mourned these dead were dead themselves, survived only by the grief they left here frozen in stone.

Alida and Jeff seated themselves on the steep slope opposite the chapel and crematorium. Traffic noises from Mount Hope Avenue were muted; the place seemed utterly peaceful.

Alida sat looking straight ahead. "It is such a quiet place for Janie."

"Wherever she is, she will quickly liven things up," Jeff said.

Alida continued to stare straight ahead. "Jeff—why?"

Jeff shook his head. "What is there to say? It was a freak accident. She fell; probably that stone had been there for a hundred years without causing any trouble, and she just happened to hit it the worst way possible."

Alida turned on him indignantly. "It was no accident. She was knocked down." She looked at her hand. "Janie never saw my ring. I don't want to be happy. I can't be happy and not know why." She turned to him. "Jeff—I've got to know why. The police aren't doing a thing."

Jeff Mardell, a stocky, good-looking man with a tumbling locke of hair his woman patients were going to love, got to his feet and helped her up. He felt Alida's unhappiness intensely, and he hadn't been able to think of a thing that could be done. It pained him to be made aware of this limitation on his powers of healing so early in his career. "If you've got to know why, then we've got to find out why," he said.

He kissed her. Then the two of them walked slowly back toward Jeff's car, arms around each other.

They drove to DuRosche Court and followed the mansion's curving drive. "This is quite a shack," Jeff said. "Who is Calvin DuRosche?"

"He comes from an old Rochester family. His ancestors were rich socialites long before Mr. Eastman thought of Kodaks."

"It's hard to imagine something like this being a private home. How would one family manage to fill it? It looks more like a public building."

"At the time it was built, they probably had loads of servants. Now there are just a few people looking after Mr. DuRosche, but once a year they hire someone to clean and air the parts of the house that aren't used. They hire someone to help with the grounds, too, whenever things get out of hand. Janie's aunt is the housekeeper, and her uncle acts as caretaker. They've been here for years. Before Mr. DuRosche had his stroke, Mrs. Kernley was his cook."

They walked up the steps to the stoop—there was a wheelchair ramp at one side—and Alida rang the bell. Mrs. Calding, the maid, was a friendly, motherly type, and she greeted them with a warm smile.

"Hello, Mrs. Calding," Alida said. "This is Jeff Mardell, my fiance."

"I saw you at the funeral," Mrs. Calding said. "What a terrible thing. Come in, come in."

She led them along a hallway and into a Victorian parlor that was tastefully furnished with antiques of a type people had been eager to throw out fifty years before—to their descendants' grief. An exquisite old roll-top desk stood in one corner. It served Mrs. Kernley as an office where she kept her household accounts and records.

Jeff and Alida seated themselves on a sofa that looked as though it might have been a prop for one of Mr. Eastman's first photographs. Mrs. Calding took a nearby chair. Alida asked, "Is Mrs. Kernley here?"

"The doctor gave her a sedative and put her to bed, the poor dear. This has been almost more than she could take."

"Is it true those men asked Janie about someone named Johnson?"

"That's what Mr. Fairchild thought. He lives in the neighborhood, and he was walking his dog. But he was across the street, and there are traffic noises from East Avenue, and he is elderly—he couldn't have heard very well. This town has got Johnsons on the brain after all those newspaper stories. He may have imagined it."

"I know there is no Johnson living here, but I wondered if someone's relatives could have been named Johnson or something like that."

"Believe me, honey, the police already thought of that. They've got Johnsons on the brain, too. On account of all the burglaries, you know. But no one here has any connection with a Johnson. The police checked. They not only checked us—they checked the whole neighborhood!"

"Of course. They would have. We thought we were being clever." Alida stood up dejectedly. "I suppose we should leave detecting to the detectives. Sorry to bother you, Mrs. Calding."

"That's all right, honey. You stop by any time. We are always happy to see you, and I'm sure Mrs. Kernley will want to talk with you when she is feeling better."

As they started back down the hallway, a door opened. Mrs. Halmer, the nurse, immaculate in her white dress, looked out, nodded at Alida, and said, "Mrs. Calding—could you give me a hand for a moment?"

Calvin DuRosche sat in a invalid's chair by the window. It was a tidy room, an immaculately clean room, with everything essential to a sick man's comfort. DuRosche was elderly, gaunt, bald-headed. He sat staring straight ahead. Mrs. Halmer lifted him easily, and Mrs. Calding rearranged his pillows. Jeff watched with professional interest.

"He has had every kind of specialist," Mrs. Halmer said. "None of them helped him. He can't talk, he can't walk, he can't do a thing for himself. All he does is exist. They say he was such an active, intelligent, man. It is a terrible thing when a person lives too long."

Alida turned away, holding back her tears. "There is a worse thing—dying too soon."

They moved down the hall to the doorway with Mrs. Calding following them. On the stoop, Alida said, "Apologies again for bothering you. I guess it was a pretty silly idea."

"The police didn't think it was silly. But I wish they would forget about Johnsons and look for those murderers."

As Jeff and Alida turned away, Mrs. Calding looked down into the shrubbery. "Hy Hyatt!" she exclaimed angrily. "What are you doing there?"

The handyman was crouched behind the clump of bushes that stood beside the entrance. He had a short length of thick pipe in one hand and a butcher knife in the other. He was a runty, ragamuffin type, dressed in cast-off clothing. He wore a white dress shirt, much in need of laundering, open at the throat; faded and patched golfing pants; and running shoes. He didn't seem to be wearing socks. His long hair was a shaggy brown mat, and any public health officer would have declared him a disaster area.

He flashed a crafty smile, showing decayed stumps of teeth. "I'm guardin' the house, Mrs. Calding. Them murderers is back. I saw 'em drive past."

"Nonsense!" Mrs. Calding exclaimed. "You don't even know what they looked like. You put those things away before you hurt yourself!"

"Now don't you worry, Mrs. Calding. I been to school, you know. I can take care of this. There won't be no murderers breaking in while I'm here."

"I'll see to you later," Mrs. Calding promised.

She followed Alida and Jeff down to the car. Alida apologized again for trying to wish the name Johnson on her.

"The only mystery about a name in this house belongs to Hy," Mrs. Calding said. "He won't tell anyone what his first name is. The 'Hy,' comes from his last name, Hyatt."

Hy had come out from behind his shrubbery. He grinned at them again. He held the pipe and knife in a way that boded no good for any intruding murderer. As they drove back down the drive, Mrs. Calding waved her hand at them. Hy stood beside her waving his butcher knife.

At the foot of the drive, Mr. Kernley, a short, fat man with graying hair and a small mustache that seemed incongruously black, stepped out and flagged them. He greeted Alida warmly; she introduced him to Jeff.

"I was looking around that place where Janie was killed," he said. "She fell back into the hedge and landed on a rock, you know. The police searched there, of course, but it was dark, and I don't think they worked very hard at it. Probably they didn't expect to find anything. Those two men never stepped off the sidewalk. Janie lost her balance and staggered backward into the hedge before she fell."

"She was pushed!" Alida said bitterly.

"Well—Mr. Fairchild thought she was, but he also said she seemed to be struggling with one of the men as though they were both pulling on something. I found this."

He opened a handkerchief and showed them a fragment of what looked like a black tube. "I thought it was metal," he said. "But it isn't—it's thin wood. See the splinters where it broke? There is something odd set in the end of it. I think one of the men had this in his hand, and Janie caught hold of it, and both of them pulled on it. When it broke, she lost her balance and stumbled backward. She must have fallen pretty hard, so I suppose she could have been pushed at the same time."

"It looks like a piece of a pocket telescope," Jeff mused. "Or maybe a microscope—one made for kids. Except that those things wouldn't have a wood tube." Holding it by the handkerchief, he scrutinized it perplexedly. "If that's a lens in the end of it, it certainly is strange-looking."

"It may have nothing to do with Janie," Mr. Kernley said. "Someone could have tossed this into the hedge to get rid of it. I pick up all kinds of junk there. Do you think I ought to take it to the police station?"

"The police certainly will want to see it. I know a sergeant who is working on the case. I can take it to him now. It should be checked for fingerprints and then analyzed scientifically. Maybe someone will know what it is."

"That's nice of you," Mr. Kernley said. "I was worried about making a fool of myself, but if you really think it is important—"

"It is. The police will thank you. Even if they don't, Alida and I thank you. You have given us a chance to do one small thing about Janie's death." He folded the handkerchief around the odd object and handed it to Alida to hold.

"Such a lovely girl with all her life ahead of her," Mr. Kernley said. He shook his head sadly. "So unnecessary. You'll see that the police get that?"

"In about fifteen minutes," Jeff promised. They waved and drove off.

*　　*　　*

There was a meeting that night in one of the row apartments. It was an exact duplicate of the apartment Alida had occupied with Janie, but its furnishings and decor were distinctly masculine, and the place had the unmistakable air of occupancy by indifferent males rather than tidy females.

Most of those present had been at the party. Bob, one of the vocalists, interrupted a babble of talk by shouting for silence. He had a wrestler's build; in fact, he was one, and his voice boomed. "Hold it! Alida and Jeff have asked us to help them."

"Where are they?" Charlie asked.

"Alida is working and Jeff had an errand. Now listen. They are trying to find Janie's murderers. This is our problem, too. Janie was one of us. Are we going to let those thugs get away with it?"

Charlie said, "Well, if the police can't catch them, how do you expect us—ouch!"

Shirley elbowed him a second time and said, "Shut up!"

"The police don't seem to be pushing this," Bob said. "In their book, it wasn't murder, it was manslaughter—there is no indication that the men wanted to hurt Janie. They certainly didn't know that rock was there, and they might even be able to plead self-defense. The guy was trying to pull away from her, and she had hold of him—or of something he had in his hand."

"Whatever the charge is, we want him caught," Shirley said.

"Right. Ed—are you still driving that cab part time?"

"What do you mean, part time?" Ed demanded mournfully. "I'm doing eight to ten hours a night!"

"If we furnish descriptions of the thugs, can you put all the cab drivers in the Rochester area on the lookout for them?"

"Sure," Ed said. "That part is easy. It's recognizing them from a description that's difficult."

"We can but try," Bob said. "A cousin of mine is a truck driver. He will ask all the truckers in this part of the state to help. Can anyone think of anything else?"

"My uncle is a postal supervisor," one of the girls said. "He can put the mail persons onto it."

Connie, a petite, dazzlingly attractive brunette, asked, "What about waiters and waitresses? Thugs have to eat, don't they."

"Great idea," Bob said. "Waiters, Waitresses, bell hops, bar tenders, newspaper boys—we need all of them. We also will need a line to the ham and citizens' band radio operators. Let's get working on it. We are calling it Operation J, for Janie. Someone will be at this phone twenty-four hours a day from now on."

*　　*　　*

Jeff's errand was an appointment with a former teacher of his. Professor Marcus Brock, a retired specialist in optics, lived in a magnificently wooded setting east of Rochester in the town of Penfield. His private laboratory, a long, low stone building, was separated from his home by an ornamental garden.

The crushed tube lay on his work bench. The odd object Jeff had thought might or might not be a lens was mounted in a testing clamp.

"The police told me you recommended me," Brock said with a grin. He was a tall, slender, gray-haired man with a neatly-trimmed beard, and he spoke with a marked English accent. "I suppose you meant it as a compliment, but you are going to be as disappointed as the police were. This thing is impossible. It doesn't exist. It can't exist."

Jeff grinned back at him. "That's interesting. When I held it in my hand, I could have sworn it was real."

"I didn't say it was unreal," the professor said testily. "I merely said it didn't exist. Look!"

He aimed a beam of light at the object. "It neither reflects nor refracts light. It *absorbs* light, which is impossible. The light must go somewhere, but it doesn't. On the other hand, this monstrosity emits light from nowhere. In a dark box with no possible light source, it manages to focus a measurable amount of light."

He placed the object in a dark box and closed the lid. The needle on the attached meter swung wildly.

"There is no light source," he said. "There can be no light source. Hence there can be no light. Nevertheless, this thing emits light. And that's impossible. I have tested it with infrared, ultraviolet, and gamma rays, and it is opaque to all of them, which also is impossible. Ionization is present—it fogs film—but the pulses are irregular, and *that* is impossible. The police said this was found near the scene of a violent death. Was anything else found there?"

Jeff shook his head.

"That's a great pity. I was hoping for another piece of this material for analysis. I would love to know what this thing is made of, but there is no way that could be determined without destroying it."

"Would the results justify destroying it?"

"A chemist would think so. Chemists believe everything can and ought to be analyzed. But what if it is made of devitrified glass? Or what if these peculiar properties are due to trace ingredients in amounts too small to be measured or even identified? I would rather have the lens to experiment with."

"Is it really a lens?" Jeff asked.

"It is hard to say what the function of an opaque piece of glass might be, but I think it is. In that mounting, what else could it be?"

"That was my thought, but the shape of the thing—"

"Ah—the shape. That is impossible, too. But you have reminded me of something."

He tilted back in his chair and meditated, his eyes on the ceiling. "The shape," he said finally. "It has a series of concentric undulations, and someone did come to me with a plan for a lens with some such configuration. That was years ago, and I can't remember who it was or what he thought the undulations would accomplish. But the shape was something like this. I remember that distinctly."

"Was it by chance someone named Johnson?"

The professor straightened with a jerk. "Let's check."

Filing cabinets stood in the corner of the room. The professor went to one containing five by eight cards and opened a drawer. "If this individual's ideas struck me as interesting or unusual—and they probably did, since I remember them—I will have notes about him. Unfortunately, there are thirty-five years of records here."

He thumbed through a section of the cards, thumbed again, and shook his head regretfully. "No," he said, pushing the drawer shut. "If I kept a card on that person, his name wasn't Johnson. I'll run those tests again, and I'll give the chemists a piece of the broken case to analyse. One never knows, there may be something unusual about the wood. Anyway, I'm grateful for the recommendation. An impossible lens doesn't happen to an optics expert more than once in a lifetime."

They walked back to Jeff's car together. Behind them on the work bench, the lens, the broken case, and an assortment of tools that chanced to be nearby, suddenly disappeared.

19

GEVIS

Roszt and Kaynor fled, leaving the girl lying crumpled in the hedge. Egarn leaped to his feet and gazed after them in horror. Arne, deeply puzzled as to what could have happened, leaned forward and stared. Inskel matter-of-factly started to adjust the len to follow the fleeing men, but Egarn snapped, "Leave it." For more than an hour they watched the drama unfolding at DuRosche Court—the people gathering in consternation about the girl, ambulance and medics, her body taken away, the shock and grief displayed by those at the DuRosche mansion.

"What were Kaynor and the girl struggling over?" Arne asked finally. "It looked like—"

"It was his weapon," Inskel said flatly.

"But why would he be carrying it in his hand? Surely there was no danger threatening. It wasn't to be used unless all else failed."

"Everything went too easily for them at first," Egarn said soberly. "Now the police are searching for them, and people are talking about them, and newspapers are printing stories about them, and they were getting jittery. Even so, Kaynor had no reason to carry his weapon in his hand. Something must have frightened him." He turned to Inskel. "Where did they go?"

Inskel first focused on their motel room, where Val was comfortably stretched out on the bed. Roszt and Kaynor weren't there. The dog raised his head hopefully whenever he heard footsteps in the hallway.

Inskel searched the entire neighborhood around the DuRosche mansion, but there was no sign of them.

"They will have to come back eventually, if only to feed and exercise the dog," Egarn said. "I will leave a message for them. They must get out of Rochester. This isn't like a breaking and entering where nothing is stolen. This is a disaster. They must leave at once and go back to Buffalo."

Egarn wrote a stern order. Gevis, who delighted in his expertise with the small machine, deftly landed it on the motel room's table. Then they checked the various hiding places Roszt and Kaynor had established for emergencies. There was no sign of them anywhere. The despairing Egarn finally slept; Inskel continued the futile search. At intervals they focused on the motel room again. It was mid-morning the next dae when they suddenly found the room empty. Roszt and Kaynor had returned for the dog. They also had taken the message but without leaving a reply.

Inskel, hoping the two men were only walking the dog and would soon return, continued to watch the motel, but there was no further sign of them. A maid put the room in order. Then a new guest checked in, a bustling, well-fed, middle-aged businessman, who dropped his suitcase, used the toilet, and then left at once.

Roszt and Kaynor had checked out.

"We need another len," Egarn complained. "I don't know why I didn't think of it before. I thought of using the small len, but it just isn't adequate for this kind of viewing. If we had been able to watch two places at once, we wouldn't have lost them."

Inskel agreed. There was a duplicate in the secret emergency room, but moving anything that bulky through the cramped escape route would be a problem. He said, "Do you want me to try to bring—"

"No," Egarn said. "It is too late now, anyway. We will grind another when we have a chance. Surely they have started for Buffalo. I told them to look up their friend the first thing. He would be willing to help them again if they paid him, and they are going to need help."

"Do you want me to look for them in Buffalo?" Inskel asked.

"Give them time to arrive there and get settled. Then we can watch for them at the check points. You try to get some sleep. Gevis can take your place. We will keep watching that house on DuRosche Court."

Only then did they notice that the young assistant schooler was missing. It seemed so odd that he would absent himself in the middle of a crisis that Arne went looking for him. The guards had come on duty only a short time before, and they knew nothing about him. Finally Arne consulted Fornzt, the housekeeper, who told him Gevis had gone scrounging. "He needed a breath of fresh air, and he thought no one had searched the herders' huts. They are widely scattered, and they don't look like places where one would find anything of value, but he said herders sometimes laid in supplies for an entire eson, including wine. There seemed no harm in looking, so I told him to go ahead."

"It is a pity he didn't tell me," Arne said. "I searched all of the huts in Midlow when I first arrived. What little I found is already in your larder."

"Anyway, he should be back soon," Fornzt said.

In the workroom, Garzot, Inskel's assistant, was watching the DuRosche mansion on the len. Nothing was happening there. Egarn and Inskel were sleeping. When they awoke, they switched the scene to Buffalo and found the checkpoints, but Roszt and Kaynor did not appear.

Neither did Gevis, but it was the two scouts they were worried about. While Egarn, Inskel, and Garzot focused and refocused the len, Arne moved a chair to a remote corner and sat there for some time, meditating. Finally he announced, "Kaynor surely knew how dangerous it was to be carrying the weapon in his hand. He wouldn't have done it without a good reason."

Egarn stopped his fussing with the len's controls. "The girl had been visiting at the house," he protested. "She was on her way home. No one else was near them. What sort of reason could he have?"

"He must have learned something—or suspected something—about that house or someone living there."

Inskel agreed excitedly. "Yes. Of course. If the inventor of the Honsun Len does live there, or even if he comes there occasionally, Kaynor would have been prepared to deal with him. And he would expect him to have a weapon of his own and be able to defend himself."

"If the girl was the Honsun Len's inventor—" Garzot began.

"But she wasn't," Egarn said impatiently. "If they had suspected that, they would have acted differently. Kaynor was trying to pull away from her."

"However it happened, Kaynor must have thought they were close to completing their mission," Arne said. "That is why he had his weapon in his hand. If I am right, they won't leave Rochester until their work is finished, and there is no need to search for them all over the city. All we have to do is keep watching DuRosche Court. They will be back."

"In that case, they certainly will be back," Egarn agreed.

Inskel made the adjustments to bring the DuRosche mansion and its grounds into focus. Egarn sat down with a sigh. "I do hope you are right," he said. He looked about him. "What *has* happened to Gevis?"

When new sentries came on duty at the entrance to the ruins, Ellar, who was acting as head sentry, conferred with Havler, who was to replace him. He remarked that Gevis had gone scrounging and hadn't yet returned.

"That is odd," Havler said. "Where did he go?"

"He went to search some herders' huts," Ellar said. "I don't think he intended to be gone this long, but maybe he found so much he is having trouble carrying it back."

"Maybe he found some wine, and he is having trouble drinking it all," Havler said. Then he added worriedly, "They shouldn't have let him go alone. He was the assistant schooler—probably he had never been outside the village. Now someone will have to look for him."

"He will be back soon," Ellar said confidently.

Half the niot was gone when Gevis finally returned.

Connol, who met him at the checkpoint, had been expecting him for hours. He identified him with a flash of light—as though Gevis's shrill voice wasn't immediately recognizable—and passed him on to Havler.

"What took you so long?" Havler asked.

"I went further than I had planned," Gevis said.

"The way back is always seems further than the way out," Havler said with a chuckle. He obligingly opened the tunnel for Gevis. As he straightened up, Gevis buried a knife in his back, pulled his body aside, and positioned himself to guard the alarm wire. That was the critical point. He had been told that over and over—he must not permit anyone to pull the alarm wire.

Only then did he shout the signal, a "Ho!" that echoed through the trees. The Lantiff, who had been stealthily edging into position in a wide circle around the ruins, surged forward. Sentries shouted the alarm and put up a token resistance, killing a number of the Lantiff with Egarn's weapon and holding the others off long enough for the head sentry to pull the alarm wire and make his own escape—or so they thought. Then they attempted to slip away themselves, but the encircling Lantiff had already blocked all of their escape routes. Arne had not foreseen the possibility of attack by an entire army of Lantiff. The sentries continued to spread death and devastation through the forest until their weapons were exhausted. Then they killed Lantiff with their knives until they bled to death from their wounds. None of them were taken alive.

With the Lantiff fully in control of the surrounding forest, Gevis led a picked squad through the tunnel to the stairwell. He paused while the Lantiff removed their shoes, and then he clumped down the stairs in his usual noisy fashion—members of Egarn's team used this ploy to let the guards below know one of their own was coming—and the Lantiff tiptoed after him, wincing with every step on the metal mesh of the stairs. They halted one flight from the bottom. Behind them a second squad, shoeless like the first, was silently descending half way. Behind it, a third squad was waiting its turn and a fourth was working its way through the tunnel.

Gevis moved haltingly forward through the darkness to the checkpoint where the candle flickered. He performed the prescribed ritual of standing under it and then moved on to the concealed door.

The door swung open. On this night the guard was Larnor, a refugee from the south and a former potter, who had been a special friend of Gevis's. Larnor had an unlikely interest in history, and he had been fascinated with what Gevis told him about the world of the past. He greeted the assistant schooler with his usual question. "Anything moving up there?"

Gevis said nothing was moving, but the weather was nice. As Larnor turned to bar the door, Gevis stabbed him in the back—and then had to stab him again because Larnor began to struggle with him. As the potter slumped to the floor, Gevis murmured, "I'm sorry, Larnor—but I don't want to be blown out like a candle."

Gevis pushed the body aside and returned to the corridor, closing the unbarred door behind him. At the stairwell, he whistled softly. The first squad of Lantiff tiptoed to the bottom. The second squad began its descent. The third waited at the top of the stairs to charge down the moment it was needed.

Gevis returned to the door where he had killed Larnor. The Lantiff followed cautiously at a distance. Now everything depended on the next guard post, where two men were posted. They had to be killed before either could give the alarm.

Gevis was challenged, gave the password, "Green," and waited tensely for the door to open. The Lantiff were already edging forward. Once inside, Gevis stabbed Dayla and turned to grapple with Lanklin. Dayla, fatally wounded but not yet dead, almost reached the alarm wire before the Lantiff were upon them. Lanklin was cut down; Dayla was hauled away from the wire and hacked repeatedly.

Now there were no more guard posts to pass. Unless they had the bad luck to encounter a member of the team who was off duty, they could count on complete surprise. The two dead guards were dragged outside, and the first squad of Lantiff waited just beyond the door for the second to arrive with a battering ram. Gevis closed the door and settled himself in the duty position. If anyone looked into the corridor from the other end, he would pretend to be acting as guard while Lanklin and Dayla had a break.

When all was ready, the Lantiff lit their torches. Gevis pivoted the section of brick wall for them, and they swept through the rooms where the off-duty men were sleeping. All of them were dispatched before they could struggle out of their blankets. Fornzt, cooking a meal, was cut down at his stove.

Only the steel door to the workroom remained. The Lantiff poised themselves to rush it. When they were in position, Gevis went to the pipe by the door, tapped the prescribed signal, and identified himself. Scrapping noises could be heard as the bars were removed. As the door began to open, the Lantiff rushed it.

*   *   *

It was the battle-wary Arne who responded to Gervis's signal—the others were occupied with adjustments to the len. He had opened the door only a crack when the Lantiff began their charge, but that glimpse was as much as he needed. He was neither startled nor frightened; he had seen thousands upon thousands of Lantiff, in far more threatening guises. He slammed the door shut, braced himself against it, and called for help. The stout latch and Arne's weight withstood the first rush; Inskel had the bars in place before the second.

They were confounded—the enemy at the door, no alarm given—but there was no time to wonder what had happened, no time to ponder Gevis's apparent treachery, no time even to indulge their astonishment. Egarn and Garzot hurried into the sleeping room where the opening to the secret tunnel was located. Inskel went to the instruments and set all of the controls askew before he hurried after them. Arne hung back until Inskel called that the others were safely away. Then, with one of Egarn's weapons, he drilled several holes through the door—and through the Lantiff congregating beyond it. The tremendous crash of his weapon drowned out the screams from the room beyond. Then he followed Inskel.

Inskel slid a panel into place behind them to conceal the secret entrance. His candle showed a tunnel stretching broadly ahead of them to a point where it curved out of sight—but that was a blind. The real escape tunnel was at one side, a hole barely large enough to crawl through. Inskel followed Arne into it. After they had inched their way along it for a few meters, he brought the ceiling down behind them. He did this four more times before they reached the end.

But that was only the beginning of the labyrinth. They labored long through concealed tunnels and passageways, each with its artfully hidden entrance, before they finally arrived at the emergency quarters Fornzt had prepared for them.

Egarn was still panting wildly from his frantic, panicky struggle through the narrow passageways. His chest was heaving violently; suddenly he pitched forward. Arne caught him, and Inskel pushed a chair into place for him.

"What happened?" Egarn gasped.

"Treachery," Arne said grimly. "The one thing we couldn't guard against."

"Treachery? Gevis?"

"It would seem so."

"Why?"

Arne shook his head.

Now there were only four of them—Egarn, Garzot, Inskel, and Arne. They sadly agreed that everyone else must be dead or captured, but they had no time for lamentations.

The room looked like the workroom they had just left except that it was larger, and there was no separate room for sleeping. Beds were placed along the walls. A small storage room had well-stocked shelves. There were large crocks of water. Fornzt had prided himself on keeping this—and an escape room on the other side of the ruins intended for the remainder of the team—ready for use.

The instruments looked identical to those in the room they had just left except for one, a small box with a len. Inskel busied himself with it. He made an adjustment, made another, and suddenly an image formed on it of the workroom they had fled from. At that moment, the Lantiff finally broke in.

The picture, of events so close in space and time, was surprisingly clear—far more so than any representation the large len produced. They watched with rage while the Lantiff poked into their possessions and gaped at the machines. Several went into the sleeping room and emerged a moment later, bewildered at finding no one there. More Lantiff entered. They began tapping the walls as though looking for hiding places.

Gevis was brought in. In spite of the success of his treachery, his new masters had no fondness for him. They handled him roughly.

Suddenly the Lantiff stiffened to attention. Through the door strode a stately female figure in a striking gold and black uniform. She was an old-young female—only Egarn could have guessed her age and he only because he knew her.

"The Peer of Lant," he murmured. "So she has actually come here. I wonder why. I wonder if she knew I was here."

Another female figure entered—equally tall, equally stately, wearing the same distinctively patterned uniform but in silver and black. Arne found a chair for himself and sat down heavily. "Now I understand," he said. "It is Deline."

"Deline?" Egarn moved closer to the len and squinted at the picture. "That is the Prince of Lant."

"It is the former Prince of Midlow," Arne said.

"She is the Prince of Lant. I know the uniform well. Remember—I was once the Prince of Lant's consort."

"Then the peer has adopted her," Arne said. "I can't say that I am surprised. A warrior peer would consider her an ideal warrior prince."

Gevis was brought forward. He spoke, gesturing with his hands. He was describing the machines—how they worked, what they did.

Inskel swore an involved chain of oaths. "He knows, curse his foul soul. He knows how to operate all of them. I taught him myself."

"His knowledge won't be of much use to him," Egarn said. "He can't interfere with Roszt and Kaynor—he doesn't know how to look for them any more than we do. Anyone he sent into the past would be helpless—he wouldn't have the language, and he would be snapped up at once as an alien or a mental case. Has the escape tunnel from this place been inspected lately?"

"I will do that now," Inskel said.

"Please do. All of you—forget Gevis. We must get back to work."

He was trying to sound cheerful, but the exhausting escape and the loss of those who had looked after him for so long had broken him. Arne persuaded him to lie down and sleep. Even when he finally dozed off, he tossed fitfully. Grief about his friends, combined with the sudden appearance of a nemesis from his past, gave him nightmares.

Garzot focused the large len on the DuRosche mansion. Arne continued to watch the small len. The peer and prince were questioning Gevis. When they didn't care for his answer, one of the Lantiff stepped forward, shook him, and slapped his face. No one loved a traitor.

Inskel finally returned to report the escape tunnel clear except for the exit. Fornzt had ended it a few feet from the surface; he didn't intend for it to be completed unless it was needed.

"You didn't have one of these in the other workroom," Arne observed, indicating the small box and len.

"I made it to use while I was building these machines," Inskel said. "Only Fornzt, Egarn, and I knew about this room, which meant there was no way Egarn could send for me if he needed me. I used this len to watch the other workroom while I worked. Then Egarn could signal if I was wanted."

"Will it show the present anywhere else?"

"I suppose. All I was interested in was the other workroom."

"You could have followed the war from here—watched every battle."

Inskel shrugged. "We couldn't have done anything to help, and it would have interfered with our work."

Garzot continued to watch DuRosche Court on the large len. Every few minutes he surveyed the nearby streets; then he searched the mansion's grounds and briefly focused the len on its front door. It was high noon in Rochester, and very little seemed to be happening. Very little ever happened at DuRosche Court. Early each afternoon, Calvin DuRosche was taken down the invalid ramp for a brief airing. Mrs. Halmer pushed his wheelchair the length of the drive and back. Then either Mr. Kernley or the decrepit-looking handyman, Hy, helped her push it up the ramp again. Otherwise, Hy, and occasionally Mr. Kernley, did a little yard work. They were the only ones seen outside until the woman employees left for the day. Hy dug in the garden; he trimmed bushes; he raked some of the previous year's leaves from places that were heavily overgrown. Whatever he did, he seemed to tire or loose patience quickly and move on to something else.

The task of watching nothing happen quickly bored Arne, and he returned his attention to the scene in the old workroom. The drama being enacted there reached some kind of conclusion. Chairs were brought in. The peer, her advisors, and the prince seated themselves, and Gevis resumed his demonstration of the large len.

"Deline may have noticed something suspicious about the ruins," Arne said thoughtfully. "The Peer of Lant told her about Egarn, and since we have the weapon, they suspected Egarn was at work here and posted a watch—which caught Gevis on his way to the herders' huts. Then the new Prince of Lant persuaded him to change sides."

Egarn was awake again. "Corrupted him into changing sides!" he snorted.

"Well—" Arne smiled sadly. "She can handle her wiles compellingly, and Gevis was already in love with her. All the young men in Midd Village fell in love with her when she was my assistant."

Egarn turned curiously. "How do you know that? Did the first server also hear confessions?"

"He heard a great many complaints," Arne said. "All of the young women complained about her influence on the young men. Gevis was in love with her, she left, his world was shattered by the Lantiff invasion, and he had nothing at all to look forward to except the end of everything when Roszt and Kaynor succeeded. Suddenly the Lantiff seized him, and he found he could choose between rewards and punishment. Not only were the rewards alluring, but he discovered he might have a future after all. What I don't understand is why the Lantiff were slapping him. He gave them exactly what they wanted."

"That is the Peer of Lant's way," Egarn said sourly. "Her word is good—if she promised him rewards, he will get rewards. But she will also have him punished severely for not coming to her voluntarily."

They watched the dae pass in Rochester, and then another. On the morning of the girl's funeral, a black limousine called at the mansion for those attending. After the funeral, it returned with them. Later, a young couple arrived. There seemed to be nothing out of the ordinary about them, but when the fat caretaker handed them something in a cloth, Egarn leaped up with a shout of dismay. A continuous flicker of light showed in it.

"It is a len!" he exclaimed. "They have a Honsun Len!"

Inskel focused on it as closely as he could, and they made out the fragment of black tube with a len in the end of it. "Part of Kaynor's weapon," Egarn breathed. "It broke off in the struggle."

They forgot their search for Roszt and Kaynor. Inskel kept the len focused on the weapon fragment all the way to police headquarters, where it was fingerprinted and photographed, and then to a suburb where an elderly, bearded man took charge of it. In a building behind his dwelling, he began to perform what Egarn recognized as scientific tests.

"A scientist!" Egarn exclaimed. "It is the worst thing that could have happened! I wonder who he is."

Inskel managed to focus on the dwelling's mail box. The scientist's name, Marcus Brock, and his street number, were displayed in luminous letters that were dazzlingly clear on the len. Of course the name of the street wasn't given.

"This is terrible," Egarn wailed. "Even if Roszt and Kaynor kill the inventor, there will still be an expert there who knows all about the len."

"Then they will have to kill him, too," Inskel said indifferently. "But maybe it won't be necessary. If we were to snatch it back—"

"Do it! Now!"

But the instrument had to be adjusted to the new location. Then the first attempts failed—perhaps one of the scientist's instruments produced a temporal distortion. They were still trying when the young man they had seen at DuRosche Court called on the scientist. The left off their efforts and waited for him to leave—Egarn was reluctant to snatch things while people were watching.

Their opportunity came when the older man turned off his instruments and escorted the young man back to his car. Inskel, with several quick passes, snatched the len, the clamp that was holding it, the piece of the weapon's tube, and several of the scientist's smaller tools.

"That settles that," Egarn said with satisfaction. "Not only do we have the len back, but the police have lost important evidence. If I had thought of this sikes ago, I could have equipped an entire laboratory with tools and equipment and saved myself a lot of trouble. Now—back to DuRosche Court!"

It was late afternoon when Inskel managed to focus on a passing car with Roszt at the steering wheel and Kaynor seated beside him. The two men had taken the precaution of changing cars—this one was a more recent model than any they had owned previously. It even had an opening in the roof. Egarn thought it much too conspicuous.

The scouts made a leisurely circuit of the neighborhood. Then, by a devious route, they drove to one of Rochester's parks where they did nothing at all for a time. When they finally left, they went directly back to the DuRosche Court neighborhood and made another leisurely circuit.

"They can't see much from the car," Inskel said. "Why don't they walk?"

"Too many people know their descriptions," Egarn said. "They aren't so recognizable in the car. They are being cautious and sensible, but I would feel better if they were miles away. I understand what they are doing, though. They are looking for something, but they are afraid they will arouse suspicion if they hang around the neighborhood too long. They must consider it important. I wish I knew what they have found out about this place."

In the old workroom, Gevis was conducting another demonstration. Peer, prince, and the peer's high advisors were grouped around the large len, staring. Arne knew how they felt—he had stared himself when he caught his first glimpses of the past. He wondered what Gevis was showing them.

Egarn was unconcerned about it. "At least it is giving the peer something to occupy herself with, and that keeps her from wreaking havoc somewhere else."

The afternoon waned; dusk set in. Roszt and Kaynor continued to make an occasional trip through the neighborhood. Not until it was completely dark did they park four blocks from the DuRosche mansion and set out on foot.

Blending with every tree and shrub they passed, they moved slowly toward DuRosche Court. They were only a block away when they stopped abruptly and slipped sideways behind a bush. There they remained, motionless, while those watching the len stirred impatiently. Egarn said for the tenth time, "I do wish I knew what they are looking for."

Suddenly a parked car at the end of the block started up. Its lights came on, and it slowly moved away. It was a police car.

Egarn took a deep breath. "Did any of you notice it? I didn't.

But they did. They certainly have developed their instincts. I don't doubt they know what they are doing. I just wish I knew what it is."

Roszt and Kaynor didn't stir for some time after the police car had gone. Then they began to move slowly, again blending with the shrubs and trees. They stealthily passed the entrance to DuRosche court and the drive to the house—both of which were well-lighted—and proceeded along the sidewalk to the break in the hedge where they had met the girl. They slipped through it and began moving across the grounds, two indistinguishable dark figures zigzagging from shrub to shrub through the darkness. They were approaching the house when Hy suddenly loomed beside them and swung his piece of pipe viciously.

He was recognizable even among the indistinct shapes on the flickering len because of his short stature and white shirt. The dark figure closest to Hy jerked away, but the pipe hit him solidly on the arm and must have hurt. The arm hung limply. Hy dropped the pipe, grabbed him, and drew back his knife.

Lightning flashed, impaling Hy and several bushes beyond him. Hy crumpled; the two dark figures slipped away into the night.

The handyman must have screamed. Yard lights came on. Only seconds passed before a police car turned in at DuRosche court and came quickly up the drive. Mr. Kernley came from the house armed with a flashlight and probed about the grounds with it. The beam came to rest on Hy's still body.

Egarn said brokenly, "Now they really must leave Rochester—and quickly. Whatever it is they have found, they will have to leave it. It won't be safe for them to be seen there again—not for sikes. The girl's death could be written off as an accident, but this time they were trespassing, and the handyman was guarding his employer's property. They are certain to get a long prison sentence. They can't finish their mission now. They don't dare."

20

ROSZT AND KAYNOR

Roszt and Kaynor also realized their time had run out, but they knew better than to leave Rochester immediately. Egarn had taught them more thoroughly than he realized. To leave a motel room without checking out would attract attention. To check out in the middle of the night would attract attention. Whatever the cost, they must avoid attracting attention.

Inskel, having seen them park their car four blocks from the DuRosche mansion, had no difficulty in picking them up there with the large len and following them to their new motel, and a terse order from Egarn arrived at their room almost as soon as they did. They ignored it. They were certain they had escaped cleanly. No one could have noticed them or their car in the dark, and just to be certain, they had driven several blocks with their lights off before they took a circuitous route to the motel. They saw no point in altering a routine they had complete confidence in.

And they were exhausted. They awoke at six the next morning and quickly packed their suitcases. Kaynor walked Val while Roszt went to the office to check out. When Kaynor returned, he put dog and suitcases in the back seat and drove the car to the office at the front of the motel to wait for Roszt.

It was almost seven o'clock by then, a popular time for checking out, and Roszt had to wait in line. He exchanged pleasantries with the clerk—they had enjoyed their stay, he murmured, and hoped to return soon—pocketed his change and the receipt, and strolled out to the waiting car like a man without a worry to his name, not to mention a possible murder or two.

The car rolled down the motel's drive to the street, waited for traffic to clear, and then drove off. In the new workroom, Egarn finally felt able to relax. He had acquired enough of a feel for the city to know the two scouts would soon be on the network of expressways that ringed and bisected Rochester, and these would take them away from the city as rapidly as they cared to drive. Inskel made the necessary adjustments and followed their flight with the len.

*　　　*　　　*

A far more dramatic scene was occurring in the restaurant adjoining the office of the motel they'd just left. Alida's friend Connie, the petite brunette, was a waitress there, and she passed the door just as Roszt strolled out to the car. She had read every description of the fugitives she could find, and somehow this character seemed to *fit*—whammo! And there was the second character waiting for him in the car! She set plates of food down on an unoccupied table and dashed outside. While Kaynor was waiting for traffic to clear, Connie hastily scribbled a license number on her order pad.

She hurried back inside. The restaurant's hostess, appalled by this breach of discipline, raised her voice a full fifty decibels above the husky whisper with which she greeted guests. "Connie!"

Connie murmured something about an emergency and dashed to the pay telephones in the lobby. When she returned, the manager was waiting for her in a towering fury. If the food was refused because it was too cold to eat, he thundered, she would pay for it herself.

Connie smiled, a martyr to a noble cause, and went to apologize to her customers.

Bob had been living and sleeping by the telephone ever since Janie's funeral. He sat in a daze for a moment, staring at the license number and car description he had scribbled, and then he got out a list of numbers and began to make calls.

So it was that cab drivers' radios all over Rochester suddenly received Code J reports with a license number and a description of the car just seen leaving the Fortley Motel with the two wanted men and a large black dog. Vehicles with citizen band radios heard something similar. So did truckers.

It was a motorcyclist with a CB radio who first spotted the car. He had just exited Interstate 490. The car was a short distance behind him, and when he glanced back at the highway, he saw it. He couldn't verify the license number, but it was the correct make and year with two men in front and a large, black dog hanging its head out of a rear window. He passed on the information, which was immediately relayed on all the networks.

The driver of a semi-trailer picked up the car next as it took the interchange to Interstate 590 and headed south. "Do tell!" he breathed. "My very first Christmas present of the year!" He reached for his microphone.

* * *

Roszt and Kaynor were astute observers—they had to be, to accustom themselves to an utterly strange civilization—and they knew how traffic normally moved. As 590 threaded its way through pleasant, open country, they suddenly decided they didn't like the behavior of the large truck that was following them. It moved out as though to pass, and Kaynor was conscious of the driver's scrutiny as the truck's cab pulled even with them. Then, for no reason at all, it dropped back again. Now it was following far more closely than normal in scattered traffic.

After a few seconds of that, Kaynor began watching for an exit. A sign ahead of them announced East Henrietta Road, Highway 15A, and he flipped his turn signal. Then he scowled. The driver of the truck had turned on his signal the moment he saw Kaynor's. They exited onto East Henrietta and drove slowly to give the truck a chance to pass—it was a five-lane road, and traffic was scattered.

The truck remained close behind them.

Kaynor flipped on his turn signal again as they approached Highway 252, Jefferson Road. The truck's signal came on at once. Kaynor slowed until the intersection traffic light was about to change; then he made his turn. The big truck slipped through behind them on the red light, ignoring horn blasts from outraged drivers on Jefferson. Before it could gather speed,

Kaynor mashed his accelerator, and the car shot ahead.

They quickly left the truck far behind. Jefferson Road spanned a long stretch of suburbs south of Rochester. They passed commercial buildings with a scattering of motels; then neat modern structures used for light industry intermixed with a variety of restaurants.

The nosy trucker was no longer in sight by the time they reached the shopping malls and plazas that clustered around the intersection of Jefferson Road and West Henrietta, Highway 15. The overpass took them over West Henrietta, and then, leaving the shopping plazas behind, they emerged in open country with occasional old houses that had shoddy commercial enterprises cluttered around them. Traffic continued light. They passed another semitrailer plodding along in the right lane— and it pulled out and followed them.

Roszt had noticed a look of startled recognition on the driver's face as they passed. It suddenly dawned on him that such vehicles might have radios, just as police cars did, and the enormity of their predicament became clear to him at once. They should have avoided heavily traveled roads where trucks were to be found. He spoke to Kaynor, who swung into the left turn lane. They made the turn, and an impressive complex of buildings loomed ahead of them. Roszt caught the name of the road, Lowenthal, and took their map of Rochester from the glove compartment.

The semitrailer followed them, but Kaynor quickly outdistanced it. They reached the buildings, which were fronted by the National Technical Institute for the Deaf, and turned right. They passed an odd, domed structure and then the vast brick building of the Rochester Institute of Technology. There were several stop signs, but these were to assist traffic exiting from parking lots, and there was no traffic. Kaynor sped through them without stopping and followed curving Andrews Drive to its junction with East River Road. By the time they reached it, Roszt had found their location on the map. If they turned south on East River Road, he thought, they could follow it out of the Rochester area.

The semitrailer was overtaking them. From the south came the sound of a police car approaching, and Kaynor's quick eyes caught the flashing light. Reacting instantly, he made a screeching turn to the north, away from the police car, and drove with the accelerator on the floor.

East River Road, which lay along the east bank of the Genesee River, had only two lanes. There was a steel guard rail along the river and sharp drop to the water just beyond it, but the bank was so overgrown with trees and shrubs that the river was almost invisible. Fortunately there was no traffic. They sped easily along the edge of the Institute of Technology's grounds, but only the dog Val was enjoying the chase. Kaynor kept the accelerator on the floor, but the police car was gradually overtaking them.

Roszt released his seat back and climbed into the rear of the car beside the dog. From his pocket he took a small tube— Egarn's weapon. He steadied it on top of the rear seat and fired once. The beam bored a hole through his own rear window and through the right side of the police car's engine. It also blew the right front tire. The car swerved off the road. There was nothing there for it to collide with, so the officer probably was not injured. At least, Roszt hoped not.

He returned to the front seat. They had reached busy Jefferson Road again, and there were both left-turn and through lanes. Miraculously the light turned green just ahead of them, and they roared through the intersection and entered the town of Brighton.

A short distance beyond, a railway bridge loomed on their left, and the road climbed abruptly to the railway tracks. At the top, they bumped over the tracks and were momentarily airborne when the road suddenly dipped down again.

Just ahead of them, a police car blocked the road, lights flashing. The officer stood beside it, weapon in hand. Beyond him, on the right, was a large building with a paved—but empty—parking lot. Several small boys were playing there with radio-controlled cars. Given a choice between hitting the police car or running down officer and children, Kaynor didn't hesitate. As the car landed, he twisted the wheel to the left.

The heavy growth along the river had resumed again, but there was a break just beyond the parked police car. They bounced wildly out of control, cleared the guard rail, shot through the gap in the trees, soared over a motor boat that was moored to the bank, and hit the water with an enormous splash.

In the new control room, Egarn sat with his face buried in his hands.

*   *   *

Word quickly reached the campus and the row apartments, and friends of Janie's who had access to transportation headed for the river bank. By the time they began to arrive, the motor boat had been moved, and a truck with a winch was waiting to pull the car out. A diver was in the water; he had located the car and was attaching a cable. There were crowds of gawkers on both river banks. The students stood together, Alida and Jeff among them, and Detective Fred Ulling, who had been working on Janie's case and also on the Johnson break-ins, came over to talk with them.

"Is anyone in the car?" Jeff asked.

"No. Talk about your ironic endings! Now I suppose we'll have to drag the river for those characters."

Someone noticed a large, black dog cowering in the shrubbery. It had been in the water; the mob of people obviously frightened it, but it seemed reluctant to leave. Alida said, "I wonder if that's their dog."

She called it. The dog backed away warily. When one of the students tried to grab it, it ran off.

Finally the winch went into operation. The car was hauled to the surface. Water poured from open windows on both sides. The winch hauled it up the bank and onto the road. There was no one in the car. There seemed to be nothing of interest in it except two ordinary-looking suitcases with disgustingly ordinary, soggy contents.

People had begun to drift away. The dramatic event had turned into a non-spectacle. Jeff said, "The bodies will be a mile downstream before they get their equipment here. Shall we go?"

Alida nodded.

*　　*　　*

In the new workroom, the large len showed the river bank. More people came, looked, and went away. Afternoon waned into evening, and then darkness set in. Those in the room were not watching with hope but because there was nothing else they could do. The small len showed Gevis, the peer and prince, and even an assortment of Lantiff watching the large len intently in the old workroom, but Arne couldn't see what it was they found so interesting.

Traffic on East River Road diminished as the niot wore on, and the road was poorly lighted. The scene on the len had become murky when Egarn suddenly cried out. Two dark shapes hauled themselves out of the water. The dog Val was there to greet them, leaping about them excitedly. Both of them embraced the dog. Then they set off on foot.

They followed East River Road as far as Genesee Valley Park, fading into the shadows whenever a car approached. Once in the park, they avoided roads until they reached the old Barge Canal. Then they took the Joseph C. Wilson Boulevard through the University of Rochester campus. Beyond Elmwood Avenue, they angled toward the back of the campus, which ran along the edge of Mount Hope Cemetery. With the dog trotting patiently on their heels, they walked the length of a downward sloping parking lot. The land on their right gradually rose to a steep bluff with the cemetery far above them. On the left were the dark campus buildings.

As the cemetery boundary curved eastward, residence halls loomed on their right, a few of the windows still lighted. Directly ahead was another parking lot, and a cinder walk ran steeply up to the residence halls. They followed the walk until, midway to the top of the slope, a dirt path branched off and angled along the side of the bluff. The path took them to the hole in the Mount Hope Cemetery fence they had located long before. They crawled through it and set out across the cemetery.

Eerie shapes confronted them wherever they looked. On their right were regimented tombstones where Rochester's Civil War veterans were buried in orderly ranks below the statue of a Civil War soldier. Roszt and Kaynor had puzzled over the statue's message on an earlier visit: "On fame's eternal camping ground, their silent tents are spread, and glory guards with solemn round, the bivouac of the dead." Beyond this area, a tall pillar topped with the statue of a fireman marked one dedicated to Rochester's fire fighters.

They threaded their way eastward and then north, dim shadows more ghostly than the ghosts that surrounded them. Exhaustion was evident in every halting stride—even the dog was exhausted—but they moved as quickly as they could until they had left the more open southern part of the cemetery far behind them. They staggered along a sheltered, wooded drive until the land dipped downward into the picturesque dell and they reached the boarded up chapel and crematorium.

It was one of the refuges they had prepared long before by hiding food, blankets, toiletries, and a change of clothing there. Now they simply pulled one of the plywood window coverings open far enough to admit them—they had already loosened it. The dog was lifted up to the window. Then Roszt climbed in and turned to help Kaynor. The board was pulled into place after them. Because they had left the padlock on the door intact, the casual passerby or even the cemetery's employees, would think the building empty and safely locked.

They changed their clothing. They ate and fed the dog. Then they wrapped themselves in blankets and fell asleep at once huddled on either side of the warm dog.

Their peril had been enormous. It still was. Their escape, however skillfully managed, was only temporary. Egarn knew they wouldn't be safe until they were far from Rochester. He also knew they would never get out of the city unless they got rid of the dog. "Two men with a large black dog" was a tag anyone could remember and apply. Probably that was why they had been followed so easily. They were marked men as long as Val was with them. They would have to get rid of the dog and separate.

It was cruel to them and to the dog, but it had to be done. Egarn wrote a message, explaining this. Inskel transferred it, landing it a mere three feet from the sleeping men's heads. Then he adjusted the large len to show an outside view of the old building, spectral in the moonlight.

In the new workroom, everyone felt as exhausted as Roszt and Kaynor had been. All except Garzot went to bed and to sleep.

Garzot awakened them with a shout. The scene on the len was unchanged except for a black figure that stood statue like in front of the building. While they stared, another figure appeared. Then another.

They turned to the small len. Gevis was sending Lantiff into the past. One at a time they positioned themselves beneath Egarn's large instrument, Gevis pulled the cord, and they vanished—to appear on the large len in front of the old building where Roszt and Kaynor slept.

Before those in the new workroom had fully grasped what was happening, there were six Lantiff gathered around the chapel door. One of them applied Egarn's weapon to the lock. As the lock fell away, the others charged the door. They rushed inside the building before Garzot could adjust the len to follow them.

He refocused on a scene of ghastly horror. Roszt and Kaynor were dead, their throats cut. The dog had been stabbed repeatedly. All three had died before they could wrest themselves from the fog of exhausted sleep.

Lantiff were searching the bodies with care. The well-filled money belts, Egarn's weapons, the odds and ends Roszt and Kaynor had carried in their pockets were placed in a neat pile at the far end of the room. Suddenly the pile disappeared. On the small len, they saw Gevis beginning to sort through the dead men's possessions.

"He uses the machine more skillfully than I do," Inskel said bitterly. "What will happen to the Lantiff? He can't bring them back. Not for a long time."

"Why would he bother?" Egarn demanded. "Lantiff are soldiers and therefore expendable."

The large len followed the Lantiff as they hurriedly left the cemetery by the route Roszt and Kaynor had followed to reach it. Dawn was approaching when the six black-cloaked figures moved quickly through Genesee Valley Park. By the time it became light, they had found themselves a hiding place in thick shrubbery along the river some distance north of where Roszt and Kaynor had made their plunge. As soon as they were settled there, Gevis dispatched a quantity of rations to them. The Lantiff ate; then they lolled about as though waiting for their next assignment.

"We were terribly, terribly wrong," Egarn said brokenly. "I said the Lantiff couldn't survive in the past, but of course they can—as long as Gevis provides them with whatever they need. Not that it would matter to the Peer of Lant either way. She can send another six, or sixty, or six thousand if she wants to. She has them to spare, and they are dedicated to dying for their peer." He turned away wearily. He had tears in his eyes. "It was a miserable death for two gallant men."

"I was the one who didn't think," Arne said angrily. "I easily could have cut the machines to pieces as I left. Instead, I killed a few Lantiff—as if any number of dead Lantiff made any difference. I will go back and do it now." He asked Inskel, "Is it possible to get through that tunnel again?"

"No," Inskel said. "It would be an enormous task to clean it out—and dangerous. The cleared dirt would have to be carried back through the tunnel, and now that the ceiling has been disturbed, it might keep on collapsing. The Lantiff would hear you coming and be waiting for you. It would be better to use our escape route and fight your way back down the stairway—but you couldn't do that, either. There are too many Lantiff."

"None of us were thinking," Egarn said. "It happened so quickly, and we never dreamed a traitor would show the Lantiff how to use the machines. This is the end of everything. We have failed utterly—unless I go back myself and try to finish what Roszt and Kaynor started." He broke into sobs. "But I am so tired—and what chance would I have against an army of Lantiff?"

"Send me," Arne said. "I have fought armies of Lantiff before."

"No. You would be helpless."

"No more than the Lantiff. You can send me what I need."

"No." Egarn shook his head. "The Lantiff's task would be different from yours. All they would have to do is keep you from carrying out your mission. They could arrive in the night, cut your throat, and then hide—as we saw. They don't need training for that. You would have to resume the search for the right Johnson and keep him from inventing his len. Look how difficult it was for Roszt and Kaynor despite their sikes of study. The Lantiff would kill you before you learned to find your way around the city."

"We can't simply quit," Arne said stubbornly. "Even if I don't know enough to do it, I still have to try."

Egarn straightened up and squared his shoulders. "You are right. The task has become impossible, but we can't quit. We will go together. We will arrive in Rochester—in one of the parks or the cemetery—as soon as it is dark. Unlike the Lantiff, I will be able to talk to people. I can show you how to behave, and after watching Roszt and Kaynor for so long, I know the city well. So we will have some important advantages. We can find a motel room to work from, and I know exactly what we must do next."

21

ARNE AND EGARN

A police car screamed past on Mount Hope Avenue. And then another. Bob, wearing a sweat suit and jogging shoes, miraculously survived a reckless dash through Mount Hope Avenue traffic and arrived panting at the row apartments. His shouts were inarticulate, but his arm waving was eloquent. Students began pouring out of the apartments.

Bob gasped, "The murderers are dead."

"How do you know?" Ruth demanded.

"They broke into the old chapel." He paused for breath. "A jogger noticed the door smashed open." Another pause. "He looked inside, and there they were."

"What killed them?"

"Don't know."

"Let's go!" Charlie said.

They poured across Mount Hope Avenue, almost stopping traffic, and rushed through the cemetery gate. At the old chapel and crematorium, police were already holding back a crowd. Alida and Jeff were among the latecomers, but they edged their way to the front.

"What has happened?" Jeff asked a police officer.

"It's those two characters we chased into the river yesterday. They holed up here last night, and someone robbed them and cut their throats."

Detective Fred Ulling emerged from the building and walked over to them. "This is more ironic than yesterday," he said. "We can call off dragging the river for these guys, but now we have to start looking for their murderers. If you don't mind an unpleasant sight, Miss Brylon, it would be helpful to know if you have seen these characters before. We are wondering how long they've been hanging around."

"I'll be glad to help," Alida said.

Alida and Jeff followed him into the chapel. The detective leaned over and pulled the blanket away from one body and then from the other. Alida gripped Jeff's arm firmly.

"Yes," she said slowly. "I have seen these men maybe three or four times, but I never connected them with anything. Janie and I saw them crossing the campus one day. Janie joked about them."

"Were they following Janie?"

"No. They were just crossing the campus. They walked past us headed in the opposite direction. I saw them do that at least two other times, and once I saw them over by the Johnson Center."

"Are you sure Janie didn't know them?"

"I'm certain she had never seen them before. What sad faces." Alida went on meditatively, "They looked on all the misery of the universe, and then they died. I thought I would hate them, but I don't."

"They looked on a lot of misery of their own making, and they died because thieves cut their throats," the detective said.

"What did they have to steal?'" Jeff asked.

"They were wearing money belts—well-filled belts according to the marks left on their skin. The thieves took them and also emptied their pockets.

"Seen enough?" Jeff asked Alida.

She nodded. "It doesn't solve anything. It just raises more questions."

"It certainly does that," the detective said. "Who were they, where did they come from, and what did they want?"

*　　*　　*

In the new workroom, the day was spent committing acts of theft. The large len was shifted to Buffalo and focused on the men's clothing section of a department store. When there seemed to be no one watching, Inskel snatched packaged shirts, underwear, pajamas. Egarn and Arne tried them on; then Inskel snatched again, from adjoining displays, until they were properly fitted. Trousers, sportcoats, and raincoats were a problem—their hangers were difficult to pull from the rack—but after a few tries he managed it. Shoes and slippers, with both members of a pair fastened together, were easy to steal, but it was difficult to find correct sizes.

When they were completely outfitted and supplied with all the spares they needed, he stole a suitcase for them to put the extra clothing in. Then, with Egarn directing him, he ranged through the store sucking up anything Egarn thought they might need: An electric razor, wallets for both of them, wrist watches, handkerchiefs, socks, neckties and tie pins, ball point pens and pocket-sized memo pads, a traveler's alarm clock— anything a traveler might carry with him. They saw no money belts, so they snatched some cloth and sewing supplies, and Garzot made two of them by hand.

Money posed a special problem. Roszt and Kaynor had needed a huge sum that would support them indefinitely and allow for expensive purchases like automobiles. Egarn and Arne could do with considerably less, but they couldn't risk running short. Egarn decided to take the money from banks located as far from the scene of their activity as possible just in case there were records of the serial numbers on bills they stole.

They switched to the West Coast, found a large city Egarn didn't bother to identify, and created mysterious shortages in several of its banks.

Finally they had every necessity Egarn could think of, they were packed, they were ready to go. Egarn used the new razor; Arne refused to. He had seen an occasional beard in 20th century society, and he was determined to keep his. While Inskel tried to focus on the time and place chosen for their landing, and Egarn rested, Arne had a last minute errand of his own to perform. With instructions from Inskel, he used the small len to scan the remnants of the war in the east.

His direst predictions had not been fulfilled—yet. Inskor had spread destruction across Lant, burning Lant Court, destroying mills, wrecking roads and bridges, laying waste to the countryside, even raiding the peer's prized stables and seizing her horses. Her people, especially her one-namers, would be suffering greatly, but the only damage the peer suffered would be to her pride. And now Inskor was in trouble, slipping out of one trap after another.

As for the trek south, it was far behind schedule. Inskor had enlarged the military escort after hearing Arne's warning, and the column was still intact. Arne recognized Bernal, so the scout had reached it safely with the train of supplies and the reinforcements. No doubt both had been desperately needed. Now food was in short supply again, Arne's caches were too far apart for the group's slow progress, and it certainly could not reach the south before winter. As a harbinger of things to come, the Peer of Easlon was dead—perhaps killed leading the column, which would have been like her. Arne knew this because the former prince now received a peer's obeisance. Her leadership was certain to be as bold and resourceful as her mother's—but the march was doomed.

When Inskel called them, Arne had seen enough, and he knew would never have the slightest desire to look again. He said nothing to the others about what he had seen, and none of them asked him. As Inskel had already said, there was no way they could help, and worrying about it would interfere with their work.

Egarn and Arne were launched into the past almost without ceremony. There had been no wine since Roszt and Kaynor left; there was no longer a team to see them off. They clasped Garzot's hands and then Inskel's, and then, one after the other, they stepped under the large machine. Inskel put them down in a deserted section of Mount Hope Cemetery shortly after dark. They strolled past the Civil War graves and exited through the same hole in the fence that Roszt and Kaynor had used coming in the other direction. They went down the residence hall path, across the parking lots, and through the campus to Joseph Wilson Boulevard, which they followed along the river.

Egarn was unaccustomed to walking, and by the time the street curved eastward to intersect Mount Hope Avenue, he was exhausted—but this was not even a problem. They hailed a cab, and he told the driver to take them to the Sharber Motel. As he registered for himself and Arne, he carelessly displayed a well-filled wallet to the desk clerk and wondered whether it would be possible to have the same room he'd had several years before. Eying the wallet, the clerk thought it would be no problem at all if the room wasn't occupied, and it wasn't.

In this simple fashion they found themselves installed in the room Roszt and Kaynor had used for so long. They wistfully hoped the two men had left behind something that would be useful—records, notes, documents—but the chambermaid had cleaned thoroughly, and the safe under the bed was unlocked and empty.

"We will have to get along with what we already know," Egarn said. "At least we have arrived safely, and we are ready to to work. Now if this scientist who was trying to study the len has a telephone listing—"

He did. The address was in Penfield, an affluent Rochester suburb, and the street number matched the one they had read on the mailbox. "We will go there now," Egarn told Arne. "If he seems sympathetic, and if I like his looks—and if he will listen to me—I just might tell him the whole story. It will be dangerous, but he is the one person who may be able to understand what we are trying to do, and we will need help—especially now that the Lantiff are interfering." He took two steps toward the door and collapsed.

Arne lifted him onto the bed. His old heart was racing wildly; his face was pale and moist with perspiration. He muttered, "I can't do it. I waited too long." He stared at Arne wildly. "And you can't even speak English. You would be helpless."

"Rest until you are feeling better," Arne suggested. "Then you can make telephone talk with the man."

"No. He would consider it a crank call. We can't do anything unless we are taken seriously."

"Then rest until you are able to write a message. Invite him to come here. I will take it to him."

Egarn shook his head. "No. You wouldn't be able to say a word. He would think you were a mental case and notify the authorities. Even with me there to explain things, this will sound preposterous. I will have to talk fast to keep us from being thrown out."

"I can show him this," Arne said. "Then he will take me seriously."

He held up one of two small tubes he carried in his pocket. Egarn's weapon.

"Yes," Egarn agreed. "Yes—that is what you must do. He has already seen the end the girl broke off Kaynor's. He is a scientist. If I offer tell him what it is, and where it came from, and how it works, he certainly will come. Yes. Let me rest for a moment, and then I will try to write."

He wrote a letter on the motel's stationery. Then he read it over and carefully rewrote it. A lifetime had passed since he composed anything in English, and he had difficulty thinking of words. On a separate sheet he wrote the scientist's address in Penfield for Arne to show the cab driver. He also gave Arne a blank sheet of stationery with the motel's name and address so Arne could show it to another cab driver if he had to return alone. If that happened, they would have to go into hiding until they found out whether the scientist had alerted the police.

After listening patiently to a long lecture about what he must and must not do, Arne put Egarn to bed, saw that he was resting comfortably, and slipped quietly from the room.

He was enormously worried about the old man. At that very moment, the six Lantiff might be leaving their retreat by the river bank and trekking toward the center of the city, and they would find Egarn exhausted and helpless—as they had found Roszt and Kaynor.

But Arne had no choice. The quest had become his.

He told the cab driver, "Penfield."

"What was that?" the driver demanded.

Arne repeated the word twice while the driver, twisting his body so he could stare into the back seat, scrutinized him severely. The driver saw a decently dressed young man with long hair and a beard, apparently sober, probably not an addict. He talked like a foreigner, in which case he was harmless and likely to tip well. "Sure," he said. "What address."

Arne handed him the slip of paper.

The driver glanced at it, returned it, said cheerfully, "Gotcha," and drove off.

The trip, through the night-time strangeness of a vast metropolitan area, seemed interminable to Arne and confusing beyond the scope of reason. He'd had no idea how fond the people of the past were of words and letters. Occasionally he had seen these displayed in scenes the large len showed them, but he hadn't realized that the night sky would be ablaze with them—for what purpose he couldn't imagine.

Eventually they put the city's clutter behind them. The scientist lived in an area of widely-scattered, wealthy-looking homes. His house was set far back from the road in a wooded, park-like setting, and they followed a winding drive to the front door. Outside lights came on while Arne was getting out of the cab. He read the fare on the meter, deftly calculated a fifteen percent tip, and added another five per cent for unusual service. As first server of the Peerdom of Midlow, he'd had to be adroit in figuring percentages—that was how he apportioned food among the villages—and he had learned about numbers and money when Roszt and Kaynor were studying them. He paid the driver and watched the cab roll away before he mounted the steps.

The door opened as he reached the stoop. The man who faced him through the screen door was same tall, slender, bearded man he had watched doing tests on the len. Arne felt comfortable in his presence at once because of the beard. A civilization of clean-shaven men, along with so many women with long hair, gave him a sensation of inferiority everywhere he turned. To Arne, all of them were peeragers.

The man said—testily, as though he didn't welcome being disturbed by late callers—"Yes?"

Arne said, "Marcus Brock?"

For a moment he thought the man was going to deny his own identity, but it was only Arne's pronunciation that he was denying. "Marcus Brock," he said, making it sound very different. "That's me. What do you want?"

"Have let-ter," Arne said and offered it.

The professor opened the screen door. "Come in."

He escorted Arne into a large room that seemed packed to the bursting point with meaningless clutter, got him seated in a plushly cushioned chair, and sat down nearby to read the letter. When he finished, he studied Arne doubtfully for a moment, and then he read it again.

"You are Arne?" he asked finally.

Arne pointed to himself. "Arne."

"And you don't understand English. 'Saving Earth from destruction' sounds serious," he went on good-naturedly, "but surely it isn't imperative to rescue it at this hour of the night. On the other hand, I certainly would like to know where that lens came from, and how it was made, and what it was used for. A pity you don't speak English. Is there any other language we could communicate in? *Parlez vous francais? Sprechen sie Deutsche?* No? But I suppose the person who wrote this letter speaks English well enough. He says you have something to show me."

Arne was gazing at him bewilderedly.

"Show me——" The professor glanced again at the letter. "Show me len."

Arne got up and went to him, holding out Egarn's weapon. He repeated the words Egarn had taught him. "Danger. Not touch. Look."

Brock squinted carefully at the end that was extended to him. When he'd had time to recognize it as identical to the fragment he had seen, Arne obligingly let him see the len in the other end.

Brock got to his feet. "The letter also mentions a demonstration. De-mon-stra-tion. Never mind, I'm sure you know."

He led Arne through rooms full of strangenesses, pausing along the way to take a handlight from a drawer. They exited through a rear door, and Brock's handlight picked out a path. They moved past flower beds and a garden, past Brock's workroom, and finally into a gully at the back of the property where a small stream flowed. Arne selected a huge boulder as his target. Lightning flashed, there was a crash of sound, and the professor hurried forward to wonderingly examine the smooth hole bored through stone. Arne waited, tube in his hand, in case another demonstration was needed.

It wasn't.

Brock led him back to the house and to the room they had occupied before. "Wait," he said and left Arne there. Arne seated himself and waited. He heard voices in a distant part of the house. Then the professor returned carrying a jacket.

"Are we going to the motel the stationery came from?" he asked. "I keep forgetting you can't understand. Where—are—we—going? Where—"

Arne showed him his own piece of stationery.

"At least it's a respectable address," Brock said. "Let's go."

He led Arne through a different door and into a room where two automobiles were parked. They got into one of them, and Arne turned wide-eyed to watch the wall behind them rise up and fold against the beams overhead. They backed out and drove away.

The night-time strangeness looked just as confusing to Arne on the return trip. At the motel, Egarn responded to the signal Arne tapped. He greeted Brock warmly; the two shook hands. Then they sat down to talk.

And talk.

And talk.

Egarn used up the remaining stationery and much of his pocket notebook drawing diagrams. The two men forgot about Arne, who finally stretched out on the bed and fell asleep.

It was almost dawn when Egarn shook him awake. Brock was talking on the telephone. "He thinks we aren't safe here,"

Egarn said. "Probably he is right. If Gevis finds out where we are, it would be only too easy for him to land a company of Lantiff in the parking lot. One of us would have to keep alert all the time, and there are things that must be done. So we will check out immediately. Brock is asking friends to look after me. They will take me to a safe place—even Brock won't know where are—but he can get in touch with me by telephone whenever he needs to. I know you wouldn't enjoy being hidden away with nothing to do, so you can go with him. Help him as much as you can and guard him well—before this day is over, the Lantiff may be after him, too."

"I can't give him much help when I can't talk with him," Arne complained.

"You can recognize a Honsun Len when you see it. Except for me, you are the only person in the world—at this moment—who can."

Brock hung up and turned to them. "Ready to go?"

He drove them to the office and waited outside with his motor running while the night clerk performed the necessary paperwork to check them out. Egarn explained that they had been called away by a business emergency but hoped to return in a day or two. The clerk diffidently accepted a large tip and breathed, "Yes, sir! We will be happy to have you back, sir."

They drove away. After threading through the downtown area, Brock turned south on Mount Hope Avenue. "He hates war as much as we do," Egarn told Arne. "He will see that the len is destroyed if he can find a way to do it. Separating us is his suggestion. Then if something happens to one of us, the other can fight on."

They turned onto Joseph Wilson Boulevard. When they reached the university campus, a parked car blinked its lights at them. They slowed and came to a stop beside it. Egarn clasped Arne's hand.

"I will be all right," he said. "You are not to worry about me. You have a job to do."

He stumbled awkwardly from the car, swung his own door

shut behind him, and scrambled into the other car. Both vehicles drove away quickly.

Arne leaned back in the rear seat and worried about Egarn. He doubted Brock's friends could be trusted to guard him properly. However capable they were, they would know nothing about dealing with an utterly ruthless Peer of Lant who possessed the means of sending an army through time. They wouldn't even be able to imagine such a thing.

22

PROFESSOR MARCUS BROCK (1)

Brock, too, was worried about Egarn, but his concern was for the incredible tale Egarn had told. He wondered if he were the biggest fool in the universe for believing it. The weapon Arne carried in his pocket fully explained what had happened to the dead handyman and the police car. Unfortunately, it was an explanation that couldn't be used, and no one would believe him without it. Egarn had furnished plenty of detail—including descriptions of the tools missing from Brock's workbench after the strange lens had mysteriously disappeared—but no one would believe that, either.

Brock had no worries at all about Egarn's safety. His friend was Colonel Jacques Lobert, a former army officer with police connections, and Brock had told him Egarn was a scientist connected with an ultra top-secret project. Espionage agents would certainly try to assassinate him if they got a chance. They had already killed two of his colleagues—maneuvered them into a police chase, and then, when that didn't finish them off, cut their throats, as the colonel no doubt had read in the papers. A third man, the handyman Hy Hyatt, was also murdered, but Brock wasn't at liberty to talk about that or about the method the fugitives had used to disable a police car. He didn't have to—one of the newscasts had made a highly publicized reference to a death ray.

"They," the espionage agents, were clever, fantastically competent, and completely ruthless. Egarn had to be taken to a hiding place with all of the slight-of-hand the colonel could manage, or he certainly would be followed. Then he had to be guarded, not by one man, but by several, with automatic weapons. "They" were capable of marshalling a small army if that quantity of brute force was required.

Brock and the colonel were were long-time friends and not

given to practical joking, but the colonel still might have accused the tee-totaling professor of drinking too much had he not known how mystified the police were about those three deaths and the damage to the police car. "I'll take the situation as you describe it," he said. "But when this is over, I want a complete explanation."

"You shall have it," Brock promised. "There simply isn't time for that now. This really is urgent."

So the colonel had taken Egarn. He and several of his friends would play musical chairs with him, passing him from car to car—when they weren't passing someone else from car to car as a decoy—until they were certain they had lost any pursuit. They would do the job thoroughly, and Brock hoped "thoroughly" would be sufficient. He had no idea how efficiently "they" could spy on such manipulations with the time-peeper Egarn had described. Eventually Egarn would be taken to a motel in a neighborhood where traffic and business congestion would make any kind of a surreptitious attack difficult.

The colonel and his friends were delighted to have a pseudo-military operation to relieve the tedium of their retirements. They were capable of being ruthless themselves, and they would keep Egarn under constant guard until the problem was resolved or until Brock had convinced himself the whole thing was the figment of someone's very active imagination.

Brock also had to account for the young old-looking man who rode so stoically in the back seat. Arne had been a combination prime minister and business manager of a sovereign state, Egarn said, and he had married a girl who would have been the state's next ruler if war hadn't struck. He also had been an important general in that war. None of this seemed believable, but if Brock accepted Egarn, he also had to accept Arne. This certainly was the night for implausible stories.

Driving back to Penfield by the most devious route he could think of, he politely addressed an occasional remark to Arne, but he might as well have been talking to himself. Arne not only didn't understand; he was lost in his own thoughts and didn't seem to hear, either.

When they arrived, he led Arne to a guest room, showed him where the bathroom was—and hoped he understood *how* it was—said, "Sleep," and closed the door. He needed sleep himself. They had a strenuous day ahead of them, and there wasn't much left of the night.

When he awoke—shortly after eight o'clock—his wife had breakfast ready for them. He called Arne, and they went to the dining room and watched her load the table with generous portions of scrambled and fried eggs, ham and sausages, hash brown potatoes, toast with butter, various jams and jellies, coffee, orange and tomato juice. Arne contemplated this profusion of food with deep puzzlement. When he finally understood he was welcome to eat whatever food he chose, Brock was fascinated by his reactions.

The ham and scrambled eggs he accepted readily; the sausages he eyed with deep suspicion and finally refused. He took potatoes and a fried egg but after a tentative taste of each left them on his plate. Neither coffee nor juices appealed to him, but he accepted milk readily. The toast obviously seemed strange at first, but he managed to eat three slices. He rejected the orange marmalade firmly; the strawberry preserves were a great success.

When they had eaten, they went to the living room and waited, Brock tense, Arne completely relaxed. Finally the telephone rang. Brock answered, wrote down a number. Then he made a call of his own and talked with his former student, Dr. Jeff Mardell.

"Now we can go to work," he told Arne. "Egarn is in a motel room with a private phone. We don't know where it is, nor does anyone else, but we can get in touch with him whenever we need to. We are going to assume 'they' are watching everything we do, but I don't think they can trace telephone calls by peeping through time."

Arne listened politely and said nothing.

Brock told his wife, "You had better invite your nephew and his wife over to spend the day with you." He didn't think there would be any danger once he left, but it did seem wise to take a few rudimentary precautions. He also telephoned several of his neighbors to ask them to be alert to strange goings on in the vicinity, and he arranged for the police to check his house periodically until further notice.

When they reached DuRosche Court, Mr. Kernley was at work trimming the shrubs around the mansion's front door. His more than ample waistline created a problem in reaching the lower branches. The handyman Hy may have done very little work, Brock reflected, but he must have been useful for jobs that required stooping.

Brock introduced himself, and Kernley said, "Doctor Mardell just telephoned about you. He said you were coming."

"Several of us are highly concerned about the strange things that have been happening here," Brock said. "We are afraid they will go right on happening if we don't figure them out."

"We are worried, too," Kernley confessed. "We can't understand what those men were trying to do. Poor Hy—he wasn't worth much, he was just about the laziest critter under the sun, but he could do good work when he wanted to. Certainly he never harmed anyone. To die like that—but the police said one of the thugs had quite a bruise on his arm, so Hy got in at least one good lick. He was a lot braver than any of us gave him credit for, guarding the house with a piece of pipe." Kernley shook his head.

"When is the funeral?"

"Day after tomorrow. We don't plan anything formal. Just Mrs. Kernley, and me, and the maids. As far as we know, no one else knew him. Since he was sort of an employee here, and since in a manner of speaking he was killed on the job, the DuRosche Estate will pay his funeral expenses. Which is fortunate—he had no relatives we know of and of course no insurance."

"Do you mind if I look around and ask questions?"

"Not at all. The police don't seem to be doing a thing, and we would like to have this over and done with. Right now we feel like we are sitting on a bomb that may go off again any minute."

He called his wife to the door and introduced Brock to her. Brock introduced Arne after first rescuing him from the car. Arne kept forgetting how the door handle worked. He nodded politely when he heard his name.

Mr. Kernley returned to his clipping. Mrs. Kernley, who looked sadly subdued and grief-stricken from the continuing tragedy that had enveloped her, asked bitterly, "Have the police figured out what those men were after?"

"No," Brock said. "That is partly why I'm here. We are concerned someone else may try to finish what they started."

"Gracious!"

"I would like to look around and ask you and the maids some questions."

"We certainly have had plenty of experience with that," she said. "The police went through the whole house, but they didn't find anything. Most of it has been closed off for years."

"The police didn't know what to look for," Brock said. "I have to confess I don't, either, but I have a better idea than they did."

"It beats me what those thugs were trying to do. We keep very little money in the house—just enough to pay the paperboy and things like that. Otherwise, I write checks for everything because there has to be a record. It couldn't have anything to do with Mr. DuRosche. He hasn't had any mind at all for years. He is completely helpless. We put him in his chair, and we put him to bed. He has to wear a diaper. Such a pity. He was a wonderful man—so nice. Lots of fun, always making jokes. Everyone liked him. He was invited everywhere. Back in those days I was his cook, and he used to have big dinner parties here. When a man's mind goes, suddenly he is nothing."

"Have you gone through Hy's things?" Brock asked.

"The police did, and it didn't take them long. Hy didn't own much. He lived in the furnace room except when he was off on a bender. Sometimes he would disappear for days or weeks and come back looking a mess. We didn't pay him anything, just gave him a little spending money. He was a quiet type and never made any trouble. Once in a while he was really useful—especially during the winter when there was snow. He mostly did his benders in warm weather. We figured he earned his keep, and all of us liked him. It can get lonely in this big house, and he was company. Once in a while he would come up in the evening and watch TV with us. But land sakes, there was nothing about Hy that anyone needs to investigate! He just happened to be out there guarding the house when the thugs came."

"Every possibility has to be looked into," Brock said.

The jumble of personal effects Hy left behind him certainly didn't seem worth an investigation. He had lived in the basement, going upstairs only for his meals, which he carried back downstairs and ate at an old oak table that an antique dealer would have prized, or to watch TV. He had slept on a camp cot behind the furnace—it was neatly made up with army blankets—and he kept his possessions in a splendid antique oak bureau with a broken mirror and in a rather battered old wardrobe that contained only a worn jacket, a much more severely worn winter coat, and a number of dirty white shirts.

He had worn nothing but the cast-offs he picked up around the neighborhood. Brock wondered how they would dress him for his funeral. Probably the undertaker would provide something appropriate.

There were no books or writing materials among his possessions, so Hy neither read nor wrote. Neither did he look at pictures—there wasn't a single girlie magazine guiltily concealed in the bureau's bottom drawer. He did no drinking at DuRosche Court unless he had a bottle cached somewhere in the depths of the cellar.

Brock sat down on the bed and looked around. Arne did the same, but he was studying the furnace and hot water heater as though he had never seen such contrivances before. Probably he hadn't. The possibility of a *primitive* far future was something Brock had never contemplated.

The present seemed perplexing enough. If he understood Egarn correctly, the only way he could solve this riddle was by connecting a Johnson with it, and the difficulty was compounded by the fact that the Johnson he sought might not show up for years. Egarn hadn't been too explicit about that, but Brock sensed his worry that he had sent his emmissaries too far back in time. Perhaps the vital connection didn't yet exist.

Nevertheless, it had to be searched for.

He asked himself how Hy—that worthy but lazy man—had passed the time when he wasn't downstairs eating or upstairs watching TV. He had no radio. Did he simply lie on his cot and daydream?

The basement was as large as the enormous house and divided into rooms. Its outer walls were built of stones in the fashion of 19th century basements. Several rooms were packed with old furniture—much of which would have interested antique dealers—plus an accumulation of junk that also looked antique. This told Brock something about Calvin DuRosch without helping him in the least.

"I suppose we will have to search the cellar," he said resignedly. "It would help immensely if we knew what we were looking for." Already it was evident he had taken on a considerable job of work. Before he finished, it might even be a career.

Arne's face remained blank, but he quickly grasped what Brock was doing and joined in.

It was Arne who found it—an old foot-locker type of chest that was buried under a stack of empty cardboard boxes in a small, whitewashed room next to the furnace room. Probably the room had been had been a coal bin in the days before oil and gas furnaces. Arne may have noticed the dark green shape under the boxes. He methodically removed one at a time until the chest was uncovered. Brock, passing the door at that moment, helped him solve the puzzle of the latch and open it. It was empty.

As Arne closed it again, Brock noticed faint lettering on the lid. He carried the chest into the furnace room where a lightbulb dangled, wiped dust from it, and stared down at a line of stenciled letters.

It read, "HYACINTH JOHNSON."

"So," Brock said with grim satisfaction. "At last we have a Johnson." He pointed to the word. "Johnson!" he said to Arne.

Arne's face brightened. That was one English word he knew.

"First we telephone Egarn," Brock said. "Then we go over the whole house as thoroughly as possible."

They hurried back up the stairs.

In the hallway outside the invalid's room, they met Dr. Jeff Mardell and Alida Brylon, who greeted Brock warmly. The invalid's room stood open; Calvin DuRosche sat in a chair, bib around his neck, staring straight ahead. Mrs. Halmer, the nurse, was trying to feed him. Mrs. Kernley was watching.

"It is so hard to make him eat," Mrs. Halmer said. "It is as though he keeps forgetting how. We are feeding him constantly, but he chews and swallows so slowly that he hardly takes in enough to keep him alive."

"May I examine him?" Mardell asked.

"I forgot you were a doctor," Mrs. Halmer said. "Go right ahead. Every other doctor in town has had a crack at him. Send the bill to his estate, he can afford it. Unfortunately, any doctor who has seen him once has seen him. The poor man's condition hasn't changed for years."

"I didn't have anything that formal in mind," Jeff said. "It's just that I thought his eyes looked peculiar." He stepped close to DuRosche, scrutinized his face, and then took a penlight from his pocket and shined it into one eye and then the other.

"Strange," he said. "His pupils don't respond to light."

Arne suddenly pushed forward. He, too, stared into DuRosche's face.

"Is this another doctor?" Mrs. Halmer asked in surprise.

Before Brock could answer, Arne turned to him and gripped his arm. "Egarn," he said.

"Yes—I must make that telephone call," Brock said. "We have finally found the mysterious Johnson. It was Hy."

None of them wanted to believe that, not even after Brock described the chest. "Are you saying those two thugs killed him just because his name was Johnson?" Mrs. Kernley demanded. "That isn't possible! How could two strangers he met in the dark for a few seconds find that out? We didn't know it, and he lived here off and on for years. We thought he was Hy Hyatt."

"I don't know," Brock said, "but his name must have been Hyacinth Johnson. He kept the 'Hyacinth' a secret by calling himself Hy—and who would blame him for that? The 'Hyatt' must have been a nickname, or maybe it was his middle name, and for some reason he came to use it instead of 'Johnson.'"

"Then those thugs were looking for all over Rochester for him," Alida said wonderingly. "When they finally found him, they killed him."

"About that, I simply don't know. I am just getting started. I must make my telephone call."

He dialed the number he had been given and asked to speak with Egarn. "We have found the Johnson," he said.

"Thank God!" Egarn exclaimed.

"If you are still worrying about having to murder him, you can stop. It is Hy, the handyman here, and he is already dead. Now I'll see what more I can find out."

He was about to hang up when Arne gripped his arm again. "Egarn!"

"I think Arne wants to talk with you," Brock said. He handed him the telephone. Then he had to show him how to hold it.

*   *   *

Egarn was feeling comfortable and at peace with the world except for the fact that he still felt terribly tired. He was in a spacious motel room, and his guardians treated him royally. The only drawback was the uneasiness he felt in being surrounded by alert men with assault rifles. It reminded him that neither he nor Arne could be safe anywhere.

The news that a link had finally been discovered between the DuRosche house and a Johnson was an enormous relief to him, but the added realization that the Johnson was already dead, that he had been killed by Roszt and Kaynor, had set his mind reeling. Had the scouts from Slorn fulfilled their quest before they died? What, if anything, was supposed to happen when they did? He needed to think.

"What is it?" he asked Arne.

"There is a man here—a rich man who owns this house—"

"Calvin DuRosche. He is an invalid, isn't he? He had a stroke, and he has been sick for years. Is that the one you mean?"

"He isn't sick at all," Arne said flatly. "He is a no-namer."

23

PROFESSOR MARCUS BROCK (2)

Jeff and Alida, Brock, and the Kernleys were being served coffee and hot pecan rolls in the dining room by Mrs. Jefferson. The rolls, fresh from the oven, were delicious. It seemed sad indeed that DuRosche, who was paying for all of this, was apparently unable to taste food.

Arne couldn't taste food either—or wouldn't. He refused with a shake of his head, and now he was walking in widening circles about the house and grounds.

"He looks," said Alida, who was watching him through the window, "like a general planning a battle. You said he was a general, didn't you?"

"Yes—in addition to those other things," Brock said. Egarn had given him permission to tell his story to a few others whose discretion could be trusted and whose help was needed.

"He seems young for it," Alida said, "but he also seems so overwhelmingly serious. Maybe that is the explanation. Do we really have to believe this?"

"Egarn insisted there was a Johnson connected with this house when everyone said there wasn't, and he was right. DuRosche's condition has baffled specialists from around the world, and Egarn immediately knew all about it. Everything that has happened has fit perfectly with what he has told me. Yes, I think we have to believe this. The weapon Arne has in his pocket would stand the Pentagon on its head—if the Pentagon knew about it. Which it must not do. Do you understand? None of us must ever breathe a word of this. Even though we don't understand how these things are possible—I'm a specialist and a presumed expert, and I can't begin to understand—a careless remark might give a clue to someone who would find a way to make use of it, and the whole terrible scenario of repeated destructions of Earth and humanity would follow."

Jeff said slowly, "And the weapon that will cause the destruction was—or will be—invented right here in Rochester?"

"Was invented, I think, and here in this house. DuRosche had some connection with it—he received brain damage from that strange lens. We must find out what the connection was. This house has to have the most thorough search possible without tearing it down. We not only will have to look around and under and in everything, but we also will have to look for all those things mystery writers are so fond of—secret panels, and hinged openings in the floor, and false partitions, and whatever. That is where I thought you two could help. Those students who organized themselves to find Janie's killers—would any of them be available for this?"

"If I tell them it is important, they will all be available," Alida said. "Anyone who doesn't have a class, that is. And some who do."

"It is a big house, but we don't want so many they would get in each other's way. Perhaps fifteen or twenty?"

"I'll telephone," Alida said.

"I have another call to make. Let me go first."

Brock telephoned his wife and sent her out to his laboratory to search the files. When she returned, she told him, "C. DuRosche is the name on the card. Dated twenty-five years ago. Shall I read your summary?"

"Please do."

"'Lens with undulating surfaces. Thinks it is the philosopher's stone of lenses with all kinds of unlikely potentialities.' Then you wrote the word 'crackpot' with a question mark."

"'Unlikely potentialities' was an understatement, and I was the 'crackpot.' Anything happening there?"

"Not a thing," his wife said cheerfully. "We are watching an old movie."

"One that would interest me?"

"No. You don't like Charles Boyer."

"He gives me an inferiority complex. I want you to do something right away. Immediately. This instant. Then come back

309

and tell me you have done it. Take that card to the fireplace and burn it. Pulverize the ashes. Make sure nothing is left. And forget what you just read."

"If you say so."

He waited. Finally she returned. "Done. Burned, ashes pulverized. I don't remember anything about it. I wouldn't have anyway. Do you want me to sprinkle the ashes on the geraniums?"

"It wouldn't hurt a bit. Enjoy Charles Boyer."

Five carloads of students arrived. Arne watched with a disapproving frown as they piled out, laughing and joking, and hurried into the house, but they went to work seriously enough. An hour later, Alida, who was helping Charlie and Shirley in the attic, turned and saw Detective Sergeant Fred Ulling standing on the stairs and eying them perplexedly.

"Hello, Sergeant," she said. "Couldn't you find anyone downstairs?"

"Someone told me Professor Brock was up here. What is going on?"

"The Kearneys gave us permission to search the house provided we leave things more or less the way we found them. We are doing our best."

"You certainly have plenty of help. What do you expect to find that the police didn't?"

"It's complicated," Alida said. "I'll let Professor Brock explain it. Did you know Hy was the mysterious Johnson."

"That's what the professor said on the telephone. He didn't explain why it mattered. He also didn't say he was bringing in a wrecking crew to tear the house apart."

"Come, now. We haven't wrecked a thing—yet. I'll see if I can find him for you." She said to Shirley and Charlie, "If you two need a hand with anything, shout."

She and the detective vanished down the stairway. Charlie applied weight and muscle and shoved a massive old bureau aside. An enormous pile of magazines had been stacked behind it.

He dusted his hands with satisfaction. "That just about does it up here. There is nowhere else to look unless you want the floorboards ripped up."

"We are just getting started," Shirley told him. "Now we've got to go through every one of those magazines, page by page—the secret plans, or the stolen treaty, or the missing will, or the formula for poison gas, or whatever it is could be hidden in one of them. After that, we've got to move everything back where it was."

"You're kidding! What does it matter which side of the attic this junk is on?"

"You are here to supply the muscle. Leave the philosophy to me. Alida said we have to put things back back where we found them."

"You mean—all the stuff we just moved from this end to that end we have to move back to this end?"

"Right. But first we tackle these magazines."

Charlie wearily slumped to the floor and picked up a magazine.

In a room below, Alida and the detective found Brock and Jeff Mardell. **Brock** was watching while Jeff wielded a yardstick from the top of a ladder.

"Just what is it you expect to find?" the detective wanted to know.

"If we knew, it might be a lot easier," Brock said. "I finally got around to taking a look at DuRosche's background. Elderly eccentric millionaire. Tinkered with things. Called himself an inventor. Years and years ago, when Mrs. Kernley was his cook, he made a few telescopes. Ground the lenses himself."

"You figure that's important?"

"Very. In the years before his illness, he suddenly got secretive about what he was doing. People were calling him a crackpot and making fun of him, and he resented that. He also resented the fact that experts he consulted—including myself—were too thick-headed to recognize his ability. So no one knows what he was doing at the time his illness struck. He had an elaborate workshop in the basement, but after he became disabled, a nephew—who has since died—cleaned the place out and took everything. Curse him."

"Then you think this funny business concerns something he was working on when he got sick? Someone got wind of it and is trying to steal it?"

"It seems so."

"If the nephew cleaned everything out, why the search for hiding places?"

Jeff spoke from the top of the ladder. "I've been wondering about that myself. Why would he bother to hid things in a false ceiling, or under the floor, or behind fake partitions? If it was something he was using regularly, he would want it where he could get at it. If he wanted a really secure hiding place, he could have rented a safe-deposit box."

"With eccentric millionaires, you never know," Brock said. "I talked to his attorney. He guarantees there was nothing in his safe except deeds, stock certificates, bonds, financial records, things of that kind. He doesn't think DuRosche had a safe-deposit box. No rental notice has ever arrived for one. Also, no important papers are missing. So we have to search."

"And how did Hy—whatever his last name was—get connected with this thing?" the detective demanded.

"That part is easy," Brock said. "He found what we are looking for."

Ulling shook his head. "You academic types have your own special brand of logic. If Hy found it, then it is no longer hidden. So why are you looking for it?"

"Because it isn't around anywhere. Therefore Hy hid it again—or left it hidden."

"If that kind of mental loop-the-loop appeals to you, I suppose you might as well look. If you have nothing better to do, that is. Unfortunately, I do, but Colonel Lobert telephoned someone at headquarters, and that someone spoke to someone else, who spoke to my boss, and I'm assigned to keep an eye on you. As long as I'm here, I might as well look, too. The sooner we finish looking, the sooner all of us can do something else."

From the first floor came an enormous clatter. Alida and the detective ran. When they reached the bottom of the stairs, the plump Mrs. Jefferson was just ahead of them, moving with surprising speed. In the kitchen, one of the students sat dejectedly on the floor surrounded by pans of every description.

Mrs. Jefferson shook her finger at him and said angrily, "There are no hiding places in my kitchen!"

By evening, the students were convinced there were no hiding places anywhere. They had examined the floor boards throughout the house except where carpets had been in place for years. They had eliminated any possibility of false ceilings, false partitions, secret rooms, hidden staircases, or even wall cavities. One carload at a time they were giving up and leaving.

Alida, descending the cellar stairs, found Jeff standing on a chair and scrutinizing with intense interest a bulge in a furnace pipe. "Have we sunken to that?" she asked.

"I'm afraid it's the only thing left," Jeff said, "except for a suspicion I've been nourishing about that old oil tank at the other end of the cellar. It easily could contain blueprints, or drawings, or notes of experiments, or even some of those strange lenses. Unfortunately, it is at least a third full of oil. I'm wondering if I should try to drain it."

"Better not," Brock said from the other side of the furnace. "I already asked about it. The oil furnace was installed after DuRosche had his stroke. When they changed to natural gas, they kept the tank just in case they decided to switch back."

"Scratch one oil tank. How are things going upstairs?"

"The same as down here," Alida said. "Our detective decided we weren't worth keeping an eye on. His superiors agreed, so he left. Most of the students had to leave for classes. The ones still here are persisting but with noticeably less enthusiasm. They want to know if they should start over again. I'm afraid it's a washout."

"Too bad," Jeff said. "It seemed like such a good idea—especially with Hy being the mysterious Johnson."

313

"The only thing the search established beyond a doubt is that Mrs. Kernley is an excellent housekeeper," Alida said. "By the way, she insists that anything connected with Hy will be hidden down here. He sometimes ranged through the rest of the house doing chores, but this is where he spent his leisure—which seems to have taken up quite a lot of his time. No one knows what he did with it except that sometimes he tinkered. Mrs. Kernley thinks he slept a lot."

"She's wrong," Jeff said. "About there being anything hidden down here, I mean. We have searched everything but the cellar walls. I thought of tapping on them, but those stones wouldn't sound hollow even if they were. Was Hy a tinkerer?"

"He fixed things, if that's what you mean. When he first came here, years ago, he would roam the alleys and pick up junk and repair it."

"And sell it?"

"He wasn't much concerned with money. He would give it away if someone wanted it.

"Then where is it? That sort of person usually converts his environment into a junk yard."

"Mrs. Kernley wouldn't have tolerated that."

Jeff picked up a hammer and tapped on the nearest wall. "See? Even if it were hollow, it wouldn't sound any different. I suppose I could look for loose stones."

He went on tapping and prying at the stones. Alida and Brock stood watching him. He worked as far as the old wardrobe, and then he resumed on the other side.

"You aren't being consistent," Alida said. "That wardrobe is the only thing down here that could be hiding something. It's right up against the wall."

Jeff grabbed the wardrobe, tried to shove it, tried to lift a corner. "It seems to be cemented down," he said.

"Let's try moving it the other way," Brock said. "I'll push and you pull."

He put his shoulder to the other side of the wardrobe. Jeff pulled. It swung aside with ridiculous ease, dumping Jeff to the floor. It was hinged, and it served as a door to an opening in the basement wall. Beyond it, in the shadows, was a small room. At the back stood a workbench and equipment.

There were papers on the bench; at one side there was a bracket with an odd-looking circular object. There were similar objects scattered on the bench.

"Finally, the Honsun Len!" Brock breathed.

The wardrobe had a spring that closed it automatically. Jeff set a chair against it to hold it open. Brock stepped into the hidden room.

"It's the old well for an outside stairway," he announced. "DuRosche must have poured a cement roof and sodded over it so he could have a secret workshop. These are technical drawings."

He pulled the chain on a dangling light bulb and bent over the drawings. "This is it," he said. There was a queer flutter of excitement in his voice. "We have got it. The important thing now is not to let anyone touch anything until we are very sure what we are going to do with it."

He continued to scrutinize the drawings. "DuRosche's name has been trimmed from one of these but not from the others. And here is a sheet of paper where someone has practiced lettering the name 'H. H. Johnson' in the same style as the lettering on the drawings. Meaning 'Hyacinth Hyatt Johnson,' I suppose. I do believe Hy was about to steal DuRosche's invention. And look—here are Hy's personal papers, including a diploma from the Mellia Technical Institute certifying that one H. H. Johnson accomplished this and that. I've never heard of it. Has anyone seen Arne?"

"He is still wandering around outside," Jeff said. "I think he is worrying about what might happen here after dark."

Professor Brock nodded. "The house is highly vulnerable, you know. As for this workshop, we simply must not let anyone else near it. Looking into this odd lens can be dangerous. That's what DuRosche did. The lens releases bursts of energy, probably at random moments, and he had the bad luck to catch the full blast of one. Probably he was at work down here. He staggered backward and collapsed on the basement floor. The wardrobe swung shut, and no one except him knew the secret workroom existed. And the doctors, who had never seen such an affliction, thought he'd had a stroke. Maybe he did, in a way. He might have suffered broken blood vessels.

"And then, long afterward, Hy discovered the workroom. He was an educated man ruined by drink. He was getting ready to claim he had invented the lens himself and patent it. Johnson lens—Honsun Len. Of course."

"Why don't we just release the wardrobe and put a guard on it?" Jeff suggested.

"There is no way we can guard it," Brock said. He was thinking about the lens that had been snatched from his own laboratory. Perhaps *they* were watching—and getting ready to suck up the drawings and lenses at any moment.

He dashed into the next room and came back with a small bookcase. He moved the lenses to the center of the bench and placed the bookcase on top of them and the drawings, open-side down.

"I need something heavy," he said.

"I saw a few bags of ready-mix cement beside the rear entrance."

"The very thing."

They brought them, one at a time, and stacked them atop the bookcase. From Egarn's description, Brock didn't think the small machine had sufficient power to deal with the weight. Even the large machine, the one that accidentally snatched Egarn out of the past and then sent him back again, would have difficulty handling that much mass, and Egarn had said it wasn't all that accurate anyway. The setup was as safe as he could make it.

"We'll leave the wardrobe open," he said. "You stand guard, Jeff. Shout if anything peculiar starts to happen. Now I must make a phone call. Then maybe I will know what to do next."

"I'll call off the search," Alida said. "Are you going to tell the detective?"

"No," Brock said. "We know how DuRosche fits into this, and we know what Hy's connection is, but we still have no explanation for the murders that would be acceptable to a police officer."

He and Alida climbed the stairs—she to look for the students, and he to make his telephone call—but the phone in Egarn's retreat rang unanswered. Brock tried again. And again. When he gave up, he was frowning worriedly.

As he turned away, the telephone rang. Brock snatched at it. It was Fred Ulling, the detective. "Any new developments there?"

"Yes," Brock said. "We found DuRosche's secret workroom. He was an amateur inventor. He had an invention he was almost ready to patent when he had his stroke. Hy found it and planned to steal it and patent it in his own name. That is as much as I'm able to explain."

"It's no explanation at all. What does all that have to do with the murders?"

"Murders are your department. Secret workrooms and inventions are mine."

"Whatever it is you're sitting on, it is hot and about to go boom. Six people from that neighborhood have telephoned complaints about loiterers and prowlers. What are they after? DuRosche's invention?"

"That's as good an answer as any."

"Then I'd better get some men in there quickly."

Brock said slowly, "If you come charging in here with an army of police, you may set off a war."

"A war? Who are those people?"

"You might call them foreign agents trying to grab DuRosche's invention."

The detective was silent for a moment. Brock had finally said something that made sense to him. "I'll move some officers in there quietly," he said. "The focus of activity seems to be

Cobbs Hill Park, which is a few blocks south of you. They must have been hiding out in the park. Now they are crossing Interstate 490 on Culver and then spreading out through the residence streets south of East Avenue. It's odd they aren't using cars."

"They aren't hiding out in the park," Brock said. "They are landing there."

"*Landing?* Are you sober?"

"Too much so, I'm afraid. When they have this neighborhood completely under control, they will start landing here."

"To do what?" the detective demanded.

"That I don't know. But this house may be under siege very shortly—if it isn't already. I am going to look around now and see what can be done."

"Help is on the way," the detective said. "Just hang on and don't do anything rash."

Alida had been listening. "Now that's cheerful advice," Brock told her, hanging up. "Don't do anything rash. How many students are still here?"

"Seven," Alida said. "They're having coffee and rolls in the dining room. They will be glad to stay as long as the rolls last. If seven aren't enough, we easily can get more."

"No. Seven are too many. This isn't a parlor game. This suddenly has become very, very dangerous business."

"It has been very, very dangerous all along," Alida said soberly. "Four people have died."

"Which is an excellent reason for not involving more people than we have to."

Brock went down the hallway to the front door and stepped outside. He was surprised to find it so dark—he hadn't been aware of how late it was. No outside lights were on. The few lighted windows on the ground floor gave out only shallow rectangles of illumination. The street light on DuRosche Court was very distant and faint. The night seemed peaceful, but a shadow suddenly scudded across the drive and vanished into the shrubbery. Brock hurried down the steps to the cover of a bush and squinted into the gathering night.

He called softly, "Arne?"

Arne slipped from the nearby shadows, making no sound at all.

Brock wanted to know if the house was surrounded. He pointed down the drive. Then he pointed to one side and the other and made a circular motion. On the third third try, Arne suddenly understood.

His limited English vocabulary included yes and no. He pointed down the drive—yes. To the side that adjoined the street, no. To the other side, no. To the rear, no.

So they weren't surrounded—yet.

Brock was worried about the students and about the servants, too. The maids and the nurse were getting ready to leave. They had stayed later than usual—the uproar caused by the search had upset their routine. Now he was wondering how the invaders would react. They might suspect the students or servants of trying to smuggle out the plans.

Should the plans be destroyed? That seemed to be Egarn's intention, but Brock hesitated to take such a drastic step without consulting him. Had the invaders found him despite Colonel Lobert's precautions?

If the invaders tried to storm the house, Arne's weapon could focus the ultimate power of the universe on them. It also could devastate the neighborhood and kill a lot of innocent people. The invaders, since they came from the same place Arne did, probably had the same weapon. If Arne used his, what would prevent them from blasting the house to splinters?

Alida called to him from the door. "Telephone," she said. "It's a Colonel Lobert."

He took all of the front steps in one leap.

The colonel said, "We spotted some suspicious-looking characters nosing around the motel we were using. They were masquerading as Zoro, or the Three Musketeers, or something. We didn't like their looks, so we smuggled Egarn out the back way and left the room's lights on and the TV going. The characters haven't missed us yet—they are still hanging around there. I just checked with the proprietor. So we may have got away cleanly, but I'm not taking any bets yet. I can't figure out how they got onto us. They must be clairvoyant."

"That's as good a way to describe it as any," Brock said.

"We are at a different motel, now—one a long, long way from the other. Better write down this number." He dictated it, and the professor wrote. "Egarn isn't feeling well—I've sent for a doctor. He doesn't look well, either. He must be rather be rather old."

"Several hundred years," the professor said.

The colonel chuckled. "No doubt. I'm sure these events have aged him. He wants to talk with you."

Egarn's voice came faintly. "Have you found it?"

"We've got the whole works," Brock said. "DuRosche was the inventor. He had a secret workroom. There are plans there for the lens and also some samples. You and Arne were right— DuRosche must have had his mind damaged while he was working on the lens. No one else knew about his workroom, but eventually Hy found it. I told you Hy's name was Johnson. I think he was going to patent the lens under his own name, H. H. Johnson. For Hyacinth Hyatt Johnson. That would have made it the Johnson Lens."

"Yes," Egarn said weakly. "Yes. That explains everything. What did you do with the plans?"

"I put a bookcase on top of them and bags of cement on top of the bookcase to keep them from being snatched. I wanted to talk with you before I did anything else. While we were waiting to hear from you, an army of characters in what look like black capes has been forming outside. The police say it has the whole neighborhood surrounded."

"The plans must be destroyed," Egarn said excitedly. "The plans and the lens. Completely. Utterly. But if you do that, the Lantiff may destroy the house and everyone in it. They are ruthless. Their minds are damaged the way DuRosche's was—

less severely but enough to burn away all of their humane impulses."

"If they have weapons like Arne's, they can cut this house to pieces any time they feel like it and us with it," Brock said.

"No. They won't dare. If they did that, they might destroy the plans. As long as you have the plans and lens intact, you are safe. But once they get their hands on them—"

"I understand. They don't really want them. They just want them preserved so future history won't be altered. If someone else took them and patented them, it wouldn't be a Honsun Len, it might be a Smith Len or a Miller Len, but that wouldn't significantly alter the future. But wait—if we destroy the plans and the lenses, then no one can patent the lens, and future history will be fractured. They will no longer exist—or will they?"

"I don't know," Egarn said soberly. "You see—even if you destroy the future, they are already in the present. Changing the future may not have any effect at all on the ones already here. How many are there?"

"I haven't any idea. They are mostly concealed in the shrubbery at the edge of the estate. From what the police told me, there could be several hundred about."

"The Peer of Lant can send an army if she wants to," Egarn gasped. "If you destroy the plans, the Lantiff will run wild. They could devastate the entire city—maybe even the entire state."

"I understand. I saw Arne demonstrate the weapon. So what do you suggest?"

"I don't know," Egarn said. "It is a terrible decision to force on you. The len has killed millions and billions already—will kill them. I feel tired and sick, and I am having trouble thinking. I just can't—"

The voice faded away. A moment later, Colonel Lobert spoke. "I'm afraid the old fellow's dying. He looks extremely bad. His breathing is fast and shallow, and his heart is racing. He wanted to talk with Arne, but I don't think he is able to. If the doctor doesn't get here quickly—did you get what you wanted?"

"No," Brock said, "but I'm afraid I got all I am going to get."

"If he improves, I'll call you again."

Brock hung up and found Alida at his elbow. She said brightly, "Don't worry. There are twenty or thirty students on the way. If those thugs try to rush the house, they will get a surprise."

"You are much too late," Brock protested. "We will soon be cut off if we aren't already. The students won't be able to get through to us."

"Yes, they will—if they come quickly, they will. There is a back way through the adjoining property. Mr. Kernley has gone to meet them."

"But this is terrible!" Brock exclaimed. "Here I am trying to find a way to get people out of here safely, and you are bringing in twenty or thirty more! I suppose it is too late to tell them to stay away."

"Much too late," Alida said. "They are already on their way. Don't worry about getting us out of here. All of us are staying. So are the maids and the nurse."

Mrs. Kernley, who was standing at the front door, called, "Professor—there is someone coming!"

Brock went to the door. A shadowy figure was strolling nonchalantly up the drive. Every few strides, the gusting breeze tugged at his black cape. He looked formidable. He looked like the Prince of Darkness calmly arriving to take over his property.

But when he stepped into the light that touched the area around the front door, he resolved into a thin, pasty-faced youth.

He said, "Marcus Brock, please."

Brock was astonished. Then he remembered that Roszt and Kaynor had spoken English well enough to get by. This youth was an emissary from the future's darker side.

"I am Marcus Brock," he said. "Who are you?"

"I am Gevis."

"You are trespassing, Gevis. This is private property, and you are here without permission. Do you have an errand?"

"You give plans," Gevis said. "We go away. No one hurt."

"If you don't go away, we will burn the plans. Do you understand?"

"Bad for you," Gevis said. "We burn house, people dead."

"Bad for you," Brock said. "The place you came from, and everyone who is there, will go 'poof!' and be gone forever. Can you understand that?"

Gevis seemed to be struggling for words.

Suddenly a voice rang out. "Gevis!"

Gevis winced and turned quickly. Even in the dim light, he suddenly looked frightened.

Arne strode up to him and spoke. Gevis raised his hands as though warding off blows, but the only violence done to him was with words, spoken softly but with unmistakable venom. Finally Gevis turned and staggered back down the drive like a man fleeing from a beating. He vanished into the shrubbery. Arne turned indifferently and faded back into the shadows. Brock had no doubt that a brief but bitter drama had been enacted, but he couldn't begin to guess what it signified.

The end of the drive was faintly touched by the DuRosche Court streetlight, and as Brock stared in that direction, a black-cloaked figure appeared out of nowhere. It stepped aside, and another followed it. And another. And another. Negotiations had failed, and the Peer of Lant was sending her army.

24

ARNE AND DELINE

Bob slammed down the telephone receiver and leaped to the door of his apartment. Outside, he faced the building and sounded three piercing whistles. Heads appeared in windows.

"Jeff and Alida need help!" he shouted. "They're being threatened by thugs from outer space. It's dangerous. Who's with me?"

Shouts came back. "I am!"

"Right on!"

"Wait for me!"

Students, male and female, began to pour from the building.

Within minutes the convoy was underway. Connie, riding with Bob, asked as they made a screeching turn onto Mt. Hope Avenue, "What sort of danger?"

"No idea," Bob said.

"Just what did you mean—'thugs from outer space?'"

"No idea about that, either. It seemed to fit what Alida told me."

"What are we supposed to do—scratch them to death? I wouldn't have trimmed my fingernails last night if I'd known."

"Good point. I've been thinking about that myself. There is no quick way to get our hands on some guns, but anything at all would be better than nothing at all. I've been trying to remember where I saw that sign."

They rocketed along for two more blocks before he remembered. He took a corner on two wheels with the convoy following. He backtracked several blocks, turned again, and eventually swerved into the parking lot beside a long block of stores. As he came to a stop, the second carload of students pulled in beside him. The others arrived and took vacant spaces.

The block of stores was only one store, a hardware and building supply business that had grown to occupy the available space. A sign in the front window advertised a fire extinguisher sale. "Better than nothing at all," Bob said cheerfully.

"I suppose," Connie said. "But it will take more than a dribble to subdue a thug from outer space. We will need *big* extinguishers, and they are expensive. Our combined wealth probably runs to about seventeen bucks."

"Trust me," Bob said confidently. "Coming in? Your good looks will add a touch of class to this otherwise vulgar-appearing mob."

The proprietor's face took on an expression of perplexity as a procession of students marched up to his counter. He said politely, "Good evening."

"Evening," Bob said. "I would like to rent about three dozen fire extinguishers."

"You would like to *rent*—"

"Just for tonight," Bob added hastily. "We are having a rally. Old building, you know, and the fire marshall thinks we ought to have more fire extinguishers."

"But we don't rent—"

"Bring 'em back tomorrow," Bob said assuringly. "Probably we won't have to take 'em out of their boxes. Chance for a quick profit for you, no risk. We store them for you overnight and return them in the morning. How about fifty bucks? We'll leave as many university ID cards as you want for security."

They closed the deal for seventy-five. Steve, a chemistry major, had a brief discussion with the proprietor about the types of extinguishers available. A few moments later, students began to emerge from the store with their arms full of boxes.

*   *   *

At the DuRosche Mansion, a worried Professor Brock continued to watch shadowy forms emerge out of nowhere and immediately fade into the shrubbery. Egarn had called them the Lantiff. Brock had no notion of what the word meant, but somehow it seemed appropriate. They continued to arrive.

Sergeant Ulling telephoned again to see how things were going, and Brock reported this latest development.

"Where are they coming from?" the sergeant demanded. "We've sealed off all the main routes. They can't be materializing out of thin air."

"It is reassuring to know that. Have your men seen several carloads of college students headed in this direction?"

"No one has mentioned it."

"Probably they aren't using a main route. Would you put out an order to have them stopped? I've got enough problems without filling the house with unarmed civilians."

"I understand. Sure, I'll have them stopped."

"And tell your men this isn't one of those damned westerns where the cavalry charges to the rescue. They are to hold back zon the heroics until all of us figure out what is going on."

"Will do."

He didn't call again, but at least the college students failed to arrive. The outlook seemed dismal in every other respect. The Lantiff were forming ranks several men deep and gradually extending them to surround the house.

Suddenly a patrol car turned off East Avenue. Its flashing light came on; so did its siren. It screamed its way toward DuRosche Court.

"There is always one idiot who doesn't get the word," Brock muttered resignedly.

Lightning flashed, thunder crashed, and with an audible "whoosh," flames enveloped the car. The two officers escaped, but one was cut down in the street by another flash of lightning. A few minutes later Mrs. Calding, who had been watching from an upstairs window, reported flames on East Avenue. The battle had been joined.

Brock was still trying to see what had happened to the two police officers when a ruckus sounded at the back of the house. The college students filed in with Mr. Kernley proudly in the lead. No scout who had successfully led a wartime expedition through enemy territory could have looked prouder.

"Are we glad to see you!" Alida said. "We were beginning to feel downright lonely."

"It was a near thing," Mr. Kernley said. "They closed in right behind us, but everyone made it through."

"Professor!" Alida called. "Reinforcements!"

"Great," Brock said sourly. "Maybe you can frighten these characters away with college yells."

"We come armed," Bob said proudly. "We are the chemical warfare unit."

He showed Brock what the students were carrying. Brock raised his eyebrows. "This is downright original of you. Congratulations. Unfortunately, your chemicals won't last forever or even very long. If we don't find a way to resolve this, a lot of people are going to get killed. Have you seen the fires? Traffic has been halted on East Avenue and probably every street in the neighborhood. You just barely made it in here, and now we are completely sealed off."

In sneaking through the grounds from the next estate, the students had missed all of the action. They dashed upstairs for a look; a moment later they shouted that two houses on East Avenue were burning. Flames also could be seen off to the south, probably on Harvard Street. In the distance, fire engines were wailing.

Brock hurried downstairs to see Jeff. "It will be our turn next," he said. "We had better get ready. If we can keep them out of the house, we will be all right. Remember, it is the plans and lenses they want. They can burn us out whenever they like, but they won't dare—I hope—because that would destroy what they are trying to save."

"Right. A fire extinguisher at every door and downstairs window should do the trick. The basement windows, too. Unless they find ladders somewhere, the second floor is secure."

"We need a special guard for DuRosche's workroom," Brock said. "If they succeed in breaking in, the plans must be destroyed at once."

Brock hurried back upstairs. Suddenly the front door opened and Arne stepped in quietly. He said something—either in his own language or in grossly mispronounced English—and at that moment the night sky fractured. The house was bathed in splashes of light as the encircling ranks of black-cloaked men began to advance slowly. Some of them were carrying tubes that spat lightning as they moved forward.

For one terrifying moment Brock thought they were doomed, but these tubes, though they turned the darkness into bright daylight, were totally unlike Arne's weapon. They seemed to do no damage at all.

"If that energy could be harnessed," Brock remarked conversationally, "the world's electric companies would go bankrupt."

"But what is it?" Alida asked.

"Time," Brock said.

"Is time an energy?"

"Of course. It is the universe's one irresistible force. All the puny works of man combined can't stop it for a single second. Fortunately for us, this particular adaptation seems harmless."

Shirley and Charley were peeking out of the rear door when Bob handed them their fire extinguishers. "Clear the decks for action," he said. "They'll be charging the house any minute."

"I hope you realize this means war," Shirley said.

In the basement, Connie and Ed were contemplating one of the high windows. It was out of reach even when Ed stood on a chair.

"Maybe I can find a box to stand on," Ed said.

"What for?" Connie demanded. "So you can stick your head up? Those beams of light may be some kind of death ray." She handed him a fire extinguisher. "Here. We will stand back until they break the window. Then when one of them looks in, you can jump up and squirt him good."

The professor and Jeff were debating what to do with the plans and the lenses. "I simply don't understand," Jeff said. "If they are destroyed, what is to prevent someone else from inventing the same thing?"

"Most inventions are the inevitable result of scientific progress. That is why several people will be working on the same thing simultaneously in widely scattered places. If one doesn't perfect it, another will. I don't think that applies here. The idea for this lens is so wildly improbable, and the lens itself is so radically unlike anything else, that there wouldn't be a chance in a billion billion of someone else inventing it."

He remembered his own reaction when DuRosche consulted him. He knew no rational scientist would even consider anything like the Honsun Len. Only a screwball amateur like DuRosche could have come up with it, and only by the wildest coincidence could he have got both the glass and the lens right. The odds against another screwball happening onto the same combination would be more than astronomical.

"*You* could invent it," Jeff said. "You know all about it."

"Not 'all.' Only a little, and I will be wise enough to forget that little the moment I have a chance."

"How come some of those flashes start fires and some don't?"

"They come from different weapons. Different kinds of lenses, arranged differently, produce different effects." Brock was wondering whether the weapons had a shutter arrangement that could store temporal energy, something comparable to a Q-switched laser, so they could release controlled bursts. That might explain some of the strangenesses. He wished he had examined Arne's weapon more closely. He also was glad that he hadn't.

He desperately wanted to talk with Egarn again, but he had a sinking feeling of certitude the old man was dead. This hot potato was his to handle—his and Arne's, and he couldn't even ask Arne a question. He picked up the phone and found it dead. The invaders from the primitive future had finally grasped the importance of telephone wires. He sent Jeff through the house looking for flashlights just in case the electrical wires were cut next. Then he ordered all lights turned off inside the mansion. The outside lights were turned on, though they weren't needed. Bright flashes continued to bathe the entire house in light.

Suddenly the Lantiff charged. Glass was broken. Every figure that attempted to climb through a window, or that approached a door, got a blast of chemicals in the face. As he crumpled, hands over his eyes, another took his place and received the same treatment. It went on, and on, until there was a pile of moaning men around each window and door.

The attack stopped as abruptly as it had started. The figures that were still uninjured drew back. The flashes of light stopped. Night closed in abruptly on the shallow areas illuminated by the outside lights. At the foot of the drive, reinforcements were arriving again. The circle around the house began to reform.

Brock went from window to window checking the fire extinguishers by gently shaking them. They were almost empty.

"This can't continue," he said to Jeff. "The extinguishers don't have enough of a charge left to beat off another attack. *Now* we must decide."

Jeff said nothing.

"All the wisdom I am capable of seems unequal to this," Brock went on, "but since the decision is mine, I will say this—if we have to sacrifice ourselves to make a better world, so be it. Take a couple of your friends. Get the plans and lenses from DuRosche's workroom. Smash the lenses with a hammer. Burn the plans. Destroy the ashes and glass fragments as thoroughly as you can. You must work quickly, or they may try to snatch them with a temporal vacuum cleaner. We will continue to resist as long as possible."

"Will do," Jeff said.

The professor went to the front door and opened it. Distant sirens could be heard. Fires seemed to be burning out of control on East Avenue. The ring of dark figures stood motionless. All of the Lantiff had been brain-damaged by the lens, Egarn had said. They were trained to fight and die; they would do whatever they were told.

Suddenly the ring parted. A different figure stepped forward. This one was a woman in a striking silver and black uniform. Her long, blonde hair tumbled carelessly onto her shoulders. She was the Queen of Darkness—poised, fearless, terrible.

She held a tube in her hand. She pointed it at a huge oak tree that stood near the house. With a flash of lightning and a crash of thunder, the tree toppled. It fell across the circle of waiting Lantiff. They scattered, but several were crushed. The others paid no attention. They reformed the circle. Watching, Brock shuddered.

She aimed again. Thunder crashed as the lightning ripped through the house. He heard fire extinguishers working behind him. "Anyone hurt?" he called over his shoulder.

Someone answered cheerfully, "Not yet."

The woman aimed at the house again, but this time nothing happened. She stood motionless, tube pointed menacingly. Her meaning was clear enough: Surrender, give us what we want, or all of you will die.

Arne stepped from the shadows and walked slowly toward her. His shabby department store clothing contrasted starkly with her flashing military apparel. He might have been a beggar about to ask alms of a queen except that his manner and poise were fully as regal as hers.

She turned her weapon on him as he approached; but he already held his weapon pointed directly at her. He halted a mere ten paces from her, and they stood facing each other.

The professor had seen one stirring encounter that night— when Arne confronted Gevis. He knew instinctively that another emotion-wracked drama was taking place and he probably would never understand it, either. The two continued to face each other. Brock held his breath and waited to see which would fire first.

Suddenly they vanished.

The ring of black-cloaked figures vanished.

At the same instant, a hellish racket sounded somewhere in the house. Brock turned and ran. In the kitchen, Mrs. Jefferson was bent over the sink. Jeff and Alida stood beside her; the Kernleys and Mrs. Calding were watching.

Jeff shouted over the noise. "We burned the plans and smashed the lenses. Now we're feeding the ashes and the glass particles into the garbage disposal. You said to destroy them completely, and this was the most effective thing we could think of."

Mrs. Jefferson laughed gleefully. "The man who sold us this thing said it would grind glass, and it sure does!"

Brock nodded. "It sure does."

"Is it over?" Alida asked.

"It is completely over. It is finished. They have gone. Vanished."

Mrs. Jefferson turned off the disposal. Alida shouted, "Hey gang—the war is over!"

Ten minutes later, with traffic beginning to move haltingly on East Avenue and firemen finally able to get to the fires, Sergeant Ulling arrived at what he knew would be the focal point of the destruction and leaped from his police car.

Off to one side, a tree had toppled. Something had blasted a hole in the wall of the house. Windows were broken. Otherwise, the scene was peaceful. Some college students had gathered on the lawn, and they were singing.

"Where is the professor?" the sergeant demanded.

"He went to find a telephone," one of the students said.

Brock had gone next door to see if the telephone line there was still intact. He dialed the number of Egarn's motel and spoke briefly to Colonel Lobert. It was an enormous relief to him to hear that everything was all right. Egarn was in bed and sound asleep, and Lobert thought he shouldn't be disturbed. "When the old man wakes up, I'll bring him to DuRosche

332

Court," the colonel said. "Mind you, I'll be expecting that full explanation."

"There are a few things I would like to have explained myself," Brock said. "I'm sure Egarn will tell us everything he can that isn't classified."

He strolled back to the DuRosch mansion, reflecting along the way on what Egarn had already told him. Roszt and Kaynor, the emissaries from the future, had prowled around the DuRosche mansion at night. There was one cellar window from which they could have looked into DuRosche's secret workroom when the wardrobe was swung out of the way. Probably they saw Hy at work there and noticed the plans and the finished lenses. Did they suspect Hy was the Johnson they were seeking and kill him deliberately?

"We will never know," Brock mused. "Certainly they did their best to carry out their mission."

As for Hy, if the course of history hadn't been interrupted, no doubt he would have committed a series of forgeries, patented the lens, and ended up owning the mansion and much of DuRosche's fortune as well. That was implied in Egarn's discovery of a future H. H. Johnson who owned a manufacturing company and who lived at 1 DuRosche Court.

Some mysteries couldn't be resolved so easily. There was that strange duel at the end between Arne and the Amazon warrior. The tension between them had almost crackled with electricity. It would have been worth delaying the destruction of the lenses and plans for another minute or two, Brock thought, just to see how that conflict would turn out.

More sirens cut through the neighborhood. As Brock headed back up the drive from DuRosche Court, an army staff car rolled past him and came to a halt beside the students. A major general got out and looked about perplexedly. "What *is* going on here?" he demanded.

"We are having a lawn party, general," one of the students called. "Would you care to join us?"

The song continued: "We'll forget the books we've read, the songs we've sung, and the cause we've led, but we'll all remember Janie. But we'll all remember Ja—a—nie."

It was Arne that Brock would remember. He would always be haunted by his recollection of that silent, strangely intense young man who had so nobly fought a desperate war against the odds. It seemed curious to him that Egarn hadn't vanished, too—but perhaps there was no reason why he should. Egarn had simply returned where he belonged. He was all right, and the colonel would soon be bringing him.

Then, perhaps, Brock would be able to fill in some blanks.

25

VLADISLAV KUZNETSOV

A telephone rang, and Vladislav Kuznetsov stirred resentfully. The ten thousand devils of a corrosive Chinese curse were holding a celebration in his head. Slowly he opened his eyes. It was nighttime; the only light that touched the room came from somewhere outside, and the drawn drapes were dimly awash with its brightness.

Before the phone could ring a second time, a voice answered it, speaking in what Kuznetsov knew was a hushed undertone although every word echoed thunderously in his wracked head. "All over, you say? Everything all right? That's great! That's splendid!" A pause. Then—"He seems to be doing okay. Had us worried for a time, but he is much better, now."

Kuznetsov tensed and began to perspire. They were talking about him. He had been sick. If his aching head was any indication, he was still sick. He felt terrible. If he was better now, he must have been close to death.

"The doctor checked him over and gave him something to make him sleep," the voice went on. "That was an hour ago. He is awfully old, you know, and he simply had overdone it. Heart very weak and tired."

Kuznetsov relaxed. They weren't talking about him.

"He was breathing easily the last time I looked." A pause. "It's perfectly all right, Mark. Pleased I could be of help. Glad everything worked out. I'll call off the guard, now. Yes—I'll bring him to DuRosche Court when he wakes up. Mind you, I'll be expecting that full explanation."

The click sounded as he replaced the phone. Then he bent over Kuznetsov, who burrowed more deeply into his pillow and feigned sleep.

The man went to the door and opened it. "It's finished," he said softly. "All done. Tell them they can go home. We will get together later and talk about it—after I find out myself what the hell we were doing. The old man will be okay, now. No one will bother him. I'm going for a bite to eat."

The door closed softly. Kuznetsov sat up and looked about him. He was in a motel room. Under the light blanket that covered him, he was fully clothed. His shirt and undershirt had been pulled from his trousers. The shirt was unbuttoned. When he started to reassemble himself, he discovered an odd object tied tightly around his stomach.

He investigated. It looked like a hand-made cloth belt, and in it . . .

He stared down at himself in disbelief. The belt had a series of pockets, and each one was stuffed with money. "What have I got myself into?" he breathed.

There was a wallet in his rear pocket. It had no identification at all, but it, too, was stuffed with money.

His clothing fit badly. The shoes on the floor by the bed had to be his, but they, also, fit badly. He put them on. There were two garments hanging on the rack, a sport coat and a light raincoat. They didn't fit any better than the other things, but he decided to take them anyway. There was nothing else in the room.

His one thought was to get out of there. He put on the sport coat and carried the rain coat. He slipped through the outside door, closed it quietly, and headed across a parking lot. He walked three blocks along a wide and heavily traveled street before he saw a cab. He hailed it and climbed in.

"Look," he said to the cabbie. "This may sound like a silly question, but I think I've been on one hell of a bender. Where am I?"

As the cabbie hesitated, he added, "I mean—what town is this? I don't recognize a thing."

"Rochester," the cabbie said.

"Minnesota?" Kuznetsov asked incredulously.

"New York. That *was* quite a bender. You got any money, fellow?"

"Plenty," Kuznetsov said. He took a twenty-dollar bill from

his wallet and held it up. "Now how the devil did I get to Rochester, New York?"

"I can think of a better question," the cabbie said. "How could you be that drunk and not get rolled? As long as you got money, you're okay. You can head back to wherever it is you think you came from."

The cabbie took him to a downtown hotel. Along the way, Kuznetsov did some intense thinking, and the more he thought, the more frightened he became. When they reached the hotel, he rewarded the cabbie generously, went inside for a quick tour of the lobby, and then came out and flagged a cab. "I don't like this hotel," he said. "Take me to another one."

When they arrived, he walked several blocks and took another cab.

Eventually he reached the bus station, and an hour later he was on a bus headed south. His fright had changed to panic. It was the money that worried him. Perhaps he should have left that strange money belt in the motel room where he regained consciousness.

"Where in God's name did it come from?" he asked himself over and over. "And where the hell have I been?"

The last thing he remembered was taking a walk on a lovely spring day and dozing off in a park near the campus. And that, according to the calendar in the station, was more than a year before. He had to get back to Mt. Harwell College, and finish his course work, and get his degree. Then—assuming there was no new slump in the auto business—he had to find a job.

But where could he have been all that time, and what had he been doing? And where did he get the money?

There was absolutely no way he could have come by that amount of cash honestly. He must have robbed a bank.

Printed in the United States
4390